TIME WILL KNIT

Fred Urquhart

TIME WILL KNIT

RICHARD DREW PUBLISHING
GLASGOW

First published 1938 by   Gerald Duckworth & Co Ltd

This edition first published 1988 by
Richard Drew Publishing Ltd
6 Clairmont Gardens, Glasgow G3 7LW
Scotland

The publisher acknowledges the financial
assistance of the Scottish Arts Council in the
publications of this book.

British Library Cataloguing in Publication Data

Urquhart, Fred, 1912-
  Time will knit.——(Scottish collection).
  I. Title
  823′.912[F]

  ISBN 0-86267-233-3

Printed and bound in Great Britain by
Cox & Wyman, Reading

FOR

MY MOTHER AND FATHER

" There'll be no great decision.   Time will knit,
    And multiply the stitches while we look.
    A few hours we shall stand, a few hours sit,
    A few hours talk, or walk, or read a book.
    The dishes will be washed, the table laid.
    Smells of sweet food will spread delicious wings.
    The daily commonplaces will be said,
    And we shall handle all the daily things.

    And so time will pass.
    Yet is there not a meaning in our looks
    That makes us kindred as the blades of grass,
    Or tree-leaves leaning over country brooks ? "
                HAROLD MONRO.   *New Day*.

As it is in Vulgar Fractions everything in this novel
has been reduced to the Lowest Common Denominator,
and the reader is invited to add, subtract or multiply
for himself.

NOTE

Because the main incident of this novel—the
eviction of the tenants from the cottages—is
based on fact, and because the locale may be
recognised by some readers, I wish to state
that no other incident is an actual incident and
that all the characters are entirely imaginary.
An author, like an artist, must have some model
on which to base his work, and it was the sight
of the ruined cottages that first made me con-
ceive and then try to tell this story.

F. U.

ONE PLAIN

I WAS raised in Little Bend, Kansas, but I came to Scotland when I was eighteen. That was in 1929. Me and Pop didn't get on so good, so I thought I'd light out. Pop was real mad. He said for me to stay home and help on the farm, but Mom said : " Let him be. There ain't no good thwartin' him an' repressin' his ego. Lookit what happened to me an' to my brother Tom."

" Yeah, lookit your Tom," Pop said. " He's a fine example, ain't he ? "

" A fine example o' what I mean," Mom said. " If Mother an' Dad hadn't thwarted him he'd never of done what he done."

" Howja make out they thwarted him ? " Pop said. " They had nothin' to do with it."

" Well, maybe not," Mom said. " Only—if Tom had had a real chance things might of been different."

" Boloney," Pop said. " Tom always was a wild guy. He'd of gone bad no matter what happened."

" Well, Spike's gonna get a chance to make good," Mom said. " He wants to be a sailor an' he can't be a sailor right in the middle o' the States—unless he aims to be a river man. An' that sure would kill me. An' it ud be enough to make his Great-Granpa turn in his grave."

" Well, let him be a sailor if he thinks it'll do him any good," Pop said. " Only there ain't no call for him

to go to Scotland to be a sailor.   He can easy go down
to Galveston, Texas or to New Orleans.   Plenty o'
boats there."

"He's goin' to Scotland," Mom said.   "Seein' as
how you an' me can't afford to go ourselves.   I'd like
Mother an' Dad to see one of their American grandchildren afore they die."

"Ain't no sense spendin' money on his passage if he
could work his way," Pop said.

"George Wilson, are you outa your senses?" Mom
said.   "Ain't you got no pride?   Wantin' to let one
o' your own flesh and blood work his way to our native
land.   Not if I have anythin' to do with it.   My folks
are gonna get a chance to see that Spike's a gentleman
afore he becomes a sailor."

Mom always spoke real dramatic like that on account
of her being an actress in small-time vaudeville afore
she married Pop.   But she always spoiled it by laughing.
We would be real carried away by her eloquence, and
then we would watch a little dimple at the corner of
her mouth going out and in like a puncture in a bicycle-
tyre, and then we would all laugh, even Pop.   But
Mom used to be pretty mad at herself.   I know how she
felt about it, for I do the same myself.   I'm like Mom
in lots of ways, far more like her than I'm like Pop.
The fact is I'm not like him at all and I often wonder
how he came to be my father.   So I felt real bad at
leaving Mom and the kids.   She'd of liked to come
with me, for she hadn't seen her old folk for near twenty
years, and she reckoned she'd never see them again
on account of Granpa being eighty-two and Granma
only four years younger.   But we couldn't afford it and,
anyway, there was the rest of the kids to look after.
They all saw me off at the station, except Pop, he was

cutting his wheat that day. The kids was near bawling.
You'd of thought I was gonna be hung or something.
I'm a tough guy but I was near bawling myself.

" You'll write an' let us know how you get on, son,
won't you ? " Mom said.

" Sure," I said, and I left them then so's I wouldn't
miss any of the lunch they was serving on the restaurant-
car. It was a pretty good feed, but it had nothing on
some of the feeds I had in New York. I was there a
week. My passage was booked on the *Berengaria*, but
it was sailing the night I got to New York so I switched
to the *Olympic* because it was sailing on the seventeenth.
That gave me a week in New York besides being on one
of my lucky days. An eight day, you see. Seven and
one make eight, like it tells you in Doctor Clifford's book
of Numerology. I'm a great guy for Numerology. I
never do nothing without calculating whether its numbers agree with the lucky numbers of my birthday—the
second of June, the second day of the sixth month,
eight. I take this offen Mom. She was a great one for
the stars afore she married Pop, and though I guess she
made a miscalculation when she married him she's still
as strong for them as ever.

I knew they'd wonder at home why I didn't sail on
the *Berengaria* so I wrote and told them I missed it. I
didn't care whether they believed this or not, I was too
busy having a swell time in New York. I met a peach
of a dame in a cinema and we stepped around some
together. But it was maybe just as well I'd switched my
passage to the *Olympic* for that dame sure could get
through the jack. I forget what her name was but we
had a swell time together.

I was crazy to go to sea, but I wasn't so crazy the first
two days out from New York. But on the third day I

was able to get out amongst the other passengers who were on deck and I told quite a few of them about how my Great-Granpa had been captain of a steamer and how I was gonna be a sailor myself. One guy was awful inquisitive.

" What was the name of the boat your Great-Granpa sailed on ? " he said.

" *The Grace Darling*," I said.

" Never heard of her," he said.

" My Mother was called after her," I said. " She was Grace Gillespie, the actress."

" Never heard of her," he said.

" She used to be on the same bills as Marie Lloyd," I said.

" Never heard of her," he said.

I didn't speak to that guy after that. For a guy who was always asking questions he didn't seem to know anything.

It always riled me to think that Mom might of been a great actress like Marie Lloyd if she hadn't fallen for Pop and quit the stage back in 1910. I reckon that's what made me so mad at Pop. He hates the stage and everything connected with it. Sometimes I wish Mom had told him to go to hell and went on being an actress, for I'd of liked to of had a famous actress for a mother. But it cuts both ways I guess, for if she hadn't married Pop where would me, and Arn, and Isa, and Kay of been ?

I'd never seen any of my relations, but I'd seen photographs of most of them. Mom didn't speak about them an awful lot. I don't think Pop liked her to speak about them, for sometimes when he was out and she got started talking about the days when she was a kid she'd dry up awful sudden when Pop came back. Both her and Pop had been raised in Harrisfield, a small town near Edinburgh. Once it had been a separate small town like Forthport, and Leith, and Portobello, all small burgs lying along the shore of the Firth of Forth, but as Edinburgh expanded it gradually took them all in till they're all part of Edinburgh now. But when Mom and Pop lived there it was a pretty one-horse burg, even smaller than Little Bend, for Mom seemed to know everybody in it. Her folks lived in what she always called The Cottages. They'd lived there for near fifty years in the same house, ever since they was married. Mom was their second eldest daughter, and they'd had seven of a family. The others was Uncle Tom, Aunt Meg, Uncle Arn, Aunt Bella, Uncle Walter and Aunt Kate.

Mom had told us a lot about Aunt Kate and her red bloomers, that Uncle Arn had called bull-tormentors, and I'd always pictured her as a tall, gawky girl with long hair, from some of the photos Mom had, so I reckon I was kinda disappointed when I found she wasn't like that at all. I knew she couldn't still be wearing the red bloomers, of course, and even if she was, she wasn't likely to let me see them. But I sure didn't expect to be met at the Waverley Station in Edinburgh by a tall, hefty dame, massive-looking, with dyed yellow hair. She wore it in a long bob down to her shoulders and it was cut in a fringe across her forehead. She'd been plucking her eyebrows and she hadn't made such a swell job of them. The powder was so thick on her face it was falling off in flakes.

Aunt Bella was with her. She was like Mom, stout and high-coloured, and she had grey, shingled hair. She was panting because Aunt Kate had made her run, thinking they was late for the train, and what with this, and her speaking awful broad Scotch, I had a tough time making out what she was saying. But I made out what Aunt Kate was saying all right. She was deaf, and she thought everybody else was deaf, too.

"Help my Jimmie Johnston!" she yelled. "Isn't he like Walter?"

"Ye're haverin', Kate," Aunt Bella said. "He's no more like Walter than fly-in-the-air. Walter's fair."

"Not your Walter," Aunt Kate said. "Our Walter."

I knew this was my uncle who had been killed in the war.

"I wonder what my mother'll say?" Aunt Kate said. "She took it terrible bad when Walter was killed."

"Listen now, Kate, ye cannie help family resemblances," Aunt Bella said. "My mother'll maybe no' notice, anyway."

They kept firing questions at me. How was my father, and mother, and all the kids, and had I had a good journey, and what did I think of Scotland, and had I been sick coming over? We began to go up the Waverley Steps, and Aunt Bella's breath gave out at last. 'Hey, I'm no' a racehorse," she cried to Aunt Kate. "Is yer mother bothered wi' breathlessness?" she asked me. "I'm awfu' short-winded. I mind how I used to be able to run up they steps, but I'm no' sae young as I used to be."

"None of us are," Aunt Kate said.

"Yer mother'll be forty-four," Aunt Bella said. "She's a year aulder than me."

"Ten years older than me," Aunt Kate said.

Aunt Bella stopped in the middle of the steps and laughed. "Listen, Kate, ye've surely been studying the advertisements for beer, an' gettin' younger every day!"

"I was thirty-four my last birthday," Aunt Kate said huffily.

"Yer last birthday must have been five years ago!" Aunt Bella said.

We reached the top of the Waverley Steps and came on to Princes Street. Mom had raved to us about Princes Street and I was real anxious to see it. But it didn't look any different to me from some of the streets in Little Bend, except that the streets in Little Bend were better. That was what I thought the first glance I got, for right opposite me was Woolworth's, and a movie-theatre, with Al Jolson in *The Singing Fool*. But while we was waiting to cross the street I looked along to my left and I saw the tall spire of Scott's Monument with the Castle on its rock in the background, and I changed my opinion a bit. I guess Mom was right. There ain't another street like it. No place elsewhere you could get the old and the new together, and blending so well.

"There's a Nine," Aunt Kate cried, and she dived across the street and left me and Aunt Bella to follow her.

"Listen now, ye didnie need to be in sich a hurry," Aunt Bella said when we got on the tram. "We're no' a' sae guid at runnin' after cars as you. We havenie a' had your experience." She turned to me and said: "Yer Aunt Kate's aye late and she's aye runnin'."

The tram was packed and I had to stand though my aunts got seats. They began to gabble to each other about hats so I looked around me at the folks on the tram. I'd never seen such folks in the States. There were two women and they were both drunk. That don't mean that I ain't seen drunk women, but I'd never seen drunk women like those two. They didn't have

hats on and one of them had on a tartan shawl. She had
a straw message-bag with bottles in it at her feet. They
was sitting at the other end of the tram from us, but we
could hear every word they said. Aunt Kate whispered :
" They're right High Street keelies, those two." Her
whisper was so loud I thought the women would hear it,
but they was so busy talking about some dame they knew
that they hadn't time to bother about what anybody was
saying about themselves. One of them said : " Her
man's a retired polisman an' she looks like a big bobby
hersel', but, by God, I dinnie care twopence for her.
One o' they days I'll smash in the bitch's face for her
though I get sixty days for it."

" That's right, Sarah," the other one said.

" Comin' to me an' tellin' me it's my turn to wash the
passage ! " She spat on the floor of the tram and rubbed
the spittle with her heel. " That for her an' her passage !
I'll wash it only when it comes up my back, an' not
before."

" That's right, Sarah," the other one said.

" They surely come from the new houses at Calderburn," Aunt Bella said. " What awfu' like tickets ! "

" It makes you wish you didn't come from Harrisfield,"
Aunt Kate said. " Harrisfield used to be a nice place
to live in, but all those new houses at Calderburn have
lowered the tone of the place."

" Yer mother wouldn't know it if she saw it now,"
Aunt Bella said to me. " Calderburn was all fields when
she went away. It used to be a big estate."

" Real classy," Aunt Kate said. " But it's changed
days ! Nowadays if you say you come from Harrisfield
folk look at you as much as to say, ' Oh, do you come
from the slum-clearance area ? ' It's not fair putting
all these new houses in our district."

"Folk have got to bide some place," Aunt Bella said. "An' mind you, some o' the hooses they folk came frae werenie up to much. All those auld tenements in the High Street and the Cowgate. It was high time they got knocked doon. They were just breedin' grounds for vermin and disease."

"But they're such awful-like people," Aunt Kate said.

"What can ye expect?" Aunt Bella said. "They've never had a chance. If you'd been brought up in the High Street you'd, maybe, be like them, too. They're not all bad."

The conductor was taking the fares and when he came to the two dames they had an awful argument with him. "Threepence is faur ower much," the one with the shawl said. "The Corporation should mak' allowances for us puir souls. They turn us oot o' the hames we ha'e lived in for years an' mak' us bide in a God-forsaken place like Calderburn, an' then they ha'e the cheek to chairge us threepence for a ride in the car. Where the hell do they think we get the money?"

"From the same place as you got the money to buy those bottles," the conductor said.

"Is it a skite on the jaw ye're wantin'?" the dame said.

"That's what he needs, Sarah," the other one said.

The conductor didn't answer her and he went on collecting the fares. But the dame with the tartan shawl had her dander up. She kept yelling at the conductor so that everybody on the tram had to listen, whether they wanted to listen or not. And when she saw that the conductor wasn't heeding her she tried to pick a quarrel with a dame in a fur coat who was sitting next to her, and who looked as if she wished she was where she should of been with a fur coat on a warm night like that. But this dame moved as soon as she saw a vacant seat. Sarah wasn't beat, though. She shifted her seat, too. "Am I no' guid enough for ye, hen ? " she said to the dame with the fur coat. " I'll claw yer e'en oot if ye look like that at me again. The stuck-up b—r ! " she said to the other people in the tram.

" That'll do now," the conductor said. " One more crack like that and off you go."

" An' whae'll do it ? " Sarah said. " It would tak' a man to put me off a car an' no' a dressed-up puggy. Wouldn't it, Aggie ? "

" That's right, Sarah," Aggie said.

For about a quarter of an hour the tram clanged through fairly busy streets, past shops and movie-theatres and churches. There sure was a helluva lot of churches, and any stranger would be bound to reckon the folks of Edinburgh were awful religious, till he got to know them better. All the way the tram was going down hill and I remembered what Mom had told me about Edinburgh being built on seven hills. Then, after a bit, the traffic wasn't so great and the appearance of the streets began to change. We were out in the suburbs. And then, suddenly, we seemed to be in open country. But that lasted only for about a couple of seconds. We were getting near more houses and we were getting near the sea. This was Harrisfield, lying in a hollow on the Firth of Forth. Away to the left, on a hill, I saw what Aunt Kate said was Calderburn ; huge tenements standing out black against the pinkish twilight of the sky. I saw that some of them were just skeletons, for the sky was shining through the window-spaces. As the car began to gather speed going down the hill towards Harrisfield I saw the harbour. There were three piers, the Middle Pier, the West Pier, and the

Breakwater, and they stood out in the water like the
letter E with a bit added to one of its sides.

"This is Harrisfield Road," Aunt Kate said, as the
tram rattled down the hill. "See, there's the school!"
But before I had time to get a real good look at it the
tram stopped with a jerk and Kate said: "Well, here
we are!"

It was the tram-terminus and the women with the
bottles got off, too. Aunt Bella was so busy looking
at them and trying to hear their parting remarks to the
conductor that she dropped her hand-bag and broke the
clasp.

"That's what you get for being inquisite," Aunt Kate
said, laughing. Aunt Bella was kinda annoyed at this,
and by the time she had recovered her dignity the women
were off the car and away. We watched them begin
to go through, what had once been a field, but what
looked now more like a gigantic mud-plaster, and they
headed for the tenements.

"Fancy having to live beside folk like that," Aunt
Kate said. "I'd go off my head."

"Well, I doot ye'll maybe land in the asylum yet,"
Aunt Bella said. "I hear there's some word o' shuttin'
the cottages an' makin' the tenants move to Calderburn."

"Who told you that?" Aunt Kate said.

"Nell Dippy," Aunt Bella said.

Aunt Kate laughed. "Nell Dippy!" she said. "Do
you mean to say you believe anything that daft creature
tells you?"

"Well, she had been speakin' to Sir Malcolm's
factor," Aunt Bella said. "An' he told her that if any
tenants left the cottages their hooses werenie to be let
again. The Sanitary ha'e been kickin' up a row aboot
them. The McRaes, an' the Stones, an' the Robertsons,

are a' thinkin' aboot flittin'. They want new hooses
wi' electric light an' a bathroom."

"Help my Jimmie Johnston!" Aunt Kate said.
"Fancy Jock McRae with his bow legs in a bathroom!"

"What would hinder him?" Aunt Bella said tartly.
"He, maybe, likes to wash himsel' though he's bandy.
Not like some folk I ken," glaring at Aunt Kate and
pressing her lips together, real annoyed. "Dinnie
mention this to my father or mother. There's no use
worryin' them. There'll be time enough for them to
worry when that crowd flits."

I knew from Mom's description of it that this wide
open space was Harrisfield Square. On one side there
was a bank, and a smithy, and a public house called the
Harrisfield Tavern, though everybody called it the
Tap for short. And on the other side there was a
police station and a pretty little church with a church hall
beside it. There was a road leading into each corner
of the square : the Harrisfield Road,t he West Road,
opposite it, the Low Road and the Forthport Road.
The harbour was at the foot of the square. Mom said
it was a busy harbour, but all the boats I could see were
two dingy old tramps and two or three little trawlers,
lying like old tin tubs. Away to the west, lying somewhere between the West Road and the Low Road, was
a huge gasometer. And beyond that, in the distance,
I could see the Forth Bridge. There ain't no call for
me to describe the Forth Bridge. You'd get a better
idea of it from a picture post-card or from a guide-book.
It was about ten miles from Harrisfield and it looked
pretty good with the sun setting behind it. Three
black arches like the sticks of three fans against a red
sky. There was a train going over the top and puffs
of smoke were blowing up like feathers in the air.

" We'll go up the West Road," Aunt Kate said. " It's quicker." And she set off at a gallop past the smithy. " That's the smiddy-seat," Aunt Bella said, nodding at a wooden bench clamped to the wall. "Maybe, ye'll ha'e heard yer mother speak aboot it? Yer grand-father used to be a great one for sittin' there." I just had time to glance at it, for we were too busy trying to keep pace with Aunt Kate. She led us for about fifty yards up the West Road beside a low wall, over the top of which I saw the roofs and chimneys of the cottages.

Jees, I sure was disappointed with my first look at the cottages. I'd only once before seen such a lotta tumbledown shacks and that was when I was on a trip to St. Joseph, Missouri, and I was walking through the Negro quarter. The nigger huts was built of wood, of course, and these was built of brick. But all the plaster was peeling offen them and the bricks was showing. And the slates was offen most of the roofs. Some of them was empty, and them that was, had the glass knocked outen the windows and some of the doors was broken in. Jees, you never saw such a lotta crocks. There was five rows of them, eight houses in a row. About two-thirds of them was occupied. One of the rows was at right-angles to the others and the houses in it was bigger than the houses in the other rows; they had three rooms, but the other houses had only two. Mom's folk lived in one of those, number twenty, and it faced the harbour and the green, where some washing was still hanging out though it was kinda late.

There was a flight of stone steps leading from the West Road down to the cottages, and we went down them. There was a lotta kids playing around, and they all stopped to watch where we was going. Two or three women were gossiping at the end of one of the rows, where there was a well. They all had pails for water, but I found out after that sometimes they took as long as an hour to fill their pails. They all stopped talking when we came up and they said " Good evening " to Aunt Kate and Aunt Bella. One of them, a dame with matted hair and no teeth and a dirty scarf around her neck, came gushing forward and shook hands with me.

" So this is Grace's boy," she said. "I knew yer mother." I didn't think Mom would be flattered at the acquaintanceship—What a map ! It was terrific !—but I shook hands and said, " Howjado ? "

" I'm Nell Dippy," she said. " Maybe ye'll ha'e heard yer mother speak aboot me ? "

I had, but I didn't think she'd be pleased to hear some of the things Mom had said about her. " Yeah," I said.

"Do ye hear that ? " Nell said to the other women. " He speaks just like they speak in they new-fangled talkies."

Granma was waiting at the door for us. She was a little thin dame, a bit bent and all shrivelled-up. I guess she wasn't really little as women go, but she seemed little to me. She sorta gasped and put up her hand to her mouth when she saw me.

" I told you," Aunt Kate whispered to Aunt Bella.

But the old dame recovered pretty quick. " Come awa' in, laddie," she said. " Welcome to Scotland." She reached up and kissed me and then she turned to my aunts and said, " Isn't he like Walter ? "

" Isn't he, mother ? " they said.

Granpa was sitting on the sofa, for he wasn't able to walk much on account of his rheumatics. It took him

all his time to walk across the floor. The same thing
struck me about him as had struck me about Granma
—they were both so clean. They were wrinkled, but
the wrinkles didn't look as if they had come with worrying. Although they were old and done, they weren't
decayed. They weren't dirty like that Nell Dippy.
Like the cottages they had seen their day, but unlike the
cottages they weren't in ruins. They had an air of
nobility. I guess nobility is the right word though it
seems sorta soppy to write it.

Aunt Kate made an awful fuss of Granpa. You'd
of thought it was her and not me that had come all the
way from the States. And you'd of thought he was a
baby from the way she spoke to him. " Oh, but he's
a nice old man," she said. " He's the nicest, cleanest
old man I know."

" And hoo mony auld men do ye ken ? " Aunt Bella
said.

Aunt Kate never let on. She bent over Granpa,
kissing him. She turned to me and she screwed up her
face, supposed to be with sympathy, but more like she
had toothache. " The dear auld cratur'," she said.
" It's sad. Poor old soul ! " And she shook her head
as if Granpa was just dying. He took it all quite coolly.
I found out later that he didn't hear half of what was
going on. I bet he'd of been kinda annoyed at Aunt
Kate for some of the daft things she said. You'd of
thought that either she or Granpa was in their second
childhood—especially her. Every time she came in
she made a fuss of him like this. Even though she'd
been only the length of the lavatory. It sickened me.
Often I'd of liked to tell her to lay off.

It was an awful small kitchen and the big old-fashioned
iron bed took up a lot of room. There was a horsehair

sofa covered with a print cover in front of the bed, with
one end of it beside the fire. This was Granpa's
favourite seat. There was a piano in the corner beside
the bed, and the table was in front of the window.
You'd of thought there wouldn't be much room for
anything else, but there was a high chest of drawers, and
a wash-hand-stand, and a few hard wooden chairs
squeezed in somehow. The walls was covered with
old calendars and pictures. There was six photos of
Rudolph Valentino above the mantelpiece. Aunt Kate
had a crush on him at that time, but later on she took
down his photos and put up some of Ivor Novello in his
place. And later than that, Gary Cooper was the big,
strong, silent man in her life. And he sure was silent.
Any man would of been with Aunt Kate.

At tea-time her and Aunt Bella jawed about this, that,
and the other, remembering things Mom had done or
said, or things they'd done or said themselves, when they
were kids. Granpa didn't hear what they was saying
and he kept stretching forward his head to see if he
could catch it. Granma chipped in occasionally, but
I sat quiet and watched everything. A good time was
had by all.

" Ye're like yer Uncle Walter in more than looks,"
Granma said. " Ye dinnie say much, George."

" They call me Spike at home, Granma," I said.

" Oh, ay, yer mother said that," Granma said.

" He's like Dad, too, don't you think ? " Aunt Bella
said. " Like Dad when he was young in yon photo in
the album."

She got the big family album off the dresser and showed
me a photo of Granpa when he was about twenty-five.
He had a big beard like he had now, only it was black.
I guess I'd of looked like that if I'd been fool enough to

grow whiskers and get my neck trussed up in a high collar and a tie like a scarf.

Aunt Bella and Aunt Kate began to turn over the pages of the album and they kept crying " Look," and laughing at what they saw. " Lookit Meg in this one," Aunt Kate said. " Help my Jimmie Johnston, she's not half fancying her buckie. You'd think she was Lady Muck."

" Meg aye fancied hersel'," Aunt Bella said. " Is that the one she got taken in a dummy aeroplane at the Carnival ? "

" Yes. She's got on a hat with a big bird stretching its wings," Aunt Kate said. " What a sketch ! She'd pass out if she saw it now. I bet she burned her copy of it years ago."

" Ye dinnie need to shout, Kate," Granma said. " We're not all deaf."

" I'm not shouting," Aunt Kate said.

" Ye're that deaf that ye dinnie hear yersel'," Granma said.

Aunt Kate flared up at this and there looked as if there was gonna be a first-class row, but Aunt Bella stepped in. " That photo was taken just before yer mother went to the States," she said to me. " Yer Aunt Meg, and yer mother, and father, and me, were all at the Carnival. It was the day after they got engaged."

" You're not very like your father, Spike," Aunt Kate said.

Aunt Bella made a noise like a horse neighing. " Ye cannie expect him to be," she said, and she looked at me in a funny sorta way. But before anybody could say anything else she said to Granma : " Ha'e ye had ony word frae Meg lately ? "

"I had a letter yesterday," Granma said. "They're all fine—only she's got the back-door trot."

"She'd be ower polite to put diarrhœa," Aunt Bella said.

"More likely she couldn't spell it," Aunt Kate said.

This reminded me that I wanted to see a man about a couple of greyhounds. I asked where the place was. Aunt Kate said she would come with me. "Aw, shucks," I said. "I can find the place myself."

But after she got the key offen the nail beside the door for me she insisted on coming to the corner of the house. "Go straight along the row and you'll come to them," she said. "The number's on the door."

There was a lotta kids playing outside the lavatories and they stopped when they saw me. One kid said: "Are you auld Gillespie's grandson frae Americy?"

"Yep," I said.

"She said she would get ye to scud ma behind," he said, laughing derisively.

"Did she?" I said. "What had you been doin'?"

"I only put chalk on her pavement," he said. "She's an auld bitch. She's aye yelpin' at us."

"I'll clip your ears if you say that again," I said.

"Awa' and raffle yersel'," he said. "Do ye think I'm feared for you, or for yer granny, either?"

I was making to give him a slap on the jaw when another one said: "Hey, mister, do ye ken Tom Mix?"

"No," I said. "I do not ken Tom Mix."

"Ye cannie come frae Americy then," he said.

"But he does so," another one said. "Ma mither said it. She said he'd focht wi' Indians."

"Indians!" the first one said. "He couldnie fight a scabbed cat."

I put the key in the door of the lavatory numbered

twenty, but I couldn't get it to turn at all. I struggled with it for a while, and then I said to one of the kids : " Do you know how to open this ? "

Immediately they all crowded round. " Ye should put it in upside down," one said. " Here, gie's the key an' I'll try."

He opened the door and they all stood gaping while I went inside. It was the first time I can remember having an audience for an occasion like this. I had an awful job shutting the door on them, for they all wanted to see inside. I heard them laughing and shuffling about after I went in.

The lavatory was painted with oil-paint, and as it was damp, it was a mighty cold place. But I found it was a darned sight colder when I sat down. It was just a hole cut in wood and placed above a tunnel. The draught was something terrific. I didn't aim to sit long, but I heard the kids all laughing outside and then I heard some of them go into the lavatory next door, so I sat still and tried to make out what they were saying. But they were giggling and spluttering so much I couldn't make out anything. And then I heard one say : " Here, gie's a look." And I'd just realised that they were looking down the hole of the lavatory next door when there was a yell and I got a helluva skelp on the behind with a stick.

I rose mighty quick then, but, of course, they was all away by the time I got out.

Granpa sure got a mighty good laugh when I told them what had happened. It was the first time since I arrived that I'd seen him so lively. " It reminds me o' the time Sam Dippy got drunk and shut himsel' in the water-closet," he said. " D'ye mind o' that, Mirren ? "

" Ay," Granma said, pressing her lips together.

" We've heard the story that often that we dinnie want
to hear it again."

" But Spike hasnie heard it," Granpa said. " Ye'd
like to hear it, wouldn't ye, Spike ? "

And he started in to tell the story. It had happened
a long time ago, when Mom and them was young.
The Dippys lived next door to the Gillespies. Old
Sam Dippy was Nell's father and he drove a horse and
cart for the railway. He got drunk pretty often. One
day he got so tight that he went to the lavatory to sleep
it off. Old Maggie, his wife, was near demented, wondering what had happened to him. She thought he'd
fallen into the harbour and she was on her way to the
police station, when somebody told her they'd seen old
Sam go into the w.c. Old Maggie went to the lavatory
and she hammered on the door, but she couldn't get
any answer. She hammered and yelled till pretty near
everybody in the cottages came up to see what was
wrong. Old Maggie was in tears. " Oh, ye dinnie
ken hoo much I love ye, Sammy," she kept on shouting.
But there wasn't no response. Things got so bad that
everybody began to think that, maybe, Sam had passed
out, so young Truth Dippy, that everybody said was
simple, was sent down the lavatory next door to see if
his father was O.K.

" What a picture he must of seen ! " Aunt Kate said.

Aunt Bella's sons, Walter and George, came about
half-past nine. Walter was seventeen, and he had a
red nose and pimples and soft fair hair. He worked in
a second-hand bookshop and he seemed to spend all
the time his boss was out in reading smutty books.
George was a couple of years younger. He'd just left
school and he wanted to go to sea like me. He was
studying at the Wireless College to be a wireless operator,

because Aunt Bella didn't want him to be a common sailor. She thought it would be a great idea if we both got on the same boat, but neither me nor George thought it would be such a great idea. All the same him and me got on pretty good together. Better than I got on with Walter.

Walter wanted to be an artist and he read a lotta queer books I wouldn't of been found dead reading. But George could talk real sensible about football, and motor-bikes, and horse-racing. He was the kinda guy you could be with for a week and though you said nothing you didn't need to worry, you knew he was thinking of nothing, the same as yourself. But if you was with Walter for ten minutes without speaking you always had the funny feeling that he was thinking a lotta unpleasant things about you.

" Where's your father ? " Granma said to them when they came in.

" He's busy in the garden," Walter said.

" That awfu' garden," Granma said. " He'd rather work in it than go to the kirk."

" And it'll do him more good than the kirk will," Aunt Bella said sharply.

" Here ! Here ! " George said. " I'll mind that on Sunday when you want me to go to the kirk."

" Dinnie think ye'll get oot o' goin' to the kirk," Aunt Bella said. " What I meant was that yer father's inside working all day, and he needs some fresh air. Besides, the garden's got to be attended to. If ye neglect it it's not long in going to wreck and ruin. Are the laddies playin' footba' the night ? " she said to Walter.

" Ay," he said.

" The minute ma back's turned," she said. " Yer

father's that saft he'll no' quarrel them. He says plenty aboot them puttin' in their ball and breakin' all his plants, but he leaves it to me to tell them where they get off."

" You're good at that ! " George said.

" The kids call her Mrs. Crabbet-face," Walter said to me.

" I'll Mrs. Crabbet-face them if I hear ony o' them ! " Aunt Bella said. " I'm the boy for them ! They're not long in liftin' up their ball and runnin' when I pop ma head outen the window."

" I took one look at you and then my heart stood still ! " George sang a few words of the song that was all the rage just then.

" More than their hearts will stand still if I catch them ! " Aunt Bella said. " They wouldnie be able to sit still if I had onythin' to do with them. I never saw such bairns as the ones nowadays. They'll not take a tellin'. I'm sure our ones werenie like that."

" They knew better ! " George said.

This started Aunt Kate. She raved about them when they was kids. " You were little angels," she said. " Little darlings. Oh, you were the bonniest bairns I ever saw. I was crazy about you."

" You've apparently never recovered," George said.

" That's enough from you, cocky," Aunt Kate said, laughing.

Me, and Walter, and George, went for a walk. They took me along the Low Road, and past the sawmill, where Granpa used to work. The railway lay alongside the road and there was nothing between it and the road to prevent people from walking on the line. We walked about a couple of miles till we came to the Quarry, where there was some dye-works and rubber-

works. The smell was pretty awful. Farther along the
beach was Granton and Cramond, but George said it
was too far to walk to-night. As we turned to go back
he pointed to a narrow lane that joined the road just
above the Quarry. " That's the Gipsy Brae," he said,
laughing. " But it should be called Lover's Lane.
It's a fine place to go with a dame."

" Thanks for the tip," I said. " It looks kinda dark."

On our way back we went down the West Pier.
There was some piles of fish-boxes and pit-props on the
waste-ground at the top of the pier. By the smell the
fish-boxes had been there since the year one. The sun
had set, but it wasn't dark yet. The Firth of Forth
was as smooth and glossy as the back of a dead whale,
and opposite Harrisfield, the coast of Fife was like one
of the whale's fins sticking up.

The wood of the pier was fairly rotten and it had been
patched in places, but I didn't think it any too safe.
There was no sign of life among all the sheds and cranes.
It was kinda creepy walking along and hearing the waves
swishing against the piles. George was humming
Moonlight on the Colorado.

" Jees, this place gives me the willies," I said.

" It gives more than you the willies," George said.

" Me, too," Walter said. " I'm crazy to get away
from it."

" You'd be crazy no matter where you went," George
said.

It was funny how I'd no bother in making out what
my cousins said. Occasionally they used words that
I didn't understand, but usually they spoke the same as
Mom and myself. But I'd an awful job making out
what Aunt Bella and Granma and Granpa said. Aunt
Kate was O.K. She spoke very la-di-da and polite,

on account of her working in a shop, but she could speak real broad when she wanted to. Maybe it was because Walter and George were nearer my own age, but I guess it was mainly because they went a lot to American talkies. I guess it shouldn't take long now before all the English-speaking nations talk the same.

" Imagine anybody livin' in this dump for fifty years," I said.

" Imagine livin' any place for fifty years," George said.

" Well, Granny and Grandpa have nearly done that," Walter said. " Next year will be their Golden Wedding."

" Jees, fifty years in the one house," I said.

" Don't you believe it," George said. " I guess they'll need to shift before the fifty years are up. The cottages are condemned. They'll need to go to one of the new houses at Calderburn."

" Do they know that ? " I said.

" Not yet," George said.

" Aw, maybe they won't need to shift," Walter said. " There's no definite word of it. Only some of the people have flitted and that's set everybody on edge. It would kill Granny and Grandpa if they had to flit now. Folk don't want to make a change at their time of life. All they've got to live for now is death."

" Christ, you should be in a pulpit," George said. " You're a right auld wife. Grandpa's good for another ten years yet. If he could only walk better you wouldn't be able to hold him in the house."

" Ach, you're haverin'," Walter said. " You know as well as me that they haven't anything to look forward to. All they're livin' on is their memories. The cottages are dead and they're practically dead, too. The whole thing reminds me of Goldsmith's ' Deserted Village.' "

" Goldsmith's deserted backside ! " George said.
" Why shouldn't they shift ? The cottages should of
been knocked down years ago. If they'd belonged to
anybody else but Sir Malcolm Harris they'd have been
declared uninhabitable ten years ago. But because they
belonged to Sir Malcolm the Sanitary have been afraid
to say anything, and they've held out till they couldn't
hold out any longer. God only knows how Granny
and Grandpa have stuck them for near fifty years.
Raisin' a family of seven in those three poky wee rooms,
and carryin' all their water, and havin' to walk a hundred
yards every time they wanted to go to the w.c. Hell,
it would of killed me years ago."

" Me, too," I said.

" I don't know," Walter said. " There's something
romantic about the cottages. All these tiny houses and
all the people that have been born and bred in them.
Where did they all go to ? To America, like your
mother and father, Spike ? Or to New Zealand, like
old Stumpy McGregor's sons ? Or to France to fight
in the war, like Uncle Walter and all the others ? Or to
wherever Uncle Tom went ? All those lives, born here
and growing up, and going out into the world. Gee,
if those walls could only speak what a lotta queer stories
they'd tell."

" You're loopy," George said.

I agreed with him. Walter was a queer cuss. All the
same there was a lot in what he said. The cottages
must of seen a lot in the last fifty years. And I couldn't
help speculating about it that night before I went to
sleep in what Granma called the East Room.

I guess I was too tired to sleep and I lay and looked
around me. The wall-paper was so dingy I couldn't
make out the pattern. The blind was down and made

a yellowish light over everything. I'd wanted to pull
it up, but Granma wouldn't let me because she said
people would look in. I'd tried to open the window,
but it was so stiff I couldn't move it. I lay and counted
the spirals on the pillars of the high, old-fashioned chest
of drawers. And I thought about all that I knew about
my relations so far.

Not very much. I knew more about people I'd met
just casually. Of course, I didn't expect them to tell
me a detailed life-story as soon as they met me. Only
hick Americans in films did that. Real folks told you
things that had happened to them last week, and then
they told you things that had happened to them years
ago. You got their life-stories in pieces, like a jig-saw
puzzle, and you had to piece them together for yourself.
So I reckoned that would be how I would learn about
Granpa and Granma. Maybe, some day, I'd be able to
realise how they'd stuck this out for near fifty years,
the chuff-chuffing of those goods trains at the foot of
the green and the shunters shouting to each other
occasionally. But just then I couldn't figure it at all;
the monotony of it would get on my nerves. And I
wondered if it had been the stuffiness and the monotony
that had driven my uncles to doing what they'd done.
And I wondered what exactly it was that they'd done,
and I was speculating about this when I fell asleep at
last.

ONE PURL

LISTENING to those engines you wonder how you've managed to thole the sound of them for nearly fifty years. Every night, in sickness and in health, in joy and in sorrow, those engines have been in the background of your thoughts, keeping time with your heart-beats. When you were moaning in child-birth, when you were worrying about Tom and Arnold, when you were thinking that you'd never see Grace again, thinking of her across the Atlantic, thinking of Walter in a grave in a foreign country. . . . But why think of them any more? The engines are there and the others are not there. The engines are the last sound you'll hear as you lie here dying. Will Grace's laddie be listening to them in the bed in the East Room, in the bed where his uncles slept for years before he was ever thought of? Ah, it's like old times again, when there were bairns in the house. Not that he's such a bairn. He's bigger than ours were when they were his age though he doesn't seem as grown up. But then, he's never had to work and all ours had to work long before they were his age. Eighteen. Ay, it's a long time since any of them were eighteen. A long, long time since you were eighteen yourself. . . . When would that be? You were twenty-nine when you married Wattie. That was in eighteen-eighty. Eleven years before that when you had just made up your mind to be a cook and your three sisters were annoyed at you.

A mere domestic servant! they said. *That's not a fitting
occupation for the youngest daughter of a sea-captain. You
should become a school teacher like us.* Poor Sybil, and
Isabella, and Katherine. A lot of good being school
teachers did them. Only Isabella got a man. And a
poor, dry stick he was. Another school teacher. But
they couldn't turn me against what I wanted. *You look
after the soul,* I said to them, *and I'll look after the belly.*
And I got a job with old Miss Jerome. A fell, crabbed,
old tarter she was, too, with her long neb poking into
all the corners. *Mirren, this corner is thick with dust.*
Do you remember the time she said that to you, and you
turned round and said, *I'm cook here, Miss Jerome, not
housemaid.* A fell, hard time, us poor slaveys had with
her. How you laughed the first time she said to you,
Leave the room, Mirren, I want to pass wind. And how
your bairns and your bairns' bairns have laughed since,
when Wattie told them about it. It was him that told
them; you wouldn't have told them yourself, and often
you felt sorry that you told Wattie in an unguarded
moment.

You put up with old Miss Jerome and her tantrums
for five years and then you went to the Mitchell-Greys.
That was a good place, as places went in those days,
though you're thinking some of the slaveys nowadays,
with their wee aprons and their high heels, would turn
up their noses at it. And you can't blame them. You
wouldn't put up with it yourself, now. Who's going
to sleep in an attic that's not big enough to swing a cat
in? When your box was in there wasn't room for
anything else and you had to stand in the passage and
put on your clothes. It was fell inconvenient sometimes.
Whiles I wonder now how servants put up with such
conditions. They can't have had much spunk or they'd

have told their mistress to stick her attic where . . .
But there, you're as bad as Wattie. That's the sort of
thing he'd say.

You mind the last time you put on your clothes in
that attic? On your wedding-morning. There was
a vivid red sky, and you stood at the sky-light, and you
remembered the old saying, *Red sky at morning is the
shepherd's warning*, and you stretched your arms wide as
if to challenge it. If you had been Grace, or Bella, or
one of your grand-children, you'd have put your fingers
to your nose. But even if you had thought about it
you wouldn't have dared to do that, in case anybody
saw you. You always thought about what other people
would think.

Your wedding-dress was a present from Mrs.
Mitchell-Grey. You would have liked to have chosen
white, but you remembered, in time, that white dirtied
too easily and you chose grey so that you'd be able to
wear it on the Sabbath after you were married. It was
a braw silk gown, good strong stuff. You wore it for
years and then you made it down into frocks for Meg
and Grace. They wore them when they went to Mr.
Oliphant's dancing classes. They used to come home
singing *A in two three, an out two three*, and imitating the
way Mr. Oliphant did the steps. Grace said he should
have been called Mr. Eliphant *only*, she said, *an elephant
never forgets and he gey often forgets what he's going to do with
his feet*. Grace was always a great one to imitate people.
They said she took it off me, that I was a good mimic.
Well, I don't know. One thing, you never had much
times for dancing, Mirren. You didn't even get a dance
at your wedding, for there wasn't a spree to dance at.
It was your mother's place to provide the spree, but
when you told her that you were going to marry Wattie

she said, *I wash my hands of you. Never, never shall you darken my door again.* Though darken *your* door she did. You were the first she ran to when the Captain got into trouble after he rammed that schooner. Oh, she was a hoighty-toighty piece of goods the Captain's Lady. A bit of an actress and a snob forbye. Thank God she didn't give you any of her snobbishness the same as she gave your sisters. They were too high and mighty to look at any man that came after them. They thought they should get Dukes, or Earls, and in consequence they got nothing. They became poor, dried sticks of old maids, always sneering at you and saying, *I told you so*, every time you were in difficulties. But you've had a better life than they had by a long chalk. Maybe your life hasn't been all it should have been, but whatever hardships you've had you've always had a man beside you, and that's more than your sisters could say. Isabella might have married another old maid for all the good her man was.

You didn't invite anybody to your wedding. Wattie had no friends except his father. So you had a quiet wedding, with only Auld Tam, and Beanie, and Tib. You might as well have been married in one of those register-offices. But it was in a kirk. You wouldn't have felt that you really were married if it hadn't been in a kirk. *Do you, Marion Alice Murdoch, take this man, Walter George Gillespie, to be your lawful wedded husband, to love, honour, and obey, till death do ye part?* Wattie was that nervous he got into a terrible fluster and Auld Tam had to give him a nip out of his bottle. He was a birkie, Auld Tam. He had just come in for the day from Penicuik and he was determined to have a good time. It's, maybe, just as well that your mother and sisters weren't at the wedding, them that were aye so genteel.

They'd have been shocked at Auld Tam. But him and the Captain always got along real well whenever they met at your house. The Captain was always sorry that he let your mother over-rule him about coming to the wedding and he tried to make it up to you later on.

After we were married we drove in a cab from the kirk in Morningside. There were no tram cars in those days. Not even the old cable-cars, they came later. We came down the Lothian Road and along Princes Street and down Leith Walk. It was a kind of round-about way to come, but Wattie wanted to show his father all the sights of the city. And some queer sights there ·were, too. Though I think Auld Tam, himself, was one of the biggest. He wanted to talk, but neither you nor Wattie gave him any encouragement, and he pulled his bowler over his eyes and his big red nose, and sat and stared at his belly. Like yon wee heathen idol that your grandson Walter has. The Buddy or something he calls it. An awful-like thing it is. I'm thinking it would need Auld Tam's checked waistcoat to help hide it.

When it reached Leith the cab turned sharply to the left and the horse began to clop-clop along the cobbles of Commercial Street. You stared out of the window on your right, but you could hardly see the Docks nor the berth where the *Grace Darling* was lying for the mist before your eyes. Not that you didn't know well enough in imagination what they looked like ; you had been born and bred within sight of them. And when the cab passed the Captain's house you pressed your lips together and Wattie reached over and patted your knee. You didn't see anything clearly until the cab came to Forthport, and then you laughed, when Auld Tam sat up with a jerk and said, *God Almighty ! What a hum !*

It's the fish, you said, and you pointed to the groups of fish-wives standing and sitting beside their creels on the esplanade. Some of them were gutting fish. Others were shelling cockles and mussels. They looked brawny and healthy, and they shouted and waved when the cab passed. There never was any trace of shyness about the Forthport folk.

They're great singers, aren't they? Auld Tam said. He put his fingers on his nostrils and sighed. *Ah, they're brave folk. It would tak' something to mak' me open ma mooth and sing wi' a smell like that knockin' aboot. So help me god!*

Not even a dram, father? Wattie asked.

Not even a dram, Auld Tam said.

Ay, the Forthport folks have become famous since those days, what with their Fish-Wives' Choir, and their Fisher-Girls' Choir, and going to London to sing before Royalty. They say that a lot of them in the Choir never carried the creel in their lives : they got into the choir because they could sing—or because other folk thought they could sing. For myself, I think they've terrible ugly voices, the Forthport folk. And they're a clannish crew. There's an old story about them watching a fight between a Forthport man and a stranger. Those on the outskirts of the crowd, who couldn't see, kept crying, *Whae's doon noo?* And when the others cried, *Oor ain man*, they cried *Help aim up*. But when they cried, *Stranger*, they cried *Kick aim*. That's an old saying in Harrisfield when you hear tell of anybody being clannish, *Stranger! Kick aim!* But, no doubt, it's true of plenty places other than Forthport.

After the cab left Forthport Wattie leaned forward and pointed. *Look, there's Harrisfield!* And you looked out of the cab window and saw the Breakwater stretching out into the water, like a long grey stick with white scallops, like fungus where the spray was dashing against it. The cab was passing some fine, stately houses, with huge gardens sloping down to the shore. *That's Trinity, where all the toffs bide,* Wattie said. Auld Tam sniffed and spat out of the window. He aye had a great dislike for the gentry and he'd instilled it well into Wattie.

The cab jogged along the Forthport road beside the railway on the embankment and you passed the pend that led on to the Breakwater. After that the railway line began to slope down, and by the time you came into the square, it was running level with the cab. You'll never forget your first look at Harrisfield. It was a busy place in those days, though it seemed farther from Edinburgh than it does now. There was more trade then, trade with the boats. Now there's no boats to speak of and no trade, although there's more folk here than ever there were ; all those folk up the hill there at Calderburn. All strangers, folk that have no work and that have been put out of their slums in the Auld Toon because of the Sanitary. But in those days there was plenty of life and bustle. Engines drawing strings of wagons full of coals ; piles and piles of pit-props. The cab had to stand for a few minutes to let an engine with a long line of wagons puff slowly up the coal-lie, and while you waited you looked out at the harbour. It was full of boats, trawlers, and schooners, and three-masters, such as they haven't got nowadays. And out of the other window you could see the green fields and gardens of Calderburn House stretching away towards the spires and the grey roofs of Edinburgh, with the Castle Rock the most prominent feature. It and Arthur's Seat, like a crouching lion, watching the city.

The whip cracked and the horse moved forward and you got your first look at the cottages. You thought you had never seen such a lot of bonnie wee houses, all whitewashed, with bright red roofs and window-boxes in a lot of the windows. The horse slowed down to a walk and you saw all the men and women standing at their doors and a crowd of bairns began to follow the cab crying, *Poor oot! Poor oot!*

The cab stopped and Wattie jumped out and helped you down. You stood, clutching your long skirts and wondering whether you should smile, or what, to the crowd standing around the door. A young woman about your own age came out smiling and Wattie said, *Mirren, this is Mrs. Dippy.* You shook hands with her and she said, *The kettle's just boiling. Ye'll be needing your tea.* Auld Tam wheezed and puffed his way out of the cab and he cried, *Steady there! Steady there!* to the bairns that were crowding round. And he put his hand in his pocket and hauled out a handful of coppers and threw them to them. Wattie and he stood laughing at the scramble while you followed Maggie Dippy into the house, and then Auld Tam gave the nearest behind a skelp as he followed us in.

It's no' a palace, Wattie said.

But you didn't mind that. You were pleased to have a house of your own after working for so long in other folk's houses. *It's lovely*, you said.

It'll do till we get something better, Wattie said.

And he meant that. He was terribly ambitious when you got married. But his ideas were greater than his deeds. He didn't try to put any of his plans into action. By the time he had finished dreaming and planning he had got tired of the plan and another idea had crowded it out of his head. He never did anything. He was nearly fifty before he really started to try to do things and then it was too late. He was too old and tired. Rearing a family and working for them had sapped all his strength and courage. Wattie should never have got married at all, really. Men like him, who want to help their fellow-men, shouldn't get married and have obligations. They should keep themselves free so that they'll be able to give all their attention to what they feel is their life's work.

You and Wattie had your first quarrel the following Sunday. After breakfast you put on your wedding-dress, which already you called Your Best, and you waited for Wattie to get ready. But he sat at the fire, smoking his pipe and whittling at a piece of wood. *Hurry up and get dressed*, you said. *The ten o'clock bell has stopped.*

What aboot it? Wattie said.

We'll be late, you said.

Late? he said, looking up, but not stopping his whittling. *Late for what?*

The kirk, you said.

Aw, Mirren, he said, and he looked at you that way that made your inside turn. But you pressed your heels to the ground and tried to keep your legs from trembling, and you said, *Get your things on.*

No' on our first Sunday, he said.

Ay, on our first Sunday, you said. *We must get kirked. It wouldnie be decent if we didnie go.*

Ach! he said. *Decent!*

Get your things on, you said.

And because he loved you, because he was an easy-going man who didn't like to quarrel with anybody, Wattie put on his Sabbath clothes and went with you. He would far rather have sat by the fire and whittled the piece of wood into a pipe-rack. That was the first time he had been at the church for years. His mother had died years before you married him and there had been nobody to see that he lived a decent, God-fearing, life. Auld Tam didn't believe in kirks. *They cramp my style*, he said, and he would hawk noisily and spit to show his independence.

But your folk were kirk folk. Your father was an Elder and every Sunday that his boat was in port he went round with the collection bag. Your mother was assiduous in doing good works; she formed women's guilds and mothers' meetings, and she liked nothing better than to visit poor folk and tell them how to bring up their children. And your sisters were Sunday- as well as Day-School teachers. So you were determined not to let them have all their own way. You'd show them! You made up your mind that Wattie was going to be an Elder. And if he was going to be an Elder there would be no time for sitting beside the fire, whittling at wood and making useless little knick-knacks, and dreaming of the good times that were coming. Dreaming! Tcha!

This led to endless bickering between you, but, as you were determined, and as Wattie was, naturally, easy-going and anxious to please, by the time your first bairn was born, kirk twice every Sunday was the regular programme in your house.

Your first bairn. . . . What a disappointment that was. You wanted a bairn so badly so as to be upsides with everybody else. Three months before your time Maggie Dippy had her first, a son whom she christened Samuel after his father. Samuel! I don't think Truth Dippy ever got called Samuel in his life. It was always Truth because the poor simple soul didn't seem able to tell a lie, even when a lie was necessary. He was a funny, wee bairn, with a shrunken red face and pale, pale eyes that never seemed to look at you but always looked beyond you at something over your shoulder. You remember that while you washed him you prayed that your bairn when the time came wouldn't have a vacant look like this one of poor Maggie's. But when the time came you would far rather have had something like Truth than the cold, still-born thing they plucked from you. You envied Maggie Dippy as she bustled around you, and you could have struck her when she said, *Ah, it's a bad time of year.*

That was always Maggie Dippy's explanation for everything. A bad age or a bad time of year. Only she didn't say a bad age to you, though she meant it. You could have screamed. You had wanted a bairn so badly, so as not to feel an outsider when the women at the well talked of those things, and you had wanted to be able to say that none of the bairns in the cottages were as well looked after as yours. The disappointment hurt you even more than the unwanted milk in your breasts. But you dug your teeth into your lips to keep from saying anything, and Wattie was surprised at your calmness when they took away the wee body and placed it in the white coffin.

The morning after the bairn was buried you got up as usual and kindled the fire and prepared the breakfast. You were stirring the porridge when Wattie awoke. He blinked sleepily at you and said, *I thocht ye'd ha'e lain a day or twa in yer bed.*

No' me, you said. *I'm a' right.* For you saw no reason why you should lie in bed any longer. You weren't a fine lady who needed coddling. You didn't complain because you had to get up at half-past four so that your man could start work at six o'clock. Most of the women in the cottages had to do that.

But Wattie complained. He said, *It's a damned shame that us puir folk should ha'e to rise at this unearthly hour, in the middle o' the night, so that a handfu' o' rich folk can live in idleness. Thank God the day is coming when everybody'll be born equal an' we'll a' ha'e to get up at the same time.*

Havers! you said. *Ye'd better get up or ye'll be late.*

Wattie worked in the sawmill that belonged, like everything else in Harrisfield, to Sir Malcolm Harris. Those with the highest pays got thirty shillings a week, but most of them got round about a pound. Wattie was getting twenty-one shillings then and he was looking forward to the time when he would get thirty. All our hardships would be over then, he thought. Ah, that thirty shillings was a long time in coming, and when it did there were so many mouths to feed that we never knew the good of it.

Every man in the cottages worked for Sir Malcolm, in some job or other. And a lot of the younger women, as well; they worked in the Net Work. Hardly any of them ever complained. They got up every morning, they went to their work, they came home at night and they went to bed. They had no pleasures, though they had plenty of hardships and sorrows. About all they had to hope for was to get drunk, or to have an occasional jaunt into Edinburgh or Leith, on a Saturday night. Sometimes in the summer time they might take the ferry across to Burntisland, but that was the farthest they ever went. One or two had been to Glasgow, and their neighbours thought they were great travellers. London was only a name to most of us. We knew the Queen lived there and that it was where Sir Malcolm and his

large family spent most of their time and most of the
money that we earned for them.

Wattie was one of the few who ever complained.
Our neighbours called him a Radical. It was an awful-
like thing in those days to be a Radical. It was like
what being a Communist is now. Folk expected him
to blow up the sawmill with a bomb or something
equally ridiculous. They all kind of looked upon him
as an enemy; they didn't realise that it was for their
good that he was a Radical; that if he got the shorter
hours and the bigger pay that he advocated for, they
would get it, too. They agreed that there was sense
in his arguments, but they would not go further than
agreement with him. Their fathers, they said, had
lived like that before them and their fathers' fathers,
and, no doubt, their sons would live like that after
them.

Wattie was furious at them. He worried himself a
lot, railing against them. *The working-man's greatest
enemy*, he often said, *is the working-man. They're all at each
others' throats, suspicious of each other.* They did not
foresee the great changes that would sweep over the
country. They did not think that their sons would
have more courage than they. They did not think that
many of the things Wattie dreamed about would come
to pass. If only some of them were alive to-day, they
would look in amazement at the things their grandchildren accept without question. And those grandchildren—they are not satisfied, either. They, too,
look forward to greater freedom. Will their grandchildren reap the fruits of their dreams, as they, themselves, have reaped the fruits of their grandparents?

You had been pregnant for about five months again
when the mill went on short-time. The men still

started at the unearthly hour of six o'clock, but they finished work at three o'clock in the afternoon. This annoyed you even more than the cut in Wattie's pay, for he came home in the afternoons and sat by the fire. He would sit there for hours, supposed to be making things for the house, but in reality dreaming of the good times coming.

You were so active, yourself, that when you saw him sitting there so lazy-like, you were furious. You hated to see him whittling. *Messing up ma clean kitchen wi' yer nonsense*, you said. *Get awa' ootside for ony favour*.

But he never went. Sometimes he didn't even trouble to answer you, and this angered you all the more, so that you bustled about feverishly, venting your spleen on the furniture.

You're a woman who has aye been fond of reading, but you don't believe in sitting down with a book until evening when all the work is done. Not like some women, who sit down in the middle of all their work, hoping, maybe, to find in their book some of the romance that life is denying them. But you wait until the gas is lit and the curtains are drawn before you get out your book. That's why you have aye liked to light the gas as soon as daylight begins to disappear. You hate the gloamin'. But Wattie likes the gloamin'. The flames of the fire, casting shadows on the wall, help to stimulate his fancies ; he doesn't like to be rudely jerked back to the harsh realities of life by the plop of the gas being lit. And how can he dream of the world to come, where all men are equal, with a gas-jet sizzling angrily two feet above his head ?

But apart from little differences like that we were very happy those first few years. Indeed, we have been happy enough those fifty years—it was other folk that

caused us all the heartbreaks we've had. Never he, nor
you. All our little differences of character and habits
have helped to bind us closer together. You understand Wattie, and he understands you. And complete
understanding is the main thing in a happy marriage.
In a working-class marriage, anyway, where you can't
afford to let other passions stir you. Once married
you stay married.

You weren't long married before the Captain visited
you, and he visited you every time he was in port after
that. Whether he told your mother of those visits you
never found out. But about this time, when Wattie
was on short-time, you got your first visit from the
Captain's Lady. She came one afternoon when Wattie
was sitting by the fire, making a footstool. She just
nodded to him, and for his part he never fashed himself
about her. He went on working, though you knew by
the set of his head that he was listening to all that you
said as you showed your mother the house.

The Captain's Lady had on a green costume and a long
yellow lace scarf, that she flirted every now and then,
when she drew back her shoulders and threw her head
up with a sniff. You knew that she was thinking, What
a poky little hole for the daughter of Captain Arnold
Murdoch of the *Grace Darling*, but she said, every now
and then, *It's very nice, I'm sure.* And she would give
the ends of her scarf another flirt. While you were
making the tea she sat down beside the fire and looked
across majestically at Wattie.

Are you not working just now, Mr. Gillespie? she said, as
distantly as she could.

You felt like striking her; her tone made you that
mad. But you chuckled to yourself when Wattie said,
Naw, ma, the mill's on short-time, in an awful common

voice. And when he spat in the fire you had to look away in case you would laugh.

The spitting fell short and it sizzled on the grate. Ordinarily you would have roared at him for making a mess of your clean grate, but you didn't say anything to-day; you smiled when you saw the disgusted look on your mother's face.

Can you not find other and better paid work? she said.

Naw, ma, Wattie said.

He knew that this familiar tone annoyed her; he told you afterwards that he'd enjoyed seeing the flush that settled like a rash on her high cheek-bones and seeing her press her thin lips tightly together.

Can the auld man no' get me a job on his boat, ma? he said.

Captain Murdoch has more to do than find work for any Tom, Dick or Harry, she snapped.

But I'm no' ony Tom, Dick or Harry, Wattie said. *I'm Wattie, his son-in-law.*

It was by no desire of ours that you entered that relationship, your mother said. *Marion has made her bed. She must lie on it.*

Who said she wouldn't? you said quietly, and you placed three chairs around the table. *Sit in, mother. I'm sorry there's nothing but bread and treacle. That's all we can afford just now.*

And you in that condition! she said. *What kind of bairn do you think you'll have? A blackamoor very likely.* She turned to Wattie, and cried furiously, *You should be ashamed of yourself. A big, able-bodied man like you sitting by the fire when you should be out earning enough to keep your wife and her child. Bread and treacle, indeed!*

What more can you expect off twelve and six a week? Wattie said. *Would ye like us to live on sheep's lichts and liver, like some o' oor neighbours? Bread and treacle may not be the staff of life but it's nourishing. Treacle's guid for ye. It keeps the bowels open.*

The bowels! The Captain's Lady gasped for breath.

Ay, the bowels, ma wumman, Wattie said. *If ye keep yer bowels open yer mind'll keep easy.*

Oh, I was never spoken to like this in all my life, your mother said, rising and drawing her scarf tight around her shoulders. *I'll have you remember that I'm the Captain's Lady.*

An' I'll have ye remember that I'm the Captain on this quarterdeck, Wattie said. *If ye dinnie like it ye ken what to do.*

You followed your mother to the door. *Remember what I told you, Mirren,* she said. *Eat something more substantial than bread and treacle, or that child of yours will be a weakling. If things get any worse you'd better come home. God knows that it was against our wish that you married that man, but I wouldn't like people to say that we allowed our daughter to die of undernourishment. Here's half a sovereign. It's all I have with me. Don't you dare spend one penny of it on that man.*

No, thank you, mother, you said, *pushing back her hand. We want nothing from you. Least of all do we want advice.*

Tom was born about six weeks after that. You felt then that your position in the cottages was secure. When you gossiped with the women at the well and the talk turned to child-birth and other things, you no longer felt embarrassed. And when Margaret was born the following year, and Arnold the year after that, you regarded yourself as a very fortunate woman, a woman, as Mr. Silver, the minister said at Arnold's christening, whom the Lord had blessed.

There was some trouble about choosing a name for Arnold. You wanted to call him Anthony, after the hero of a novel you were reading, when he was born. But Wattie wouldn't agree to that. *The first two are after ma faither and mither*, he said. *This one'll ha'e to be after your side.*

And the Captain who came at once to see his new grandson approved of this. *One of them'll have to be called after me*, he said. *I'll make a sailor of him.*

I doot ye'll ha'e a job, Wattie said, thinking about the row the bairn made when he was getting bathed. *He doesnie like the water at a'.*

You called him Anthony Arnold, but he never got called anything but Arn. He was a delicate bairn, fair like yourself. The first two were dark, like Wattie, and real strong little Gillespies. But Arn was puny and aye ailing. Oh, Arn, Arn, my poor laddie, after all the trouble we had in rearing you, to think that you would end like that. It would have been better if you'd died one of those times when you were wee and we'd given up hope of ever getting you to be strong and rosy-cheeked like the others. We might have known that because you were so different from the others you would end differently.

Arn was two and Grace was hardly a year when Bella was born. While you were waiting on her you took the other four and went to stay with Auld Tam. Tom was just about school age and the other bairns in the cottages had their summer holidays, and you were afraid he'd learn a lot of ill off them. You thought you'd take him safely out of their road and give yourself less worry while you were expecting.

But you were wrong. Tom didn't need other bairns to make him wild. He had a wild, wayward strain of his own that he must have got from his grandfather; Auld Tam had been a birkie in his day. He'd been a soldier, and when he'd served his time he was pensioned off with the rank of sergeant-major. The army had left its mark on him, for he couldn't abide women-folk fussing around him. He lived in a wee cottage at Penicuik, ten miles on the other side of Edinburgh, and he kept it cleaner than many a woman would have done. Most of his army life had been spent at Glencorse Barracks, and as they were within walking distance of Penicuik, he never allowed a day to pass without walking over to have a crack with the soldiers there about old times.

You got on fine with him, though he couldn't abide the sight of the bairns. It was queer, for he seemed to like them all right any time he visited the cottages. Perhaps it was because in Penicuik they upset the peace and quiet of his little house. Especially his garden. Oh, that awful garden! It was Auld Tam's god. The garden and his hens. You don't know yet, after forty years, which of them he treasured the most. One of his hens had hatched ten chickens two or three days before you took the bairns to stay with their grandfather. It was kept in a box that he'd made into a coop, and the very first night Auld Tam took Tom and Meg down the garden to show them the chickens and told them not to dare to go near the coop unless he was with them. They promised faithfully that they wouldn't.

The first morning you sent them out to play while you were cleaning up the house, and for a while you thought they were getting on fine, and you were congratulating yourself for having brought Tom here, out of reach of the bad language and tricks of the cottage-laddies. You looked out at them once or twice, but they seemed to be playing fine and you went on making the dinner, quite unconcerned. You were peeling the tatties when you heard an awful uproar. The bairns were yelling and greeting, and above them all, you could hear Auld Tam bullering and swearing.

Ye young b—r, ye'll be the death o' me, he cried.

What's wrong, father? you asked, when you ran outside and found wee Tom struggling with his grandfather.

What's wrong? Auld Tam roared. *This wean o' yours has let oot a' ma chickens and he's shut the hen up in the coop. I was takin' a dander doon by the burn an' when I cam' back I found him an' Maggie throwin' the chickens ower the berry-bushes.*

We only wanted to see if they could fly, Tom said.

And they couldn't, Meg said.

You had a gey hard job trying to soothe Auld Tam, but you managed to get him to go into the house while you put the chickens back into the coop beside the hen. You never saw a hen make so much fuss. It was fair demented. Tom wanted to hold it while you put the chickens in, but you sent him into the next field with Meg and Arn. *Now, play there till I call you*, you said. *And don't make any noise for wee Grace is sleeping.*

When dinner was ready you went to the hedge and called them. But the field was empty. *I'll warm that Tom's arse*, you said to yourself, as you scrambled through the gap in the hedge and ran across the field to look for them. But there was no sign of them in the adjoining field either, and you were going to go back to the house, thinking that, maybe, they were at the front, when you heard them shouting in a meadow on the other side of the burn. You shouted to them, but they took no notice, so you thought you'd go for them and you were making up your mind to go for Tom in another way when you got him. You had to cross the stepping-stones farther down the burn, and then you had to cross a ploughed field, and you were fair swearing to yourself when you got to the gate of the meadow.

But when you reached it you stood and stared. You opened your mouth to shout, but before the sound came something made you strangle it.

A big cart-horse was grazing and the bairns were playing round about it. Tom had picked a switch from the hedge and he was tickling the horse's belly with it. The horse wasn't fashing itself about them, but every minute you expected to see them getting trampled to death beneath its huge hoofs. Even now, after all those years, you can't remember clearly what happened. But you think that it was Arn who saw you and came toddling towards you. Meg followed. And then you found courage to call to Tom. *I'm coming*, he called. And he stepped back and gave the horse an awful swipe with the switch before he ran and joined you at the gate. The thunder of the horse's hoofs as it galloped across the field still rings in your ears. But you were that thankful that they were all safe that you never quarrelled Tom.

The next day you took them home. You have all the town-bred woman's fear of the country. Far better, you thought, for Tom to swear and get into mischief with the other laddies than that he should be trampled to death beneath the hoofs of a wild animal. Auld Tam thought it was on his account that you were taking them home and he pleaded with you to stay. But you wouldn't listen to him, and he said, *You're an independent bitch, Mirren.*

Well, you had to be independent. You hated to accept anything from anybody. You can't rear seven children in a three-roomed cottage on thirty shillings a week without finding out that life isn't a bed of roses.

Many's the time you'd have been glad of a little help, yet whenever it was offered you refused it—not very politely sometimes. When the Captain offered you money after Bella was born you near jumped down his throat, and he said, *You're as short as cat's dirt in the morning.*

Back in the cottages Tom got wilder than ever. His holiday in Penicuik wasn't very long, but it was long enough for him to boast to the other laddies and tell lies about things he'd never seen. *We were at London,* he told them. *We passed London on the way to Penicuik.* You felt like skelping his behind for him at the time, but since then it's become a regular family joke.

Many's the time you had to skelp him. Sometimes you thought your hand would be more sore than his bottom, and devil a bit of good it seemed to do him either. When he went to school he got fair outrageous. Will you ever forget his first day? He had on a pair of new tacketty boots and he was fell proud of them. He came home at dinner time and told you that Danny Brown had a pair of tacketty boots, too. *But they're no' as big as mine,* he said.

How do ye ken? you said.

He laughed and said proudly, *Because the b—r's no' as as big as me.*

You warmed his ears well for him and sent him off to school for the afternoon. After you'd washed the dishes you dressed yourself, and Meg, and the other three, and you put Grace and Bella in the pram and set out for a walk. You went down the green and up the coal-lie, and on to the West Road, and when you got round the corner of the square you near fell back over with surprise. There were Tom and Danny Brown, sitting on the smiddy-seat, holding out their feet and measuring their

boots to see who had the biggest! Poor bairns, they
had no more sense—they didn't know they had to go
back to the school for the afternoon—and you still think
it gey brutal of Ginger Grant, the schoolmaster, to palmy
them when you took them up to the school.

And will you ever forget the time you caught Tom
saying *that* word? He was about four at the time, a
wee shaver, with black eyes and a red jersey. He had
learned it from some of the bigger boys and really he
wasn't to blame. But you skelped his ears sore for
him and sent him into the house. Then you started
to tell the other laddies what you thought of them.
You were telling them off good and proper when they
all started to snigger. *Don't you laugh at me*, you said to
them. *I've a good mind to go straight to your mothers and
tell them what you've been doing. Teaching a bairn to swear!
I've a good mind to wallop some of your lugs.* But they still
went on laughing, and you saw that they were laughing
at something behind you. And when you turned round
there was the bold Tom leaning out of the window,
putting his fingers to his nose.

Go inside, ye bad boy, you said. But he didn't budge.
Go inside at once, you said, for you couldn't very well tell
the laddies off with him there. But not an inch did he
move. And then, when you made to go for him, he
put out his tongue and said *that word*.

Oh, he was a wild laddie. He never came straight
home from the school. If he did, he just flung his bag
into the lobby and bolted before you could catch him.
If you needed any messages from the Store you had to
wait till Meg came walking in sedately and placed her
bag in the corner by the fire. You could aye depend
on her being home on time. But Tom never came home
until hunger drove him in at tea-time. Arn was never

in a hurry to get home either, but he didn't come because of different reasons from Tom. Arn walked home dreamily. The only times you ever saw Arn in a hurry to get home were the times when Mr. Bennett was in the offing.

That was old Mr. Bennett, the father of the Mr. Bennett who's Sir Malcolm's factor now. Old Mr. Bennett was a little man with a big sticking-out belly and a walking stick. He strutted along importantly and he aye poked all the bairns he met in the belly with his stick. Probably this was his way of getting his own back on folk who had poked him in the belly when he was a bairn, and God knows you couldn't blame them if his belly *then* was anything like his belly when he was Sir Malcolm's factor. But it didn't endear him to the bairns in the cottages. You always knew when Mr. Bennett was in the offing, for Arn would come in screaming, *Here's yon funny wee man wi' the stick!*

But, although Arn was feared for Mr. Bennett, Tom wasn't, and one of his most mischievous pranks was the day he hid behind the coal-lie dyke and threw stones at Mr. Bennett.

You were washing that afternoon. Like all the other women you washed your clothes in a tub at the door, if the weather was dry. But it had been dull and overcast that forenoon and you had washed in the house. It was getting near dinner time, so you carried the tub to the door and left it standing full of clothes on the pavement, thinking you'd leave it there till dinner was over. You were going in when you heard cries at the foot of the row, and when you stopped to see what was wrong you saw Wattie coming round the corner dragging Tom by the ear. Tom was yelling at the pitch of his voice, *Let me go, ye b—r! Let me go!*

What's wrong? you asked, like to burst out laughing at the look on Wattie's face.

What's wrong! he said. *This young devil has been throwin' stones at Mr. Bennett, that's what's wrong! Do ye want me to lose ma job?* he said to Tom.

Well, he poked me in the belly, Tom said. *Let me go, ye b—r,* and he wrenched free from Wattie and ran to the other side of the wash-tub. Wattie made as if to run after him, but the next minute Tom shoved over the tub and splashed us both with the soapy water, forbye emptying the clothes on the dirty pavement.

That was one time when Wattie didn't laugh at Tom's wildness. Not that he ever laughed much at his wildness when he grew up. It was when he was wee that Wattie saw the funny side of Tom's mischievousness.

Wattie always saw the funny side of everything. Often, in fact, he laughed when you didn't see anything to laugh at. Like the time when poor wee Truth Dippy put the po on his head and it stuck. If it had been made of pig, of course, there would have been no need for anybody to know. Maggie could just have given it a knock with a hammer or something, and if she had cut Truth's head while she was doing it she could have said that he fell and hurt himself. But, unfortunately, it was made of enamel, and no amount of tugging would bring it off. So she had to take him to the Infirmary to get it taken off there. It was no laughing matter; the poor bairn might have suffocated himself or something, but Wattie roared and laughed when he saw Maggie Dippy all dressed up in her Sunday best leading Truth along the row and him with the patty down over his lugs. *My God, but the folk in the tram-car'll get their money's worth the day,* he said.

There's a coarseness about Wattie that you've never

been able to understand. A quieter man there never
was in the cottages. He never got drunk on Saturday
nights and quarrelled with you, like some of our neighbours. And he wasn't a man that cursed and swore
much. Indeed, if anything, he was just a wee thing too
quiet. If he'd been a man that ranted and roared, and
went to the Tap with the other men, he might have got
some of them to listen to his Radical opinions. But
he wasn't a man like that. The only thing about him
that might have appealed to his drinking neighbours
was his fondness for stories that you didn't like to hear
repeated. It was he who remembered all those stories
about Tom, and he has repeated them so often that you
can't forget them. You would like better if you could
mind some of the pleasant things about him. But you
can't. You can't remember anything much about him
at all except all the sorrow he caused you.

*Oh, Tom, Tom, you were easily the worst of our seven
bairns, but I don't love you the less for that—wherever you are
now. And fine I'd like to see you again before I die.* . . .
Ach, you're havering like a fool, Mirren Gillespie.
After all the trouble he's caused you you'd fall on his
neck as though nothing had happened if he were to
come home to-morrow. Ay, my woman, but if he did,
you wouldn't know him. He'd be a middle-aged
stranger. All you'd have in common with him would
be a few memories of the past. And most of those are
of the kind that are best buried and forgotten.

Buried and forgotten. . . . My three laddies. . . .
Walter's dead, and Arn's dead, and you don't know if
Tom's dead or not. There are only the lassies left now.
. . . Lassies! Eh, losh preserve us! That puts me in
mind of Tib, the housemaid, at the Mitchell-Greys.
Mrs. Mitchell-Grey always called her sons, The Boys,

though the youngest was as old as you, and that made
Tib say once, when she was in a temper, *Gey auld-arsed
boys !* So your daughters are gey auld-arsed lassies,
Mirren, with laddies and lassies of their own. Though
none of them have had as many as you. Meg, with her
five, has had the most. And there's Grace, with four,
and Bella, with only two. And Kate not married yet,
and if she doesn't hurry up she'll soon be too old to have
any. But big families aren't the fashion nowadays,
they tell me. The fashion ! Whether they were in the
fashion, or not, when you were young you had them,
and so had everybody you knew, if they were able.
You did your best to stop having them sometimes.
After Grace was born you thought four was enough,
but the others just seemed to come and once they were
there you didn't mind a bit. You didn't love any of
them any the less because you hadn't wanted them before
they were born or because their coming meant more
struggle to make ends meet. You loved them all ;
you tried to have no favourites. But if you had a soft
spot at all it was for Arnold and Walter, they were that
like each other, bonny, fair-haired laddies with red
cheeks. . . . But there's nothing left of their red cheeks
now. . . .

Was that six struck ? Ay, time you were up. Wattie's
still snoring, so easy now, easy. . . .

TWO PLAIN

MY first morning in the cottages I was wakened about eight o'clock by kids shouting outside. I lay for a while and looked around me, but everything looked so dim and fusty that it gave me the willies, so I got up and pulled up the blind, and saw the sun sparkling on the sea and I felt better. I heard somebody moving about in the kitchen and when I went through I found it was Granma. She said she'd been up since six o'clock, lighting the fire and preparing the breakfast. "I like to take my time," she said. "I'm no' sae soople as I aince was. Besides, I've been in the habit o' gettin' up at six."

Granpa was still in bed though he wasn't sleeping. I asked him how he was and he said: "No' very great. I didnie sleep well."

"Havers!" Granma said. "Ye didnie sleep ony worse than usual. Ye cannie expect to sleep sound when ye're never oot to get ony exercise and ye're half-sleepin' most o' the day. He's aye like this in the mornin'," she said to me. "Ye'd think that he was the only one that didnie sleep."

Aunt Kate came in with an awful bang of her bedroom door. She just grunted "Mornin'," and dived at the wash-hand-stand. She poured a little water into the basin, about enough to fill two tea-cups, and she dipped a bit of dirty-looking rag into it and gave her face a lick. Jees, she sure looked a sketch without her war-paint. Her eyes was bleary, and her nose was red, and she had her hair screwed into a lotta curling-pins. It must of been sorta uncomfortable sleeping with all that iron around her head. As soon as she'd given her face a dab with a towel she sat down at the table and said: "I'll take my breakfast, mother. I'll have to hurry. I'm late."

"Can ye mind o' a mornin' when ye werenie late?" Granma said, as she took a plate of porridge from the oven and dumped it before Aunt Kate. "It's no' for the want o' me cryin' at ye, onyway. I shouted at ye five times."

Aunt Kate was too busy eating to answer. Maybe she didn't hear, I don't know. Granma gave Granpa his porridge in bed and she told me to sit down at the table. But before she could give me anything, Aunt Kate was finished and ready for her ham and egg. I never saw such a dame to eat. Pete knows where she put it all. I guess she ate too quick for her meat to do her any good, she just galloped it off as if she was afraid somebody would beat her to it. I always laughed when she was having tea or supper at the Andersons'. Uncle Jim and the boys always made fun of the way she grabbed at things. Uncle Jim would lift the plate of cakes and put them as far from Aunt Kate as he could get them and he'd say, "No, you've had enough. I'd rather keep you a week than a fortnight." And Walter and George made a mug of her, grabbing out for whatever she was gonna take and snatching it away in front of her. All the time Aunt Bella would laugh and Aunt Kate would say, "Help my Jimmie Johnston, I never saw such laddies." And it usually ended with Walter knocking over his tea-cup or something.

As soon as she'd finished breakfast Aunt Kate filled a

bowl with hot water. She put menthol in it. Then
she wrapped a towel around her head and she bent
over the bowl and inhaled the steam. I was watching
her, and I guess I must of had a queer look on my puss
for Granma said, " She does that for her deafness. The
doctor didnie do her any guid, so she went to a quack
and he told her to do this."

" He charged me thirty shillings for advice," Aunt
Kate said. " I didn't half grudge it. Thirty shillings !
I help my kilt, it wasn't worth it."

" Is it doin' you any good ? " I said.

" No' it," Granma said. " Just a lot o' plowters."

" Sometimes I think it does, and sometimes the buzzing
noises are just as bad as ever," Aunt Kate said. She
pushed two plugs of cotton-wool up her nostrils. " I'm
supposed to keep them there for twenty minutes, but
help my Jimmie Johnston, where can I get time in the
morning for that ? "

" You should get up earlier," Granma said. She
took Granpa's empty porridge-plate, and gave him his
ham and egg, all chopped-up into little bits, on account
of his not having enough teeth to chew it. " If ye're
goin' to be deaf, ye'll be deaf and a' the plugs in the
world'll no' stop it. Look at yer father. What a
carry-on we'd ha'e if we had to put cotton-wool up his
nose ! "

" He's a dear auld cratur'," Aunt Kate said, rushing
over to the bed and about smothering Granpa with a hug.
" He's the dearest, nicest old man, I know."

She looked at the clock and she let out a yell. " My
God, I'll miss my train if I don't run." And she rushed
into her room and scurried about for a few minutes.
She came in all dressed except for her face and she started
in to make it up. Jees, she sure had a bold slash ; she

should of been a landscape artist or a house-painter or something. " I'll away then," she said. " I'll be seein' you," she said to me and she kissed me. Then she kissed Granma and made Granpa about choke with a mouthful of ham and egg when she kissed him again.

She left half her lipstick on my cheek, and I rubbed it off as I stood at the door and watched her running along the row. She ran as if she was knock-kneed, with her heels kicking out as if she was doing the Charleston.

" Ha'e ye had enough breakfast, father? " Granma said to Granpa.

He raised his hands to show he'd had enough. " Quite sufficed, my dear," he said. " Richard's himself again ! " And he chuckled.

I helped Granma wash the dishes and then I fetched water from the well. Nell Dippy popped her head outen her door when I passed and she said, " Good mornin'," and looked as if she was gonna come out and talk. But I didn't stop. I told Granma that I guessed I'd go for a walk till Granpa got up.

I went down the West Pier. One of the boats that had been there the night before was away. The other was called *Red Biddy*. A crane was hoisting bales of esparto grass outen its hold and I stood to watch the operation. I was standing when a guy, leaning over the side of the boat said, " Good mornin'."

" Hello," I said.

" It's a rare mornin'," he said.

" It sure is," I said. " But I can see that for myself without you tellin' me."

" I knew you were a stranger," he said, laughing. " If you hadn't been you wouldn't have said that. You'd ha'e said, ' Yes, isn't it ? ' and then you'd ha'e stood

E

lookin' as if you'd swallowed yer tonsils until I'd ha'e felt like sayin', ' It's another rare mornin'.' "

" Yeah, I'm from the States," I said.

" Oh, ye'll be Grace Gillespie's laddie," he said. " I heard ye were comin'. Kate told me they were expecting you. How's yer mother ? "

" She's O.K.," I said.

" My name's Danny Brown," he said. " Maybe ye'll ha'e heard yer mother speak aboot me. I used to bide in the cottages."

" Sure," I said.

" I'm an auld flame o' yer mother's," he said.

" Mom always had good taste," I said.

" Ye're like yer mother," he said, laughing. " She was a great flatterer. Many's the time she's told me that I was like Henry Irving, or Sir George Alexander, when I hadnie shaved for three days and the backside was hanging oot o' ma breeks."

" Maybe she was right," I said. " I'll be able to tell when I see you with a clean face. Just now you look more like Wallace Beery."

" I'll Wallace Beery you," he said. " Comin' aboard ? "

" Sure," I said.

" I was a great spark wi' the ladies when I was young," he said, as I climbed aboard and followed him across some bales of esparto grass to the fo'c'sle. " You ask yer mother and she'll tell you. It must be because I'm a sailor. Even yet I get them. The last time I went away for a holiday with the wife, to a wee village in the Highlands, I met in with a daft-like woman. She stopped me in the street and said, ' Is that yer Sunday face ? ' "

" And what did you say ? " I said.

" I told her that it wasn't, but that I'd soon show her

my Sunday face if I let down my trousers ! " He laughed.
" Her and me got on fine after that. We skipped up
the street, arm in arm, singin' ' Cinnamon Brown'll soon
have them down ! ' "

" What did your wife say ? " I said.

" She just came on ahint, laughin'," he said. " She's
been married to me for seventeen years so she kens me
by this time."

" Seventeen years ! " I said. " So you weren't
faithful to Mom ? "

" He's faithful to none o' his lady-friends," a man said,
as we went into the fo'c'sle. " Aren't ye no',
Cinnamon ? "

There was three guys smoking in the fo'c'sle. Two
was about the same age as Cinnamon, and the other one
was a bit older than me. Cinnamon was the cook,
and everybody called him that on account of him putting
it into everything he made. The two old guys was
called Tubby, and Blisters, and the young chap was called
Sugar. He was a hefty big guy and didn't say much,
so I didn't take much notice of him at the time. It's
funny often how people who make you notice them later
on sorta creep into your life. You can't remember
sometimes how you first met them. It just sorta happened.
Well, it was like that with Sugar. I was too busy
listening to the others to notice him. They was talking
about the good old days when they was young and the
cottages was in their prime.

" Them were the days ! " Cinnamon said. " The
good old days when you courted your girl at the lavatory
door ! "

" Kate tells me ye want to be a sailor," Cinnamon said
to me as I was climbing ashore.

" Sure," I said.

" Would ye like to come on this auld tub ? " he said.

" I guess I'd risk it," I said.

" I'll speak to the skipper about you," he said.

" O.K.," I said. Then I said quick, " Just a minute ! "
And I went along to the bows and counted the number
of letters in the ship's name. There were eight. " That's
O.K.," I said. " I'm game."

Granpa was sitting on the sofa all dressed up when I
got back. He was a whole lot brighter than I'd seen
him yet. I noticed that he always was brighter in the
middle of the day, unless there was somebody in at
night who interested him an awful lot. I told them
about Cinnamon Brown and the *Red Biddy*, and both of
them started in to tell me about him. They both talked
at once and neither of them would stop to let the other
tell the story, so my head was dizzy, turning it from one
to the other.

" Danny'll keep ye cheery," Granma said. " He's
an awfu' daft man."

" He's a great lad to drink," Granpa said. " He's
waur to water than corn." And he hobbled and laughed
at his own joke, showing his gums and the stumps of
two or three yellowish teeth.

" He takes it off his mother," Granma said. " Mrs.
Brown was aye well soaked. She was a daughter o'
Grannie McLeish, who had a wee shop in number four."

" They were a real wild lot, the McLeishes," Granpa
said. " But Liz Brown was one o' the wildest. And
she was the dirtiest woman God ever put guts into."

" I dinnie think Danny's muckle better," Granma
said. " So it's no' likely that yer meat'll be cooked the
same as ye'd get it cooked at home."

" I guess not," I said.

" Danny was a great pal o' oor Tom's," Granpa said.

" They went to the school together. Danny used to run the cutter for his mother and whiles Tom went with him."

" Say, what does that mean ? " I said. " Run the cutter."

" It means to go to the Tap for drink for his mother," Granma said. " But they didnie call it drink, of course. The Browns aye called it ' currants.' I mind the first time oor Tom went wi' Danny, Danny told him he was goin' to Peter McTavish, the grocer's, in the Forthport Road, for currants. ' I'll race ye, Tom,' he said. So away they ran and Tom got to Peter McTavish's first. But when he turned round the bold Danny wasnie there, he had slipped into the Tap and let Tom run on ahead."

" Currants ! " Granpa said, chuckling. " I bet Danny has swallowed a lot o' currants in his time."

" See you and no' take any," Granma said to me.

" Oh, no," I said.

They told me a whole lot more about the time when they was younger and the cottages was crowded with folk, but I got a bit mixed trying to sort out all the relationships, for everybody seemed to be a brother of this one, or a sister of that one. Granpa got going good and strong, and he was starting in to tell a story about Stumpy McGregor, who, apparently, had been quite a character, but Granma gave him the frozen mitt and told him that this wasn't the sawmill or the Tap. " Ye can tell Spike all about it sometime when ye're in yersels," she said. But how she figured Granpa was going to be able to do that, when she, evidently, never went out, I don't know.

After dinner Granpa got kinda drowsy and he lay down on the sofa after Aunt Kate went back to work. *The People's Friend* had come in the forenoon and after

I'd helped her dry the dishes Granma sat down to read it. " There's an awfu' guid story in it the now by Annie Swan," she said. "I'm fair anxious to ken how it's gettin' on. I think Mary'll get the Laird's son, but I doot she'll ha'e to fecht for him. That besom, Sonia Sangtry, has her eye on him, the bold hissy."

So I left her to find out whether Sonia had got him, and I went up to the Andersons', at Henderson Gardens, to see what was doing there. It was in the suburb called Bickerside, near Acresgreen, and the houses were a cut above the houses at Calderburn. The people in them were mostly clerks and small civil servants, and they wore bowlers and spats to their work, and voted Conservative.

It was Walter's half-day, Wednesday, and me and him sat out in the back garden. Walter was helluva shy and I put in the worst quarter of an hour I'd put in since I'd landed. He hadn't been shy the night before, but I guess it was because George and all the rest of them were there to back him up. You'd of thought that working in a shop would of knocked all the shyness outa him, but he was so self-conscious it was painful to see how he struggled to carry on a conversation. However, I asked him about his drawing and that started to open him out. I'd seen some of the Christmas cards he drew himself, and I asked him if he thought he'd be able to be an artist like he wanted to be.

" Not as things are just now," he said. " I'd need to go to the Art College before I could ever hope to be able to draw properly, far less to be able to make a living out of it."

" Don't you go just now ? " I said.

" No," he said. " But I hope to go to evening classes next winter. I'm savin' up." He laughed sorta bitter-

like. " But you can't save very much out of four bob
pocket money. Most of it goes in tram fares. I walk
home every night and that saves twopence. That's
only a shilling a week, so you can imagine how long it'll
take to get the dibs."

" Won't your mother give you the money ? " I
said.

" How can she ? " he said. " I only earn fourteen
shillings a week. She gives me four, so you see, that
ten bob hardly keeps me."

I guess he was right. Folks like the Andersons have
to count every penny. It took all Uncle Jim's pay to
keep them ; they didn't save anything. When Uncle
Jim got too old to work he would get the old age
pension, same as Granpa, and then when Aunt Bella
was sixty-five she'd get it, too. All Walter's ambition
to get out of the rut wouldn't help him none. It didn't
matter if he had the genius of a Michael Angelo, he said,
he'd just need to go on slaving in the book shop. " And
I'm no Michael Angelo," he said. " I've got talent.
I know I've got talent. But you need something more
than talent to lift you out of the rut. People say that
if you work hard enough you'll reap your ambitions.
But I guess those people never worked in a book shop.
I start at half-past eight in the morning and I finish at
seven o'clock at night, and by the time I come home I'm
too damned tired to do anything. It's not that it's hard
work—it isn't—but the hours are so enervating that
when I come home at nights I just want to sit and do
nothin'. Sometimes I'm too tired even to think.
Unless it's to feel sorry for myself and wish that I'd been
born with a private income. Maybe I'm bitter—I
dunno—but it maddens me when I think of what I'm
missing, how I'm wasting my life. There's nothing

more maddening than to waste your life and to *know* that you're wasting your life."

" Aw, you're only seventeen yet," I said. " There's time enough to feel like that when you're old—twenty-seven or thereabouts—you'll get on O.K. Don't worry. Lookit all the great artists who've been poor, and who've become famous, and done the things they wanted to do. Lookit all the artists who've starved in garrets."

" Yeah, lookit them ! " he said. " They were all poor, accordin' to the guys who wrote their biographies. Starvin' on wine and tinned fruit. They had only a mere hundred or two hundred a year to bum along on, poor souls ! Maybe they had only fifty pounds a year, but that was enough to let them do nothing else but paint. But lookit me. I haven't got a private income. I've got to work to keep myself alive. Alive ! Gee, I don't even earn enough to keep myself. If Dad hadn't a fairly decent job, I wouldn't even be as comfortable as I am."

" Well, why worry about bein' an artist ? " I said.

" Because I've got to," he said. " There's something inside me that drives me on. Oh, I can't explain it to you. It's just something that makes me want to get away from all this. Away from this hum-drum, useless, sort of existence. You must understand. It's the same feeling as the one that makes you want to go to sea."

" But that's different," I said. " I don't want to become famous or anything like that."

" No, but you want to do something," he said. " You want to do something with your life. You don't want to stay put where you found yourself when you were born. It's, maybe, the call of adventure, maybe, the desire for fame or money—I dunno. Whatever it is, though, you've gotta obey it or you'll go under. I simply couldn't stay put all my life like Granny and Grandpa."

" What's wrong with them ? " I said.

" You don't need me to tell you that," he said. " Would you say that they had lived ? "

" Sure, they've lived," I said. " They married and raised a family. What more do you want than that ? "

" Has your mother lived ? " he said.

That was a nasty one. It was a sore point with me, so I asked him to let me see some of his drawings. He brought out two portfolios, one that he showed to visitors and one that he kept for drawings that he knew would shock people. While I was looking through them Walter went on talking as if he couldn't hold it in any longer.

The working-class, he said, could produce as many great actors, and authors, and artists, as any other class. In fact they could produce more, for the working-class was greater in numbers. And they would be greater geniuses, for the working-class was nearer to life. But actors, and artists, and authors, needed economic security if they were to get the fullest expression into their work, and economic security was the very thing the working-class hadn't got. A few isolated cases managed to get the world to recognise their genius, but in the main their stage was the family circle, their canvas the garden railings, and their literary activities were confined to writing letters, that amused or interested their friends, but that, eventually, were burned.

" Couldn't you get a scholarship to the Art College ? " I said. " There are such things, aren't there ? "

" Yeah," he said with a sneer. " But, unfortunately, to get one you need to be good at French, Mathematics,

History and all the rest of it. You need to stay at school till you're eighteen or thereabouts, and get what they call your Highers. Then you go around all the fat-headed Baillies in town and get them to sign papers for you. And even then it's a thousand to one if you get a scholarship. Some other fellow who's canvassed two more Baillies gets it. Anyway, I had to leave school when I was fifteen and go to work, so you see what a bloody poor chance I've got of getting a scholarship now."

"You might if you showed some of the Baillies the drawings in this portfolio," I said. "This one alone—Oh, boy!"

"You're like all the rest," he said. "You've got a dirty mind. That's art."

"I don't know whether it's art or not," I said. "But it sure is an arse!"

Walter got real sore at this. "People think it's me that's got the dirty mind," he said. "But it's themselves. They don't know the proper way to look at things. George and Douglas, my pal, laugh at the books I read in the shop and pass dirty remarks about them and me. And they do the same about my drawings —the ones I show to them, for lately I've stopped showing them to them. They don't look at those things in the way they should look at them. I don't read those books because I want to get a kick out of them—I do get a kick out of them, of course. Who wouldn't?—but I read them primarily because I want to learn things. That's the trouble with people in our class—they don't know anything about psychology and things like that. Especially sexual-psychology. They, naturally, divide human beings into two species, man and woman. They don't realise that these species are subdivided into numerous other species. Men-loving men, women-loving women, narcissists, masochists, sadists—oh, ever so many different sub-stratas."

" But what's this got to do with your drawing ? " I said.

" I'm trying to explain it to you," he said. " I read those books so's I'll understand myself and other people. Lookit what happened to Uncle Arnold."

" Yeah, what happened to him ? " I said.

" You knew that he wanted to be an artist ? " he said.

" Yeah," I said. " But that's all I know about him. Nobody's ever given me the low-down on his story."

" And you're not likely to get it from any of our dear relations," Walter said. " I've never been told it either. It's one of those dark secrets they keep safely under cover. We're supposed to be too young to know about such things, and if a word or two slips out occasionally, why, we're too young to understand ! But it's they who don't understand, they who don't look at it in the proper light. I've picked up a few stray threads by kidding I wasn't listening, and I've put two and two together. This is what happened, as far as I can make out. . . ."

Just then Aunt Bella came out and Walter began to shove his drawings into the portfolio pretty quick, so I didn't hear until later what happened to Uncle Arnold.

" Well, has the artist been showin' ye his drawin's ? " Aunt Bella said. " He'd ha'e been better employed cuttin' the grass for his father. Yer drawin' won't get ye anywhere, ma man. We're for no long-haired artists in this family."

I met Uncle Jim for the first time when he came home for his tea after five o'clock. He worked in a Bond, and this led Walter and George to crack one of their most

popular family jokes about them having been brought
up on whisky. Uncle Jim was a big, stout man, with
a bright red face. Aunt Bella said it was high-blood
pressure and she always lamented to folk about it, just in
case, she said, they thought it was something else. He
was a great guy for backing horses and he was always
hoping to make a pile so's he'd be able to retire. But as
it was all small bets and as he usually crossed his winnings
on to something else he sure had a poor chance of ever
being a millionaire. He was always studying form and
he kept all the newspapers for weeks back so's he could
refer to them. There was a big heap of them in a cupboard under the stair and Aunt Bella was always swearing
at them. Uncle Jim never thought of throwing out the
old papers he was finished with, but somehow or other
the heap never got any higher than a certain height.
But if he yoked her Aunt Bella always said that she never
threw any of them out; she blamed it on Walter and
George.

" There's surely been an awful lot of aeroplanes flying
about to-day," Uncle Jim said at tea time. " The
R.A.F. flying school at Turnhouse must have been on
manœuvres."

" Oh, boy, you should of seen some of them looping
the loop," Walter said. " One of them went like this,"
describing the motions with his hands.

" Mind and no' knock over the tea-pot," Aunt Bella
said. And then she said, " Looping the loop with
Lucy ! "

" I don't know whether Lucy was there or not,"
Walter said. " But they sure were looping the loop.
Gee, I wish I'd been in one of them."

" You'll, maybe, get into one of them soon enough,"
George said.

" I'm not going to join the Air Force," Walter said. " I'm going to buy one of my own."

" Howja expect to get it ? " George said. " On the instalment system for half-a-crown a week ? "

" Listen now, ye're daft enough without goin' up in an aeroplane," Aunt Bella said. " I ken I wouldnie like to get ma belly shoogled upside doon."

She was starting to pour herself a third cup of tea when she put down the tea-pot quick and let out one helluva yell. We all thought she'd burned herself or something, but she got up with a bang and rushed to the window. " If you come in here again," she cried, " I'll come out and ring your ears for you. Get away to your own place and play football there."

George, and me, and Walter, were watching the fun and we laughed at the expressions on the kids' faces. They moved away two or three yards down the street and one of them cried, " Don't put it into Crabby's."

" I'll Crabby them ! " Aunt Bella said, and she opened the window and shouted, " That's enough of your cheek, Cyril Chisolm. And you two, you don't belong here. Get away this minute or I'll get the police on your track."

She banged to the window and went back to the table, real boiling. " I'll football them," she said. " Folk tryin' to keep their gardens tidy, and then they come in after their ball, and run all over it with their big feet."

She wasn't sitting long before she cried, " There, it's in again ! " And she rushed to the window and cried, " Don't you dare come in for it. Leave it." The kids had the gate open and they were all set to dive in for the ball, but they hesitated when she cried to them. She rushed to the door, but before she could get out they had run in for it and they were out safely in the street again by the time she got the door open.

"Listen now," she cried. "If I get you I'll give you gip."

"I'll get you!" George said, laughing and imitating her. "And if I don't get you the cows'll get you!"

"Leave the bairns alone," Uncle Jim said. "You were young once, yourself."

"I never annoyed folk the way those ones do," Aunt Bella said.

"Did ye no'?" Uncle Jim said. "I've heard ye tell some gey strange stories about the times when you were a bairn in the cottages. I bet you annoyed old Miss Motion, and Stumpy McGregor, more than those bairns annoy you."

"Maybe we did," Aunt Bella said, laughing. "I daresay we were gey wild young devils—though we could take a tellin', which is more than those ones can take."

"Say, who was this Stumpy McGregor?" I said.

"Who was he?" George said. "Who is he, you mean."

"Listen now, ha'e ye no' heard yer mother speak aboot him?" Aunt Bella said. "He was a great friend o' hers—and I don't think! She used to annoy the puir auld man somethin' terrible, imitatin' his limp and the way he spoke. He's a Highlander, and he's got only one leg. He stays in number three. His wife died when we were a' bairns, and he got Jessie Motion, an auld maid, who lived opposite him, to look after him and his sons. Jessie aye thought she'd be Stumpy's second wife, but she got her specs. knocked off."

"No wonder," George said. "She was no oil-painting."

" Ah, well, she's dead now, puir soul," Aunt Bella said. " Ye shouldnie speak ill o' the dead."

" Haven't you seen Stumpy yet ? " George said.

" Not as far as I'm aware," I said.

" It's a wonder he hasnie been in to see you," Aunt Bella said. " He comes in often and cracks wi' yer grandfather and tells him a' the news about the harbour. He's able to get about fine though he's got only the one leg. I thought curiosity would ha'e driven him in to see what like ye were. He was awfu' feared that he was goin' to be yer grandfather."

" You bet that he'll have had a squint at Spike out of the window," George said.

" No doubt," Aunt Bella said. " He'd be wantin' to set his mind at rest." She laughed. " Eh, he was awfu' feared yer mother was goin' to marry his son Alistair. But he didnie need to fash himsel'. Yer mother wouldnie ha'e touched Alistair wi' a ten-foot pole. She was just takin' a rise oot o' him, but the muckle sumph thought she was in earnest."

" Tell Spike about Stumpy and Uncle Tom," George said.

Aunt Bella laughed. " Listen, ye'd ha'e died if ye'd been there. It was when yer Uncle Tom was about twelve. Oh, he was a wild devil ! If ony o' you ones had been as wild," she said to Walter and George, " I'd ha'e skinned ye alive. Ye wouldnie be sittin' listenin' to this. I dinnie ken where he got all his wildness, for ma father's an awfu' lawabidin' man. Well, this day Tom, and a few others, tied a rope from Stumpy's door to Jessie Motion's, then they threw stones at the doors, and, of course, when Jessie and Stumpy tried to get oot to see whae was makin' all the noise they couldnie get their doors open. God, how I laughed ! Grace was there, and she was as wild as Tom. She began to strut up and down the row, imitatin' Stumpy's limp and sayin', *Dear, oh, dear, what laughs!* just like Stumpy says it himsel'. Puir Stumpy was fair frothin' at the mooth. He leaned oot o' the window and cried, *If I get ye, ye limmer, I'll gi'e ye such a sore backside that ye'll need to get a wooden one. We'll see who'll laugh then when the other bairns cry Stiff-arse to ye*."

Aunt Bella laughed at the recollection. " But Grace didnie gi'e a hoot. She put her fingers to her nose and cried, *Ye've got to get oot before ye can do that.* And her and Tom did a jig in the middle o' the row. Jessie Motion was fair wild, too. She kept cryin', *I'll go to the polis, ye young hooligans*, and she hauled at her door till it's a wonder she didnie pull her arms oot o' the sockets. But that wasnie the biggest laugh. For when baith her and Stumpy were haulin' at once Tom got a knife oot his pooch and cut the rope. We a' ran, so I dinnie ken what Stumpy and Jessie would look like, but we heard their yells. Stumpy had to get Willie Brown and Gibbie Taylor to help him up. He was fair boilin'. He came along and kicked up a row wi' yer grandfather and said he'd send the polis after us. He didnie, of course. Stumpy's bark was aye worse than his bite. It was Jessie Motion, the auld bitch, that sent for Plates, the sergeant. But Plates just laughed at her : he kenned she was kind o' daft."

" Tom was an awfu' fellow," Uncle Jim said. " He was up to all kinds o' tricks. He kept us all lively when we were grooms together in Lord Caimes' stables. Do ye mind the time he sent Nell Dippy a birthday present ? "

" Will I ever forget it ? " Aunt Bella said. " It was her sixteenth birthday and in the morning she came

bargin' into oor hoose, carryin' a parcel and simperin'
like a nanny-goat."

" Fancy yon face simpering," George said.

" *See what your Tom's sent me*, she said, holdin' oot the
parcel. *Hoo do ye ken it's frae Tom if ye havenie opened it?*
ma mother said. *I ken his writin'*, Nell said, *and the post-
mark's Jedburgh. Well, open it*, I said. So she started
to do that. My, ye'd ha'e died if ye'd seen the way he
had it tied up. All tied with fancy string and sealed
with red sealing-wax. Then, when Nell had got the
first brown paper off we saw that there was another
layer o' white paper, all covered wi' wee lovers' knots
pasted on it. Nell simpered and blushed all over.
Oh, my, she said, *I dinnie ken what to think. Neither do I*,
ma mother said. *He must be oot o' his mind.* Nell was
that hot and bothered that she couldnie unfasten the red
ribbon it was tied with, so I unloosed it for her. It was
an awful fancy box tied with more red ribbon. *God
save us*, ma mother said. *He must ha'e spent a week's pay
on red ribbon.* There was an envelope stuck in the ribbon,
so Nell opened it and took oot a card. On it was written
—Oh, I'll never forget the look on Nell's face when she
read it !—*To my sweet Nell, my orange blossom of old Drury,
may you soon wear these, my blushing bride. Sweets to the
sweet.*"

Aunt Bella had to stop, she couldn't say any more for
laughing. The rest of them were helpless, too, for they'd
heard the story so often they knew it backwards. " Oh,
I wish I'd had a camera to snap the look on Nell's face
when she opened the box." Aunt Bella said, near
choking.

" Well, what was in it?" I said, wishing she'd hurry
up and tell me so's I could laugh, too.

" Horse's dung," she said.

F

When she was clearing the table Aunt Bella dropped a knife. " That's a gentleman comin' to visit us," she said.

" You're as bad as Mom," I said. " She's real superstitious."

" Your mother aye was superstitious," Aunt Bella said. " She used to believe in the stars and a whole lot of other boloney. She must ha'e spent a fortune goin' and gettin' her hand read and her fortune told by cards. There was a time, when she was sixteen or seventeen, when she thought that people had auras, or some such blethers, and she used to go about sayin', *What colour's your aura?* And I remember when she was interested in astrology she used to say that yer Uncle Arn was aye dafter when it was full moon. As if the moon bein' full made any difference ! "

" I guess the moon must always be full in this house," George said.

" Speak for yourself," Aunt Bella said.

" Mom's still like that," I said. " She takes turns. She believed in Spiritualism for a while, then it was Palmistry, then Phrenology. She was a Christian Scientist for a while, too, but that stopped kinda quick when Pop fell outa the loft and broke his leg ; she sent me for the doctor at once. Her latest craze is Numerology. I kinda believe in it myself."

" Well, I'm no' that superstitious," Aunt Bella said. " The only things I dinnie like to do are to open an umbrella in the hoose, or to walk under a ladder. That's a sensible sorta superstition. Ye never ken what whoever's on the ladder might drop on ye."

Aunt Bella was washing the dishes when there was a knock at the door, and George said, " Here's your knife ! " But it was only Walter's pal, Douglas. Aunt

Bella said, " It's you, is it ?   I thought it was a gentleman."

Uncle Jim and me stood and looked out the back door while she was washing-up.   " Is your Aunt Kate comin' here the night ? " he said.

" I guess so," I said.   " She said at lunch-time that she'd be seein' you."

" I hope she comes hersel'," Aunt Bella said sourly.

" Now, Bella," Uncle Jim said.

Aunt Bella sniffed and rattled the dishes so much I reckoned some of them would get broken.   " Well, I dinnie like him," she said.   " And I never will."

I waited to see if she'd say any more, but she began to sing *Sonny Boy*.   I looked at Uncle Jim, but he was filling his pipe and looking out at the garden.

" It's funny Aunt Kate never got married," I said.

" What's funny about it ? " Aunt Bella said, breaking off her singing like she was snapping a thread.

" Well," I said, " she's been a fine-looking woman."

" Ay, she was a fine-looking girl when she was young," Uncle Jim said, rubbing tobacco between the palms of his hands.   " She would ha'e been married long before this if yer Granny hadnie been so narrow-minded."

" Listen now, it would never have done at all," Aunt Bella said snappily.

" It would ha'e worked out all right, Bella," he said. " I still think your mother made a great mistake."

" How ? " I said.

But there was nothing doing.   Uncle Jim said, " I think I'll have to cut the hedge," and Aunt Bella began to rattle the dishes more and more, and to sing :

> *There's no way of knowing, there's no way of showing*
> *What you mean to me, Sonny Boy !*

So I didn't press them; I reckoned that I'd find out for myself, sooner or later. They say that everything comes to those who wait, and I kinda flatter myself on being a patient sorta guy. Maybe Walter or George would give me the low-down on Aunt Kate's love-life, if they knew it. But I couldn't help speculating about it when she came in after she'd finished work, wondering what like the guy could of been. For Aunt Kate was up to High Doh. A kid could of told you that she'd something she wanted to spill, and she was so keen on spilling it that she couldn't take time to take off her hat and coat.

"I came down in the car with Nell Dippy," she roared as soon as she came in.

"What a treat for the folk in the car!" Aunt Bella said. "Ye'd be roarin' at each other like a couple o' fish-wives."

"Well, I can't help being deaf," Aunt Kate said huffily. "You have no idea what an affliction it is."

"All right," Aunt Bella said, trying to gloss it over. "What was Nell talkin' aboot?"

"She was on again about the cottages being condemned," Aunt Kate said. "She'd been speaking to Mr. Bennett——"

"Ay, she told me that yesterday," Aunt Bella said.

"Yes, but she'd been speaking to him to-day again," Aunt Kate said. "He told her that the Sanitary wanted everybody to be out of the cottages by the end of the year."

"Listen now, that's a lot o' havers," Aunt Bella said. "The Sanitary'll have to give folk longer notice than that, and they'll have to find new houses for the dispossessed tenants."

"God knows what we'll do," Aunt Kate said.

" Sit still till ye hear frae the Sanitary," Aunt Bella said.

" It'll kill my father and mother," Aunt Kate said. " They don't want to flit at their time of life."

" They'll just ha'e to make the best o' it," Aunt Bella said. " They'd be better off in a new hoose if they only knew it."

" There's no use talking about it till they hear from the Sanitary," Uncle Jim said. " Time enough then to make a molligrant about it. They'll, maybe, not need to shift. It's just that daft Nell Dippy and her tales. There's no use worrying about snow till it comes on."

Aunt Kate blethered and worried about having to flit all the time we was at supper. But it didn't seem to hurt her appetite none. She sampled pretty near everything on the table. She was sitting looking around to see if there was anything she'd missed when Aunt Bella said, " Try a bit of that gingerbread, Kate."

" That quack doctor said I wasn't to eat anything sweet because of my deafness," Aunt Kate said, eyeing the gingerbread. Walter and George looked at each other and George made loud smacking noises with his lips. " I don't know when I tasted such good gingerbread," he said.

" I wonder if I should ? " Aunt Kate said.

" You'd better not," George said, reaching out and taking another bit. " I notice that you seem deafer than ever to-night."

" It's an awful job being on a diet," Aunt Kate said. " If it was doing me any good I wouldn't mind so much. But sometimes I think it isn't helping me at all. I sometimes think I'd have been as well to put my thirty shillings down the drain." She looked again at the gingerbread and then she looked around at everybody.

She sniffed, and drew back her shoulders. "Ach, to hang!" she said, reaching forward and grabbing a piece of gingerbread, like she was afraid somebody would beat her to it. "I might as well!"

The next day Cinnamon Brown came to Granma's, and told me that he had spoken to the Captain about me and he reckoned it would be O.K. for me getting a job on the *Red Biddy*. He stayed for quite a while and talked to Granma and Granpa. They sure were tickled to see him. They liked when somebody like him came in, somebody who could talk about the people in the cottages years ago. "See and not be long in comin' back," Granpa said when Cinnamon was going away. "I enjoyed yer crack fine, Danny. It was as guid as a week doon the water!" They all laughed at what was evidently an old joke, and Cinnamon said he wouldn't be long in coming back. "Ye'll come doon to see the skipper the morn?" he said to me when we was standing at the door.

"Sure," I said.

Cinnamon was moving off when Nell Dippy popped her head outen her door. She had on a man's old cap instead of a dust-cap, and her hair was hanging out like string at the sides. "I thought it was you, Danny," she said, simpering. "I kenned yer voice."

"Ay, many's the time it's cried after ye, Nellie," Cinnamon said. "The Voice of Love!"

"Ay," Nell said, giggling like a kid.

"Nell and me are auld sweethearts," Cinnamon said, winking at me. "Many's the bit cuddle we've had together doon among the fish-boxes."

"Aw, Danny," Nell said, giggling worse than ever.

"I aye thocht that if ma wife was to want to divorce me she wouldnie ha'e ony bother to get it," Cinnamon

said. " She'd just need to name Nell as co-respondent !
Ha'e ye still got a' ma love-letters, Nellie ? "

" Aw, Danny, ye're an awfu' man," Nell said, squirm-
ing with pleasure.

" I suppose ye'll ha'e them all tied-up wi' tartan
ribbon at the foot o' yer Hope Chest ? " Cinnamon said.

Nell was blushing at this and trying to hide her tooth-
less gums with one big red hand when a middle-aged
guy, who sure reckoned he was the king-pin around
there, came strutting along the row.

" Mornin', Nell," he said.

" Good mornin', Mr. Bennett," she said.

He had come to get the rent, so while Nell was inside
getting her purse Cinnamon lighted out, giving me a
wink and a cheery wave. Mr. Bennett came in to see
Granpa for a few minutes to ask how he was keeping.

" I'm no' sae bad the day," the old man said. " If
only ma rheumatics would keep awa'. It's them that
bothers me. Man, if I could just get oot to see what
was goin' on, I'd be pleased."

" We'll have to get a bath-chair for you," Mr. Bennett
said, laughing.

" Bath-chair ! " Granpa said, shaking his head. " I
doot that's oot o' the question."

" Ay, whae would push him ? " Granma said.

" Surely one of your grandsons would oblige," Mr.
Bennett said.

" I dinnie want to ha'e a corpse on ma hands," Granma
said.

" And how are you keeping yourself, Mrs. Gillespie ? "
the factor said.

" I'm as well as I'll ever be," Granma said. " There's
no use in me complainin'. It would never do if I was
to fall ill."

" No, mother, the game would be up then," Granpa
said.

" It's aboot up as it is," Granma said.

" Nonsense, Mrs. Gillespie," Mr. Bennett said.
" You'll surely be spared for a long time yet."

" I hope so," Granma said. " But I doot it. I'm
seventy-eight now, ye ken. We'll soon be celebratin'
oor Golden Weddin'—if we're spared ! "

" Oh, let's hope you'll see both it, and your Diamond
one," Mr. Bennett said.

" If we see the Golden one we'll be pleased," Granma
said. " Especially if we see it here. Do ye think we'll
ha'e to move, Mr. Bennett ? "

" Well—um—I don't know, Mrs. Gillespie," he said,
beating around the bush. " There's nothing definite
yet."

" The McRaes are flitting next week," Granma said.

" They're doing it of their own free will, of course,"
Mr. Bennett said. " They want a bigger house with
conveniences. There's no question of them having
been put out."

" I hope we'll never come to that," Granpa said
sadly.

" Surely not, surely not," Mr. Bennett said. He got
up awful quick then. I thought he was in one hell of a
hurry to get out. He sure didn't like the subject of
flitting.

But Granma and Granpa liked it all right. They could
speak about nothing else. They was worried to death
themselves and they nearly rode it to death. They
thought they was bound to shift because everybody else
was shifting, and Aunt Bella and me was never done
pointing out to them that they wouldn't need to quit
till they got notice to quit. They was afraid they'd

soon be the only ones left in the cottages, but Aunt
Bella told them they didn't need to worry none about
that. "Nell Dippy and Stumpy McGregor won't shift
till they have to shift," she said.

Stumpy McGregor told them that himself the next
day. It was the first time I'd seen him, though Aunt
Kate said she'd bet her false teeth he'd seen me two or
three times through his window. He was a tall old
guy, a Highlander, with red hair streaked with grey
and a big moustache waxed into long points. He
stumped along pretty good with his pin-leg and his
trouser-leg flapped around it like a triumphant banner.
It beats me how he managed to keep his balance, for he
had a real big belly and it was all cluttered up with
waistcoats and woollen jackets, and a watch-chain, like
a ship's cable, stretched across it.

"So this iss Grace's boy," he said when he saw me.
"Welcome to Scotland, my man. I hope your mother
wass well when you left her?"

"Sure," I said. "She was fine."

"I havenie been so well myself," he said, and right
away he got started in to tell Granpa and Granma all
about his ailments. Jees, if he'd been suffering from all
he said he'd been suffering from he should of been
celebrating his funeral. But he didn't look like conking
out yet. Neither did Granpa; he got wakened up good
and proper when Stumpy began to spill his news. And
as soon as Stumpy was forced to pause for breath, Granpa
waded in and told him all about his own aches and pains.
They went on like that for a while with Granma chipping
in occasionally. A good time was had by all.

The day after Cinnamon came to the cottages I signed
on as a deck-hand on the *Red Biddy*, and we sailed late
on the Saturday night for the Baltic.

Granma was kinda like crying when I said good-bye to her. " Ye've had a short stay, laddie," she said. " I hope it'll no' be long till ye're back, and I hope that we'll still be here when ye do come."

" You bet you will, Granma," I said cheerily.

" I wonder," she said.

I thought she looked awful small and pathetic standing there at the door as I turned at the corner and waved to her. And I wondered what she was thinking about. But I guess, maybe, she wasn't thinking of anything except what she was gonna order from the Co-operative Store van for the next day's dinner.

TWO PURL

ALTHOUGH you're watching Grace's laddie you
don't really see him, just as you don't see that the
cottages are broken-down and dilapidated. You see
them as they were between thirty and forty years ago,
and you see the other folk that left this house to go out
into the world.

Meg was the first to go. You didn't think it strange
at the time, but you think it strange now. For Meg was
a quiet lassie and she has aye been a quiet, unadventurous
woman. But she was the eldest lassie and, maybe, that
was what did it. She left school at the same time as
Tom. She was thirteen and for nearly a year she stayed
at home and helped you. But she pined to start work.
She wanted to go and be a lady's maid. Wattie was
awful angry at her. *You bloody fool*, he said, him that
hardly ever swore. *What do you want to be a maid for?
Haven't you got any pride?*

What's pride got to do with it? Meg said. *I'm not going
to stay here all my life. I've got to work and the kind of work
I want is to be a lady's maid.*

Ay, you've got to work, Wattie said. *But ye can surely get
a better job than helpin' some namby-pamby bitch off and on
wi' her clothes. There's nothin' wrong wi' work—if ye don't
get too much o' it. But that! That's slavery. You might
as well be livin' in the dark ages.*

And I might as well not be living at all as living here,
Meg said. *What fun do I ever get? Helping to get the*

*other kids up in the morning and helping to put them to bed
at night. Do you call that life?*

No, Wattie said. *I don't. I should give you a ring on
the ear for your cheek, but I know how you feel about it. I
know how it is to feel that there's no use living when you're
doing the same things at the same time every day. But being
a lady's maid won't help you.*

There's nothing wrong with being a lady's maid, Meg said.
Mother was a maid.

Your mother was a cook, Wattie said. *A queer difference
frae bein' a lackey."*

I won't be a lackey, Meg said.

Will ye no'? Wattie said. *If ye dinnie ca' waitin' hand
and foot on another woman bein' a lackey, what do ye ca' it?*

Miss Guthrie is gentry, Meg said. *Her uncle is Lord
Clanroon.*

My God! Wattie said. *There's no hope for this bloody
world as long as there are folk like you in it.*

He was furious at Meg, not so much because she wanted
to go into service, but because of her attitude. *She's
sayin' that she's no' as guid as this Guthrie woman,* he said.
*God knows she doesn't take it off me. I say that there's
nobody better than myself in this world and damned few as good.*

And she doesn't take it off me, you said.

She must take it off the Captain's Lady or her aunties,
Wattie said.

That must have been it. Meg stayed with your
mother and sisters for a while and they must have
instilled that fawning before gentry into her. She was a
right snob when she was a lassie and wouldn't play with
the other bairns in the cottages because she thought
they weren't good enough for her, and she's no better
now that she's a full-grown woman. They say that
character changes as one gets older and you can well

believe it in your own case. There's lots of things
you'd do now that you wouldn't have done fifty years
ago, like going to the Kirk twice on a Sunday and
bothering what your neighbours thought about you.
You're not able to go to the Kirk, of course, but even
though you were you wouldn't fash yourself; you've
seen through the stupidity and hypocrisy of it all. But
Meg's character hasn't changed any with the passing of
time. She still fawns afore those she thinks are better
than herself and looks down her nose at those she thinks
are not so good. Her and her man are a pair. And
her bairns are not any better; they were brought up on
the Sheringwall estate and they can ape the manners of
the gentry to a T. God help them when they go out
into the world to fend for themselves. They have such
a good opinion of themselves that ordinary work will be
beneath them. Meg and Bernard Ashe have a lot to
answer for. Meg still reads all she can about the royal
family, and about lord this, and lord that. I'm sure the
last letter you had from her had more in it about the
royal family and the lovely pictures of the smiling duchess
than it had about herself and her own bairns. A lot of
havers!

She didn't half fancy her buckie that day she went
away. She had on a big straw sailor hat and a grey
costume with a tight waist and leg of mutton sleeves.
She was aye awful pernickety about her clothes and liked
to be in the fashion if she could. That was why she
was so pleased that morning. *Thank goodness I'm in the
fashion for once*, she said. *I hope I'll never be out of it again.*
A lassie of fourteen talking about being in the fashion!
You were that annoyed at her tone that you said snappily,
*Wait till ye get married and ha'e a family, ma lassie, ye'll
see whether ye'll be able to stay fashionable for long then. If*

yer bairns are like yersel' and aye want to be decked oot in finery ye'll find that ye'll no' ha'e much o' yer man's pay left for yersel'.

Grace and Bella were fair taken up with Meg's new clothes, and both of them tried on the hat and the costume, though it was too big for them. They went to the car with her and Tom carried her case. He went with her to the Caley station, where she was to meet Miss Guthrie. They were going to London for a few weeks. Meg was more excited about going into service than she was at going to London. But Tom said, *I wish I was going to London.* And that night, instead of going out with his pals as usual, he sat and brooded beside the fire.

There was a post-card from Meg a day or two later. Wee Kate got it from the postman and she brought it in crying, *This must be for me because there's a chicken on it.* It was a picture of a chicken coming out of the egg and underneath it was written, *Does your mother know you're out?* Grace laughed when she saw it and she said, *Meg must be feeling like that.* But there was no sign of her being home-sick in the screed on the back. It was covered with writing but there was very little news. It was filled with the names of the grand folk who were staying in the house where Meg was serving and it ended, *Your affectionate daughter, Margaret Marion Gillespie.*

After Meg left, Tom began to talk about going away, too. He was working in the sawmill beside his father, but he didn't like the work at all. But when he mentioned leaving Wattie was furious. *Ye'd better stop at hame, ma man*, he said. *Yer pay's no' very big, but yer mither needs it.*

But Meg's not here now, Tom said. *That's one mouth less to feed.*

Maybe, Wattie said. *But ye must mind that ye're all gettin' bigger and that it takes more to keep ye now than it did when ye were all wee.*

Meg'll likely send some money home, Tom said.

I'm no' lippenin' on her, Wattie said. *Lady Margaret's awa' and I'll no' be surprised if her motto after this is " Oot o' sight, oot o' mind." Ye'll stay here.*

But Tom sulked about it and at nights instead of getting into mischief, hanging about at the top of the pier and the square with Truth Dippy and Danny Brown and a wheen others, he began to dress himself and go up the town. He never told any of us where he went, but one day, about two months after Meg had gone, he came to you and he said, *I've got a job, ma. I'm going to Caimes House at Jedburgh, to be a groom in Lord Caimes' stables.*

You didn't know how to break the news to Wattie. You began to speak about Tom always being fond of horses and wondering if it wouldn't be better to let him take a job amongst them instead of having him eat his heart out in a job he didn't like. Wattie glowered at you. *Ye've got somethin' to tell me*, he said. *What is it?*

So you told him and bonny and mad he was. *He can gang*, he said. *But if he doesnie like it he doesnie need to come hame here greetin' and whinin'.* He was that angry that he didn't say good-bye to Tom when he went away at the end of the week. He went off to his work in the morning without speaking to anybody.

But the rest of you made up for it. You all helped Tom to pack the old Gladstone bag, and you all stood and admired him wearing the new suit he had bought to go in. It had terrible loud checks, and you thought it wasn't quite the thing for a laddie of fifteen, but you said nothing. He had bought a bowler, too, and he had to put up with an awful lot of chaff from the others when he put it on. But he just grinned and said, *How do I look, ma?*

Real horsey-looking! Grace said, laughing.

Never mind her, you said. *You look fine. You'll be gettin' all the maids at Lord Caimes' after you.*

No fear, he said. *Nell Dippy's got my heart.* And you all laughed, for everybody in the cottages knew that poor daft Nell was sweet on Tom and followed him about like a wee dog. He couldn't be bothered with her either, that was the funny part of it. You would have said something too, if you had thought he had bothered.

Will ye send me a post-card with a chicken on it? wee Kate said.

I'll send you two! he said.

Remember to say your prayers and wash behind the back of your ears, Grace said.

Oh, I'll do that all right, he said. *And I'll get my hand read every week and send you the result.*

Grace began to sing " The Gipsy's Warning," and Arn beat time with the poker on the watering-can. Tom picked up his bag and said, *Well, I'll away.* Just like that, quite matter of fact, as if he was going across to Burntisland for the day instead of away to Jedburgh. *Good luck, laddie,* you said, *see and take care of yourself,* and you were leaning forward to kiss him, but he must have guessed what you were going to do, for he backed out quick and started to walk along the row. He had to stop at the Dippys' door, though, for Nell and her mother to say good-bye. *Ta-ta, Tom,* Nell said, simpering and twisting her apron with her muckle red hands. *I'll look forward to gettin' a post-card frae ye.*

Sure, Tom said. *Maybe I'll send ye somethin' better than a post-card.* And he laughed and raised his bowler with a flourish.

The poor silly lassie was that flabbergasted that she was near greeting with pleasure. Grace told you about it after, for you were too upset yourself at the time to see how other folk behaved. You had a queer ache at your heart as you watched him walk smartly along the row, a stranger feeling than you'd had when Meg went away. You knew that you'd see her again, but you weren't so sure about Tom. You knew that he was starting his life, that a man never comes back to his home in the same way as a woman does. When he came back he would be changed; he wouldn't be a bairn any longer. Maybe, he would have a wife. . . . You said to yourself, *G'wa and no' be daft, Mirren Gillespie*, and you waved to Tom when he stopped and turned round at the corner. If it hadn't been for the other bairns and the Dippys you'd have gret. You'd have thrown your apron over your head and gret as you hadn't gret since you were a bairn yourself, younger than Tom was now. But you didn't gret like you were feared you would. You threw back your head and you laughed with all the rest when Grace cried the catch-word that was all the go at the time, *Mind the horses!* And you smiled and waved until Tom was out of sight.

You came inside and you sat down while Grace made a cup of tea. She was only twelve, but she was a real help to you. She understood how you felt. *Cheer up, ma!* she said, as she handed you the tea. *He's not goin' that far. Jedburgh's only about fifty miles from Edinburgh.* But you thought as you sipped the tea that it might as well be five hundred miles. But you didn't think about it long. You had to forget that you felt like crying and you had to tell Arnold to stop capering. He was an awful laddie. He wasn't wild and mischievous like Tom, but he did awful daft-like things. He had a knife under

G

the milk jug and he was trying to balance the jug on the end of the knife. *Will you stop that?* you said. *Do ye want to drive me crazy wi' yer daft tricks?*

This is the full moon, Grace said.

Full moon your grandmother! Arn said.

Don't talk aboot your grandmother like that, you said. *She's, maybe, an auld besom, but that doesn't go to say that you should be disrespectful about her.*

Aw, ma, I was only saying that, he said, and he came up close to you and smiled in that way that you couldn't help smiling back. *It's only an expression,* he said.

Well, ye'd better not let her hear you say it, you said.

She's not likely to, he said, *seeing that she hasn't been here since Kate had the scarlet fever.*

And even then she didn't come in for fear she'd catch it, Grace said.

Nevertheless, she's your granny, you said. *You should aye speak respectful of folk aulder than yourself.*

Can I sleep with Arn and Walter the night, ma? Kate said.

Indeed, ye cannie, you said. *What put that idea into your head?*

Well, seeing that Tom's away there'll be only two in their bed, she said. *But we still have three, and Grace and Bella take up so much room, they squash me between them.*

Away ye go! Grace said. *Ye ken fine that it's no' nearly so bad as it was when Meg was at home.*

I wish Grace would go away, too, Kate said. *Then Bella and me would have more room.*

I hope Grace'll no' go away for a while, you said. *We need her at home.*

Can I leave school and help you at home, ma? Grace said.

We'll see what your father says, you said.

Meg left when she was thirteen, Grace said.

You're only twelve, you said.

But she left school. She was always a determined
lassie, and if she'd set her mind on it she didn't stop
till she'd got whatever she wanted. She was a big help
to you, a far bigger help than Meg had ever been. Meg
was too fond of decking herself up in her best clothes
and looking at herself in the mirror. Grace was a great
one for looking in the mirror, too, but she didn't gaze
soulfully at her reflection the way Meg did ; she was
always making funny faces and striking daft attitudes.
She and Arn fooled a lot together. Grace was always
singing ; she knew all the latest songs. It was she you
first heard singing, *Good-bye Dolly, I must leave you*, and
The Lass o' Killiecrankie. You mind how you laughed
when you saw her leaning over the wash-tub, her arms
soap-suds to the elbows, singing :

> *Jean, says I, you're looking smart,*
> *Could you masticate a tart?*
> *Tra-la-la-la-la-di-da-*
> *The lass that stole my hankie !*

She went to the music-halls whenever she could
scrape together the money, and she used to come home
either raving about the actresses, or saying she could do
far better herself. Often she used to say, *I'll be a greater
actress than any of them yet*. But you always told her to
get away and not blether. You aye were kind of dubious
about letting her go to these music-halls ; you'd heard
so many strange stories about the men who went to
them. So very often you gave Grace money to take
Bella with her. You always felt safer when Bella was
there. Although she was a year younger than Grace
she was far more practical and she had her head screwed
on the right way. It was she who told you if any

man had spoken to them, or if they'd seen anything she thought they shouldn't have seen.

Meg had been away for a year before she came home for a holiday. She was a terrible swell. She had a lot of Miss Guthrie's old clothes made-down to fit her, and she gave Grace and Bella some of them. Wattie wasn't pleased at her. *Puttin' ideas into the lassies' heads*, he said.

You don't need to worry, Dad, Grace said. *She can't put any more ideas into my head that aren't there already.*

We're for no more lady's maids in this family, Wattie said.

Don't worry yourself, Grace said. *I've no notion to be a lady's maid. It's something higher in the social scale for yours truly.*

After Meg went back to Miss Guthrie's, Grace began to get restless. Meg's stories about London and Brighton had upset her. She got more superstitious than ever. She was always running along to old Granny McLeish's to get her tea-cup read. Bella used to get fair annoyed at her. *Runnin' along there and leavin' other folk to wash the dishes*, she said. *Can ye no' wash the dishes first and get yer cup read after ?*

Ah, it's your destiny to wash dishes all your days, Grace said. *But me—Ah, I shall go up into the heights !*

And ye'll come doon with a hell of a bang one of they days, Bella said.

She stuck it for a while and then she complained to you one day. *I might as well leave the school, too*, she said. *I'm no' learnin' anythin' at the school, anyway. Auld Ginger Grant cannie teach me to wash clothes or cook a dinner.*

We'll see what yer father says about it, you said. *Ye're young enough yet.*

I'm twelve, she said, *and Grace was twelve when she left school*.

You were fair irritable when Grace came back from

Granny McLeish's. *Well*, you said, *what did the gipsy tell ye the day?*

The gipsy said I was going through fire and water—into the heights and down into the depths.

Arn laughed, and began to sing, *Don't go down the mine, daddy!*

Be quiet, you said to him, then you said to Grace, *A lot o' havers.*

She said I was going on a long journey, Grace said.

She was right, you said. *You're goin' to Acresgreen, to the Co-operative Stores for messages. And hurry back. Dinnie put off yer time blethering to the men in the Grocery. I want you to iron that frock o' Kate's.*

Grace got a job in the Net Work just after that, so Bella left school. There really was no need for her to help you in the house; you were quite capable of doing all the work; so it wasn't long before she got a job, too. Mr. Silver, the minister, got her a job as a housemaid with some friends of his. Things were a wee thing easier then; you were able to afford wee luxuries that you hadn't been able to afford before. Bella's pay was paltry, but she aye tried to give you something off it. But Grace spent most of her money on herself. She was terribly extravagant. She was aye buying books about the stars and hand-reading, and she would pore over them for hours. *See this, ma*, she would say, holding out her hand. *Do you see that line there? That's the line of fortune. See what it says about it in the book.*

An' do ye see they lines there? you said, holding out your palm. *They're lines made by hard work.*

But no amount of chaffing and quarrelling would make her stop her daft notions. *I'm fated to be a great actress*, she said, *and it's high time I started my career.*

Ye can career oot o' here and get a pail o' water, you said.

Arn'll get it, she said.

I'm not going, Arn said. But he always said that. He would say, *I'm not going*, and tell you all the reasons why somebody else should go, while he was emptying the old water down the siver at the door and preparing to go to the well for more. Arn was always an awful good-natured laddie; you never saw him lose his temper, or if he did he didn't bide in a temper for long. Not like Tom. Tom would sulk for hours if things didn't go the way he wanted them to go. He always seemed to bear a grudge. When he was wee, if you hit him, he would wait for, maybe, hours, and then he would hit you when he saw his chance. Often you had to laugh at him, it was that funny. But Arn wasn't like that at all. He was working in the sawmill, but although he didn't like it any better than Tom had done he didn't grouse about it. *I'll get out of it some day*, he said. *I'll be a great artist, ma, and then I'll take you to Paris, and Madrid, and Vienna.* He always thought about his mother; he considered your feelings far more than the rest of them ever did. You figured in all his ambitious plans. Whiles you would say, chaffing him, *Ye'll no' want to trail yer auld mother around wi' ye when ye become famous. Ye'll ha'e a wife and bairns o' yer ain.* But he laughed and said, *No, I'll never marry.*

Hoots! you said. *Jean Brown'll ha'e somethin' to say to that.*

Jean Brown has nothing to do with it, he said.

But you laughed and as you laughed you were a wee thing jealous of poor Jean Brown. You knew that she had her eye on Arn, and although you didn't want to lose him for a long time yet—deed no, and him only fifteen, a mere bairn—you thought you'd rather have Jean Brown for a daughter-in-law than any other lassie in the cottages. But Arn didn't seem to trouble himself about her. Not that he wasn't civil enough to her and walked home from the Bible Class with her, but they never went out walking at nights like the rest of the lads and lassies in the cottages. *Ay, poor Jean, you had great patience with him ; there's not many would have been faithful to him for so long. You recognised the goodness in him, though. Which was more than other people would do ; even those who'd known him since he was a laddie turned against him as if he was a wild beast. But even after it happened you wanted to marry him.* Arn would rather sit in the house with his drawings, or if he did go out he always went with Willie Taylor, him that was a clerk in Sir Malcolm's office, and was always such a swell with a handkerchief up his sleeve. A swell! He wasn't such a swell underneath. You mind the first time Arn went away with him for a holiday and he came home and told you that Willie Taylor hadn't a decent pair of socks. *They were all full of holes*, he said. You never liked Willie Taylor, there was something sleeked about him. He was two years older than Arn and you've aye blamed him for being a bad influence on Arn. Wild Willie, the men in the sawmill called him. Why, you don't know, unless it was, as Maggie Dippy suggested, after that blackguard, Oscar Wilde, who was so much in the papers at the time.

Grace was in the Net Work for two years, and then she fell out with the foreman about dancing and singing when she should have been working. It was bad enough not working herself, he said, but it was a damned sight worse when she kept the other girls off their work watching her make a fool of herself. *A fool of myself!* Grace said when she came home fair boiling, *I'll fool him ! I'll give him something to think about. He was getting*

free entertainment and he hadn't the sense to appreciate it.
I'll see that he pays for it the next time he hears me sing. And
straightaway she went up to the old Tivoli Music hall
and persuaded the manager to let her into the chorus.
None of us knew anything about it till she came home
and gave us some free passes for the show.

Wattie didn't say anything. He seemed fell proud of
her. It was you that made the fuss. *An actress!* you
said. *After all I've done to keep you decent and respectable!*
What will folk think?

They can think whatever they like, Grace said. *I've always*
wanted to be an actress and now that I'm going to realise my
ambition, I don't give a damn for anybody.

You turned to Wattie, who was sitting, puffing his
pipe up the lum, and you said, *See, there she is already!*
Swearing like a trooper! An actress! Oh, I'll never be able
to hold up ma head again for shame.

Ach, awa' and no' blether, woman, Wattie said, and he
spat into the fire.

Mind ma clean grate, you said, though there was no
trace of spittle on it.

Wattie never let on. *Ye'll be prood o' her bein' an*
actress yet, he said.

Will I? you said. *Everybody in the cottages will be*
laughin' at us. Stumpy McGregor aye said she'd come to a
bad end. He'll not half chortle.

Let him chortle, Wattie said. *If he says anything ye can*
draw his attention to the fact that the Queen receives actresses
now at her courts. That should settle his hash! For
Stumpy was very patriotic and a great admirer of the
Queen, though God alone knows what he got to admire
in her, seeing that he'd lost his leg in one of her wars.

I don't know what my mother'll say about it, you said.

The Captain's Lady doesn't need to come pokin' her nose

in here, Wattie said.   *If she does I'll gi'e her a piece o' ma mind.*

You laughed snootily and said, *You've given her a piece of your mind so often that it's a wonder you've got any mind left.*

All the same you went to see Grace make her debut. You all went.   Bella got the night off from her place, and she came home for tea, and helped you to get Kate and yourself ready.   You had on a brown dolman and a black bonnet with violets, and you looked real smart, although you do say it yourself.   Wattie had on his Sabbath clothes, his lum-hat and his tail-coat, that he never wore through the week except for funerals. Arn was at the gawky stage and he seemed to be all red wrists and fair hair plastered down on his brow with water, but he was a bonnie laddie and you didn't notice the awkwardness.   We were a braw family as we walked along the row, and most of the folk came to their doors to tell us to be sure to enjoy ourselves and to wish Grace the best of luck.   You bowed real affably to Stumpy McGregor when you passed him at the smiddy-seat, and Wattie said, *We're on our way to see our daughter, Grace, make her dieboo.*   And he lifted his hat and half-bowed to Stumpy as if he were the minister himself.

You took the cable-car up to the Register House, but you got out there and Wattie hailed a cab.   Young Walter wanted to sit up on the box beside the driver, and he fair made you squirm with annoyance when he howled because you wouldn't let him.   You all sat up straight in the cab and you affected not to notice the racket he was making as the cab bowled along Princes Street.   But it began to get on your nerves and you leaned forward and hissed, *Ma man, if ye dinnie hold yer wheesht it's a well-skelpit backside ye'll be gettin'.*   You don't know

whether it was that or because Wattie leaned forward
at the same time and said, *I'll buy ye sweeties if ye be quiet*,
but by the time the cab stopped at the Tivoli wee Walter
had quite forgotten that he wanted to be a cab-driver,
and he chummed Arn into Low's for a Holiday Parcel.

Your seats were about four rows from the front and
you felt real proud as you marched down the aisle to
them.   You felt like saying, *My daughter is appearing
here to-night*, to the folk that looked at you, as much as
to say, What the devil is that crowd doing here, and you
straightened your shoulders and jerked back your head
Just like the Captain's Lady! Wattie told you afterwards.   You sat at one end and Wattie sat at the other,
and you looked around to see if there was anybody
there that you knew.   And you were fell pleased to see
Alistair and Hector McGregor standing away at the
back.   Alistair was sweet on Grace, poor laddie, but
she never as much as looked at him.   You nodded real
dignified to them.

Arn was sitting in the middle, with the Holiday Parcel
on his knee, and he was that nervous and excited that
when the firs turn finished and he began to clap he
knocked the parcel off his knee, and all the conversation
sweeties and ju-jubes scattered on the floor.   Walter
and Kate got down and began to hunt for them, but the
rest of you pretended that they weren't with you.   Poor
Arn was blushing like a red-herring.   He kept touching
his celluloid collar, but it couldn't have been tight because
it was an old one of Wattie's, and made Arn's head look
like a flower growing out of a pot.   *I think we've got them
all now, pa*, wee Walter said.   Wattie kidded he didn't
hear him, so Walter went on groping under the seats,
thinking that his father meant him to look until he found
them all.   *Here's some more*, Kate cried, and thinking

that nobody was looking at her she popped three into her mouth at once. *Spit them out at once, you dirty girl,* you whispered. But whether Kate did or not you don't know for just then your attention was distracted by the woman in front turning round, and saying that wee Walter was touching her ankles. *Well, some o' the sweeties were under her skirt,* Walter said. *She shouldnie wear such long skirts, shouldn't she not, pa?*

Grace did fine, but you were disappointed that she didn't have more to do. She just came on and sang and danced with some other lassies. She didn't get a chance to show what she could do at all. You felt like complaining to the manager about it, but you knew it would come to Grace's ears and you didn't want her to know that you were interested, so you said nothing. After the show was over you walked out, feeling prouder than ever, and you knew that it was taking Wattie all his time to keep from tapping utter strangers on the shoulder and saying, *That's my daughter, the fair-haired girl with the big smile who danced third from the end.* You drew yourself up as straight as you could and you stood in the front hall of the theatre drawing on your gloves while they all collected around you and Wattie, and Arn and Bella debated whether we should take a cab. Wattie was going to hail one at once, but you grabbed his arm and said *Wait!* So you took a cable-car along Princes Street and another one as far as Acresgreen. Then you hired a cab and drove down to the cottages in style. You've always felt real pleased about that, because it only cost you a shilling, whereas if Wattie had had his way it would have cost you at least two-and-six.

The Captain's Lady came to see you the following week. You were filling the coal-scuttle at the bunker outside when you saw her sailing majestically along the row, and you went on filling it till she came up to you.

What's this I hear? she said.

What's what, mother? you said, eyeing her and thinking that she didn't look a day more than sixty though she was seventy-two. She was as straight and trim as the mast of the Captain's ship.

What's this about Grace dancing and singing like a strumpet in some low music-hall? she said, tapping the pavement with her umbrella.

It's not a low music hall, you said. *It's the Tivoli, a very respectable place patronised by all the best people.*

Nonsense, she said. *The best people don't go to such places.*

Don't shout like that at me, mother, you said. *If you're going to say something you'd better come in and not let everybody in the cottages hear it.*

Don't be afraid, you said, when you saw her hesitating. *Nobody's got the scarlet fever now.*

She tossed her head and marched in. She went on full blast about Grace, but you never let on; you started to make the tea. And she was parading up and down the floor as if it was the bridge of the *Grace Darling,* when Wattie came in. *Hello,* he said. *What airt's the wind blowin' the day?*

Due north, Walter Gillespie, she snapped at him. *What do you mean by allowing my grandchild to make an exhibition of herself before a lot of depraved creatures?*

There must be a lot of depraved creatures in Edinburgh, Wattie said. *Grace tells me there's about five hundred there every night.*

I don't know how you can allow it, she said.

Why shouldn't I? Wattie said.

An actress! your mother snorted. *A low vulgar*

music-hall actress!   To think that one of my granddaughters should come to this!

She could come to worse, Wattie said.

Well, she's on the right road, your mother said.   *You'll have only yourself to blame if she goes any further.   I wash my hands of her.*

We're quite capable of washing our bairns ourselves if they need washing, Wattie said.

The Captain's Lady was so sore put about that she couldn't find an answer for him, and she sat and sipped her tea with her little pinkie cocked out genteelly. Wattie watched her, grinning to himself.   He wiped his beard and moustache with the back of his hand. *The stage is a more honourable profession now than it was when you were a lassie,* he said.   *They tell me that Her Gracious Majesty the Queen even deigns to receive actresses nowadays.*

But the sarcasm was lost on your mother.   She was staring at the fire and you couldn't help feeling a bit sorry for her when you saw the look on her face.   *I had hoped for so much from my grandchildren,* she said.   *But there's Tom a stable-boy.   A stable-boy!   The grandson of the Captain of the Grace Darling, a stable-boy!*

Tom wouldnie be very pleased if he heard ye, Wattie said. *He's a groom and he seems to ha'e a guid enough job.*

And Arnold, your mother said.   *A manual worker in a sawmill!*

Ye'll, maybe, hear aboot Arnold yet, Wattie said.   *I'm hoping to get him into Sir Malcolm's office.*

I had hoped that one of them would follow their aunts' example and become a school teacher.   I had hopes of Meg for a while, but, unfortunately, the girl has no brains.

I could ha'e told ye that long ago, Wattie said.   *If she had, she wouldnie be servin' as a lackey to a woman that's not fit to black her boots—brains or no brains.*

Meg has a very good post, your mother said stiffly. *In the circumstances, she is in a better position than any of my grandchildren. Miss Guthrie is an excellent mistress, and she is a niece of Lord Clanroon, and a cousin of Lady Axelby.*

And we're all forty-second cousins of the apes at the zoo, Wattie said.

I want you to let me educate Walter, your mother said, disregarding Wattie entirely. *I think that the boy should be given a chance. Mr. Grant tells me that he's very clever at school. His aunts will coach him and he will have every chance of making a place for himself in the world.*

What as? Wattie said. *A nincompoop of a teacher putting a lot of shit into bairns' heads about king this and king that, and when was the date of the battle of Waterloo? No, no, ma woman, we're perfectly able to give him every chance that he needs. If I let him be a teacher I'll see that he has the proper home background to offset the rubbish that the authorities would teach him and have him teach. You can trust me to give him the proper coaching to make a place for himself in the world.*

Let's hope you make a better job of him than you've made of the others, she said, and with that she rose and stamped out. You didn't see her for a long time after that, and that was the time when she came in great distress because the Captain had rammed a schooner. As if you could do anything about it.

Grace getting started as an actress gave you a lot of worry, for she was meeting all kinds of strange people, and you hoped that nothing would happen to her. Wattie wasn't worried when she went on the stage at first, but he began to worry when she started to come home later and later at nights. She usually said that she'd been rehearsing and once or twice she said she'd been at parties. Wattie told her that she hadn't time for parties if she wanted to succeed in her profession. *You've got to work hard to succeed in anything,* he said, *unless you're born into the upper classes and have a lot of friends ready-made, and ready to shove you into success.* He was annoyed when she came home sometimes in a cab after the show. *Your brother can easy come and meet you if you're feared to walk home from Acresgreen,* he said. *Ye've more need to gi'e yer mother some money than to spend it on jaunting in a cab. Dinnie think that ye're gettin' folk to take notice o' ye, for ye're no'. Folk here are all in their beds by the time ye come home.*

All the same, folk talked about her coming home so late at nights in cabs, and there were a few kind-hearted souls who told you that they'd seen men in the cabs with her. *Ye'll ha'e to keep yer weather-eye on her, Missis Gillespie,* Maggie Dippy said. *She's at a bad age.*

Keep yer own weather-eye on Nell, you said to her. *She's more need o' it than Grace. She never was, and she never will be at anything else, but a bad age.*

For Nell Dippy had started her capers. She was the same age as Meg, but if Meg had looked as fast and been as quick developed you'd have had something to say about it. Nell was always standing at the top of the pier, chaffing the young fellows. A glaikit-looking besom she was, too. God knows what the men saw in her. Very likely they didn't see anything except the chance of taking a rise out of her. But Nell fair fancied herself as a man-killer. She had quite given up hope of catching our Tom after he sent her that parcel, and you were real thankful about it. You wanted none of Nell Dippy's kind for a daughter-in-law, and you're more thankful than ever now that you've seen what she's turned into. But though she'd given up hope of catching Tom that didn't stop her from coming in to

simper and ogle like a muckle tattie-bogle when he came
home for the week-end sometimes and brought two other
young chaps with him, Bernard Ashe and Jim Anderson.
They were fair tickled at Nell and they took an awful
rise out of her, calling her *Miss Dippy*. Wattie sat by
the fire and egged them on. He got them to tell all
the horsiest stories they knew, and he even would have
let them tell her the story about Bernard's brown boots
if you hadn't stopped them.

That was an awful story. Wattie still roars and laughs
as much as ever he did whenever Jim Anderson starts
to tell it, though he must have heard it, or told it, himself,
hundreds of times.

It seems that they were all out late one night and came
back to their bothy well-sprung. Bernard had on a pair
of new brown boots and he was that drunk that he just
hauled them off and tumbled into bed. But he wasn't
in bed long before he needed to make water, so he got
up, and, instead of going to the w.c., he pe-ed out of
the window beside his bed. The window was usually
open, but this night it was shut, and in the morning
he discovered that one of his boots was full. So he had
to treat the other one in the same way to make them both
the same colour.

Nell Dippy didn't need to fash herself making sheeps'
eyes at Jim Anderson, for he was kind of struck with
Bella though she was only a lassie. You noticed it the
first time he came with Tom, and you noticed it even
more every time he came after that. Bella seemed to
have a notion of him, too, so you weren't surprised
when she left her place and got another one near Melrose.
It was near Jedburgh, and you got Tom to promise
he'd keep his eye on her. He was never a great hand
to write, but he sent you a post-card occasionally, and

you thought that he, and Jim, and Bernard, were oftener over at Bella's place than, maybe, her mistress would like. But you could trust Bella not to get into any mischief; she had her head screwed on the right way. You only wish that Grace had been a bit more level-headed.

It was just about that time that Grace went away to tour what she called the provinces. She was away for six months and when she came back to the Tivoli she had left the chorus and was doing an act of her own. She sang and did a few skips, for you couldn't call it a dance. She was very funny and folk said she was on a fair way to being as great a comedienne as Marie Lloyd. There was a freshness about Grace that took. She was earning money, but very little of it came your way. It wasn't that she wasn't generous enough with it—she was too generous sometimes—but she seemed to spend an awful lot of it on useless presents. She was extravagant. It was she who insisted upon buying a piano and giving Kate music-lessons. But mostly she spent her money on clothes and useless gew-gaws for herself. You were aye impressing upon her that she should save up for a rainy day, but she just laughed and said that her horoscope said she'd always be well-provided for. *And when I know that*, she said, laughing, *what's the good of saving? I might as well enjoy myself while I'm young.* Often she got presents from folk, mostly men who were admirers of her acting, but you told her not to accept anything except flowers or sweeties. Two or three times she got jewellery, but you made her give it back. She was a great worry to you.

She wasn't long home after the tour of the provinces before she wanted us to remove to another house. She said she couldn't invite any of her friends to the

H

cottages. You, half-heartedly, thought about shifting, but Wattie put his foot down. Which was funny when you think that on your wedding-day he told you that it wouldn't be long before you'd be able to go to a better house. It was practically the first time he'd gone against any of Grace's ideas. He said she was quite right to want to get on in the world, but he said that wanting to leave the cottages was just snobbery. *Ye'll be saying that we're no' guid enough for ye next*, he told her. *If we go to another hoose we'll no' be long there afore ye want to go to a grander one still. We're stayin' here, ma lassie ; the cottages suit us fine.*

And here we stayed, though Grace left to bide with another lassie in a wee flat in Northumberland Street. She didn't cast-out with you over it, and she came to see you every week. But although she was always asking you, you didn't go to Northumberland Street very often. You didn't like the girl Grace stayed with. Her name was Lizzie Butcher, but she called herself Lisa de Laine. She sang awful sentimental songs. She leaned against a piano and twirled a fancy hankie in her hands and made eyes at the toffs in the boxes. You were fair scunnered at her, but the toffs seemed to like it all right. She aye had a crowd of them dangling around her and taking her out to supper. She brought them to the flat and you warned Grace to have nothing to do with them. She said she wouldn't, so you had to leave it at that. You thought you could trust her ; she was seventeen and old enough to take care of herself. If you'd known then what you know now, you'd have packed her off home at once. But, unfortunately, you didn't know about the ploys that went on. You didn't find out until it was too late. And then you said nothing. You'd have had to go across the Atlantic if you'd wanted to say anything to Grace, and it was no good saying anything to Bella. She had done her best to cover up Grace, so you let her think she'd succeeded. She doesn't know yet that I know far more than she thinks I do. Maybe one of those days I'll surprise her. Eighteen years is a long time to keep a shut mouth.

You had plenty of worries on your mind round about then—the turn of the century—to worry over much about Grace. There was the Boer War, and it hadn't long started before we got word from Bella that Tom had enlisted.

The letter came in the morning and you were that worried all forenoon that you couldn't do any work. Everything that you started to do seemed just beyond you; you couldn't see the end of it at all. And as a result you started a lot of things and never finished them. *I'll finish them in the afternoon*, you said to yourself, and you started to get the dinner ready. You wondered what Wattie would say, for he was terrible bitter about the war. He was all for the Boers. He and Stumpy McGregor had some awful arguments about it. Stumpy said that if he'd had both his legs and had been a bit younger he'd have gone off at once. *And get both legs off this time!* Wattie said. *My God, it's terrible. Some folk never learn sense.*

Stumpy was furious at this. *Ye dinnie deserve to be called a Britisher, Walter Gillespie*, he said.

I dinnie want to be called a Britisher, Wattie said. *I'm a citizen of the world.*

Oh dear, oh dear! Stumpy said. *I'd just like to get a whack at those Boers.*

Well, I wouldn't, Wattie said. *They're an oppressed people. They're in the right.*

Do ye mean to tell me, man, that ye wouldn't fight for your

home and family if an invader was to come to Harrisfield?
Stumpy said.

Of course, Wattie said. *Only in this case it's the British that are the invaders.*

Wattie was terribly angry when he read Bella's letter. *To think that a son of mine would go and help to oppress a free people,* he said. *After all I've drummed into him about being on the side of the downtrodden and exploited.*

Auld Tam chuckled when he heard that Tom had 'listed. *He's a real chip o' the auld block,* he said. *Dinnie go on so sore aboot it, Wattie. The laddie's young. He's lookin' for adventure.*

I'll adventure him! Wattie said. *I'll gi'e him somethin' more than adventure to think aboot when I get him hame.*

When you get him hame, you thought. If you get him hame, you mean. If you get him hame. . . .

For soon news began to come of all those who'd been killed. Oh, that war, it dragged on and on, and you thought it would never stop. Every time you saw the postie coming along the row you expected to get news that Tom was dead. You stood at the window, keeking from behind the curtain, for you didn't want to let folk see that you were so anxious. And then when you saw him look at his bundle just before he came to your door, and then make for the door, how your heart thumped. You stood, feared to go, wondering . . . and then how slowly you went to the lobby. And then how relieved you were when you saw it was just a letter from Meg or Bella, and how happy when it was a badly-written post-card from Tom himself.

Waiting for the postman . . . What a feature of your life that has been. What a common occurrence it was to become in years after that. Waiting and waiting. . . . In that war and in the next one, the greater war that was to end wars. Ay, you've aye been waiting for something, Mirren. Even now, when your life's almost finished, you're not done waiting. You watch every day for the postman to bring something from the Sanitary. Waiting for death or for the notice to quit. And you wonder which will get here first. . . .

THREE PLAIN

I'D read plenty of sea stories and Pop had warned me, trying to turn me against it, so I was prepared for the rough-and-ready life aboard the *Red Biddy*. It suited me O.K. We left Harrisfield late on the Saturday night and headed for Methil, where we loaded coal for Gefle, in Sweden.

Cinnamon and me got along swell. He was a great guy. He kept the whole crew in fits at the daft things he did and said. One night in Gefle we had a real good laugh at him. We'd finished discharging and we were cleaning out the bunkers. We was all black with coal-dust, when a couple of natives came aboard and produced bottles of some kinda liquor that would of knocked the eyelashes offen a snake. I took one little snifter and that sure was enough for me. But Cinnamon looked like his lips had got stuck to the bottle. I left him trying to talk to the natives with the two three words and phrases of their lingo he'd picked up at different times and I went aft to wash myself. About an hour after that, when I went to the galley, I found Cinnamon staggering around and trying to make the bread. He hadn't washed. He was dipping in the flour-bag and he was putting more flour over himself than he was putting in the basin. He sure looked a sketch. " An advertisement for Buchanan's Black and White Whisky," I told him. And the dough looked like a big mud pie.

" Say, we can't eat that," I said. " You better leave
it till you sober up and wash yourself."

" You'll eat it before it eats you," he said, and he was
all set to put it in the oven.

" The hell we will," I said, and I grabbed the basin
and dived up on deck with it, aiming to throw it over-
board. But Cinnamon was quicker than I'd reckoned
in that state, and he ran after me and made a pass at the
basin. I ran across the deck and up on to the poop,
but Cinnamon wasn't far behind me. I slipped at the
top of the ladder, and when I was trying to save myself,
I fell against Cinnamon and he fell on to the deck.
Jees, I was scared stiff he'd broken something, but by
the time I'd gotten down to him he was sitting up as
sober as a judge with his face all bleeding where he'd
bumped it, and he said, " If only this coal-dust was blue
I'd be able to call the bloody Union Jack my forty-
second cousin."

I reckon Cinnamon was a Communist, though he
wasn't a member of the C.P., and didn't know a thing
about Marxian Ideology and Dialectical Materialism.
But I reckon he was a better Communist than most of
them, and one good thing about him he didn't call you
Comrade. He was a real good skate. Occasionally,
when you got him started, he'd talk politics, but not
often. One of those times was when we were coming
back from Gefle to Middlesbrough, and him and me
were leaning on the rail, talking. I don't know
what started it but he got talking about the way
some folk voted at election time, and Cinnamon said
he reckoned nine people outa ten voted for the wrong
guy.

" Lookit Stumpy McGregor for instance," he said.
" He never votes anythin' else but Conservative. If

there's not a Conservative standin' at an election—and
that's not likely !—Stumpy doesnie vote at all."

Cinnamon spat over the side to relieve his feelings.
" And look at him," he said. " All he has is his old
age pension and what his sons send him from New
Zealand, and God knows they'll have a helluva hard
struggle to scrimp enough to send him, puir souls.
If I were them I wouldn't send the old bastard anything after what he's made them come through."

" Why ? " I said.

" He's their father, of course," Cinnamon said, " and
I suppose blood's thicker than water. All the same I'd
let the old B. stew in his own juice. They haven't
anything to thank him for unless it was for bringing
them into this bloody vale of tears."

" What did he do to them ? " I said.

" What did he not do to them ! " Cinnamon said.
" He made their lives a bloody misery when they were
bairns wi' his kirk-going, and what he called, bringing
them up in the faith. Even when they were young men
they couldn't call their lives their own. Then one of
the worst things he ever did to them was when he made
them enlist in the Boer War."

" Didn't they want to go ? " I said.

" They were keen enough to go to South Africa, like
all the other young fellows," Cinnamon said. " But
they weren't too keen to go and fight. But Stumpy
forced them to enlist. For the glory of their Queen
and Country ! He's a great patriot, is Stumpy."

" What did they go for if they didn't want to fight ? "
I said. " Surely to Pete he couldn't force them to go ?
If they were old enough to fight, surely they were old
enough to defy him ? "

" They could have knocked him down with one hand,"

Cinnamon said. "But they were afraid of him and of what the other folk in the cottages would say. Going against their own father! Dear, oh dear," he imitated the way Stumpy said this. "That would never do at all, at all. They thought folk would call them cowards, and they weren't far wrong there." Cinnamon chuckled. "I had that experience."

"What did you not go for?" I said.

"I'm daft, laddie," Cinnamon said. "But I wasn't that daft. I had no illusions about patriotism or the glory o' ma country. I kenned that a wee bullet would soon stop that. No, no, I thought it was better to bide in Harrisfield, although I couldnie walk along the row wi'oot everybody lookin' at me as if I was a lump of dog's dirt on the pavement."

He spat again into the Baltic. "And a very small lump at that!" he said. "Folk only spoke to me on sufferance. I got many a hint about the best place for a young man o' eighteen when his country was at war. But I just looked at them and grinned. 'I'm soft,' I said, 'and they dinnie want soft folk in the war; they want somebody that's so hard that the bullets'll bounce off them and go back and kill the one that fired them.'"

"I bet you'd of been annoyed if they'd called you soft," I said.

"You bet," Cinnamon said. "But what I aye say is, 'kid you're daft and you'll get a long hurl.' I made a note o' all the folk I told I was soft and I paid them back after the war was over. The only man that stuck up for me was yer grandfather. And that was funny because he had a son at the war, too."

Cinnamon took his pipe out of his mouth and spat at a gull that was flying beside the bulwarks. "Missed the b—r!" he said.

"It was queer that your uncle Tom should go," he said after a while. "And yet it wasn't queer either. His grandfather was a soldier, and your uncle Tom had the wanderlust, anyway. But it was a queer thing for your grandfather's son. Your grandfather hated the war like poison. Him and Stumpy McGregor were at logger-heads all the time the war was on, and I'll never forget the row they had on Mafeking Night."

Cinnamon stood so long watching the gull swooping up and down over its shadow on the waves that I began to get impatient. "Well, what happened on Mafeking Night?" I said.

"I don't suppose I need to tell you what Mafeking Night was?"

"I've read about it," I said. "I guess it must of been a great sight."

"Nothing you've read could ever do it full justice," Cinnamon said. "It was as if everybody had gone mad. It was as if somebody had left each of them a million pounds instead of them having helped to put a colony of hard-working people, like themselves, under a foreign yoke."

"But it wasn't a foreign yoke," I said. "It was the British that won the Boer War."

"Put yourself in the Boers place," Cinnamon said. "Who'd be the foreigner then?"

"I guess you're right," I said.

"I guess I am," Cinnamon said.

He told me what happened when the young men from the cottages came back from the war. Hamish and Alistair McGregor stayed at home for a while, then they had a row with their old man and lit out for New Zealand. Uncle Tom got his job as groom with Lord Caimes back again because he was one of the brave

lads who'd helped to win a very rich slice of the British
Empire for the gentlemen who controlled it. Lord
Caimes was one of those guys and he was helluva proud
of Uncle Tom for a little while.

"What made him change his opinion?" I said.

"Haven't you heard the story?" he said.

I said I hadn't and he said he didn't reckon he should
tell me on account of Uncle Tom being one of the
skeletons in the Gillespie cupboard. "Maybe your
granny would be mad if I told you," he said.

"Aw, go on," I said. "I ain't never heard nothin'
about him except that he ran away from home and they
don't know where he is now."

"If he ain't dead," Cinnamon said. "I shouldn't
wonder but what he is. He'd be in the last war, you
bet. Nothin' would of kept him out o' it. He was a
great lad, Tom, he liked to be in the thick of everything.
Him and me were great pals when we were younger, but
after he went to Lord Caimes' I didn't see so much of
him."

"Well, what made him leave there?" I said.

"It's not a very nice story," Cinnamon said. "But
I'll tell ye it. You'd hear from somebody sooner or
later, anyway."

He refilled his pipe and leaned over the rail and made
himself comfortable.

"Your uncle Tom was aye a great guy for horses,"
he said. "I guess that must ha'e been the reason he
went back to Lord Caimes' after the war, for it must
ha'e seemed tame after South Africa. But he liked the
stables. And he liked the company that was there.
Yer uncle Bernard and yer uncle Jim were grooms
there along wi' him. I was down at Caimes House,
once or twice, at the week-ends to stay wi' them in

their bothy. I'd an idea at that time that I wanted to become their brother-in-law. Jim Anderson and yer Aunt Bella were courting, and Bernard had just met yer Aunt Meg and seemed interested, and, of course, ye ken how I felt about yer mother. But that didn't come off." He sighed with mock seriousness. "What would ye ha'e said if ye'd been born and found that I was yer father?"

"I'd of asked the stork to take me right back," I said, laughing.

"Ye young devil!" he said. "I wouldnie ha'e liked a son like you, anyway. Ye're too big. Ye'd ha'e been wantin' ower much o' yer ain way."

"I might of been afraid of you like Stumpy's sons," I said.

"Ay, ye might!" he said. "Ye're like yer mother, ma lad. Ye've got spirit. I never knew where I was wi' her. She led me a fine dance, I can tell you. And she led yer father a fine dance, too, before he nabbed her. I dropped out of the race pretty quick. I decided I didnie want to marry a woman who was aye winkin' to all the young lads in the gallery."

"Competition is the life of trade," I said.

"There was too much competition for me," he said. "So I said to yer father, 'Ye're welcome to her, Geordie,' and I lifted ma hat and curtsied three times. Puir man, he wasnie made up wi' her when she presented him wi' a son like you."

"You're jealous," I said.

He laughed, but he sobered up kinda quick when he remembered what he'd been talking to me about before that.

"Ay, your Uncle Tom was fond o' horses," he said. "They were his undoin', puir chap."

" Was he tarred with the same brush as Uncle Jim ? "
I said.

" No, your Uncle Tom didn't bet at all," he said.
" At least he didn't bet any more than the average young
man of his age. What I meant was that he was too fond
of horses to work among them. He couldn't bear to
see a horse ill-treated. He never used a whip or spur
himself and he fair hated to see the way those toffs
used them. They had no mercy. He aye managed to
control his temper, though. And that was a sore trial
to him. He was terrible bad-tempered and flew off
the handle at the slightest provocation. So he was hard
put to it at Lord Caimes', for his lordship entertained all
kinds o' folk. But it was bound to come sooner or
later, and it came when the Earl of something-or-other
was staying with Lord Caimes. I just forget what he
was Earl of. But it won't matter, he was of no account,
anyway. All I know about him was that he had a vicious
temper. He was a real unpleasant sort of brute, but he
had plenty of money, and old Lord Caimes was hanging
in with him so that he would marry his daughter. Well,
this Earl came into the stables one day and asked for a
horse called Mephisto, a bonny horse, a stallion as black
as coal. Your Uncle Tom wasn't keen that he should
take him, for Mephisto didn't like strangers. But my
bold Earl said that he wanted Mephisto and that he
wasn't going to take any other horse. So at last your
Uncle Tom saddles Mephisto and the bold Earl
mounted."

Cinnamon rammed the tobacco down into his pipe
with a savage forefinger. I guess he wished it was the
Earl he was ramming into a sewage-pipe.

" Mephisto took the huff, of course, and he plunged
and reared, so the bold Earl got busy with his whip and

spurs. But he didn't use the whip for long. It soon
took him all his time to hold on. He rammed his
spurs into the horse's side until the blood came, and all
the time he wouldn't let the beast have its head. He
curbed it. He evidently thought it should stand still
till he'd finished thrashin' it. Your Uncle Tom saw
red then and he darted forward and got a hold of the
Earl's leg. 'Leave the beast alone, you swine,' he
cried. 'Leave the beast alone.' But the Earl made a
swipe at him with the whip, so Tom gave him a yank
and hauled him off the horse. And then there was hell
to pay. Boy, I'd ha'e liked fine to see that fight!"
Cinnamon smacked his lips. "I doubt, though, that
it would be a gey one-sided affair, for accordin' to all
reports Tom made that Earl look like something the
cat had been tryin' to chew and had found indigestionable.
He looked as if a steam-roller had run over him when he
appeared in court."

"In court?" I said.

"Your Uncle Tom was arrested and charged with
assault and battery," Cinnamon said. "Lord Caimes
was that anxious to keep in the Earl's good books that
he wouldn't listen to one word your Uncle Tom said.
He called him a ruffian and phoned for the police himsel'."

"And what happened at the trial?" I said.

"Nobody believed your Uncle Tom's story. The
sheriff was a bloody auld wife. He was all over the
Earl. He was trying to hang in with both him and
Lord Caimes, and he sentenced Tom to three months.
And he said he was sorry it was beyond his jurisdiction
to order him to be flogged."

"Flogged!" Cinnamon said with a short laugh.
"That was what cut up your Uncle Tom more than

anything else. I saw him afore they took him away to the jail. He was fair white wi' anger. 'I couldnie ha'e stood that, Danny,' he said. 'Honest to God, it would ha'e killed me. Thank God the old bastard couldnie do it.' Flogged! The old bastard," Cinnamon said. "I know what I'd ha'e done to both him and the Earl. Your Uncle Tom was only twenty-two."

Cinnamon didn't speak for a good long time, then he said, " That's just a sample of one law for the rich and another for the poor. Nobody says anything when the gentry ill-treat their horses—or their servants for that matter—but if a puir carter gives his horse a big crack to encourage it to do better the S.P.C.A. are down on him like a ton of bricks."

" What happened when Uncle Tom got outa the jug ? " I said.

" Your Granny expected him home, of course," Cinnamon said. " It wasn't as if he'd done anything to be ashamed of. In fact your grandfather was quite proud of him, and used the incident to illustrate the inequality of the classes when he spoke at Labour meetings. He spoke at a lot of meetings about that time. A queer thing, for your grandfather was aye an awful quiet man. But he got very bitter after Tom was arrested. Your granny didn't say much. She's never been a woman that's complained, though God knows she's had more than her share o' trouble. She accepted it like everything else that's happened to her, saying nothing to nobody. She waited for Tom's sentence to finish, just as she had waited for him to come home from the Boer War. And that day his time was up she got everything ready for him coming home. In the afternoon she set the table and she had the kettle boiling by the side of the fire. She had got in lots o' things that she knew Tom liked—fancy cakes, and tongue, and tomatoes, and God knows what. I know because she invited me to ma tea."

Cinnamon sighed and stared over the side of the boat. " I went along to Number Twenty about half-past six, after I'd finished work—I was workin' in the Net Work at the time—and I found everything ready. The table was set and your Granny was in her Sunday clothes, prepared to do the thing in style as if it were the minister himsel' who was comin' to his tea and not her son comin' hame frae jail. She was a fine lookin' woman, your Granny. Her hair was just beginning to turn grey at the time, but it was still thick. Tom hadn't arrived yet, so we sat down to wait for him. You would have thought that Mrs. Gillespie would have got used to waiting by that time, but devil a bit o' it. She kept goin' to the door and she kept repeatin' the same things. If she said once that it had been a fine day but that it didn't look too promising for the morrow, she said it a hundred times. There was no need for her to be conversational with me about the weather; I was too old a friend o' the family for that. However, I agreed wi' her. And when your grandfather came in I said to him that it had been a fine day and we all talked about the weather. Seven o'clock came, but still no Tom. Half-past seven, and then eight. Your Granny was beginnin' to get near demented. I could see that from the way she kept pleatin' her fancy apron. We had our tea at half-past seven, and when it was over Kate washed the dishes, and Arn and Walter and me dried them. At nine o'clock I said I'd be goin' and that I'd see Tom the next day. But I didn't see him the next day, nor the next, nor the day after that, either. For he never came home. Nobody in Harrisfield has seen him from that

day to this. God knows if they'd know him if they
saw him. There must be a big difference in him from
the time he was twenty-two to whatever he is now—
forty-seven, I think. Puir Tom, he was a wild devil,
but I cannie help feelin' sorry for him. But I'm most
sorry for yer Granny. He was her eldest son and he
was the apple o' her eye. Him not coming home
must ha'e meant more to her than she's ever told anybody. And yet to see her you wouldnie think she's
come through all that she's come through."

I guess Cinnamon was right. Nobody looking at
Granma would reckon she had any troubles in her time.
But she sure has had all the grief.

We went to the Mediterranean after we left Middlesbrough and we got a cargo of esparto grass at Nemours,
in North Africa, and brought it back to Harrisfield.
We was away for a couple of months, and when I got
back I found Granma and Granpa pretty much the
same as they was when I left them. But somehow or
other I couldn't help looking at them with new eyes.
I guess that's a soppy way of putting it, but hell, I'm
a sailor, not an author. I never got no education to
speak of, so nobody can expect me to write the same
as a guy with all the answers at his finger-tips. Anyway, it shows O.K. what I mean.

Granpa wasn't in a very good mood when I went in
just after tea. "He hasnie been at the stool to-day,"
Granma said. "That's what's worryin' him."

"I like to go once a day," Granpa said. "It's a great
mistake not to keep the bowels open." He shook his
head from side to side and pursed his lips.

"Havers!" Granma said. "Ye cannie expect to
go regularly every day, you that never takes any exercise."

I began to tell what kinda voyage I'd had and about

I

all the things I'd seen when I was away. But it was tough going. Granma listened, but Granpa couldn't hear a lot of what I was saying. Most of the time he sat with his head on his chest, looking into the fire and occasionally leaning forward to spit. It wasn't that they weren't interested, but I guess they couldn't visualise things that were so remote from them. They had had such full lives themselves and everything that could of happened had happened to them. They lived so much in the past that they couldn't be bothered listening to anything new. What they liked best was to recall old stories and old sayings about people they knew or had known. They always brightened up considerable when Aunt Bella or somebody like that came in.

Aunt Bella and Uncle Jim and the boys came in about eight o'clock. Aunt Bella was laughing fit to burst. We heard her laughing when she was coming along the row, and Granpa sat up quite perky when Granma said, " I think this is Bella comin'."

" We met Nell Dippy," Aunt Bella said when she came in, and Granma asked her what she was laughing at. " And Jim asked her if she'd had the winner the day."

" Well, I was only tryin' to be polite," Uncle Jim said. " What was funny about that ? "

" It was the way you said it," Aunt Bella said. " You were that polite callin' her Miss Dippy."

" What was I goin' to call her ? " Uncle Jim said.

" You could ha'e called her Nell, like everybody else," Aunt Bella said. " Makin' her simper and blush like that, the daft bitch. Ye'd ha'e thought the King was speakin' to her."

" Well, somebody as guid as the King was speakin' to her," Granpa said.

"I didn't know Nell betted," I said.

"That's only one of her vices," George said.

"Jees," I said. "I didn't know she had any vices."

"Let me weep on your shoulder!" George said. "Didn't you know that Nell was the Village Bad Woman? Her folks made a mistake when they christened her Nell."

"But she saved the Old Homestead!" Walter said.

"Listen, now, that's enough," Aunt Bella said. "Ye can tell Spike all about that sometime when ye're by yourselves." She turned to Granpa and said, "Nell was speakin' aboot havin' to flit."

"Ach, Nell's aye on about that," Granma said. "She's got flittin' on the brain."

"That's what I told her," Aunt Bella said. "I said, 'Listen now, Nell, there's no use worryin' yourself about the milk afore it's spilt. If ye have to flit ye'll have to flit, but listen,' I said, 'there's no sense in worryin' about it afore it happens.'"

"Would she be awa' up to the Register House?" Granpa said with a chuckle.

"Very likely," Aunt Bella said.

"I dinnie ken what like the Register House would look like wi'oot Nell," Granpa said.

"How do you ken what like it looks wi' her?" Aunt Bella said. "Ye've never seen her standin' there."

"No, but I've heard plenty aboot her bein' there," Granpa said.

"That's been her stance for a long time," Uncle Jim said.

"She used to stand at the Theatre Royal for years afore that though," Aunt Bella said. "She stood there for a guid lot o' years after the war."

"That was after she got ower auld to walk Princes

Street," Uncle Jim shouted in Granpa's ear, and he winked.

Granpa chuckled. "She walked Princes Street well," he said. "All through the war. She was well known. They used to call her Naughty Nell. She used to wear a mustard-coloured costume with big black buttons down the front. God knows what the buttons were for, but the wags used to shout after her, 'Can I press your bell, Nellie?'"

"The awfu' like besom," Granma said.

"Ay, she had a bad time during the war," Uncle Jim said. "She could get only auld men or laddies."

Granma tut-tutted with annoyance and looked warningly at Uncle Jim, but neither him nor Aunt Bella let on; they knew that anything like this livened Granpa up.

"It was a bad time o' year!" Aunt Bella said, laughing.

Granma sighed. "Puir Maggie Dippy," she said. "It was a blessin' she died when she did. I wouldnie ha'e liked her to see Nell now. I'm glad none o' mine turned oot like that."

"I wonder how she'll do?" Granpa said. "She must ha'e a hard struggle."

"Oh, Nell'll find money lyin' around at the Register House," Granma said sharply. "There's aye some daft body ready to fling awa' his money."

Me and George was sitting in the corner between the bed and the piano, and he whispered to me, "Come listen to the story of Dippy Nell, she'll let you water your cuddy at her well." I spluttered so much I couldn't hear what Granma was saying.

"I'm sure everybody in Edinburgh knows Nell Dippy by sight," Aunt Bella said. "They all know she comes from Harrisfield. Do ye mind that day we got on the tram-car at the Post Office, Mother?"

"Ay," Granma said. "The car was packed, and there at the other end was Nell sittin' as bold as ye please. 'Hello, Mrs. Gillespie,' she cries, 'Hello, Bella.'"

"I could ha'e planted her," Aunt Bella said. "Especially when the conductor said, 'She wants everybody to ken that you come from Harrisfield.'"

"The awfu' like besom," Granma said.

"Do ye mind the time when Nell was a lassie and the foreign sailors said something to her in the square?" Aunt Bella said, laughing. "She stood with her hands straight down by her sides and her thumbs up, and she said, 'Fer shoo vant to go?' She thought she was speakin' foreign to them, puir soul!"

Granpa laughed real hearty. "But do ye mind when ye were wee yersel'?" he said. "And ye met some foreign sailors with bonnets like balmorals and ye sang to them, 'What's the price o' yer tammy-shanter?'"

Aunt Bella laughed and, of course, when Aunt Bella laughed everybody laughed, for her laugh was sorta infectious. She sure cheered Granma and Granpa up no end even though it was a lotta boloney she usually talked.

"Listen," Aunt Bella said sudden. "Is that the time already? Kate's surely late to-night."

"She's awa' to the choir practice," Granma said.

"I thought she was goin' to give up the choir?" Aunt Bella said. "It's high time she was. Wastin' her time wi' a lot o' havers. It would be wicer-like if she came home at nights and kept you company. She's developin' into a right auld maid."

"The choir'll do her no harm," Granma said. "Ye were in the choir yersel' when ye were young."

"It was the only chance we got to go out on a Sunday," Aunt Bella said. "Ay, ye may well laugh," she said, turning to Walter and George, who were helpless at this information. "We didnie get to gallivant the way the young folk nowadays get to gallivant. We had to give an account of ourselves, and where we'd been."

"Was Mom in the choir?" I said.

"No, yer mother and yer Uncle Tom were the only two that werenie in it," Granma said. "And they were the best singers o' the lot."

"Kate'll see Matt Renton at the practice, I suppose," Aunt Bella said. "She'd better watch hersel'. If she's no' careful she'll maybe get caught and folk'll think she's another Nell Dippy."

"Who's Matt Renton?" I said.

"Yer Aunt Kate's flame," Aunt Bella said.

"A pretty old flame!" George said. "He's so dim he'll soon be out."

"That's enough from you," Granma said kinda snappy. "Mr. Renton and your Aunt Kate are just friends."

"He used to lodge with your Granny," Aunt Bella said before George could give any more of his wise-cracks.

"I didn't know you'd had a lodger, Granma," I said.

"No' me," Granma said. "Your other Granny."

"Wiggy Wilson," George said.

Both Aunt Bella and Granma made clucking noises of disapproval, but George just laughed. "Everybody called her that," he said. "Somebody's bound to tell him sooner or later."

"She lived in Number Thirty-three," Granma said. "Your father was her only child."

"Well, she sure made a fine job of him," I said.

"Really, Spike," Granma said.

" What a like way to speak about yer father ! " Aunt Bella said. But she said it sorta mechanically and it gave me the hunch she didn't like Pop no better than I did. She looked at me in a sorta queer way, looking and looking like she was looking for a dirty mark on my face or something.

" What did they call the old dame Wiggy for ? " I said.

" She was as bald as a billiard ball," Aunt Bella said.

" Howja know ? " George said. " You never saw her without her wig, did you ? "

" Once," Aunt Bella said. " It was the night your father and mother got engaged," she said to me.

" Jees," I said, and I put my hand up to my head. " I hope it's not hereditary."

" Don't worry," George said. " Thick heads, thick hair."

" You can't go by that," I said. " Pop's gettin' kinda thin on top."

" You don't need to worry," Aunt Bella said, and she looked at me with that queer kinda look again. Jees, she sure made me feel funny. Just like she knew something about me that I didn't want anybody to know. It was sorta as if she hated me. Yet it couldn't be that either, for her and me got along swell. I wish I could be sure she was right about my hair though. I get helluva afraid sometimes I'm gonna be bald the way Pop's getting bald, and I wouldn't like to wear a wig like Granma Wilson. But I reckon I would wear a wig if I got that bald. I reckon it's up to everybody to try to make the best of himself and to look as good as he's able.

" Matt Renton lodged wi' yer Granny for a while durin' the war," Aunt Bella said. " He wasnie at the war. He took good care to make his heart as weak as he could. But he got fed-up stayin' wi' Wiggy, because she didnie cook enough to please him. That's the real reason, though he said it was because he didnie like the view."

"Well, ye cannie blame him for that," Granma said. "Since Wiggy's windows looked out on the lavatories."

"Inspiring prospect!" George said.

"So he left," Aunt Bella said. "An' he'd been awa' for a good while and staying in Forthport before he took up wi' our Kate. He hadnie noticed her much when he was bidin' in the cottages and she hadnie noticed him at all. She was too taken up with somebody else, but that's a different story.

"An' it's a story that ye'd better keep to yersel'," Granma said, real annoyed.

"It's all right," Aunt Bella said. "I wasnie thinkin' aboot tellin' him it. It's ancient history now, anyway." She turned to me and said, "Well, he started to come to Harrisfield Choir and he fell in wi' Kate, and he thought he'd like to come back to the cottages. But Wiggy wasn't havin' anything. 'I'm not takin' any more lodgers, Mr. Renton,' she said. 'Besides, the view's still the same!'"

Aunt Kate came in about half-past ten and she brought Matt Renton with her. She had on a short fur jacket and a bright red scarf, that didn't go with the colour of her lipstick. You couldn't help noticing the colour of the lipstick because it wasn't put on so good. It looked kinda like as if Aunt Kate had dabbed her mouth with it in the dark.

"You've surely got on your bum-freezer to-night," George said.

Aunt Kate glared at him; she wasn't so deaf sometimes. But she didn't say nothing before Matt Renton.

Granpa had heard it though and he hadn't caught it proper. But he knew by the way George said it and by the laugh Aunt Bella gave that it was something he shouldn't miss, so he said, " What was that, George ? "

" I said Aunt Kate surely had on her monkey-jacket to-night," George said.

" Her monkey-jacket ! " Granpa opened his mouth wide and laughed fit to kill. He was all set to say something about it, but Aunt Kate was afraid he'd say something worse than George had said and she said quick :

" Sit down, Matt, and I'll make a cup of cocoa."

I don't think Granma was any too pleased to see Matt Renton at that time of night. He was a tall, thin guy, with an awful big adam's apple, and a stiff collar that was too wide for him. He was dressed real prim in a dark suit with a black tie, and there was a real Sunday-go-to-meeting look about him. He sat on the edge of the sofa with his bowler in his hands like he was afraid to put it down.

" Oh, don't trouble," he said to Aunt Kate. " Don't trouble."

" It's no bother," Aunt Kate said. " Help my Jimmie Johnston, it's no bother at all. I want a cup myself. I think a cup of cocoa last thing makes me sleep. Really, you've no idea how I miss it if I don't take it."

" We'll awa'," Aunt Bella said, rising and putting on her hat and coat. " It's gettin' late."

" Oh, don't let me drive you away," Matt Renton said.

" You're not," Aunt Bella said. " It's time we were goin', anyway."

" Will you not stop and have a cup of cocoa ? " Aunt

Kate said. " It'll warm you up before you go out.
It's awful cold outside."

" No," Aunt Bella said. " I'll be warm enough by
the time I walk home."

" It's awful cold," Aunt Kate said.

" You'd better give me a loan of your monkey-
jacket," George said.

" That's enough from you, cocky ! " Aunt Kate said.

Granpa said, " Dinnie be long in comin' back," to
Aunt Bella and them as they went out.   I reckon he was
kinda sad because they were going ; he'd of liked them
to stay a while and help to carry along the conversation.
Matt Renton spoke so low that even Granma had a job
hearing him, and Granpa couldn't hear him at all.   Not
that he missed much, for Matt Renton didn't seem able
to talk about anything intelligent.   All he could speak
about was the choir practice and about the way the
organist gave all his special pals the solo parts to sing.
And about his dog.   Jees, he sure could say a lot about
that dog.   He reckoned it was the most wonderful and
most intelligent animal under the sun, but it doesn't
say much for its intelligence if it had anything to do
with him.

Nobody spoke all the time Matt and Aunt Kate were
drinking their cocoa and eating biscuits and buns.
I didn't know what to say, and Granma and Granpa
looked as if they were too tired to think of anything,
and Matt and Aunt Kate were too busy eating.   Jees,
they sure shifted a lotta buns and biscuits between them.
Nobody would of thought to see Matt that he had such
an appetite.   I guess he must of had a tape-worm.

When they'd finished eating they sat, and Matt told
us some more about his dog.   But he couldn't speak
about the dog all night, so pretty soon he began to talk

about the weather, and then pretty soon after that he sat and looked in front of him. Granma yawned and Granpa's head was falling forward on his chest, but Matt sat still and made no move to go. Jees, I sure was tried. I felt like giving him a kick to make him rise. I could of given Aunt Kate a kick, too, for she sat and stared in front of her with a dreamy sorta expression on her face I'd liked to have wiped off with a good slap. She didn't help the conversation none and that was a funny thing for her because she usually talked nineteen to the dozen. I guess it must of been love. Anyway, I couldn't stand it any longer so I got up and said I reckoned I'd go get myself some sleep. And when I said that Matt Renton got woke up sudden and he said he'd better be going. Don't get me wrong when I say I near kissed him when he said good night.

Aunt Kate went to the door with him and as soon as she got to the door she began to wake up. Maybe she'd just thought of all the things she should of said when we were sitting. Maybe it was just the moon and all those crazy things lovers say to each other. (Though I reckon it couldn't of been that, because I guess their friendship was purely platonic. It couldn't of been anything else with a guy like Matt Renton, who was so cuckoo about his dog.) Whatever it was, anyway, she kept on talking and talking. She was still talking when I said good night to Granma and Granpa, and when I went into the lobby to go to my room they were both standing behind the door in the dark. I said good night and went into my room.

They were still standing there muttering, and Aunt Kate was giving a giggle occasionally, like a High School kid on a petting party long after I was in bed. It was a quarter to twelve the last time I looked at my watch.

I reckon Matt Renton would have to walk to Forthport. I wondered, before I fell asleep, if this was the way Mom and Pop had carried on when they was courting. And I wondered, too, how Aunt Kate had carried on when she was having the affair Aunt Bella had hinted at once or twice, seeing this was as Granma said, only friendship.

THREE PURL

I COULDN'T help looking at Spike to-night, he was so like his father. He's like Grace and Walter, of course, but there's a look of his father about him, too. That long nose and the sarcastic curl of his upper lip. No wonder he doesn't get on with George Wilson. You can't blame George, either. Every time he looks at Spike it's bound to remind him of how Grace tricked him. And calling him ' Spike '—better than calling him George, perhaps, but our Grace had some nerve. Every time she calls him that she must remind George Wilson of that night.

I can't think how she had the nerve to do what she did. If it had been me I wouldn't have dared. I'm not blate, God knows, at saying what I think and doing what I like—I've always gone my own way—but I'd never have had the nerve to hook George Wilson like Grace hooked him. Of course, I wouldn't have got myself into a pickle like that in the first place ; I always had more sense than Grace in things like that ; I always kept a grip of myself. Mother was always afraid of things like that happening to Grace. That's why she used to send me with her to the music-halls long before she ever became an actress herself. I didn't know at the time, but I know now that mother sent me with her to keep an eye on her. God knows what might have happened if she'd been allowed to go by herself. It was bad enough when it happened later, but it would have been awful if it had happened then when Grace was too young to be able to know what it meant. There would have been hell to pay.

There was hell to pay as it was, but neither Mother nor Dad knew that. They didn't hear about it till after, and then they didn't hear the full story. They guessed only part of it and they blamed poor George Wilson. Poor George? I wonder if I should call him poor? After all, he ran well after Grace. He was keen to get her. And he did get her—though, maybe, he got more than he bargained for !

Although she's my own sister I can't say that I really knew Grace well after she went on the stage. She was away from home so much. Sometimes she toured the music-halls in an act of her own ; sometimes she was in musical comedies. She was in *The Merry Widow* and *Miss Hook of Holland*, and though she had only small parts in them she got noticed ; everybody said she was developing into a first-rate comedienne, and that, in time, she'd be a rival to Marie Lloyd. At the old Tivoli, of course, she was a star ; she was the Tiv.'s main attraction. She was there, off and on, for years. I was a lot away from home myself ; I was five years at Melrose with the Cruickshanks and then I was at Perth for a year. Then I got a job as head-housemaid with Mrs. Wynne-Greig, in Ainslie Place, and I began to see more of Grace. I often went to her flat on my evenings off. Jim had just left private service and had started in the Bond, and we used to make Grace's our meeting-place. Sometimes there were other people there, friends of Grace, and sometimes there would only be Lisa de Laine, who shared the flat with Grace. I liked best when there was nobody there. I didn't mind Lizzie, of course. She was just an ordinary girl, like

Grace and myself, though she dressed in great style and spoke awful la-di-dah, and always had a crowd of toffs hanging around her. Our Grace spoke and dressed like that, too, but she didn't encourage the toffs in the way Lizzie did. She flirted with them, but she never took any of them seriously. She didn't have time for anything but her career. I daresay Mother was to account for this; she had drummed it so well into Grace that she must be respectable and hard-working, that she was afraid to be anything else. She wasn't nearly so wild as she made out. She always carried on at a great length when there were parties at her flat, but I think she was just acting the same as when she acted on the stage. She really had no time for stage-door mashers. That's why I still can't understand why she took up with Montague Seton-Blair.

Meg, and Mother, and Dad, always lament about Grace marrying George Wilson and giving up her career. To hear them you'd think she'd been another Lily Elsie or Marie Studholm, but she wasn't in that class, of course. Still, if she'd held on a bit she might have been. She was well on the way. But she saw the goal in front of her and she thought she'd rest on her oars for a bit. That's where she made the mistake. No goal's ever reached until you're actually at it. She should have struggled on a bit longer before she took it easy. She shouldn't have had anything to do with Seton-Blair.

You can't blame her, of course. She'd been working hard for ten years—the ten years when most other girls have their fling—and she thought that she could begin to take it easy. She should have picked on somebody better than Seton-Blair to have her fling with, however.

I still can't see what she saw in him. He wasn't bad-looking, but he wasn't exactly my idea of Love's Young Dream. He was tall and dark, and he had a sarcastic face, with his mouth always twisted in a smile. Lisa de Laine said he was satanic, and she always called him Your Black Majesty. But Grace always called him Spike, the nick-name his pals gave him.

I didn't like him and I know he didn't like me, but we met each other a lot. We couldn't help meeting each other at Grace's. Give him his due, he always tried to put me at my ease, but I knew that to him I was never Grace's sister, I was just a housemaid having her night off. And he was just another young toff to me. I always felt I should call him *sir* and wait till I was spoken to. I couldn't bring myself to call him either Your Black Majesty, or Spike, and I couldn't laugh and joke with him in the way Lisa and Grace laughed and joked with him. Of course, most of the crowd who came to the flat had that effect on me. I always felt I was an outsider, just there on sufferance because I was Grace Gillespie's sister. I used to envy the way Grace could accept them all in a natural way. She was at home with them in a way I never could have been. She's like my father there; he doesn't recognise any class barriers; he speaks the same way to a beggar at the door as he would speak to Sir Malcolm Harris, or the King, for that matter. If the King were to call on him to-morrow he'd ask him if he'd have a 'wee thimbleful,' and he'd tell him how many hours he hadn't slept the night before, and that he hadn't been to the stool that morning. Grace was like that, too. Natural. She chaffed Seton-Blair in exactly the same way as she chaffed Danny Brown and George Wilson.

At first I thought Seton-Blair was just another stage-door masher. I thought that before long he'd drop off the same as the others had dropped off when they saw there was nothing doing with Grace. But months passed and that didn't happen. Instead of seeing him less I began to see him more. Every time I went to Grace's flat he was there, lounging about as if he owned it. He made me fair uncomfortable, for the more I saw him the less I knew what to say to him. You couldn't speak about the weather every time. So pretty soon I just said, *hello*, and then I'd sit and say nothing, and he'd sit and say as much. That was when Grace wasn't in, of course. If she was in the room or if Lisa was there things were lively enough.

But when I saw Seton-Blair there so often I began to get anxious. I didn't like to say anything to Grace so I tackled Lisa.

" Listen, Lizzie," I said. " How often does Seton-Blair come here ? "

" Every night," she said. " Or nearly every night."

" Do you think there's anything in it ? " I said.

" How ? " she said.

" I mean do you think he wants to marry her. . . ."

" Oh, Bella ! " Lizzie said, laughing. " Don't be early-Victorian. Of course, Spike isn't thinking about marrying Grace. He'll be Lord Blairbonny when his uncle dies."

" What's that got to do with it ? " I said.

" Everything," she said. " You don't expect his uncle would let him marry an actress, do you ? "

" Why not ? " I said. " Lots of lords have married actresses, haven't they ? "

" But they were *famous* actresses," she said. " Now, I'm not saying anything against Grace, but you couldn't say she was a *famous* actress, could you ? "

" No, but she will be," I said.

K

"Not if she doesn't give Seton-Blair the heave," Lizzie said. "She'll not get on very fast with him tagging around at her apron-strings."

"Why?" I said.

"Did Grace not tell you about the London contract?"

"No."

"I don't know if I should tell you," she said.

"Listen," I said. "If you don't tell me I'll tear every hair out of your head."

Of course, I was just joking, but she knew I could do it if I made up my mind to do it. So she told me of how Grace had got an offer to star in a musical comedy, on a tour of the Dominions, and then to star in London when the tour was over. But she had refused to sign the contract because she didn't want to leave Edinburgh. "And by Edinburgh, of course, she meant Seton-Blair," Lizzie said with a laugh.

I couldn't believe it. London had always been Grace's goal. She'd often said that she'd never be really able to call herself an actress till she'd appeared before a London audience. Yet here she was throwing away what she'd worked for all these years for a man like Seton-Blair.

"She's mad," I said.

"You should know," Lizzie said. "She's your sister."

I tackled Grace as soon as she came in. "What's this I hear about you gettin' an offer to tour the Dominions?" I said.

"I'm not going to take it," she said. "It wasn't very good. I'll wait till I get a better offer."

"You'll, maybe, wait a while," I said.

"Oh, I'm doing all right as I am here," she said.

"But London," I said. "You've always wanted to go to London."

"I can't help it," she said. "I'm staying here in the meantime."

"Has Spike Seton-Blair got something to do with this ? " I said.

"What if he has ? " she said.

"Is he going to marry you ? "

"I don't know." She laughed and gave her shoulders a shrug. "I haven't asked him."

"I would think it would be his place to ask you," I said.

"Maybe," she said. She went to the mirror and looked at herself. "You didn't say how you liked my new hat," she said.

"It's very nice," I said. "That orange osprey goes well with the blue velvet."

"I'll put it on the next time I go home," she said. "My, won't the cottages stare ! "

"Are you in love with him ? " I said.

"I suppose so," she said.

"Have you——? " I said, and then I stopped. It was the kind of question you couldn't put even to your own sister. But Grace had none of my false modesty.

"Of course, I've slept with him," she said. "My God, what do you think I am ? An icicle ? What do you think I've encouraged him for at all ? Don't you think I've got a right to have some fun ? I've worked hard and never had any fun. All around me I see other girls having their fling. Why shouldn't I have mine ? "

"You might have waited a wee bit longer," I said. "What's the good of throwing away everything you've worked so hard for, for the sake of a man ? "

" I'm not throwing it away," she said.   " I'll get other offers to go to London."

" Why can't he go on the tour with you ? " I said. " He's got plenty of money and he doesn't work."

" His uncle needs him here," she said.   " He won't let Spike out of his sight."

" What'll he say when he finds out that his heir is carrying on with an actress ? "

" He can say what he likes."

" Does he want to marry you ? " I said.

" I don't know."

" Do you want to marry him ? "

" I don't know," she said.   " I kind of fancy the idea of being Lady Blairbonny."

" You're the only one, then ! " I said.   " What do you think Mother and Dad would say ? "

" Meg would be pleased," Grace said, and she chuckled.

" My brother-in-law, Lord Blairbonny," I said, imitating Meg's polite tone.   " Ay, she'd be the only one that would get any kick out of it.   Mother and Dad wouldn't like it at all.   Dad especially.   What would he say if one of his daughters married one of the class he despises ? "

" He'd get used to it," she said.

" Would he ? " I said.   " Listen now, you know it would be uncomfortable for all of us.   It's bad enough coming to visit you here, but what like would it be coming to visit you if you were staying at Blairbonny Castle, with servants waiting on us and everything ? Everybody would be ill-at-ease.   Mother and Dad would feel more at home with the butler and the cook, than they'd feel at home with Spike."

" I'm not married to him yet," she said.

" And you never will be," I said. " He's no more intention of marrying you than fly-in-the-air."

We left it at that because I hoped it would gradually peter out. I knew that Seton-Blair would never marry Grace. Old Lord Blairbonny hated actresses. He never would have allowed his nephew to marry one even if she'd been as famous as Ellen Terry or Mrs. Langtry, and God knows our Grace was nothing like that. And I knew that Seton-Blair had neither the guts nor the wish to defy his uncle. He was keen enough on Grace the way they were, but he didn't want to marry her. Our Grace should have known that for herself and have had the sense to be more careful. After all my Mother had told her you'd have thought she'd have known better. But it just shows you.

That night, about a week before Christmas, she was in a fair panic when she came back from the Tivoli. I'd been down at the cottages and I'd looked in at Grace's flat for two or three minutes before I went back to Ainslie Place. I didn't bother to take off my hat and coat, and I was sitting, wondering if I dared stay any longer when Grace came in. I'll never forget how she looked. She had on a brown velvet frock with a salmon-pink corsage and a salmon-pink hat with brown velvet leaves sewn over the crown. It was a big hat, round as a cartwheel, and sitting flat on the top of her bunched-up hair, the sort of hat nobody would be seen dead in nowadays, though it was the height of fashion then. I hadn't time to admire it or take it in, however, for I couldn't take my eyes off Grace's face. She was as white as a sheet and she had been putting rouge on her face, a thing she never did off the stage. Her eyes were all circled with black. I thought at first that she'd been in too big a hurry to wipe off her make-up properly,

but when I saw the look in her eyes I knew it wasn't
that.

" Oh, Bella ! " she said.

I just stared at her.   For the life of me I didn't know
what to say.

" Oh, Bella ! " she said.

" Well, what is it ? " I said.   " What are you ' Oh,
Bella-ing ' about ?   What's wrong ? "

" I'm going to have a bairn," she said.

That took the wind out of my sails.   But only for a
minute.   " Listen now," I said.   " Are you sure ?
Have you seen a doctor ? "

She shook her head.

" Well, how do ye ken ? " I said.

" I just ken," she said.

That should have satisfied me, for our Grace never
spoke broad unless she was doing it on purpose on the
stage, or if she hadn't control of herself.   But it didn't
satisfy me at the time, and the next afternoon I asked off
and I took her to a doctor.   There was no getting away
from it.   She was nearly three months gone.

" He'll ha'e to marry ye noo," I said.

God knows I wasn't keen to have Seton-Blair for a
brother-in-law, but it was the only thing for it.   I just
couldn't think what would happen if my mother found
out.   It was two or three years since Tom had disappeared, but she hadn't got over it yet.   She still
thought she'd get word from him with every post.
She wasn't too well at the time, anyway.   And this, I
felt, would kill her.   Besides, what would the folk in
the cottages have thought ?   They were all decent
hard-working folk in the cottages.   Maybe they drank
a little, some of them, but they were decent ; they
weren't riff-raff.   There had never been anything like

illegitimate bairns as far back as I could mind. And
I was determined that a Gillespie wasn't going to be the
one to have the first. The Gillespies had always been
looked up to as one of the best families in the cottages.
It had been bad enough when Tom got the jail. My
mother had been sore put about, though everybody
said it wasn't Tom's fault ; that it was the man he'd hit
who ought to have been shut up. But more than my
mother would be put about if Grace produced a father-
less bairn. It would be a grand chance for a lot of folk
to wag their heads and say, " I told you the lassie
Gillespie would come to this ! Going on the stage ! "

" What made you do it ? " I asked her.

Grace laughed and gave a bit skip, twirling her skirts.
Even with that in front of her she still remained cheery
and full of fun. " We went for a ride on the cars ! "
she said, laughing. And she began to sing :

> *The seats are too small,*
> *There's not much to pay,*
> *So many a miss will be missis some day*
> *From riding on top of the cars !*

" Listen now," I said. " If I thought you *would* be a
missis I wouldn't mind so much. But will you ? "

" I dunno," she said. And she went on skipping
about as if she couldn't find anything better to do.
That was Grace all over. Once started she couldn't
stop. She had to go on to the bitter end. She'd been
like that when she was a lassie, too. She always started
to be daft when it was time to go to bed. Her and Arn.
They backed each other up, firing back-chat backwards
and forwards till they had us all in stitches. But, of
course, it couldn't last. Mother would look at the clock

and say, " Come on, it's time you were in bed." And
they would have to stop and go, although they did it
with a grudge. Occasionally they defied Mother and
then, of course, all their laughing and fooling ended
in a greeting match.

" We sat close together and spooned all the way,"
Grace carolled. " As we went for a ride on the cars ! "

" Does Seton-Blair know ? " I said.

" No," she said.

" But listen," I said. " You should have told him
before this."

" I haven't seen him for nearly a month," she said.

I stared at this ; it was so unusual ; he was always
running after her. " Is he away just now ? " I said.

" I don't know."

" Is he cooling off ? "

" Of course not," she said quickly. But I saw the lie
in her eyes. Our Grace was never good at hiding
anything though she was an actress. That was why she
was a comedian. She hadn't the makings of a tragedian ;
she would have been sure to have seen the funny side
of it and laughed when she was being most dramatic.
Though God knows she wasn't laughing then. I knew
she was afraid he'd left her. She wouldn't have come
rushing to tell me if she'd had him to go to.

" You fool," I said.

I was fair mad at her. I could have struck her. Really,
she had awful little sense for a woman of her age, a
woman who'd seen as much. No wonder I always
felt that I was the elder, not she. She had absolutely
no reasoning. She was just like a bairn. She was as
helpless as a bairn when it came to doing anything
that ordinary folk with no intelligence do without
batting their eye-lashes. I knew she'd never have the

savvy to tell Seton-Blair that he'd have to marry her. So I made up my mind I'd do it for her. It's funny, but I was always like that about Grace; she was so impracticable I felt I had to take care of her.

I was prepared to give Seton-Blair gip, so all the way to his flat in Melville Street, I rehearsed what I was going to say to him. I wasn't going to leave him with a name. I told the servant, in my haughtiest voice, that Miss Gillespie wanted to see Mr. Seton-Blair, and then, while I was waiting I picked out a few of the mildest names to begin with. I expected opposition and I was prepared to work up to a grand climax. I'd show His Black Majesty that Grace wasn't the only dramatic member of the Gillespie family! But I fair got a drop when the servant came back and said Seton-Blair wasn't at home.

It's easy enough to say now what I should have done. I should have barged in and tackled Seton-Blair. I would know better what to do now. But, after all, I was little better than a lassie at the time and I just goggled at the man and said, " Oh, is he ? " and went out.

Of course, the next three times I went back the man said the same thing to me, only he didn't need to go and see his master ; he was able to say, " Not at home " as soon as he saw me. The impudent brute even had the cheek to try to get away with me. But I soon put him in his place.

Grace was nearly demented all the time. Then a couple of days before the new year she came and told me she'd got a letter from Seton-Blair. He was going away with his uncle for a tour round the world, and he wouldn't be back in Edinburgh for at least a year. He hoped that her tour of the Dominions would be very successful, and hoped that they might run up against each other on their travels. And he remained her sincere friend and admirer, Montague Seton-Blair.

"What are you going to do now?" I said.

"I suppose I could sue him," she said. "I think I'm entitled to compensation," she said, laughing as if it were a great joke. "But I don't think I'll bother. The fat would be in the fire with a vengeance then. All my life I've wanted publicity, but not that kind of publicity."

"Are you going to take the Dominions contract now?"

"It's too late," she said. "Besides, how can I with this coming on? I'll probably have it in June. I'll need to rest for a month or two. I couldn't go on the stage like that."

"Couldn't you 'rest' for a few months?" I said. "Give out that you're in ill-health, and go away some place and have it?"

"No, that wouldn't do," she said. "A few months absence makes a big difference in show business. Besides, what would I do with the kid?"

"Somebody would adopt it," I said.

"No, I couldn't let that happen to his child," she said. "No, I have a better idea."

"What?"

"I'll tell you about it later," she said.

I was fair curious to know. I tried to think of all the things it could be, but I could think of nothing. I was annoyed at Grace for keeping me in suspense like that. She knew fine that it would worry me, for I've always been bothered with my nose, as my mother says. However, I just had to try to wait calmly till she told me about it. I hadn't that long to wait. But God knows I'd rather have waited longer and been told something different. I still think Grace could have got a better way out of it. But I daresay she was in a panic and couldn't think of a better way. Her imagination must have dried up on her. And none of the palmists and fortune-tellers she consulted seemed to be able to tell her the best way either ; they just bamboozled her.

On Hogmonay we were all invited to a spree at the Browns. I wasn't going till after twelve o'clock, for there was to be a party at the Wynne-Greigs before that. All the slaveys had asked their fellows. Jim was there, of course, and the butler had asked me to ask Meg and Bernard. All the girls got on fine with Bernard. His jokes sometimes weren't fit for mixed company, but they all enjoyed hearing him tell his stories of the different " places " he'd been in. Which is more than I've ever been able to do. Of course, I've heard his stories that often I could repeat them backward. It's not the stories I mind so much ; it's the self-satisfied way that Bernard tells them. He's fair proud of having been a groom to Lord Caimes—the old sod—and coachman and chauffeur to Lord Sheringwall. You'd think, by the way he speaks, that it was a great honour for Lord Sheringwall to tell him he was a bloody fool. My father always gets annoyed with him when he tells stories about the grand gentry, and what this one said to that one, and what relation this one was to somebody else. " Ye're no' a man, Bernard," he said to him once. " Ye have the soul of a slave—and a low, base-born slave at that." Meg's like him, of course. She was always fond of bowing and scraping to those she thought were better than herself. That's how Bernard and her first got acquainted. They could talk to each other for hours about the aristocracy and nobody told them to shut up. He was Meg's last chance, anyway. God knows I wouldn't have had him in a gift.

The spree in the servants' hall was a real cheery affair and we all enjoyed ourselves fine. But as soon as we'd seen in the New Year I said we'd better be going. "It's a wee bit down to Harrisfield," I said, "and you know what it'll be when we get down there. We'll not get any sleep to-night if we don't hurry up."

"Who cares about sleeping?" Bernard said. "We can easy make up for it again. After all, it's only once a year."

"I'll have to have my beauty-sleep," I said, laughing.

"You need it!" Jim said, and he winked at the rest of the company.

"Listen now, that'll do you," I said, giving him a cuff. "I'd like to know what you'd think of me if I didn't get my beauty-sleep."

We were making for the door when there was a ring at the area-bell.

"Guidsakes!" the cook said. "Whae can this be?"

"Guisers," the under-housemaid said.

"First-footers," the butler said. "Let's hope they've brought something decent with them."

But it was our Grace who was standing at the top of the area-steps when the kitchen-maid opened the door. "I'm not coming in," she shouted down the steps to me. "I've got a cab here to take you all down to the cottages."

But when the other servants heard who it was they wouldn't rest until they'd got her to come in and drink their healths. She laughed, and said, all right, and she brought the cabby in with her. I was surprised at the way she was looking. When I'd seen her the day before she was pale and tired, but now she was as bright as

the copper-pans hanging around the Wynne-Greigs'
kitchen. I hadn't seen her looking so well for a while.
She had on a red silk dress, all flounced and puckered,
with little sprays of pink roses sewn on to it. I
recognised it as a dress she had got lately for one of her
' numbers.' She must be mad, I thought, she'll not be
long in mucking it up if she wears it off the stage. And
what would my mother and father and all the others
think, I wondered, when they saw her bare arms and the
mass of flesh she was showing about her chest and neck.
But I had to admit that she looked well. She was
easily the most spectacular figure in the hall. Not that
it was hard to be that, of course, since most of the
servants had on their uniforms and Meg and me had on
just ordinary frocks.

Grace and the cabby drunk the company's health and
then Grace didn't need very much coaxing to get on
top of the big table and sing one of her songs. When
she got up she said she would sing only one and then
we'd have to get on our way. But after she'd danced
and pattered a bit the way she did in her act, and had
another drink, she didn't need any coaxing to sing
another song and another. She sung *Lily of Laguna*,
and *After The Ball*, but I can't remember all the other
songs she sang. Only one of them sticks out in my
memory and it was *In The Shade of The Sheltering Palm*.
I'll never forget Grace standing on that white-scrubbed
table in her beautiful red frock, with her bare arms spread
out and her face lifted to the ceiling, singing :

> *Farewell to Eden,*
> *Queen of the Eastern Sea,*
> *My star will be shining bright,*
> *Look to the West for me.*

It's only since then that I've realised what the singing of that song meant to her. It was one of the *hits* of *Floradora*, the musical comedy that she was to have starred in on the tour of the Dominions.

After she'd sung seven or eight times Grace said we'd better go before the cabby got too drunk to drive us. She had drunk a lot herself, but she was by no means tipsy. She was just gay. I don't think I ever saw her so gay.

The nearest way to Harrisfield was over the Dean Bridge and down the Orchard Brae, but Grace insisted upon the cabby driving us round by the West End and along Princes Street. It was daft, I thought, with the cabby in that condition. However, Grace insisted. She insisted, too, that he take down his hood. It wasn't a cold night, so Bernard and Jim took down the hood, seeing the cabby didn't look as if he'd be able to take it down himself. And Bernard sat on the box beside him, and we started, with all the other servants standing at the top of the area-steps, waving and shouting after us.

As we were going through the West End Grace stood up in the cab and began to sing *In The Shade of The Sheltering Palm*. We all laughed and told her to shut up. But she wouldn't sit down. She braced herself against the seat and stood with her arms wide out, as she did when she was singing on the stage. She had taken off her hat, and the frosty moonlight shone on her fair hair and the jewels around her neck (it just struck me then that she was wearing an awful lot of jewellery). The pavements at the West End and along Princes Street were crowded, and there were plenty of other cabs out with folk in them, yelling and shouting. I thought it wasn't likely that we'd attract any attention.

But somebody recognised Grace and then, before we knew where we were, there was a crowd following us. I had never realised before that just how famous our Grace was. I'd seen the Tivoli ' rise ' to her, of course, but this was the first time that it struck me what it might have been like if Grace hadn't been such a fool about that Dominions contract. If an Edinburgh crowd could be so enthusiastic what triumphs could she not have had when she became known to a wider circle ? She sang all the way along Princes Street and the crowd followed us. Poor Jim and Meg were in a fair sweat. They sat pretending they weren't in the cab. One minute they would grin foolishly and the next they would stare up at the sky, as if they were looking for better weather or for a thunderbolt to fall on Grace and make her shut up. But me, and Bernard, and the cabby, enjoyed it fine. Especially the cabby. For lots of young fellows jumped up on the box beside him and Bernard and offered them swigs out of their bottles. The cabby enjoyed it so much that he wanted to turn when we came to the Register House and go back along Princes Street. He said he wouldn't charge any extra for it. But Grace told him to drive on down Leith Street. "That's enough," she said. "That was my swan-song."

The funny faint way she said it made me say, "What ?"

" My swan-song," she said.

" What do you mean ? " Meg said.

" I left the stage to-night," Grace said.

We couldn't believe it. But it was true enough. Grace hadn't a contract with the Tivoli. She was on a weekly arrangement, and she'd told the manager a few days before that she was leaving to-night. None of us had noticed it, but there had been special announcements on the bills, *Farewell Appearance of Grace Gillespie*. She had got a great send-off. There had been a party after the show and Grace had been about smothered with presents. Most of the jewellery she was wearing had been given her by the other artistes and by admirers. "God knows I'll, maybe, need it all yet," she said.

I couldn't ask her what she was going to do now because of the others. But she knew I was dying to hear and she patted my knee and whispered, "It's all right, Bella. You'll see it'll be all right." It was a good job that Meg's and Jim's attention was taken up by the erratic way the horse was going from side to side. Bernard was driving, but he was as drunk as the cabby, so Jim got up on the box and took the reins for the rest of the way to Harrisfield. Meg was kept occupied with trying to keep Bernard at his distance, but Grace didn't take advantage of the chance and tell me what she was going to do; she sat low down in her corner and hummed softly, *After the ball is over, after the break of morn, after the dancers leaving . . . Many a heart is aching if you could read them all, many the hopes that have vanished . . . after the ball. . . .*

Everybody at the Browns was surprised to see Grace. Nobody had thought she'd be there. "We thought you'd be awa' to some grand party, drinkin' champagne and eatin' vinegar with a fork!" Danny Brown said.

"No," Grace said. "I belong to the cottages— and to-night the cottages belong to me!" And she threw her arms wide with a flourish that made everybody laugh.

Right away Grace was the centre of the party. Everybody who was anybody in the cottages was there.

Stumpy McGregor, and Maggie Dippy, and Truth, and Nell, and George Wilson, and old Wiggy, his mother. Miss Motion was sitting in a corner with a crabbed smile on her face, not very sure whether she was disgusted at finding herself there or whether she should enjoy herself for once in her life. Granny McLeish, Mrs. Brown's mother, was there in the corner by the fire, sucking her clay pipe and looking at everybody from under her shaggy white eyebrows. The Taylors were there : Wild Willie, with a stiff collar so high he couldn't bend his neck. And, of course, the Browns and the Gillespies were there in full force. You couldn't have got another soul squeezed in for love or money. They were all falling over each other, but nobody minded that ; they were all in grand fettle. My mother, and Mrs. Wilson, and Maggie Dippy, were sitting with their backs to the window, where they could watch all the fun and keep an eye on the younger ones to see that they didn't get anything stronger than invalid port. Dad, and Stumpy McGregor, and Gibbie Taylor, were by the fire having a great argument about the approaching coronation. Old Neddy had died in May, and George the Fifth was to be crowned the following June. Lots of places had coronation decorations out already, and my father said it was a piece of nonsense. " Damned tomfoolery ! " he called it. " It's all the poorer quarters that have it, too. All those slums in Leith and the Cannongate are a mass of red, white and blue. Some of them must have spent gey near a week's wages. They'd be better spending their money on food and clothes for their bairns. What has the king ever done for them ? "

Stumpy was furious. " There have always been kings, and there always will be kings," he said. " And

L

you can talk your Socialism till you're black in the face, Wattie Gillespie, but you won't change it."

"More's the pity," my father said. "But I'd just like to go around some of them with a stick and knock some sense into them. They swallow everything the papers tell them about royalty. They can't see that the whole thing's a gigantic swindle, built up by the moneyed classes to keep the workers in subjugation."

Most of their argument was drowned in the noise the rest of us were making. Mrs. Brown was staggering around with a tray. There were a lot of glasses of whisky on it, but she was staggering so much that most of the whisky had slopped on to the tray.

"Put doon that bloody tray, Liz," her man said, "and gie's a' a cup o' tea."

But it was Jean Brown, and Meg, and me, who made the tea. While we were making it Grace sang *Obadiah*, and some other songs. All the time she was singing Dad and Stumpy went on with their argument. It was pure thrawness on Stumpy's part, for he had no more reason to bless the royal family than any of us. But he was getting fair annoyed, and things were beginning to look as if they'd develop into a free fight, when Grace stepped in. She took a paper out of her bag and gave it to my father. "There you are, Dad," she said. "There's a New Year present for you. You and Stumpy have been letting off a lot of hot air, so there's some more of it for you."

Dad opened the paper and looked at it. His eyes crinkled at the corners and he began to laugh. "Look, Stumpy!" he said.

Stumpy looked and his eyes opened wide with surprise. "Dear, oh dear!" he said.

Of course, everybody crowded round to see what the

paper was about. It was a printed list of forms of
farts.

" Really, Grace," Mother said. " I'm surprised at
you giving your father a paper like that."

" Ach, away ! " Grace said. " You know you'll
enjoy reading it as much as anybody.

And right enough my mother laughed as loudly as
anybody when Dad read out some of the items. Even
Miss Motion laughed. It's funny how folk laugh at
anything like that when they get gathered together and
have a few drinks. People might say that only common,
vulgar, people laugh at such things, but no matter what
class they belong to everybody laughs. I've heard the
actors and actresses who came to Grace's flat laughing
at things folk like Stumpy and my father would be
shocked at—if they'd understood what was meant.

" Dear, oh dear," Stumpy said. " The polite girl
blames it on the baby . . . Dear, oh dear, what laughs ! "

In the corner, by the fireside, Granny McLeish was
reading Grace's cup. " Ah, I see a journey here," she
croaked, laying her brown wrinkled hand, like a rotten
leaf, on Grace's smooth white arm. " You are going
into the depths, but you will rise suddenly and go up
into the heights."

" She must be going to dive off the end of the breakwater," Arn said.

Granny McLeish looked at him as if he were something unpleasant she had just spat from her thin lips.
" Ye'll not always scoff at destiny, Arnold Gillespie,"
she said solemnly. " The time is coming when your
fate will swamp and engulf you."

We all laughed, but it was more to hide the eeriness
that had crept into the party than because we dis-
believed what Granny McLeish said. If we hadn't

believed her we wouldn't have laughed so noisily. I sometimes wonder if Arn ever thought about that prophecy later when it happened.

Grace stood up and moved into the middle of the floor. She always had the star's instinct for the centre of the stage. "I've an announcement to make," she said.

We all waited.

"Granny was right," she said. "I'm going on a long journey. I'm going to America."

There was a short, sharp silence, and then we all began to speak at once. "Have you got an offer from an American producer?" Mother said, when she could make herself heard.

"No," Grace said. "I've left the stage."

There was more questions at this, and Grace had to tell them about having made her farewell appearance that night. "I'm going to be married," she said.

We all stared at her. Grace stood and smiled at us all, her eyes moving from one to another. We were all waiting, wondering who the man was. But nobody said, "Who is it?"

Grace looked from Danny Brown to George Wilson, and I think she hesitated for a moment. Maybe it's just my imagination. Maybe it's because I know what was going on inside her, but I think there was a pause before she said, "George and I are engaged."

There wasn't a more surprised man there than George Wilson. But nobody noticed his surprise. They thought that his look like a fish gasping on a hook was bashfulness, and they all rushed forward to congratulate him and Grace. And, of course, all the girls wanted to see the engagement ring. This'll stump you, I thought. But, no, Grace had bought a ring and she was wearing it. I'd never noticed it for all the other jewels she had on.

Danny Brown was one of the first to congratulate them and he thumped George on the back. I often wish he'd thumped a bit harded and broken George's back for him. However, there it was. She wasn't in love with any of them; they were just chaps she'd known ever since she could remember and she liked them both about equally well. They were both crazy about her, so what was the odds?

I think she made a mistake, though. It's a pity she didn't pick Danny Brown. She'd have been far better with him. He's an awful drouth, of course, but he'd have made her a good man. And he and Spike would have got on far better than George and Spike ever have got on—or ever will get on. Spike seems to be fond of Cinnamon, too, as he calls Danny. Cinnamon! Eh, my God, what a name to go to bed with!

"I was right, Gracie, ma lass," Granny McLeish croaked, chuckling. "Ye see that I was right. Ye're going on a journey. I've tellt ye that for years, haven't I?" she said, looking across at our Arn, as much as to say, That's one for you, you unbeliever.

"Yes, Granny," Grace said. "You've told me that for years."

I still can't think why Grace chose America, though. She had saved three hundred pounds. She easily could have gone somewhere with that, where nobody knew her, had her bairn and then have gone back to the stage, and nobody would have been any the wiser. She didn't need to marry anybody. I told her that two or three days after. But she said she'd been forced to do it. "It wasn't me," she said. "It was written in my stars that I was to go for a long journey."

"Hoots!" I said. "What does Granny McLeish ken aboot destiny? You could easily have gone to Glasgow or London. That would have been a long enough journey for you. It would have been a long enough journey for Granny McLeish, anyway, seeing that she's never been any farther than Portobello."

The party broke up with a bit of an argument between Stumpy McGregor and Wiggy Wilson. Stumpy was fair pleased that Grace was engaged to George, for he had always been afraid that Alistair wanted her. So he congratulated Wiggy Wilson on her future daughter-in-law much more heartily than he needed to, and much more heartily than he should have done, seeing that Wiggy couldn't abide Grace. They were saying good night at the time and when Stumpy went on with his drunken compliments, praising up Grace to the skies and saying she'd exceeded his expectations, that he'd always thought she'd come to a bad end, but that he couldn't think of a better end for her than to become George's wife, Wiggy couldn't stand it any longer and she said, "Ye can stick yer congratulations up yer arse, Stumpy McGregor." And she marched away with her head in the air.

But the moon had disappeared and Wiggy had drunk much more than was enough for an old woman of her age, and Mrs. Brown had forgotten to take in her clothes rope, and it was stretched across the row. And before we had time to laugh at Wiggy's farewell to Stumpy there was a yell and the next thing we saw was Wiggy's bald head bending down, while she groped for her wig, which had been knocked off by the clothes rope.

The next night, to celebrate the engagement, Grace and George, Meg and Bernard, Arn and Jean Brown, and Jim and I, went to the Carnival. We had a great time. I never saw our Grace in such good spirits. It was as if she had made up her mind to eat, drink and be merry because the next day she would die. There was a model aeroplane suspended to the roof of the Waverley Market, where the Carnival was being held, and folks were all getting their photos taken in it. George wanted Grace to come up with him and get theirs taken. But she wasn't having any. "Granny McLeish said I was going into the heights," she said. "But you must remember that she said I was going into the depths, too. And those wires don't look any too safe."

I thought the same thing myself. However, Meg and Bernard went up and stood like a couple of Sammy-dreeps while they got their photos taken. My mother still has the photo in the family album. A bonny-like sketch it is, too!

Jim and Bernard had a great time at a stall that was laid out like a fish-pond. It was full of wee tin fish with holes in their heads and you were supposed to catch three within a certain time. There was a crowd around it, and for a while Jim and Bernard couldn't catch any more than one or two in the given time. Then suddenly they began to catch them. Every time they had three fish each. They went on like this till they had about a dozen boxes of chocolates each and the man at the stall was fair demented. I think he was on the point of closing down when Bernard and Jim gave it up.

"How did you manage it?" I said to Jim, as we came away with our arms full of chocolate boxes.

"Oh, it was easy," he said. "The first two or three fish we caught we didn't put back in the water. We kept them in our hands and then it was easy enough to cry *three*. Besides, there's a knack in it. If you drew the hook along the side where the fish were thickest you were sure to nab two or three. Most people put their rods into the centre where the current was."

Grace and George were married in the February. Everybody thought it was an awful short engagement. George wanted it to be longer. I was surprised at him. After he had run so well after Grace and been so keen on her he didn't seem so gasping to get her once they were engaged. He said he was in no hurry to get married. But Grace was. She was afraid people would begin to notice before she got safely married, so she hurried on the ceremony. She made all the arrangements with the Rev. Mr. Silver, herself, and she made all the arrangements about passports and sailings for the States. George Wilson was fair annoyed because she booked second class passages ; he said it was a waste of money and that they could easily go steerage. But Grace said that she would have gone first class if she'd felt like it. " Only," she said, " I didn't want to cause you any embarrassment. I knew you hadn't an evening suit and wouldn't be comfortable among all the toffs in the first class." That just shows what a poor, spineless, creature George Wilson was. If he'd been a man at all he'd have told her to go to hell, and he'd have broadcasted how she tricked him into being engaged. But he was that pleased to get her that he sang dumb. I'm sure Danny Brown would have had more Go about him.

They sailed as soon as they were married. Meg and Bernard, and Jim and I, went to Glasgow with them to see them off. That was the last I saw of Grace. A fair-haired woman with a blue velour hat and a blue costume standing on the deck of an ocean liner, waving and waving. And smiling . . . smiling the smile she'd smiled so often across the footlights, the smile she had smiled whether she had felt like smiling or not.

The bairn was born in June, and she christened him George. Everybody was taken up with the Coronation at the time, and the quarrel my father and Stumpy had about the flags Stumpy strung across the row, and with the marriage of Meg and Bernard, so scarcely anybody noticed that it was kind of sudden. It just shows how unintelligent some folk are about things like that. A few of them did some counting, but they didn't spread it much. Anyway, they weren't to know how well acquainted Grace and George had been before they got married. My mother found out, of course, but she thought that the bairn was really George's and she still thinks that.

Thank God, there was nothing like that about me and Jim when we got married the following November.

So that was Grace and Seton-Blair. I wonder at our Grace being so soft. If there had been anything in Seton-Blair I'd have seen the force of it. But there wasn't. He was a real bad lot. I remember hearing a while after Grace left for America, that he hadn't gone on a world tour after all, but was away to Paris with another girl. That was him all over. A girl for every day in the week and two for Sundays. I can't imagine how he stayed faithful to our Grace even for as long as he did. It must have been because she held him off at first. He wasn't long in dropping her, anyway, when he got what he wanted. I mind I was quite pleased when I read that he had been killed in the war. I met Lisa de Laine a while after that and she told me that there were rumours that one of his own men had shot him in the back. I wouldn't wonder but what it was true.

Spike's gey like him about the face and the way he walks. I only hope to God he's not like him in other things, too. I wouldn't like him to lead my sons astray. I'm not feared for Walter; I think he's got more sense. But I hope he'll not have a bad influence on George. Him and George are too chummy for my taste.

FOUR PLAIN

IN the afternoon I was at the well when I saw the postman at the corner, at Stumpy's door. I thought there might be a letter from Mom and I filled the pail mighty quick and got going. But Nell Dippy was at her bunker, filling her coal-scuttle, and she straightened up when she saw me.

" So ye're back again ? " she said.

" Yeah," I said.

" Are ye stayin' long ? " she said, and she watched the postman as he knocked at Granma's door and threw in a couple of letters.

" I dunno," I said, edging away.

" Ye'll ha'e to come in and ha'e tea wi' me some time," she said.

" Yeah," I said.

The postman stopped and handed Nell a letter. " Here's a love-letter for you to-day, Nellie," he said, with a laugh.

I took the opportunity and I said, " I'll be seeing you."

Granma was holding a blue paper and hunting for her specs. A long empty envelope was lying beside a letter from Mom on the table. " Here, laddie, ye might read this," she said. I put the pail and the watering-can under the wash-hand-stand, and I took the paper and read :

These houses having been declared insanitary by the Dean of Guild Court and His Majesty's Inspectors of Health, the

*occupants are hereby warned that they must vacate the said
premises by a date not later than 1st March, 1930.*

There was a lot more but Granma didn't listen to it.

" It's come," she said to Granpa.

He had been lying on the sofa, sleeping with a plaid
over him.

He yawned so wide that you could see the roof of
his mouth.

" Eh ? " he said.

" It's come," Granma said.   " The notice to quit."

He sat up slowly.   " The notice to quit ? " he said in
a bewildered sorta way.

" Ay," Granma said.   " We'll ha'e to be oot o' here
by the 1st of March."

The old man shook his head slowly from side to side.
There was a vacant look on his face.   He put up his
hand and brushed away a drip at the end of his nose.
" Ay, man do ye tell me ? " he muttered.

" Read it again, Spike," Granma said.

So I read it again.   " There's no need to worry," I
said, trying to appear cheerful.   " It says here that
houses'll be found for all dispossessed tenants.   And
there's a bit here for you to fill in, applying for one of
the new houses at Calderburn."

" Calderburn," Granma said.

She sat down on the stool beside the fire and stared
at the flames.   The kettle was boiling and steam was
sputtering out in bursts from the spout, but she didn't
make any move to shift it.   Her hands were pleating
her apron.   I couldn't help watching them as they
pleated the hem into neat folds and took it out and
pleated it again.

" Fifty years," the old man said.   " Ay, it's a long
time.   Ye get attached to a hoose in that time."

He sat with his hands lying loosely on his knees and stared at the worn fringe of the rug. Granma rose stiffly and put the blue paper behind the brown tea-caddy on the mantelpiece. Then she began to infuse the tea. She took Mom's letter off the table and said, " Here's yer mother's letter. Ye'd better read it. I'll read it after tea."

Granpa was still staring mutely at the worn fringe of the rug. He put out his foot and touched the fringe with his toe, moving his toe backwards and forwards.

" Leave the rug alone ! " Granma cried irritably. " Is it no' torn enough wi'oot you tryin' to make it ony waur ? Ye'll ha'e me trippin' on it ain o' they days."

Granpa said nothing. He slowly drew in his foot. And he lifted his left hand and placed it on the mantel-piece, fumbling for his pipe. He didn't watch the movements of his hands, but habit found the pipe and he put it in his mouth.

" Ye'd better not start and smoke the now," Granma snapped. " The tea's masked. Sit in."

Granpa put back the pipe docilely. He rose and clutched at the mantelpiece for support. He groped in the corner beside him for his stick. But he couldn't find it and he cried angrily, " Where's ma stick ? Damn it ! Damn it ! Where's ma stick ? "

" It's fallen down, Granpa," I said. " I'll get it for you."

I couldn't find it at first and by the time I had he was half-way across the floor, swaying and stumbling. I sprang and got a grip of one arm and Granma took him by the other. " Gently does it ! " she said. The old man gasped with relief when he sat down at the table. Then he opened his mouth wide, showing the yellowish stumps of his teeth, and he gripped his left knee with

both hands and cried, " Eh, that knee o' mine's bad
again."

" Drink up yer tea and, maybe, that'll help it," Granma
said cheerfully. " Will I spread ye a piece with butter ?
Or would ye like a wee thing jam ? "

" Butter, if ye please, Mirren," the old man said, just
like a kid.

He munched steadily, rolling the bread from side to
side in his mouth, his wrinkled cheeks sucked in by the
effort and his white whiskers moving up and down with
the motion. And he supped noisily at his tea. " A
cup of tea's very upliftin'," he said. And he cackled
weakly at the humour he saw in this expression he'd used
for years and years.

" What does yer mother say ? " Granma said to me.

" Ain't you gonna read it ? " I said.

" I'll read it after," she said.

" She says they're all fine and she hopes you're the
same. She says she guesses you'll be preparin' for your
Golden Weddin'."

" Golden Weddin'," Granma said.

" Ay, it'll be on the 19th of April," Granpa said.
" We're not even going to see it through here."

Granma said nothing. She was staring out the window
at the harbour. Although she and Granpa couldn't see
small print without glasses they were able to make out
every object on the pier. Of course, long habit had
made them familiar with the view, so familiar that it
sometimes took them a while to notice anything new.
They looked out now at the still cranes, the closed sheds
and the three trawlers that lay like rusted cans beside
the pier. The water was turgid and lifeless, smooth as
gun-metal, and a dull leaden sky hung gloomily above
like an undertaker's pall ready to descend at any moment.

"We'll miss the harbour," Granpa said.

Granma looked from the harbour to the ragged and grey unkept grass of the green. She looked at the boarded-up windows and doors. She looked at the weeds growing between the cobbles. And then she looked at Granpa and the pictures on the walls. She looked especially at the coloured enlargement of Uncle Walter in his soldier's uniform, a young fellow with bright red cheeks and yellow hair.

"We'll miss more than the harbour," she said.

We were finishing tea when Stumpy McGregor arrived, wheezing breathlessly. "Dear, oh dear," he said as he came in. "This iss an awful to-do. Dear, oh dear, that I should have lived to see this day."

"Sit doon, Stumpy," Granma said. "Will ye take a cup o' tea?"

"No, thank you, mistress Gillespie, I have shust risen from my tea," Stumpy said. "But I will smoke if you don't mind."

"Not at all," Granma said.

"Dear, oh dear," Stumpy said, filling his pipe. "This iss a terrible business. That we should have to go away at our time of life."

"I dinnie ken what their idea is at all," Granpa said.

"Insanitary!" Granma said. "Tcha!"

"They're as good as ever they were," Granpa said. "And they've done us a long time."

"I don't know what Sir Malcolm can be thinking about whatever," Stumpy said.

"If they'd let those ains that want to go go and leave us auld ains in peace," Granma said. "Whae wants to flit at oor time o' life?"

"I'm sure Sir Malcolm would let us bide if it wass brought to his notice," Stumpy said.

" Sir Malcolm! Pah ! " Granpa said. " He doesnie
ken onything aboot it. And he doesnie care. All that
he'll ken is that he'll get more money by selling the ground
than by collecting the rents from the wee crowd that's
here. The cottages have served his purpose and he has
no further use for them. And he has no further use
for us, either—if he kens that the likes o' you and me
exist. I served his father and him for over forty years,
and what thanks did I ever get for it ? He's goin' to
put me oot o' the hoose I've lived in all ma married life."

" Ay, Walter, man, you should be getting a pension,"
Stumpy said condolingly.

" The auld age pension ! " Granpa said indignantly.
" Ten bob a week, ten for me and ten for the wife.
What's that ! A pound's nothin' for keepin' two folk.
If it weren't for Kate workin' I dinnie ken what we'd
do."

" Ye're lucky, Wattie, man," Stumpy said. " I have
only the one ten shillings."

" Ay," Granpa said.

" There's talk of raisin' the pension," Granma said.

" Ay, and there's talk of raisin' the dead," Granpa
said sarcastically. " But what has it ever come to ? "

" Have patience, Wattie, have patience," Stumpy said.

" Ma patience is like masel'—worn oot," Granpa said.
" There's aye been talk o' raisin' the pension. But what
has it ever come to ? Talk ! Talk ! Ointment to
soothe the sores of the people and keep them quiet."

" It was only five shillings at first," Stumpy said.

" Ay, five shillings," Granpa said. " What could
you do with five shillings a week ? Just hang on,
half-starving a wee thing longer. Then they raised it
to seven and six. Then to ten shillings. And it's been
ten shillings for a damned long time. I'm sure they

could easily make it a pound. I don't think a pound a week's very much for a man or woman who's had to work hard all their lives."

" It's high time they were giving us it then," Granma said. " The rents'll be dearer at Calderburn. God knows how we're going to manage."

" We'll manage some way," Granpa said. " We'll manage the same way as we ha'e had to manage in the past."

" It says in the paper that dispossessed tenants will get their rents cheaper," I said.

" That's no compensation," Granpa said.

" No, it is not," Stumpy said. " They're a terrible bad class o' people at Calderburn. Dear, oh dear, that we should have to go and live among the likes of them. We have always been decent folk in the cottages."

" They cannie a' be bad," Granpa said. " There's bound to be a lot o' decent folk among them. They've just no' had our chances, puir souls."

Well, this started him and Stumpy on a great argument. Granma and me said nothing. I looked from one to the other and Granma sat and pleated her apron.

Stumpy reckoned there were ever so many different classes of folk, arranged in layers, from the king and the royal family, who were on the topmost layer, down to the people who lived at Calderburn. He reckoned that him and Granpa were a layer or two above those people, but they were layers and layers below the king and the aristocracy. Granpa didn't hold with this, of course. He said there was only one layer of people, only some of them started off with or got better chances than the others. " It's just like picking a straw," he said. " There's a huge hand with lots of straws in it and most people pick the short straws."

M

While they were arguing there was a knock at the door. It was a big, fat, beggar-wife, with so much dirt in the creases of her fat face you could of scraped it out with your finger-nail. She had on a shawl and she was carrying a basket with dishes, and shoelaces, and stuff.

" Any shoelaces, dearie ? " she said, and she grinned all over at me with her yellow teeth, that were almost as yellow as the gold of her Woolworth ear-rings.

" Nothin' to-day, thank you," I said.

" Any nice cups and saucers ? Buttons ? Thread ? "

" Nothin', thank you," I said.

" Aw, dearie," she said. " Surely you want somethin' ? "

" Nothin', thank you," I said.

" Could you give me a cup o' tea then ? " she said. " I've no' had anything since breakfast time and that's the honest truth."

" Sorry," I said, and I began to push the door a little, hoping she'd take the hint.

" Ask your wife if she hasnie any auld clothes she could gi'e me," she said. She'd heard Granma's voice and she leaned in the door and cried, " Are ye there, sis ? "

" What is it ? " Granma said, coming to the door.

" Ha'e ye ony auld clothes ye dinnie need, dearie ? " the rag-wife said.

Granma shook her head.

" Are ye sure, sis ? " the rag-wife said, and she leaned forward beseechingly. " No auld chemises or blouses ? I havenie a stitch on ma back. See ! " And she threw open her shawl and, jees, she sure had said a mouthful. She had nothing on under the shawl.

" Get oot o' here, ye awfu'-like limmer ! " Granma cried, and she slammed the door in the rag-wife's face.

And she shuffled into the kitchen in front of me muttering,
" The glaikit besom, it's the polis she's needin' on her
track."

She told Granpa and Stumpy. " I havenie seen the
likes o' her around here for a long time," she said. " We
havenie been bothered much wi' beggars lately."

" No, it's not like the auld days," Granpa said.
" Beggars dinnie bother wi' the cottages now. They
ken by the broken-doon look o' them that it's not worth
their while tryin'."

" Ah, but the cottages used to be a happy hunting-
ground for beggars," Granma said. " I wouldnie ha'e
dreamed o' turnin' the likes o' that woman awa' in the
auld days."

Well, this got them started in to recall all the beggars
who'd been in the habit of coming. Some of them had
come so regularly that Granma said you could set your
clock by them. " There was Bumbee Bob for instance,"
she said. " He came every Tuesday forenoon about
twelve o'clock."

" And do ye mind o' Treacle Tommy, who aye wanted
a treacle piece ? " Granpa said.

" And the Soap Box Loon ? " Stumpy said.

I sat and listened to their tales, but I didn't listen any
too carefully. All the time I couldn't get the sight of
the beggar-wife's breasts out of my mind. You know
how it is when you get an edge on you. You try to
think about other things, but all the time you can't get
away from it. It wasn't that I'd of had anything to do
with the beggar-wife. The hell I would. But it was
just that the sight of her big fat breasts with the dark
line of dirt and hair between them had got me going.
You know how it is. I felt like I'd feel after I'd been
looking at some of the dirty post-cards you buy in places

I've been in. I had a right edge on and I guessed I had to get out of there. So I said to Granma that I'd go up to Henderson Gardens and see if George was going to the pictures.

George's classes in the Wireless College finished around four o'clock. He'd just finished his tea when I went in, and Aunt Bella was preparing the tea for Uncle Jim. I told them about the letter from the Sanitary, and then I wished I hadn't told them for Aunt Bella got started in to talk about it and we couldn't get away to the pictures.

" It's just as well it's come," she said. " Listen now, they should have been out of that house years ago. It's no' for the likes of them. They should have a house like this where they'd have everything at their hands."

" Except money ! " George said.

" Ye dinnie need to speak," Aunt Bella said. " Ye dinnie want for very much. Ye're a sight better off than I was when I was your age. Not that we were ever starved or anything like that, ye ken. But things are different when there's only two in a family. A big difference from seven o' us. It says a lot for yer Granny and Grandpa that they brought us all up decently. We were aye fed and clad, though they had a hard struggle to do it. Some o' the folk nowdays dinnie ken they're born—they get everything flung at them."

" Bombs and stuff," George said.

" Ye're awful funny," Aunt Bella said. " But ye're not as funny as yer face."

George and me thought that this would be a good thing to go out on, but Aunt Bella hadn't finished with us yet.

" Of course, yer Granny and Grandpa will be sore

put aboot at havin' to flit at their time o' life," Aunt
Bella said. "But it won't really be any trouble to
them. There'll be plenty o' folk there to do everything for them. They won't need to do anything
themselves. It's just the *thought* o' shifting that'll worry
them."

She was all set, planning and plotting about the
flitting. To hear the way she talked you'd of thought
it was going to be the next week. She was in her
element, but, jees, she was the only one. Me and George
were rarin' to get away to the pictures. We wasn't
that interested in the flitting. And it was such a long
time away yet. There was no good getting all het-up
about it till it came. Anyway, I still had that edge on ;
that was the main thing.

We went to see *The Broadway Melody*. It was a pretty
good show and we got a good laugh. For the life of
me I can't remember any of the wisecracks, but George
was able to reel off a lot of them when we came out.
He didn't need to try to remember any of them. He had
a pretty good line of wisecracks himself, only I reckon
most of them would hardly of done for the talkies. I
guess the audience would of enjoyed them okay, but
the trouble would of been to get them past the censors,
who believe in not giving audiences anything they don't
think is good for them.

"What forms some of those chorus girls had,"
George said.

"Yeah, I wouldn't mind a night with one of them
babies," I said. "I wouldn't mind one of them right
now."

"Any night would do me," George said. "To-night
or next week."

"I want one to-night," I said.

He laughed, but he didn't say anything. He pointed to a news-bill we were passing.

SHEEP WORRYING IN SCOTLAND

"Christ," George said. "What the hell have they got to worry about ? "

"Maybe they feel the way I do now," I said.

"How's that ? " he said.

So I told him. "Do you know any place ? " I said.

"What kind of place ? " he said. His eyes were wide open. He was trying to act as if this was just a common occurrence with him, but hell, he was only about sixteen and he couldn't know much.

"A kip-shop," I said.

"There's some in Flower Street," he said.

"Lead me to them," I said.

"But I don't know where they are," he said. "I only heard about them."

"Just my luck," I said.

We walked on for a bit, then I said, "Will Walter know ? "

George hooted. "Don't make me laugh ! "

"What about his pal, Douglas ? " I said.

"You'll give me hysterics if you're not careful," George said. "Douglas would be scared stiff to go into one of those places."

"But he's always talkin' about them," I said.

"Talkin'," George said. "That's as far as he'll go."

I wished Cinnamon was with me. Cinnamon always knew where to find those kinda places when we were in foreign ports. Of course, I don't know whether he knew where to find them in Edinburgh. Maybe he 'idn't want to find them there, seeing his wife was there. But I guess he'd of known where to find them, anyway. Jees, it sure was a pity George was so young.

"I tell you what," George said. "Let's walk along Flower Street. Maybe we'll meet some tarts."

"O.K.," I said.

Flower Street was a pretty narrow street that ran parallel with Princes Street. It was dark and kinda gloomy. There was an awful lot of dark doorways with groups of young men and girls standing in them. There was a good lot of fish and chip shops, and cafes, and shops with books about birth control and rubber goods in their windows. George and me walked from one end to the other, about three-quarters of a mile, but though we seen plenty of dames who looked like tarts none of them spoke to us. And I didn't see one red lamp. Which sure was annoying. Different from being in a foreign port.

"We'll walk back again," I said.

So we walked back again, but although we looked hard at all the dames we saw standing in the doorways, and although we hung around in front of the shops with the rubber goods, waiting for somebody to see us, nobody spoke to us.

"Are you sure this is the right place?" I said.

"Sure," George said. "This is the street that gets the worst reputation in Edinburgh."

"I don't see any sign of that reputation," I said.

"Well, it's not my fault," George said.

Just then a couple of dames passed us, so I said, "Howya, baby?" to the one nearest me. But she never let on. She clattered along in her high heels with her nose in the air.

"Gee, I wish I could see a red lamp," I said. "Don't they hang them out in this god-damned town."

" No, they kid there's not such a thing," George said.

" Let's go in here," I said, nodding at a cafe.   " This looks a likely place."

We went in but there was nobody there but an old guy eating chips in a corner, and a young fellow behind the counter, reading a racing paper.   I ordered ices and we sat down.   I tried to get on the talk with the young fellow when he brought us the ices, but he was a dumb cluck.   I tried him with a line of hot talk, but he didn't seem to have no sense.   All he could talk about was what won the Cesarwitch, and what looked like winning the November Handicap.

" Hell, I don't need him to tell me that," George whispered.   " I hear so much about racing at home, I could teach him."

I thought I'd try the guy with a dirty story, so I told him one.   But he just giggled and spluttered, and came out with one about a travelling salesman that's growing whiskers.   Jees, I was sore.   But I didn't feel like giving up.   The hell I did.   Seeing I'd come that far I reckoned I'd see the thing through to its natural conclusion.   I took out some post-cards I'd bought offen a sailor in Gefle.   " Ever seen any of those kinda things around here, buddy ? " I said, and I handed them over to the sodajerker.

Boy, did that guy's mouth open ?   He slobbered at them real bad.   His eyes were sticking outen his head with surprise.   I guess he'd never seen anything like them.

" Lemme see," George said, and he reached out for the cards.   He looked at them for a while.   " Better not leave those lyin' around in your clothes in case Kate has a pryin' fit," he said.

" Trust me," I said.

I glanced at them as I put them back in my pocket and though I'd looked at them dozens of times they kinda got me again. But, of course, you know how it is and the way I was.

"See any nice dames like those around here?" I said to the clerk.

He shook his head. He didn't seem able to speak, and his eyes were sticking outen his head, like automobile lamps full on.

"Sure?" I said.

He nodded and went back to the counter. He kept looking at us after that, but he kept at the other end of the counter and didn't say nothing. Jees, he was a dumb cluck.

"Maybe he's a Sunday School teacher," George said.

We sat around till we couldn't sit any longer, so we went home. I felt real mad at not getting what I wanted, but I reckon I wouldn't of enjoyed it if I had got it after all that bother. Anyway, there was George. I don't know what the hell I'd of done about him. Reckon it was kinda silly to take him with me in the first place.

It was about eleven when I got back to the cottages. There was a light in Nell Dippy's and for a minute I'd a crazy notion to knock her up. But jees, I wasn't as bad as all that. It was just a notion.

I thought the gas in Granma's was out and I slipped in quiet, but when I got in I found that the gas was in a peep, and I found Aunt Kate sitting by the fire like an anxious mother. The old folks were in bed. Granma opened her eyes when she saw me, but she just grunted. I grinned at Aunt Kate and said, "I had my supper. I'll away to bed."

" There's a pie for you in the oven," she said.   " Don't you want it ? "

" No, I had my supper at Henderson Gardens," I said.

" What did you have ? " she said.

I told her and then I began to draw the door towards me, but she still persisted in talking.   " That was some feed," she said.   " I wish I'd been there.   I must say our Bella knows how to feed you."

" Yeah," I said.   I was itching to get to bed in case Aunt Kate would begin to speak about the letter from the Sanitary.

" It's a pity to waste that pie," she said.   " Are you sure you don't want it ? "

" Sure," I said.

" Well, I guess I'll have it," she said.   " It's over an hour since I had my supper and I'm beginning to feel hungry."

" O.K.," I said.   " Good night."

But I was just turning the handle, as soft as I could so as not to disturb the old folk, when I felt Aunt Kate's hand on it at the other side.   She came into the lobby.

" Isn't it terrible ? " she said.

" Sure," I said.

" It's sad," she said.   " Help my Jimmie Johnston, this'll kill my mother and father.   The poor old souls."

" Yeah," I said.   " It's tough."

" The First of March," she said.   " That's three months yet.   It'll give us time to get things packed, but really I don't know how we're going to manage."

" We'll manage somehow," I said, opening the door of the East Room.

" The rents at Calderburn are dearer," she said.   " I don't know how we're going to manage, really I don't."

" They aren't so much dearer," I said.

" It's not that so much," she said. " They won't want to go. They've been here so long."

She would have rambled on like this for hours, but I had visions of another night, like the night she stood there with Matt Renton, so I said, " Well, I gotta get some shut-eye. I'll see you in the mornin'." And I went into my room and got to bed. But I couldn't sleep. I guess I still was mad at not being able to get what I wanted. I was sorry for Granpa and Granma, too, of course, because they would have to leave their home. But they were old and I reckon they'd been expecting this for a long time. There wasn't much good crying about spilt milk, was there? What was more important to me was that edge I had on. I was still mad at not having found a place in Flower Street, and I was inclined to blame George because we'd been unsuccessful. But I guess it couldn't of been one of my lucky days. I lay and calculated. Fifth November, 1929. Five and eleven made sixteen, and one seventeen and nine, twenty-six, and two twenty-eight and nine, thirty-seven, and three and seven were ten. No, that was no bloody good. How could I expect my luck to hold good with a sonofabitch of a number like ten?

Aunt Kate had no time to talk about flitting the next morning; she was too busy with all the manœuvres she went through with for her deafness. " Do you think they're doin' her any good? " I said to Granma after she'd gone.

" God knows," Granma said. " They're no' makin' her any better tempered, anyway. I dinnie ken how the lassies in her shop put up wi' her if she's as short wi' them as she is wi' us. It's high time Matt Renton was poppin' the question."

" He's, maybe, waitin' till we pop off ! " Granpa said, chuckling.

" That'll, maybe, no' be long then," Granma said.

I was helping Granma to wash the breakfast dishes when I saw Nell Dippy go past. She was half running and there was a grim sorta expression on her face, and she didn't look either to left or right.

" That's Nell awa' wi' her line," Granma shouted to Granpa, who was still in bed.

" Line ? " I said.

" Her betting-line," Granma said. " She goes doon every mornin' wi' her line to the bookie's runner in the Square."

" I wonder what she'll do when she goes to Calderburn ? " Granpa said.

Granma rubbed round the greasy ring the water had left in the basin and she didn't answer for a while. Then she said, " I wonder what we'll all do ? "

After that everything hinged upon Calderburn and the flitting. No matter what anybody said or did, Granma and Granpa always looked at it in relation to the flitting. In a way it was kinda ridiculous ; you'd of thought they was gonna be hung or something. The First of March, 1930. That was execution day. It seemed that nothing would matter after that. They would start on a new life then, but what use had they for a new life at their age ?

Aunt Kate was as bad as them. In fact she was worse. She made a helluva moan about it. Which was funny, Walter Anderson said, seeing that twice or thrice years ago, when Granpa and Granma were more able, she'd wanted them to flit to a house with more conveniences. But now to hear her, you'd think she'd never done that ; you'd of thought she was chained to 'the puir auld hoose,' as she persisted in calling it.

But this only lasted for a week or two. It was like all the rest of the things Aunt Kate did. She made a helluva splutter about them and then she lost interest in them and all the spluttering died away. In a way she was acting to the gallery, like she acted to the gallery when she made a fuss over Granpa, and called him a 'dear auld cratur!' She thought that people expected her to be in a panic about having to quit the cottages, so she gave them good measure. But as soon as she got tired of being in a panic she began to plan what she was gonna do when they moved to Calderburn.

It was George and Walter who told me this, for the *Red Biddy* sailed a few days after they got the notice to quit. The day I went away both Granma and Granpa were awful low. "We'll, maybe, no' be here when ye come back, laddie," Granma said.

"Boloney," I said. "I'll be back before March."

"But, maybe, ye'll no' come back," Granpa said.

"Sure I'll come back," I said. "What would hinder me?"

"Ah, there's lots o' things," Granpa said. "We never know what's comin' to us from one day to another. We can make as many plans as we like, but there's almost sure to be somebody who'll upset them for us. Don't be too sure, laddie, ye'll no' be the first one who's gone oot o' that door sayin' it wouldn't be long till he was back. And if ye dinnie come back ye'll no' be the first. . . ."

FOUR PURL

"DON'T *be too sure, laddie, ye'll no' be the first one who's gone out o' that door and never come back.*"
I remember that was what I said to Walter the day he went away to the war. His mother was nearly crying and Kate was howling holy murder, but Walter stood in the middle of the floor with his uniform and all his accoutrements and laughed, and asked them what they were kicking up all the row about. " I'll soon be back," he said. " The war'll be over in a few weeks. It'll be a nice wee holiday for me." That was what he and a lot of other young fellows like him thought. They all thought the war was a picnic. They set out prepared to give the Germans hell in the way they'd have set out to give a drunk man biff for ill-treating a child. They didn't know of what lay behind the war or of what far-reaching effects it would have.

None of us did, of course. The war fell on us like the lash of a whip on our backs, searing us. The whip had been cracking for years—there were always rumours of war—and we had got so used to hearing it crack that we thought the men who were wielding the whip were joking and we were astonished when the blow fell. We were so surprised that we could do nothing; we couldn't even think properly. All we seemed able to do was obey.

When the Boer War was on I was an ardent pacifist —though nobody would have called me that then;

when they called me anything it was more likely to be a
bloody old fool. And after the Boer War I had so
many other things to think about that I hadn't time to
think of the whys and wherefores of war. All my life
I've burned with the sense of social injustice, but I was
never able to put it into words. I wish now that I'd
spent my spare time more profitably. If I'd only read
more, read the books that would have taught me the·
arguments to use when men, whom I knew were in the
wrong, supported the State and the people who kept
them down. But I didn't read—I always left the reading
in the house to Mirren, and it was novels and such-like
trash that she read. So I was always stumped when I
tried to find corroboration for my own statements when
I spoke at Trade Union meetings. And so I was
stumped when I tried to speak sanely about the war.
I didn't know what to think or what to believe. All
around me men, who were great Socialists, were as
belligerent as those who were Imperialistic. Everybody wanted to give the Germans hell. Everybody
believed the atrocity stories they read in the newspapers. They forgot their commonsense and their
knowledge that most Germans were a decent hard-
working lot of people like ourselves.

I'll never forget the day Walter enlisted. It was one
night in December, 1914, a wet, blustery sort of night.
I was bent nearly double as I came along the road from
the sawmill, struggling against the wind that was
blowing in from the Forth. The wartime regulations
about lights were already in force and it was a difficult
job coming along the Low Road. You couldn't see
whether you were on the road or not: you were liable
to bump any minute into the sleepers of the railway
line or into a rut. My rheumatics were bothering me

at the time. I mind that Willie Brown had to give me an arm along one bad bit of the road, and I was annoyed at that, for Willie Brown was older than me by a year or two. He was well over seventy.

I was soaking when I got in. I opened the kitchen door, so that the light would shine into the lobby while I took off my coat and shook it and hung it up. "Here's yer father now," I heard Mirren say. "We'll see what he has to say to this." I took my beard in my hand and rinsed the raindrops off it. My hand was wet and I rubbed it on the backside of my trousers as I went into the kitchen.

"What'll your father have to say to what?" I said.

Mirren lifted the kettle off the hob and began to mask the tea. "His Nabs has enlisted," she said, nodding at Walter, who was sitting as pleased as punch on the sofa.

"So you've enlisted, have you?" I said.

"Ay," he said.

I sat down at the table and began to eat. Walter rose and yawned, stretching himself. He was a fine big chap, plenty of bone and muscle, with a fresh complexion and bonny fair hair. He was about twenty-seven. Just a nice age to be shot.

"I aye suspected ye were a fool," I said, taking a drink of tea. "Now I know it."

"How?" he said.

"I don't need to tell you," I said. "Ye've heard often enough how I feel about war and the people who make it."

"Ay, and I feel the same thing myself," he said. "But I don't see why I'm a fool."

"Ye could ha'e waited till they asked you to fight,"

I said. "Let other fools rush in first. Time enough for a sensible man to go when he's called upon."

Arnold was sitting at the piano ; he had been trying to play some of Kate's music. He laughed and banged out a note or two. Walter turned round and glared at him. They were very like each other, only Arnold's face was thinner, older looking. He looked his age, but Walter didn't look his.

"You don't need to laugh," Walter said. "You'll have to go, too."

"Oh, we don't want to lose you, but we guess you'll have to go!" Arnold sang a few lines of the song that silly actresses, with sillier empty faces, were singing to young men, exhorting them to go and get blown to bits. "Catch me!" he said. "I'm too old to die!"

"You're not too old, my mannie," Walter said. "Don't you kid yourself. Thirty's just a nice age. Don't you think that you'll get off when conscription comes."

"I thought you told us before Dad came in that there would be no need for conscription," Arn said. "You said that you and the others like you would knock the Germans into hell and the war would be over in a few weeks."

"Well," Walter said. "So it will."

"Will it!" Arnold said. "That's what everybody said last August and the war's not finished yet. A few weeks, a few months, a few years—what's the odds ? "

"If every able-bodied man enlisted at once the war would be over in no time," Walter said.

"Would it!" Arn jeered. "Not on your life, duckie, not on your sweet life."

"Sit in and get your tea," Mirren said, "and stop quarrelling like a couple of bairns."

N

They sat in and we ate for a while without speaking. Mirren was sitting with a tight-looking face, hardly eating. I knew what she was thinking, but she was too proud to show it. She refilled our cups without opening her mouth. All the time she kept her eyes on the table, not looking at any of us. At last I said, " When do you go ? "

" I report at the barracks to-morrow morning," Walter said.

" What made you do it ? " I said. " Knowing and feeling as ye do—at least I hope ye feel as I do about war."

" I do, father," he said. " But it doesn't alter it. I've *got* to go. All the other men are going."

" Not all of them ! " Arn said, laughing. " Some of them have more sense."

" You're not speaking about yourself, are you ? " Walter said sarcastically. " No, you can't be," he said. " You're not a man."

" Look, father," he said to me. " I know that wars are made by the rich for profit. I know all your arguments against war and I believe in them. But I think of it like this. If we don't enlist and go, they'll pass laws to make us go. Better to get it over and be done with."

" That's where you're wrong," Arn said. " If everybody refused to go, even although they passed laws for conscription, they couldn't force them. They haven't enough people in authority to enforce their laws."

" That's what you think," Walter said. " But it just shows what a child-like mind you've got. It's true that they're less in number than us, but they've got the guns to bring us to heel. What could we do against guns ?

It's either their guns or the Germans' guns. We're better to face the Germans."

So it went on, the argument for and against enlisting. I was thankful that Walter had none of that patriotism that so many young fellows of his age had. He knew that he was fighting for the interests of a few rich men, and that he'd get no reward for it. He knew that the bulk of the German people weren't our enemies and that we weren't theirs. He knew, too, that he might die. But he thought it better to dive in and get it over with, and then he would get back to his ordinary life. Besides, he had a girl, some servant lassie that was in service up the town, and, no doubt, it was for her as much as for anybody that he'd enlisted. She wanted a boy in the trenches. She was consumed by patriotism and anti-Germanism. She wailed to Walter, *What'll become of me if the Germans conquer us? Some Prussian officer'll rape me.* Walter knew that nothing like that was likely to happen to her; that although Germany won the war we couldn't be much worse off under their exhorbitant peace-terms than we were already under our own god-damned Government. But because a woman wailed at him and was ready to call him a coward if he didn't do what she told him, he forgot all the sense I'd instilled into him. In a way I'm thankful that lassie never became my daughter-in-law. I've no use for the likes of her, empty, senseless creatures. Thank God, I never got any daughters-in-law, I couldn't have tholed them, empty chattering bitches as they would probably have been. Jean Brown was the only one I'd have cared for, and, of course, I didn't get her.

None of my sons-in-law were at the war. Bernard's boss, Lord Sheringwall, took damned good care that he wasn't going to lose a reliable chauffeur. And Jim

Anderson's heart kept him from being taken, though he was called up for examination two or three times. Bella was in a fair panic in case he would have to go. She had just had George a few months and she was still not very strong. The night before Walter left Edinburgh for the training-camp they were all here, all talking about the war. I mind I had wee Walter on my knee, and I stroked his soft fair hair as I listened to what they were all saying. Arnold was making a fool of those who were foolish enough to enlist, and Walter was defending them. They went at it tooth and nail. Bella sat with her bairn on her lap and clutched it as if the Germans were going to burst in straightway and bayonet it before her eyes. Jim sat and smoked; he was ready to go to the war to defend Bella and his bairns but he didn't want to go any earlier than he needed to go. Kate sat at the piano, but she wasn't playing. I mind that she had *Alexander's Ragtime Band* propped up in front of her. And Mirren sat with a stony face beside the fire, pleating her apron, and saying nothing.

There must have been millions of homes like ours, both in Britain and Germany, where some of the sons were going out to fight because they thought their mothers and sisters and sweethearts were in danger of being assaulted as the lying pro-rich-man-and-his-profits papers said. Millions of homes where the other sons held the view that if everybody refused to fight the war would automatically stop and those who engineered it would need to sue for whatever peace-terms they could get. Millions of homes where young mothers, like Bella, were torn between anxiety for their bairns and undecided whether to force their husbands to go and fight for them at the front or to stay and defend them at home. Millions of homes where young women, like Kate, were being proud and happy because their brothers were soldiers, because it allowed them to crow over their less fortunate (or more!) friends who had no brothers or fathers in uniform. Millions of husbands like Jim Anderson who didn't want to go and be killed, but who, above all, didn't want their wives and families to perish. Millions of mothers, like Mirren, who were uncomplaining, and said nothing either in praise or in blame, who accepted everything that came with courage. Millions of grandfathers like myself, too old to fight, too old even to work, who began to think as the war went on that they, too, would need to take a gun and go and defend their little grandchildren.

So Walter went to the war, and Mirren cried quietly every night for weeks after he'd gone, beside me in the kitchen-bed, after she thought I was asleep. She wasn't the only one who was unhappy. There was Arnold worrying about the war, too, although he did his best not to show it. He never made any move to enlist, not even when the Derby Scheme came into force, and then later, when conscription was first talked about. Not even when those bloody interfering women got busy with their white feathers did he turn a hair. I suppose he must have suffered: all the young men at home suffered almost as much as the young men at the front. If their parents didn't nag at them to join up, their consciences or other people nagged at them. It must have been hell to be a conscientious objector. For they were all men with intelligence, sensitive men who had the good of humanity at heart. And it's always sensitive people like those who suffer the most. I wonder how they felt when they saw those other people, those dull fools who didn't give a damn for humanity, stupid people who obeyed the herd-instinct,

getting praised and honoured, while they got kicked
and reviled and spat upon? Ah, God, what truth there
is in that old saying, *A prophet is without honour in his
own country.* For they were all prophets, those conscientious objectors, prophets of the great future when
men will live at peace with themselves and with others,
when none will have any doubt, and be able to reason
and feel intelligently. But God knows when that
future will become the present.

I know that Arn got white feathers given to him a
good few times, but he didn't seem to worry about it.
He made a fool of the way the women gave them to
him in the way he made a fool of everything. He laughed
and kidded even more than ever, trying, I suppose, to
make Mirren forget about Walter being at the front.
But there was a big difference in him after he went for
that holiday to Leven with Willie Taylor.

It was late in September and they went for a fortnight.
But they came home at the end of the first week, and
Willie Taylor enlisted at once. Some gang of girls
had made their lives unbearable by presenting them
with white feathers every time they met them on the
promenade. Arnold laughed about it when he came
home, singing :

> Oh, it's nice to be beside the seaside,
>   Oh, it's nice to be beside the sea,
> Where the girls give you feathers on the Prom-Prom-
>   Prom,
> In the hope that you'll join-up
> And be a Tom-Tom-Tom.
> Oh, it's nice to be beside the sea !

Arn could take it, but Wild Willie couldn't. After

he joined-up Arn got miserable. They had been inseparable for years, and now Arn had nobody to confide in. There were no other young fellows of his age in the cottages or at his work. There were only old men and boys. And boys, so young that Arn couldn't possibly have anything in common with them, any ground where they could meet. He looked at them, those boys, and he wanted to know them. But they were chary of him; he was so old. To them he was middle-aged. Thirty-one was practically a Methuselah to their sixteens and seventeens.

Only with Jean Brown could he find any sympathy, a place where he could tell something of what he was suffering.

Jean Brown was getting on; she was twenty-nine. She could have married long before that, but she thought Arnold cared for her and she threw away other chances because of him. Him that didn't care twopence for her in that way. Poor lassie. He liked her, but only as a good pal. But neither she, nor anybody else, could see that. She thought that Arn wanted to marry her but was too bashful to propose, and she tried by all the means she could to bring him up to scratch. I'm not blaming her. She did only what any other girl in her place would have done. She was gentler and more patient about it, too, than many of them would have been. If I'd had to have a daughter-in-law I'd rather have had her than anybody else. But Arnold, of course, poor laddie, wasn't meant to get married. He should have been born with a silver spoon in his mouth. In another class he would have been recognised at once as a genius and his talent for drawing would have been fostered. He would have been sent to Paris to study. He'd have got every opportunity; he'd have met

artists who would have helped him, people like himself,
who would have recognised his genius. But being a
poor man's son, having to work for a living and be a
poor man himself, he got none of those chances. He
struggled for a while. He painted in his spare time ;
he always hoped that some day somebody would come
along and notice his paintings and help him. But that
somebody never came, and bye and bye Arn ceased to
hope for him. And gradually he ceased to paint.
By the time he was twenty-nine or so he had stopped
thinking about painting. I believe it was that sterility,
that frustration, added to the terrible ache that the war
gave to him, the turmoil and the indecision it made in
his mind, that led him to doing what he did. Perhaps
it was abnormal, but the people who condemned him
should have remembered that the time, too, was abnormal. He was, by no means, as much to blame as
they made out. I'm his father and I can excuse him, of
course. But I maintained at the time, and I still maintain,
that he did it under great stress. Normally, although
he may have wanted to, he would never have allowed
his passions to get out of control. Anyway, there was
a big difference in him after Willie Taylor enlisted.

Walter came home on leave at the end of 1915. He
was bitter about Arnold not having joined-up. Already
he had assimilated some of the senseless patriotism and
stupidity of the regular soldier. He said Arn should be
doing his bit like every other able-bodied man. And for
the first time in their lives he and Arn quarrelled. They
quarrelled not as they had quarrelled when they were
bairns, wrangling over some toy. They quarrelled not
as they had quarrelled when they were young men
because one was wearing the other's socks or because
they thought their mother hadn't given them equal

helpings of meat. But they quarrelled like animals, watching each other savagely, circling round and round each other, ready to spring and sink their teeth into each other's throat.

" You'd better enjoy your freedom while you can ! " Walter said tauntingly. " There'll be conscription soon."

" But I've got a sore belly," Arn said, showing his teeth as if he were laughing, but really in a snarl of hatred. " I can't go. You wouldn't want me to fight with a sore belly, would you ? "

" No, I'd like to stick a bayonet into it," Walter said. " I'd like to rip the guts out of you—only you haven't any guts to rip."

Mirren was sore put about when they quarrelled. " Ye've awfu' little to do," she said to them. " Quarrellin' like that when ye'll maybe never see each other again. God knows Walter's leave is short enough without making it miserable for everybody."

They laughed at her fears and they did their best to forget their differences. But all the time the enmity was there ; the cancer ; the " why shouldn't you do what I've got to do "—standing between them like a pillar of fire. And it was still there when Walter went back to the front.

After he'd gone Arn became more miserable than ever. After that he stopped any pretence at being cheerful. He went about with a hang-dog expression, afraid to go out. He knew that everybody in the cottages was talking about him, wondering why an able-bodied man like him without a wife or family should still be here when everybody else in the cottages, except Truth Dippy and he didn't count, the poor vacant creature, was away fighting in France.

At last Mirren couldn't stand it any longer. " Ye'd

better speak to him, Wattie," she said to me. "God knows I dinnie want him to go. One son in this war's enough. But I cannie bear to see Arn so miserable. He's never been miserable in his life afore. Can ye no' speak to him?"

"What can I say?" I said.

"It's only because of you he stays at home," she said. "He doesnie want to let you down. He knows how ye feel about war. He doesnie want to let ye down as Tom and Walter let ye down. Could ye no' tell him ye've changed yer mind about it and that ye think it would be better if he went?"

But I couldn't do that. Arn would have known at once that I was telling a lie, that I was doing it because I thought he was a coward. Though God knows I didn't think that. If he'd been a coward he'd have enlisted long before that as Willie Taylor enlisted. No coward could have borne the looks and the things that folk said about him when he went past, and no coward could have borne those women with their white feathers. Oh, God, what those women have to answer for. Silly senseless bitches trying to be clever, how many fine young men did you send to their deaths with your daft dramatic capers? The pity is that you hadn't to suffer as the young men and their folk had to suffer.

Mirren tried to help Arn herself when I wouldn't speak. She urged him to marry Jean Brown.

"But I don't want to get married," he said.

"Maybe not," she said. "But all the same ye'd better. Don't ye see that if ye're married, folk won't think so badly of you for not enlisting?"

"I don't care what they think of me," he said.

"But I care," Mirren said. "I want no son o' mine to be called a coward."

" Do ye think that, mother ? " he said quietly.

" No, laddie, no," she said, beginning to greet. " Oh, God," she cried. " Why ha'e we to suffer all this ? Could ye no' ha'e let us ha'e oor auld age in peace ? One son gone God knows where and another facin' death at every minute. Could ye no' ha'e left us the last one ? "

" Marrying Jean Brown won't make any difference," Arn said. " Folk won't think any better of me. Those who know me well enough don't think any ill of me at all. They know I've got to stay at home, that some-body's got to look after you and Dad in your old age. Dad can't work for ever. By rights, he should be retired now."

And by rights I should. I was sixty-eight, long past the age when I should have had to work. But I couldn't get the old age pension till I was seventy, and it wouldn't be much help to us when I did get it. And it wasn't. Seven and sixpence a week is a big difference from thirty shillings. If it hadn't been for Kate's pay and the help that Meg and Grace and Bella gave us, little though they could afford it themselves, God knows what would have happened to us when I retired. It was then that we missed Arn. We saw that he'd been right after they took him away from us. We missed what he'd been bringing into the house—and that was more than money, more, more, ah God, money could not have bought what they took away from us with their stupidity.

We had a hard struggle till Mirren was old enough to get the pension, too. For there was not only Arn's pay wanting, there was Walter's as well. Of course, we got a pension for him. A pension ! As if that would compensate for all that their war had done to us. A skittery pittance that wouldn't have kept a dog far less a man and a woman who had struggled so hard to bring up the man they killed.

We didn't get a pension for Arnold, but the war killed him as surely as it killed Walter. And it made him suffer more. Walter got blown to bits by a German shell, and his death was instantaneous. But Arn got killed slowly, tortured by malice and hatred and rank stupidity.

Poor laddie, he would have had to go to the war sooner or later because conscription came in. Whether he'd have had the guts to be a conscientious objector, I don't know. But I think that being his mother's son and mine he would have had that courage.

On the day I heard that conscription was passed I thought about him all the way home from the sawmill at night. The workmen had been talking about it all day. A lot of them had asked my opinion, knowing that Arn was bound to be conscripted and wondering what I'd have to say about it. But I gave them no cuttings. I told those who asked me that I'd stopped passing an opinion about anything that happened nowadays because the world and the people who ran it were getting madder and madder. But all the way home I thought plenty about it; I thought so much that two or three times I nearly tripped over the sleepers of the railway.

Mirren was sitting on the sofa when I went in. She made no move to rise when she saw me, neither to mask the tea, nor to help me off with my coat. She just looked at me, saying nothing. I thought at first that she'd heard about the conscription law, but I realised from the look on her face that it was more than that. I knew it was Walter. But I tried to delude myself into thinking it wasn't. I tried to put off the evil day.

" Where's Arn ? " I said.   " I thought he'd be home
by this time."

" He's out," she said.

I went to the fire and warmed my hands.   I saw the
telegram behind the tea-caddy and I knew that what I'd
guessed was true.   It was exactly twenty minutes past
six and I noticed that the rim of the clock face was dusty.

" Where's Kate ? " I said.   " This is her half-holiday,
isn't it ? "

" She's away to the pictures to see Mary Pickford,"
Mirren said.

Away to the pictures and that telegram on the mantelpiece !   I knew then that it couldn't have been long since
it arrived.   I sat down beside her and put my hand on
her arm.

" When did it come, lass ? " I said.

" At five o'clock," she said.

She rose and began to mask the tea.   She said nothing
more.   I could see no signs of tears on her face ; it was
sulky-looking and her lips were pressed together so
tightly that the lines running down to her chin stood out
more sharply than they usually did.   It struck me for
the first time that her hair was nearly all grey now ; there
were few golden strands in it.   Funny I'd never noticed
it before.

I began to take my tea, but I couldn't eat.   I had
spread a piece of bread and margarine, but I thought the
first bite would choke me.   I sat with my forefinger
looped in the handle of my cup, but I never lifted it to
my lips.   The clock seemed to be making a terrible loud
ticking.

Mirren didn't sit down at the table.   She went back
to the sofa.   She took a cup of tea and a piece with her,
but she put the cup on top of the grate and the bread in

the saucer and she never touched them. Neither of us spoke. I wasn't thinking of anything. I don't know whether Mirren was thinking of anything or not. When you get grief suddenly like that you don't analyse it. It's later when you realise what it implies that you rail against it, scream against it, kicking against the pricks. But at the time you accept it quietly, because you don't realise what it means. You're kind of deadened and dumb. You only notice exterior things. Like the clock ticking.

It was the clock striking half-past seven that made me sit up. I took a mouthful of tea, but it was stone-cold ; it ran down my gullet·like lead. It took all my strength of will to keep from spitting it out. I rose and began to clear the table. Every minute I expected to hear Mirren say " Sit down and I'll do that," but she didn't. I was busy doing it when there was a knock at the door.

It was Plates the police-sergeant and there was another policeman and a man I didn't know with him.

" Good evening, Wattie," Plates said. " Is your son in ? "

" What son ? " I said.

" What son would it be, man ? " he said. " What son would it be but that Arnold one who lives with you ? The one who's a clerk in Sir Malcolm's office."

" He's out," I said. " What do ye want with him ? "

Plates cleared his throat and coughed a wee thing bashful. " Well, man, I wouldn't like to say," he said. " I wouldn't like to be the one who would have to tell you." He inclined his head a bit as if he would keek round the door. " Is Mistress Gillespie in ? "

" Ay," I said.

" Ah, that's bad," he said.

He shoved back his helmet and gave his brow a bit

wipe with his sleeve. I've thought often since then that it must have been a sore thing for him, poor man, to have to come to us with such news.

"Will you take a bit walk along to the corner with us, Wattie man?" he said.

"Well," I said. "My wife...." I shook my head and leaned against the door. "My wife——" I said again. "We have just heard that Walter ..."

"Ah, there's a fine young man now," Plates said. "A credit to yourself, Wattie, and a credit to Harrisfield. Doing his bit for his king and country. How is he getting on?"

"He was killed yesterday," I said.

"Ah, man, that's terrible," he said, putting his hand on my arm. "Such a fine young man.... This awful war.... God help us all, when will it end?"

Plates fidgeted and shuffled his feet on the pavement. The other bobby stood at the edge of the cobbles. I couldn't see his face; it was just a dark blur. The other man stood beside him. I could see by the way he was hopping from one leg to another that he was greatly agitated. I leaned against the door. I knew I should say something, but I didn't know what to say. What was the good of speaking, anyway? All the words in the world wouldn't alter what was in that telegram.

Plates must have sensed this with his Gaelic second-sight. He was terribly embarrassed; he would no doubt have done anything to be elsewhere at the time. He wasn't really a representative of the law; he was a friend of mostly everybody in Harrisfield, and he felt his position keenly. But the strange man who was with him had none of Plates' delicacy.

"I want your son," he cried, shoving Plates aside.

" Just let me get my hands on him and I'll tear him limb from limb."

" Now, calm yourself, Mr. Simmons, man, calm yourself," Plates said. " That's no way to talk. Calm yourself and we'll come back again when Arnold's in, and perhaps things will be a little brighter then."

But the man Simmons wouldn't budge. He began to kick up a terrible row, crying out against Arnold, and saying what he'd do to him when he got him. I was afraid Mirren would come out. Indeed, I can't think why she didn't. She was bound to hear most of what was being said. Unless her feelings were too numbed. . . .

I pulled to the door behind me, and I took the man Simmons by the arm. " I'll come along to the corner wi' ye," I said. " And then ye can tell me what the bit of trouble is."

" Bit of trouble ! " Simmons cried. " Bit of trouble he calls it ! " He laughed in a high, unnatural, sort of way, and poked Plates in the ribs.

" Had ye not better put on a jacket, Wattie man," Plates said. " Ye'll catch your death o' cold in your shirt-sleeves."

I went into the lobby and put on my jacket. I listened at the kitchen door, but I could hear nothing, so I looked round the door. Mirren was still sitting on the sofa. She hadn't moved. She was staring straight in front of her, perfectly quiet, except that one of her hands was pleating her apron.

" I'm going out for a minute, Mirren," I said.

But she didn't answer me. I said it again. Still she paid no heed, so I went out.

" Well, what is it ? " I said, when we got along to the corner. " What's the trouble ? "

" I don't think I'd better tell ye, Wattie," Plates said. " Man, if I'd known about . . . *this*, I'd not have come to trouble you to-night at all."

" And why not ? " the man Simmons cried. " And why not, I'd like to know ? "

" Have ye no respect for a parent's feelings, man ? " Plates said.

" Feelings ! A parent's feelings ! " Simmons began to laugh again, that horrible, hysterical laughter. " I like that. By God, I like that. What about my feelings ? Am I not a parent, too ? Aren't my feelings just as important as his ? Did his son think about my feelings when he did that to my boy ? "

" What is it ? " I said wearily. " What have you come about ? "

" I'm afraid this'll be a shock for ye, Wattie, man," Plates said slowly. I knew he was trying to spare my feelings and that in doing so he'd go round all the corners, moving along ponderously like a giant steamroller.

But the man Simmons wasn't inclined to wait till Plates told the story in his own way. He jumped right in at once and said :

" That son of yours has been interfering with my boy."

I looked at him, puzzled. " What do you mean ? " I said. " How has Arnold been interfering with your boy ? "

" How would he interfere with him ? " he cried.

" How the hell should I know ? " I said. " It's you that's telling the story, isn't it ? "

But since he had got that far he seemed to dry up all of a sudden. He just said again, " He's been interfering with my boy and I won't have it." And both Plates

o

and the other bobby didn't seem able to know what
to say either.   They all mumbled away and cleared their
throats and coughed.

"It was like this," Plates said at last.   "This boy,
Archie Simmons, is in the office beside Arnold."

"Yes, I know him," I said.   "What about him?"

"Well," Plates said, and he coughed.   "To-night
he came home and told his father that Arnold had been
. . . well, interfering with him."

"So you've said already," I said.   "Interfering!
How the hell had he been interfering with him?"

"Well, it was like this," Plates said.   "He misbehaved himself with the boy."

"Misbehaved?" I said.

"Yes, you know," Plates said.   "He . . ."   But
he couldn't say any more : he was an Elder of the kirk,
like myself, and Elders of the kirk don't speak about
such things.   But I thought I understood what he
meant.

"What do you want me to do?" I said.

I don't think I listened to what they said.   I knew
that the man Simmons meant to get Arnold sent to
prison, and I was wondering what I could do to stop
that; I knew Mirren would never bear up with this
added to Walter's death.   I was standing like a stooky,
wondering about it and beginning to feel cold, when
somebody came up the brae from the Low Road.   He
passed quite close to us and I saw that it was Truth
Dippy.

"Have ye seen Arn?" I said to him, hoping that the
poor simple soul wouldn't have done so, and that he'd
say, "No."

"Ay," he said.

"Where?" Plates said.

"I saw him going down the breakwater," Truth said.

I'll never forget that walk along the Forthport Road. You'd have thought I was the man Simmons; I was that anxious to get Arn. I was the first to reach the pend under the railway line. There was a goods train standing on it at the time, and I saw the driver's and the fireman's faces glowing red from the flames of the furnace like devils' faces in the blackness above me as I ran into the black pipe of the pend. The sergeant and the bobby panted as they followed me. Simmons was last; he'd got a stitch in his side from running. I wish the bastard had got a stitch in his throat that would have choked him.

A terrible gust of wind met me as I came out of the tunnel and I was forced to halt for a minute at the beginning of the breakwater. The wind stung my eyeballs and the spray from the sea stung me saltily. I could see only a few yards in front of me, but I began to stagger along blindly. I knew every yard of the breakwater as well as I knew every corner of my own house, but once or twice, if it hadn't been for Plates, I'd have fallen on the rough stones. I could hear Simmons, moaning and panting, behind me. But I didn't heed him. I was terrified of what we'd find at the end of the breakwater. If we found anything. Oh, God, not that, not that, I prayed. I tried to tell myself that we'd meet Arn walking towards us, but every step there was no sign of him coming towards us. He couldn't have come down here for pleasure, I thought. The spray was dashing right over the breakwater. Anybody who came down here on a night like this must be mad. But he couldn't be down here. Poor simple Truth Dippy must have made a mistake. If we didn't find him it would be because he had never

come here.   But if we did find him ?   I wanted to find
him, and I didn't want to find him.   If we found him
it would mean prison.   And if we didn't find him. . . .
¡ All sorts of things passed through my mind.   I
couldn't reason sensibly with myself.   I was sure Arn
had come down here only for one thing.   And if we
didn't find him it would mean that his body would be
floating out there somewhere among the snarling
black waves.   I was terrified we'd find nothing at the
end of the breakwater by the green lamp.

But God knows I'd rather have found nothing than
have found him as we did.   He was lying on the cold,
wet stones, at the end, and the spray was dashing over
him, soaking him.   He was moaning and muttering to
himself.   He didn't seem to know us when we spoke,
and when Plates touched him he made a convulsive
movement towards the side.   We had to hold him
back by main force, and all the way back he moaned
and talked unintelligently to himself.   None of us
could make anything of what he was saying.   I could
make out the words *Walter,* and *conscription*, and *no
guts*, but that was all I could make head or tail of.   It
wasn't difficult to get him certified after what we'd
seen.

FIVE PLAIN

IT was Cinnamon who told me Uncle Arn had been a fairy, but I reckon he'd never of told me if it hadn't been on account of Sugar.

They say you gotta live with people to know them, but if anybody had said anything to me about Sugar after that first voyage I'd of laughed at them, and said they was nuts. I'd of said Sugar was a very quiet, decent sorta guy, who wouldn't do or say a thing outa place. But it just shows how you can be wrong.

The first voyage I didn't take much notice of Sugar, which was funny, I guess, seeing how he was the one of the crew nearest to my own age. He was about twenty-six or so. We were friendly enough, of course, but all the time I seemed to be with Cinnamon. You know how it is, Cinnamon was such a great guy and he told so many tales he kept me interested all the time. Anyway, Sugar was a real quiet guy. He never seemed to say much, but all the time he sat around staring in front of him. It just goes to show you them quiet kind are often the worst.

This voyage we was going to Alexandria. One night, when we was going down the Bay of Biscay, I was leaning on the rail, looking at nothing and thinking about nothing, when Sugar came up and leaned on the rail beside me. We stood like that for a long time, his shoulder touching mine, for we were both about the same height though he was a bit broader than me,

being older. We smoked, but we didn't say nothing.
It was a fine night, and there was a cute-looking moon
sailing along like a gondola right above us. The sea
was pretty calm, considering it was November, and the
Bay having a reputation like what it's got.

" Goin' to have a good time in Alexandria, Spike ? "
Sugar said after a while.

" Sure, I'm gonna have a good time," I said.

" You better be careful," he said.

" Trust me," I said.

" You can't be too careful," he said.

" I'll watch out," I said.

" You never know what you might get," he said.

" Nuts," I said.

" They say a dose is a pretty painful thing," he said.

" I'll take my chance," I said.

" It would be a pity if you got it," he said. " It
would, maybe, spoil that pretty face of yours."

" That would be too bad," I said.

" They say it goes for the complexion somethin'
awful," he said. " Pimples and scabs and boils."

" Howja know ? " I said. " You had it ? "

" Me ! " he said. " No, sir ! I don't take any
chances."

" Whadja do then ? " I said.

" Whadja think ? " he said.

" You ain't one of them whadja-calls-it, are you ? "
I said.

" Whadja call what ? " he said.

" One of them hermits," I said. " A monk."

" Catch me," he said.

But he should of said, *Watch me !* for the next minute
he crotched me. I laughed. I thought he was fooling.
And I crotched him. But then he put his arm round

my waist, so I gave him a dig with my elbow and it made him splutter.

" Whadja want to do that for ? " he said.

" Whadja think ? " I said.

I leaned over the rail and watched the moon. Sugar stood close to me again. I could hear him breathing kinda heavy. " You can get a lotta fun without goin' to them places," he said. " An' you don't run any risks."

" I like runnin' risks," I said.

" So do I," he said. " But not that kinda risk."

He tried to come funny then. I laughed a bit and started to wrestle with him. But he was stronger than me and anyway I was only fooling because I thought he was fooling, too. But he soon let me see he wasn't. I knew what he wanted all right. So I began to get tough. " Lay off me," I said. " There's nothin' doin'."

" C'mon, Spike," he said. " You're a nice guy."

" Sure I'm a nice guy," I said, and I gave him a smack in the kisser.

Jees, I never saw a guy get so startled. He sure looked as if he was gonna cry and he went away to the fo'c'stle mighty quick. He never looked at me when I went to turn in, and he never looked at me next morning at breakfast, and every time he came near me he turned away and looked at something else. This sure got me down. I hate quarrelling with folks, so by night I was helping Sugar to avoid looking at me, for if I thought he was gonna lamp me I looked away. Things went on like this till we passed Gib., then I began to feel sore, so one morning I tackled him.

" See here," I said. " Snap outa it. I can't help if you're mad at me for what happened the other night. You asked for it."

"I know I did," he said.

"Well, forget it," I said.

"It's not that," he said. "I'm mad at myself. I like you, Spike, and I'm mad at myself for makin' you mad at me."

"Forget it," I said. "I wouldn't of thought any more about it if you hadn't acted like you done the last day or two."

So after that Sugar and me got along swell. I felt sorry for Sugar. I guess it was kinda hard for him to be on the same boat as me when he was built like that. Of course, lots of sailors are like that when they're at sea, but they're quite different when they're ashore. There's a reason for it like Walter Anderson told me he saw written in one of them psychology books he reads, but it just escapes me at the moment. Anyway, it's the same reason why men go like that after they been in jail for a while. But Sugar wasn't like other sailors, he didn't go after the dames as soon as he got ashore. He must of been born like that, and I guess he will always be like that. Tough luck for him. And tough luck for other people like him. We oughta thank our lucky stars we ain't like that—that is if we can be sure we ain't like that. For lots of people are like that and they don't know it, like Walter Anderson told me. Come to think of it there ain't no hard and fast rules. I guess that was what Walter was trying to explain to me that afternoon in the garden when he started in to tell me about Uncle Arn and didn't get finished because Aunt Bella came out.

So it was Cinnamon who told me about Uncle Arn. He told me after I told him about Sugar. Maybe I shouldn't of told him about Sugar, but it kinda worried me, and I thought I'd better ask somebody older than me. I knew that Cinnamon would keep it under his hat if he thought it shouldn't go any farther. He did, too. And after he'd told me not to think any the worse of Sugar for what happened he started in to tell me about Uncle Arn.

It seems everybody reckoned Uncle Arn was trying to make Cinnamon's sister so they was all shocked when it happened, and it was only because Granpa got the minister and the doctor and some other guys to speak for him that Uncle Arn got shoved into the bug-house instead of into the jug.

"I was in the navy at the time," Cinnamon told me, "and I went to see your Uncle Arn when I got leave. I wasn't as shocked as most folk, for I'd seen a lot o' queer things in the navy. But I was shocked when I went into the asylum. Even though you weren't daft when you went in, the place would be enough to drive you daft. All those bolts and bars and warders gave me the creeps."

He told me what happened when he saw my uncle and what they said, so I've put it all down in my own words. I reckon they wouldn't of spoken like this, but you can figure it out for yourself whether they would or not. Anyway, the sense is all here.

"You see why I couldn't marry Jean, don't you, Danny?" Arn said.

"Sure," Cinnamon said.

"I'm fond of her," Arn said. "She's one of the nicest girls I know. But I'm not cut out for marrying. What's the good of masking it? I know that lots of men like me get married, either because they don't know they're like that or because they think marriage 'll cure them. But they make their own lives and their wives' lives hells upon earth. There's no sense in that, is there, Danny?"

" I reckon not," Cinnamon said.

" If only people would understand," Arn said. " I'm
not bad. All those people who put me in here—the
minister and the doctor and them—they've shut me in
here because they say I'm an enemy of society. But I'm
not that, Danny. I've never done anybody any harm."

" There was that Simmons kid," Cinnamon said.
" His father reckons you've ruined him."

" More like him that's ruined me," Arn said bitterly.
" I don't know what made me touch him. He's not a
helluva attractive kid. I've seen hundreds of nicer-
looking chaps and resisted the temptation to touch them.
But I guess it was the mood I was in."

" What mood was that ? " Cinnamon said.

" The usual war mood," Arn said, laughing. " I've
been worried since the war started. God alone knows
how worried I've been. Do you know how many times
women have given me white feathers ? Silly bitches of
women, senseless, with nothing in their heads but what
comes out with the comb. But the war has made
heroines of them. The war has allowed them to think
they've got brains, that they're the saviours of their
country because they shame the slackers and show them
where their duty lies. They gave white feathers to me !
To me, whose boots they aren't worthy to dust ! "

Cinnamon began to get the wind up at this. He
watched the door and he began to wonder if maybe he
wasn't wrong and those people who said Arn was mad
were right. But Arn saw the look and laughed.

" I'm sorry, Danny," he said. " I simply can't help
being melodramatic. Maybe I should have gone on the
stage like Grace. Maybe I'd have been a bigger success
on it than I've ever been as an artist. An artist ! " He
laughed. " Any hope I ever had of that has been effect-

ively killed by those silly women with their white
feathers. And I'm not the only one. How many fine
minds have they sent to their deaths because they chose
the proper moment for an ostentatious presentation of
their emblem ? "

" But they didn't send you to your death " Cinnamon
objected. " You never took up their challenge."

" That's true," Arn said. " If I had I might be lying
in a grave in Flanders now instead of waiting here for
a slower death. I would of been commended for enlisting, for doing my duty to my king and country. But
because I thought my mind was of more importance
than my body, this is where I've landed."

" You would of had to go sooner or later," Cinnamon
said. " Conscription is in force now."

" That was what worried me," Arn said. " That and
what Walter said to me before he left. He said I'd no
guts. I wondered if I had, I wondered if I'd the nerve
to be a conscientious objector when I was conscripted
and go to jail. But I reckon that would have killed my
mother even more than if I'd had to go to the front.
My mother and father—I'm worried about them, too.
They're old, Danny. They need somebody to look after
them in their old age, and there's nobody else but me and
Walter. It's not fair to expect Kate to keep them, poor
kid. Life 'll be tough enough for her without her having
Mother and Dad hanging round her neck. No, it was
up to me and Walter to try to make their old age comfortable. Me and Walter ! And he had a girl. He'd
of got married if *that* hadn't happened to him. As for
me. . . ." He put his head in his hands. " That's what
I think about all day in here. All day and all night. I
can't sleep for wondering what's going to happen to
them now that they've got nobody but Kate. I reckon

it was that and worrying about Jean that made me forget myself with the Simmons kid ; I had to have something to take it off my mind."

" What did you need to worry about Jean for ? " Cinnamon said.

" She expected me to marry her. She couldn't see why I didn't make love to her and get engaged like other people. She didn't understand that I wasn't in love with her, that I liked her only as a pal. She thought I was too shy to propose. And she kept hanging on to me, letting other chances go past. I wanted to tell her that. But I couldn't. Oh, I can't tell you all I've been suffering. All that I'm suffering in here, going over and over it in my mind."

" But what made you touch the Simmons kid ? " Cinnamon said. " Hadn't you plenty on your mind without thinking about that ? "

" I expect so. But you know how it is. It was a way of escape." Arn laughed kinda wild. " A way of shoving myself in the bug-house ! "

" But didn't he—— ? " Cinnamon didn't know very well how to put it.

" No, that was the funny thing. The little swine didn't make any fuss. He seemed quite proud to be taken notice of. Any other kid in his place would have laughed and taken it all in fun. But this Simmons kid kept quiet. It just shows what a sneakin' sorta little rat he was to go home and tell his old man. Most other kids wouldn't of thought about it. They wouldn't of liked to say anything even although they'd felt like it. They wouldn't though. They'd have thought it was great fun."

" Maybe," Cinnamon said. " It depends on the kid."

" Sure, it depends on the kid," Arn said. " That

Simmons kid was the worst sorta kid I could of chosen.
I bet that kid turns out to be a real bad case.   His old
man 'll blame me, but I reckon he had badness in him if
ever any kid had it.   But I could kick myself when I
think of all the attractive-lookin' kids it might of been
with."

"What I can't figure out is this," Cinnamon said.
"What made you go down the breakwater that night?
Were you really goin' to do yourself in?   How did you
guess the kid Simmons' old man would send the police
after you?"

"I didn't," Arn said.   "I never figured the kid
would tell his old man at all.   I wasn't even thinkin'
about him."

"Why did you go then?" Cinnamon said.

"I was worried about Walter and what I'd heard that
day about conscription.   When I got home I found the
wire saying Walter had been bumped off, and when I saw
the shock my mother had got I reckoned if she got
another when I was conscripted it would finish her.   So
I went for a walk to think it over, and I just seemed
to go naturally to the breakwater."

Cinnamon reckoned it was a funny sorta place to go
for a walk on a dark winter night, but he guessed that
because Arn was in a state like that one place was as good
as another to go for a walk.

"Do you remember what your Granny said to me
that night our Grace got engaged, Danny?" Arn said.

"No," Cinnamon said.

"She said my fate was goin' to swamp me.   I couldn't
help thinkin' about her and what she said when I was
goin' down the breakwater.   I knew I was the only
son my mother and father had left.   I knew I should
stand by them, but I knew the authorities wouldn't let

me stand by them. You can't imagine what a turmoil my brain was in. I was ill with worry. I knew that if I went to the war I'd be killed. It was always people like me who got killed. I knew that it would kill my mother. I knew that if I'd the guts to be a conscientious objector I'd get sent to jail. And I knew that would kill my mother, too. I didn't know what way to look at it. And the thought came to me that I'd be as well to end it all there and then at the end of the breakwater. I remembered what Granny McLeish had told me. It would be a nice clean death. Better than being blown to bits by a shell. Better than beating out one's brains in a prison cell—or having them beaten out for me. Oh, it would be lovely, I thought, lovely, lovely, so quietly and calmly to float down, down into the cool green water with the moon and the stars shining on it. To laugh up at the stars and to curse them for what Granny McLeish had seen written in them. To laugh up at the moon! The moon! Diana, Queen and Huntress, chaste and fair. No, no, she was never my love. She would never be my love. I had no need of her. . . ."

Cinnamon came away then. He reckoned it was time. All the same he didn't figure that Uncle Arn was mad. He figured that it was the attitude of other people that was mad. "Your Uncle Arn lived at least twenty years afore his time," he said. "Fifty years afore his time. It's quite fashionable in high society now for folk to do what he got shoved in the bug-house for. But it's only fashionable in high society. Anybody in the working classes trying to do the same gets the nick, and the judges are aye helluva hard on them. You just take a look at the *News of the World* any Sunday. It's the only paper you'll find any mention of this so-called heinous crime. Other papers never mention it. That's why people are ignorant of it, and suspicious, and narrow-minded. The lower classes don't understand it. Maybe, in fifty years time they will. And a lot of the so-called, upper classes, don't understand it either. It's only intelligent people who understand it, and the mass of people are profoundly unintelligent. You've only got to look around you to see that."

That was why Cinnamon was helluva cut-up when Uncle Arn cut his throat after he'd been in the asylum for about a year. "You can't blame him," he said to me. "Yon place would of made anybody do that. I don't say that Arn took the most sensible way out of it, though. If I'd been him, I'd of tried a less painful method. I'd of tried to steal some poison, or I'd of shoved my head in a gas oven. But you've got to hand it to him for havin' guts."

"The funny thing was, however," Cinnamon said after a bit, "that what your Uncle Arn was feared for didn't happen. The shock didn't kill your Granny, as everybody expected."

"She must of been a tough old dame," I said.

"She was a tough auld dame sure enough," Cinnamon said.

After Cinnamon had told me about Uncle Arn I began to reckon that, maybe, Sugar wasn't to blame for what had happened. And when I saw him going into a place for boys in Alexandria I didn't think any the worse of him. Of course, I couldn't figure what he could see in boys when there were so many swell dames knocking around, but there's no accounting for tastes. What I always say is: You gotta be broadminded in this world. Only the trouble is that other people don't always say that. The narrower they are the bigger the yen they got to make everybody as narrow as themselves.

After Alexandria we was at Port Said, and it sure was the bow-wows. I sure would like to take some of them narrow-minded folks to some of the places there and then, maybe, they would snap outa themselves. Jees, did we have fun!

After that we was at one or two places in the Black Sea, and it was about the middle of January when we got back to Harrisfield. The *Red Biddy* got tied-up then, for trade was bad. This was plenty bad, for I didn't get no dole like the other guys. But I had what pay was due me and I still had some jack laid by that I hadn't touched when I came over from the States. So I didn't worry much. Anyway, it was kinda handy me not working at the time, for Granpa and Granma were getting ready to flit.

They had fixed on a house at Calderburn, and although they didn't need to be out of the cottages till the end of February, they reckoned they might as well quit because everything was ready. They aimed to move the first week in February. That was a bit more than a fortnight they still had to go, and there was no call for them to get ready yet. But Granma had done some of the packing herself and she hadn't told Aunt Kate what she'd packed. And this made Aunt Kate mad, for she reckoned there was a lotta things she wasn't going to take to the new house with them.

None of them had seen the new house yet except Aunt Kate. Granpa wasn't able to go, and it would of taken Granma all her time to walk to it. Besides, everybody said it was too rough for her to walk. It wasn't that it was far, but the way led through what had once been fields, through what everybody called the Piggeries, on account of them having been a place for pigs years and years ago. Both Granma and Granpa were helluva keen to know what like the house was, and whether you could see the sea and the harbour from the windows. Aunt Kate said they could. But she told Aunt Bella and us that it wouldn't be long before there was more houses built in front of them, shutting out the view entirely. She didn't tell the old folks this because if they'd known they'd of gone off the deep end. It was bad enough as it was with them having to go before their Golden Wedding in April. " If we could just have had it in the auld hoose," Granpa said, " I wouldn't have cared." Aunt Kate spoke about this at the City Chambers when she went to get the key of the new house. She asked if they couldn't possibly be allowed to stay in the cottages for at least another six weeks after the First of March. But they said, no, everybody had to be out by that date. Sentiment had no place in regard to sanitation. " As if it mattered," Aunt Kate said. " The houses have been insanitary for years and they've never done a damned thing about them. But they've just wakened up to the fact and we've to go out at the toot to please them. Help my Jimmie Johnston, I'm sure if we've had to live here with those insanitary conditions for so long, another six weeks wouldn't hurt us." But the authorities were very polite and very firm, and they said they'd have to go, Golden Wedding or no Golden Wedding.

So they all said there was no good prolonging the agony and that they'd flit at the beginning of February, and we began to prepare in good earnest. You wouldn't of thought there was so much stuff to pack in such a small space. But I sure was amazed at all the stuff Granma had under the beds. Boxes of old clothes, and photographs, and old picture-frames, and blocks of wood, and God knows what. Aunt Kate wanted

P

to throw most of it out, but Granma wouldn't hear of it. She went through it all carefully, laying aside what she was gonna take with them and hesitating before she threw out the stuff that was no good. Sometimes she'd lay a thing aside and say she'd throw it out, but a little while after she would have it among the things she was taking. Aunt Kate was real mad at her. If she'd of had her way she'd of scrapped everything but her clothes. "What's the good of going to a new house with all that old furniture?" she said.

But Granma wouldn't hear of buying anything new. "We're ower auld noo to bother aboot new-fangled things," she said. "Even if we could afford them."

But Aunt Kate positively refused to take the old-fashioned iron bed that she slept in. She said she'd go buy herself a new wooden bed and a suite of bedroom furniture to match. "I saw a gorgeous suite in a shop in Shandwick Place," she said. "It was really gorgeous. And it was only eighteen pounds. Eighteen pounds for all that lovely furniture!"

"All very well if you've got eighteen pounds," Granma said.

Aunt Kate said she'd lift it out the bank and Granma raised hell when she heard this. But Aunt Kate aimed to have her own way; she said it was her own money and she'd do what she liked with it. So Granma piped down.

Granpa never said anything to all this. All the time he sat quiet by the fire and looked at his hands or stared into the fire. Occasionally he would shake his head and say, "Ay, man, do ye tell me?" as if somebody was speaking to him. I guess it was kinda pathetic to see him, but I didn't have much time to speculate about it on account of helping Granma pack. Come to

think of it, Granma didn't seem so cut-up as you might
of looked for. You would of thought she'd of sighed
and cried a bit whenever she was throwing out or packing
things that must of minded her of things that had
happened long ago. But she done nothing like that.
Maybe, she hadn't time, what with arranging and packing,
and having to attend to Granpa at the same time; I
don't know. Anyways, she was pretty business-like.

I guess she must of been just as business-like about
everything that had ever happened to her. When it was
over she must of said to herself, Well, it's over and done
with, no good moping. It was Granpa that seemed to
do all the moping. But then I reckon Granpa had been
a dreamer all his days; he hadn't the snap and go that
Granma had. He took the flitting to heart worse nor
anybody. He sat there right in the middle of things,
as helpless as a kid, and did nothing. I guess Granma
could of choked him sometimes.

Aunt Kate wasn't much good at packing either.
About all she ever did was talk. She reckoned she was
a pretty slick hand at arranging things, and all the time
she went around giving out orders like a sergeant-
major. But me and Granma never let on we heard
her.

Aunt Bella helped a lot. It was her that took me
up to the new house two three days after I came ashore.
She was gonna wash the floors and have them all ready
so that Uncle Jim could lay the linoleum in time for the
flitting. Aunt Kate would of been no good at washing
the floors; she could hardly wash her face far less wash
a floor. But she came with us; it was her half-day.
And George came along, too. He took the half-day
off the wireless college. " I'm not learning anything,
anyway," he said. " It's just a waste of money. I'd

of been better to go to sea as a deck-hand, like I wanted. I'd of had more chance of getting on."

The new houses at Calderburn were huge tenements. They were a drab grey-colour and they looked like jails. On account of that, and on account of the folks that lived in them, most everybody called the district Sing-Sing. The whole place was in a state of being built. Houses that was occupied stood next to houses that still had painters and plasterers working in them. The scheme was all laid out like the architects had planned, but some of the streets was still ankle-deep in mud, what with the heavy builders' lorries always going along them and all the labourers. And there was piles of bricks and heaps of mortar everywhere. All the houses had gardens and some of the people had started in to try to cultivate theirs, but others again hadn't started yet, because I reckon they thought it wasn't worth while yet with all that building going on around them. Oh, it sure was a wonderful place. Something like what it would look like after an air raid, only that ain't come yet, which seems kinda like a waste of time on the part of them builders. They'd be better not to build at all seeing how the houses are liable to get knocked down any time. Maybe, that was why they was just slapping the houses up, of course. Maybe, they got a wire to say there would be a war most any time and that it wasn't worth their while to take too much trouble with them. Thrown up quick they'd be easy to throw down again quick. And what did it matter if there was a lotta folks living in them when they fell? The builders should worry. The hell they should. They would have their dough, and they would get the chance to build more houses after the air raids was over. Anyways, what the hell did it matter?

The kids of the district was having a good time playing around in the half-built houses just now.

" Listen now," Aunt Bella said.   " Did you ever see such an awfu'-like place ? "

" It's only half-built yet," George said.   " Give it half a chance."

" It'll never look any better than this, judging by the folk we see," Aunt Bella said.   " They're the kind o' folk that'll no' help themselves."

" They're the kind who will help themselves, you mean ! " he said.

" Oh, they'll do that all right," Aunt Bella said. " Only, they'll no' help themselves to get out o' the bit. They came frae a slum and they'll make this a slum as quick as they can.   It looks like a slum the now."

And it sure did.   Them folks who lived in the houses in the streets that was finished all seemed to be hanging out of their windows or standing in their doorways. Some of them looked as if they hadn't washed for weeks. " God knows what like their houses are like inside ! " Aunt Bella said.   Most of them was women with their hair hanging down on their shoulders and wearing what had once been helluva bright overalls, but there was a good lotta men around, too, standing at the corners or leaning on the railings.   " Unemployed," Aunt Bella said   " God knows how they manage.   The rents o' those houses are dearer than the rents in the slums they came from, and some o' them haven't worked for years."

George was carrying a pail for Aunt Bella to wash the floors, so we sure got plenty of folks to take notice of us.   " Help my Jimmie Johnston ! " Aunt Kate said. " You'd think we were a lot of animals in the zoo."

" Well, we're on the right side o' the bars ! " Aunt

Bella said. " And that's more than you can say about the most of them."

" I don't know how we'll be able to live among such folk," Aunt Kate said. " We're not accustomed to the likes of them."

" Listen now, you'll just need to make the best of it," Aunt Bella said.

Aunt Kate was always lamenting about this. You'd of thought she was gonna live among cannibals from the way she went on. Her attitude was always that, ' Oh, I'll never be able to hold up my head again for shame ' one, and I reckoned it was real snobbish. I ain't saying that all the folks in Calderburn were gems of the purest ray serene, but they weren't all as bad as Aunt Kate and Stumpy McGregor made out. The trouble was as Granpa said, that they'd never had a chance or seen anything better.

None of the houses in the street where Granma was gonna live was occupied yet. There was four tenements, three storeys high, and each tenement had twenty-four houses in it ; six houses in a stair. Granma's house was on the bottom flat. " Let's hope we don't get a noisy crowd above us," Aunt Kate said.

" Listen now, what difference will it make ? " Aunt Bella said. " None o' ye would hear them ; ye're all that deaf."

It was a pretty decent kinda house with a living-room, a kitchenette, two bedrooms and a bath-room. " Though I don't expect many of them'll use it much ! " Aunt Kate said. George winked at me and said, " Will you ? "

Aunt Bella got started in to washing the floors and I began to clean the windows. George measured the floors for linoleum. That was the only new thing

Granma wanted to buy, because the stuff on the floors in their cottage was so old it was rotten and it all came away in bits when you tried to lift it. Aunt Kate went around touching things and saying, she'd put this here, and that there, till we was all pretty well fed to the teeth listening to her. She didn't touch anything she needed to work at though. About all she managed to do was to get in Aunt Bella's road and Aunt Bella began to get kinda mad at her.

"Listen here, Kate," she said. "How the hell do you expect me to wash this floor wi' you dug-dancin' about like that? For God's sake awa' and sit doon somewhere."

Aunt Kate was kinda annoyed at this and things looked black, so I took out my packet and offered them cigarettes. Aunt Bella leaned on the window-sill while she was smoking. "There's a wife away into that house over there," she said. "I wonder who she can be?"

"You should go out and ask her, ma," George said sarcastically.

Aunt Bella ignored him, but a bit after she said, "There she is, sweepin' down the walls. She's no' makin' a very good job o' it, is she?"

"It's an awful job to be bothered with your nose!" George said.

"I'm no' bothered wi' ma nose at all," Aunt Bella said. "I just wondered who she could be. But I daresay we'll find out soon enough."

"We'll live in hope, anyway!" George said.

"There's no' a bad view o' the Forth from here, Kate," Aunt Bella said. "My father'll be able to sit here and see as much as he sees from the cottages."

"For how long?" Aunt Kate said. "See those buildings along there! How long will it be before more spread along here in front of us and shut out the harbour altogether ? "

"Maybe they'll leave a bit space we'll be able to see through," Aunt Bella said cheerfully.

"Maybe," Aunt Kate said.

After I'd got all the windows cleaned and George had got his measuring done there wasn't anything else we could do. Aunt Bella still had one of the bedrooms to wash out and Aunt Kate was banging about the scullery, measuring the sink and the washing-tub, for she'd decided to cover them with boards and put oil-cloth, out of Woolworth's, on the boards. "Are you afraid you'll fall down the sink ? " George chaffed her, and he whispered to me, "There's not much danger ! " There was nothing George and me could do, and it wasn't very comfortable standing around in the empty house, so we said we'd light out.

"All right," Aunt Bella said. "Tell your Granny we won't be long."

It was only about five minutes walk to the cottages, but me and George took pretty near half an hour to make it. We wandered around the half-built houses, speaking to some of the workmen and looking into everything. Jees, we sure got our feet in some mess. I'd on a pair of light flannel pants and the bottoms was all stiff with mud.

The tea was ready, but we couldn't get started, for there was a guy in Granma's when we got in. A middle-aged guy, with a sanctimonious expression and a drip at the end of his nose. "This is Mr. Webb, one of the Elders of the Kirk," Granma said to me. "My grandson, Spike Wilson, frae Americy."

The guy's hand felt like the bulwark of the boat after it had been raining. But I put my hand on the sofa as

I sat down and wiped my hand on the cover. The guy was awful polite, asking for Mom, and Pop, and the kids, and I was awful polite answering him. I hoped he wouldn't sit too long. It was almost five o'clock, and me and George reckoned we'd go to the pictures as soon as we'd got our tea. But the guy didn't look like moving. He kept telling Granpa what a lotta good the new minister, Mr. Reid, was doing in the slum-clearance area at Calderburn.

"He's a very fine young man," he said. "He takes a great interest in the boys, too, a thing that old Mr. Silver never did."

"Ah, but old Mr. Silver was a fine man," Granpa said.

"Oh, yes, he was a good preacher. But a good preacher isn't enough, Mr. Gillespie. The minister should take an interest in the physical well-being of his parishioners as well as an interest in their spiritual well-being. Now, Mr. Reid, for instance, comes to my class of Boy Scouts and gives the lads exercises."

I tried to catch George's eye, but he was looking down at his knees. I thought there was a sarcastic sorta smile on his face. I guess he was having a mental picture, like I was, of this guy Webb in shorts and a scout's hat, doing drill with a lotta boys.

"Mr. Reid used to be an International Rugger player," this guy Webb said, looking at me as if he expected me to stand up and cheer this news. But nothing happened, except that International Rugger players went down in my estimation. This guy Webb looked then at George and said, " It's a wonder you never joined the Scouts, George."

"Why?" George said.

I reckon the guy Webb was sorta stumped at this.

I reckon he expected George to show more enthusiasm.
" It's the life for a fine young fellow like you," he said.
" It's the life, lad. It's the life. Out in the open and
under canvas. You'll have to come along some night
and I'll get Mr. Reid to speak to you."

" I haven't time," George said.

He said it just like that, no apologies or nothing.
I haven't time. Which was as much as to say stick
your Boy Scouts you know where. I could of died
at the expression on the guy Webb's face. There was
so much laughter surging up inside me I thought I was
gonna choke.

The guy Webb got up on his hind legs then, and if
he had sported a tail he would of curled it between them.
He took no further notice of George. " I'm glad to
see you looking so well, Mr. Gillespie," he said to Granpa.
" And you, too, Mrs. Gillespie. May the Lord long
spare you to one another, and may he long continue to
shower his bountiful mercies upon you. Shall we
thank the Lord for his kindness ? "

And suddenly, without any more ado, he got down on
his knees and he put his elbows on a chair and he began
to pray. It was so sudden I couldn't believe it. I
looked at Granma and Granpa, but both of them had
their hands clasped and their eyes shut. I looked at
George, but he was staring at the guy Webb. So I
shut my eyes, too, so as not to see it, and I clasped my
hands between my knees with my nails digging into my
palms so as not to laugh. Jees, it sure was some prayer.
The guy Webb wasn't an educated guy like a minister
—or so far as you can call a minister an educated guy
—and his vocabulary wasn't so good. He hadn't class.
But what he lost in pronunciation and not knowing
a lotta big words, he sure made up for in lung-power.

Boy, I'll say he was determined the Lord should hear his prayer. It was all Praise the Lords, and Hallelujahs, and Thank You Gods, but what the guy Webb was thanking the Lord for I couldn't figure, unless it was because he was a boy scout and such a powerful hand at praying.

"Amen," he said suddenly, getting up from his knees as quick as he'd gotten down on them.

"Amen," Granma and Granpa said.

Me and George said nothing. We shook hands with the guy Webb as he went out and then we wiped our hands with our handkerchiefs and made a dive at the table.

We was near finished tea when Aunt Bella and Aunt Kate arrived. Aunt Bella was fairly letting off some hot air about the people she'd seen at Calderburn. "It's no' fair o' the Sanitary to ask you to go and bide among the likes o' them," she said. She sure considered herself a cut above them, and I don't say she wasn't. But at the same time you would of been hard put to it sometimes to figure from the way she talked whether she was a cut above them or not, or whether she was just better dressed and lived in a better house. Anyways, she ran them down plenty.

When Granma could get a word in edgeways she told them that she and Granpa had had a visit from Mr. Webb.

"Webb? Who's he when he's at home?" Aunt Bella said.

"You know," Aunt Kate said. "The Elder. He's a plumber."

"Yon daft-lookin' b—r, that goes around dressed like a boy scout?" Aunt Bella said.

Granpa laughed at this, but Granma said, "Really, Bella!"

"He's a right jessypunt," Aunt Kate said. "He's always sookin' in with the new minister. What did he want?"

"Oh, he was just payin' a call," Granma said. "He was tellin' us the new minister would call on us sometime."

"Ay, sometime!" Aunt Bella said. "He should ha'e called on you before he called on anybody else. You're the auldest members on the Kirk Roll."

"He's too much taken up with trying to make new members in Calderburn," Aunt Kate said. "He'll get round to see you sometime."

"We'll, maybe, be dead by that time," Granma said. "But I daresay it won't make much difference! Sit in and get your tea."

"Webb put up a prayer," George said.

Aunt Bella near choked and she had to take a drink of tea before she recovered. "What?" she said.

"Webb put up a prayer," George said.

"A prayer!" Aunt Bella said. "Listen now, a plumber puttin' up a prayer for your Granny and Grandfather! What impiddence!"

That was what I thought, too, but I reckon I couldn't of put it into words with such swell scorn as Aunt Bella put it into. All the same I guess Granma was kinda annoyed, because, I reckon, she thought it was okay of the guy to put up such a swell prayer.

FIVE PURL

BELLA'S right above it being impudence for a slavering fellow like Webb to come and pray for Wattie and you, but you can't feel as angry about it as you know you should feel. There was a time when you'd have told Webb to get to hell out of here and to take his prayers with him. And there was a time before that when you would have felt highly honoured because he was praying in your house—though at the same time you would have wished it was a better man that was putting up the prayer. But those times have passed. You're too old now to bother who prays or who doesn't pray. What's the good of fashing yourself? It's of so little consequence, and there's so little time left that it's silly to waste it in quarrelling with folk.

If you'd been able to see this far ahead when you were a young woman, if you'd been able then to see what you would think now, you wouldn't have believed it. You would have said that it was another woman. But it's not another woman. You're still the same Mirren in many ways; you don't feel any older than you did when you were nineteen; it's only when you look in the mirror that you realise that you're seventy-nine, or when you think of all the things that have happened to you. But you still have your independence and your toughness. Only in that one thing have you changed: your attitude to the kirk and to the folk who profess its religion. All your early life you believed in the Church,

and you did your utmost to obey its teaching.   But since
middle age, although you still do your best to be
Christian-like, you no longer think of the Church as
something to be worshipped.   You no longer think of
it at all.   If you do, you see what a hollow, empty farce
it is—it, and all those sanctimonious goody-goodies,
who yelp along beside it.   Of course, you always tell
your grandchildren that they should go to the kirk,
but you don't tell them because you believe it will do
them any good.   You tell them because you hope they'll
go and see how much hypocrisy there is, and act accord-
ingly, and grow up to be better men and women than
most of those around them.   Going to the kirk will do
them no harm so long as they aren't carried away by it
and become religious maniacs.   It'll help to mould their
characters, as it has helped to mould yours.   For one
thing it will teach them the elements of Christianity.
And the elements of Christianity are the same as the
elements of Socialism.   The only thing they'll have
to watch is that they don't allow wool to be pulled over
their eyes by people who also profess Christianity.
And people who profess Socialism, too.   The best
Socialists, like the best Christians, aren't those who beat
the big drum of Socialism.

It must have been after Tom went away that you
began to change.   You changed without realising that
you were changing.   For years after Tom disappeared,
if you had any doubts about the truth of the Church's
teaching you did your best to stifle them.   You were
feared you were a wicked woman, and sometimes you
had visions of being dragged down into hell-fire for
allowing such thoughts to enter your mind.   But after
the war started you were in greater doubt than ever.
How could any God, any kind father as the kirk did its

best to show him to be, how could he allow all that to happen? All that killing, and bombing, and murder. We were Christians, we British, and the Germans were Christians, too. We all prayed to him, each of us believed that God was exclusively on our side and that we were his chosen children. How, how could a God allow such things to happen to his children?

If it had been your children fighting you'd have stopped them before they did any damage to themselves or to anybody else. But God didn't do that. He let them fight and kill each other. So you began to feel that your doubts must be right. And when first, Walter was taken, and then Arnold. . . . Lots of women in cases like that, when their sons were killed, became more religious than ever, turning into religious maniacs, thanking their God for bringing sorrow upon them. But you didn't do that, Mirren. You cursed God and reviled him. And you wished he was a real person so that you could give him a piece of your mind.

You still continued to go to the kirk, of course. The habits of a lifetime are hard to break. But you no longer believed in what you heard. You still believed in what Wattie calls the ethics of Christian Socialism, of course; all your life you've done your best to live up to them. But you no longer believed that there was a God, all-powerful Jehovah watching lovingly over the children of this earth. You no longer thanked the Lord for his bountiful mercy, like that fool, Webb, because you knew there was no bountiful mercy in the world. Any mercies were those that one sincere Christian did to another. And by a Christian you don't mean somebody who goes twice to the kirk every Sunday.

You continued to go to the kirk because you had been

in the habit of going and because you liked Mr. Silver.
You knew that if everybody felt like you and stopped
going to the kirk Mr. Silver would lose his job. And
you didn't want that to happen, for he was one of the
best men you've ever known. He was sincere and
really lived up to what he taught. Not that he ever
talked about religion. Never in his life in all the times
he came to this house, and he came regularly every
fortnight, for years and years, never once did he get
down on his knees and put up a prayer like that man
Webb. And never once for as often as he had tea
here did he say a grace—he just dived in. He laughed
and joked with Wattie and you, as if you were his brother
and sister. He was a real Christian, but never a word
of Christianity came out of his mouth.

So that was why you still went to the kirk. For
Mr. Silver's sake. Often and often, after Walter was
killed, and Arn was in there, you thought you wouldn't
go. But every Sunday you got ready and went. For
Mr. Silver's sake. And for your own, too. Because
you knew that if you stayed away, catty folk would
speak about it when they came out after the service,
and say that you were ashamed of what Arnold had done,
*and no wonder, such a terrible thing, he ought to be hanged or
sent to the front like our other brave young men*. You knew
that they said those things behind your back, so you were
determined to go to the kirk and face them out as long
as you were able. Let any of them dare say any of those
things to your face ! He was your son and you'd stick
up for him no matter though he had murdered somebody.
He was no worse than anybody else. Worse ? My
God, he was so much better than most of them. They
weren't fit to be in the same street as him. That man,
Webb, now. Is it natural for a man of his age to go

galloping around with a troop of laddies? What he's
got is a mother-complex. The fool. Him and his
prayer. You would have liked to tell him to stick his
prayer where the monkey stuck the nuts, but you
remembered in time that you were a lady. Besides,
you had to show a good example to Spike and George.
You could see that they were bursting themselves,
the young devils. . . . And no wonder. Webb looked
such a fool. The Plumber's Prayer! You wonder
what Wattie thought of it. He was sitting gey reverent,
but, no doubt, he was chortling to himself all the time.
Webb wouldn't see that, of course. He would think
what a fine, simple old man Wattie Gillespie was, sitting
there so peacefully and so humbly with his white beard
flowing on his breast, listening to the words of wisdom
that fell from the man Webb's lips. Words of wisdom
about Boy Scouts and such-like havers!

Him and his Boy Scouts reminds you of the song that
folk used to sing a few years ago. We all used to chaff
Wattie about it. It was called *Grandfather's Whiskers*,
and it went like this :

> *Grandfather's whiskers, Grandfather's beard,*
> *Never had it shingled, never had it sheared,*
> *What made all the boy scouts jealous*
> *When they volunteered?*
> *Grandfather's whiskers, Grandfather's beard!*

He used to laugh and take it all in good part. He's
aye been an awful good-natured man, Wattie. He
could make a joke and take a joke against himself with
equal ease. There was the time at the smiddy-seat
when he was sitting, and a wee laddie came up to him
and said, *Beaver!* Wattie never let on he heard him,

Q

he sat and stared in front of him at the boats in the
harbour. But the bairn was determined to make him
lose his rag. *Beaver!* he cried again. *Beaver!* But
still Wattie never let on he heard him. So the bairn
touched him. *Hey, beaver!* he cried. *Are ye dead?*

Wattie used to sit a lot at the smiddy-seat in the years
after the war. He, and Stumpy McGregor, and Willie
Brown, and a lot of other old men used to meet there
every day and talk. About politics mostly. Wattie
wouldn't have sat there and talked if it had been horse
racing or football. The other old men were too old
for that, anyway. Wattie's tongue was always to be
heard laying down the law, telling them what should
be done to save the country, and what laws that were in
existence shouldn't be in existence if the majority of
folk were ever going to get a square deal. He and
Stumpy had many an argument, and all the other old
men listened respectfully to them. Ah, many's the
time you wish now that he was still able to go to the
smiddy-seat; it would take him out of your road for a
while. But there's no chance of that. Poor Wattie,
he takes ill-out with having to sit in the house. God
knows he sat often enough in the house when he was a
younger man and able to go out. But now that he's
old and not able he must often wish that he had his
youth and strength back again.

You wish you had your youth and strength back again
yourself. If only you had the strength you wouldn't
mind the youth so much. Old age brings lots of things
with it and above all it brings illness and poverty, but
sometimes it brings things that you wouldn't be without.
Wisdom and memories. Wisdom. . . . Ay, there's
many a thing you think and do nowadays that you
wouldn't have thought and done when you were younger

because you'd have been feared. Like what you've just been thinking. As for memories. . . .

They're not all sad. You've had a lot of laughs in your time. Though it's the sad memories that persist in coming to you when you don't want them ; like when you're trying to fall asleep, and you can't sleep because they come crowding upon you. Sitting in your best clothes with the table set, waiting for Tom to come home from jail. Saying good-bye at the Waverley Station to Grace, knowing you would never see her bright face again once she'd crossed the Atlantic. Opening the telegram about Walter, knowing before you opened it what was in it. Ah, you were hard hit then, Mirren, harder hit than you'd ever been in your life before, harder hit than you've ever been since. Even harder hit than when Wattie told you about Arn. You were that concerned about Walter that you didn't seem able to take in what had happened to Arn. One grief overlapped the other. But God knows you realised it plenty in the next twelve months, knowing that he was in there behind bars, him that was aye so full of life and go, aye wanting to be out and about, seeing things. To be shut away in there. . . . It was almost a relief to you when they told you that he had done away with himself. But the way, oh God, the way—it was so terrible, so unlike my Arn, my bonnie, laughing Arn, who wouldn't have hurt a fly, who used to chuck you under the chin and say, *What would I get married for when I've got a sweetheart like yourself already ?*

It was things like that that swamped your faith in religion and in most of your fellowmen. After knocks like that you tell yourself that you're prepared for anything. And yet when other knocks come you're surprised; you just can't help it.

After Arn you thought there wasn't much more that you could endure, yet it wasn't long before they sent you medals that would have been given to Walter if he hadn't been killed. Medals! You stood with them in your hand. Two wee coins with a bit ribbon on them, the kind of things they give to school bairns on Coronation days and occasions like that. Cheap little things that they turn out two a penny. For conspicuous gallantry on the field of battle!

Oh, Absolam, Absolam, my son Absolam!

You were like David crying for your son that was dead. You were only one of millions of mothers. You stood there before the fire with the little bits of cheap tin in your hand, and you looked up at the photograph of Walter in his soldier's uniform, so young, so proud, so bursting with life and energy. And there was something in your beast that was struggling to get out. And you threw the medals in the fire and cried:

They winnie gi'e me back my son!

It was a cheap way to act; it was the sort of daft-like, dramatic thing you would have expected to see on the stage. But it helped you a wee thing. It eased a little the tension in your heart. You got some satisfaction from seeing the flames lick the coloured red, white and blue ribbons into ashes. You felt as if it really were the men who had started the war who were burning in hell-fire. And you laughed as you watched them burn.

But when you found the fire-tarnished pieces of metal in the ash-pan the next morning it brought it all back to you worse than ever.

Wattie never said anything when you told him what you had done. He just gave you a bit pat on the shoulder as much as to say, *There, there, lass, never heed them.* But other folks were curious about the medals, for they saw in the papers that Walter had been awarded them. They couldn't keep from coming and prying and saying, *You'll have to let us see the medals, Mrs. Gillespie. My, you must be proud of him.*

Ay, you said, *I'll let ye see them sometime.*

But you never let anybody see them. You put what the fire had left of them into a box and put the box away at the bottom of a kist. Out of sight, but not out of mind.

He'll never be out of your mind. None of your sons will ever be. They're there, always, in all sorts of shapes and sizes. Tom, a wee shaver, in a red jersey, swearing at you out of the window. Arnold, putting a knife under the milk-jug and canting it up, and laughing when you told him he'd coup it. Walter, in a navy blue suit and a bowler and looking awful spruce, standing at the kitchen-door, and telling you not to worry if he wasn't home till late. You knew he was going to meet his lass—that servant girl you saw only twice.

The first time was after he'd been killed. She came one afternoon, a red-haired hussy, with a white felt hat and a white feather boa. *Are you Mrs. Gillespie?* she said, as bold as brass when you answered the door.

I am, you said.

I'm Walter's young lady, she said, awful genteel and simpering.

Come in, you said.

You didn't know what to say to her, so you started to make the tea. It was early enough for Wattie to be home, but you thought you'd make the tea at once. Maybe, it would be past and she'd be away before he came home. You didn't know what he'd think when he saw those peery heels and the powder on her nose. She looked a real fast one. You thought that if Walter had been there you'd have slapped his jaws for being fool enough to be taken in by such a creature.

I see in the paper that Walter was awarded two medals, she said.

Ay, you said.

I wonder if I could see them? she said.

No, ye cannie, you said, speaking as broad as you could, seeing that she was so affected and polite.

She looked at me, fair flabbergasted. *But why not?* she said. *I've a right to see them.*

Maybe you think so, you said. *But for all that you cannie see them.*

And why not, I should like to know? she said, up in arms.

Because they're burned, you said.

Oh, what a way she went on at this! *The audacity!* she cried. *The impudence! What right have you to do such a thing? It's an insult to the king and to the country. It's an insult to Walter. And it's an insult to me. How dare you?*

And what about me? you said. *What about my feelings in the matter? Is it not an insult to me for those medals to be sent to me? Will they atone in any way for what I've lost?*

But she couldn't see your point of view at all. All that she could see was that she wasn't going to get those medals to pin on her breast. That was what she came for. She thought you would be soft enough to give them to her. Well, she was wrong. Devil the medal did she get, and devil anything else. She had the impudence to ask for Walter's watch as a keepsake. *He would have wanted me to have it*, she said. But there was nothing doing. If she'd been a different kind of lassie, if she'd carried on differently about the medals, you might have given it to her. But not after that.

You never told Wattie or any of them that she'd been here. You did your best to forget her. But you saw her once after that.

That was on the day the Harrisfield War Memorial was unveiled. It was a fine Sunday morning in the autumn of nineteen nineteen. You had on a parson's grey costume trimmed with black braid—you still wear the skirt in the forenoons; it was good tough stuff, that—and you had on a black hat with jet spangles sewn on the crown. Some old women of your age still wore bonnets, but not many of them. Bonnets were going out of fashion, and you thought you might as well be in the fashion as out of it. Wattie was ready and away to the kirk, in his tile-hat and swallow-tail, long before Kate and you were ready. He had given up being an Elder a while before this, but seeing that it was a special occasion Mr. Silver had asked him if he wouldn't take his place beside the other Elders.

Kate was late as usual, running around half-dressed. The bells had started before she was ready. *Hurry up, Kate*, you said. *Ye ken fine that I dinnie like to go in after the bells ha'e stopped*. For everybody looked at you, and it was a fine example for an Elder's wife to be late! However, Kate got ready braw and quick. She had on a navy blue coat-frock with embroidery on the neck and breast, and you thought she looked real bonnie as she walked across the square beside you. She was twenty-nine and you thought it was high time she was thinking about getting married. If she didn't watch she'd develop into an old maid. You were twenty-nine yourself when you married Wattie, but he had been courting you for years and you would have married him sooner if your mother and sisters hadn't been so against it. But Kate had no lad in the offing. All the young fellows she might have had had been killed in the war. You wondered again if you hadn't made a mistake about her and Harold McAllister. Did she still think about him? Was he the reason why she'd never taken up with anybody else? You would have liked to have asked her, but you daren't: it's a subject that you've never spoken about from that day to this. . . . Ay, I think you made a mistake that time, Mirren. You thought that it wouldn't do at the time, but you've changed your views a lot since then. Maybe, it would have turned out all right. It would have been better, anyway, than for Kate to have become what she is now. . . . You should have known better with the example of your own sisters before you.

There was an awful lot of folk going into the kirk, all hurrying to get in before the bells stopped. You passed Wattie in the vestibule and he whispered, *Bella's in*.

She was sitting between wee Walter and wee George in our pew, and they moved up to let you in. The two bairns had on sailor-suits, and you whispered, *Well, ye've got your sailor-soopen on the day*, as you sat down beside George. He was only newly started to the school and he hadn't got out of calling his suit that. You were well pleased to see them, for it made the pew look like old times again when all the bairns were young. You watched Kate take her place in the choir, and you thought that once you had two sons there, too.

The kirk was packed as you hadn't seen it packed for many a long day. You noticed a lot of chaps there who'd served in the war. Some of them had medals pinned on their chests. Some of them had only one arm or one leg. And one of them, poor Willie Taylor, was totally blind.

The text was, *Love your enemies*, and Mr. Silver preached

a grand sermon on it. But I wonder how many of them listened to him? It went in at one ear and out at the other. They were all too busy looking about to see who was there and who wasn't, and to see what this one or the next one was wearing.

After the Benediction, instead of going into the vestry, Mr. Silver walked up the aisle, and the choir followed him. Everybody stood up. The Beadle opened the door and we all followed Mr. Silver and the Elders out. There was a cold nip in the air. You were glad that you hadn't on a low-necked dress like Bella. You thought it gey silly of her to come out on a day like this with only a thin voile frock on.

The War Memorial had been erected in the wee garden in front of the kirk. There was a sheet over it and a Union Jack. The congregation stood around, while Mr. Silver and the Elders stood before the Memorial. A cable-car clanged into the square, and the driver and the conductor stood to watch the ceremony. It was just before Mr. Silver began to pray that you noticed Walter's girl. She must have been sitting in the gallery of the kirk, for you hadn't seen her anywhere else. She was dressed in black with a black busby sticking up in her hat. She nodded to you and gave her lips a twist.

Who's that? Bella whispered.

I dinnie ken, you said.

Bella was beginning to speculate about who it could be, but you gave her a nudge and told her to be quiet and listen to the ceremony. But you didn't hear very much of it yourself. You were thinking that all over the country, in villages and in towns, they were putting up memorials like this, lumps of granite and stone in place of the millions of men and laddies who had been killed for something they knew nothing about. *Oh Absolam, my son Absolam!*

The sheet fell and the Union Jack fell and there was a big granite cross with all the names of Harrisfield's dead. *Their Name Liveth* . . . There was a mist before your eyes and you could hardly see the names, but you made out *L.-Cple. Walter Gillespie, D.C.M., M.M.,* and you began to look then for Arnold's name. . . . But you remembered, and you clutched wee George's hand and pulled him after you through the crowd.

It's not finished yet, Granny, he said. *Everybody's looking.*

But you didn't heed. You were past caring whether folk looked or not. You just walked on, and you could hardly see for the tears that were running down your face. But you didn't bother to take your hankie and dry them. What was the use? You held George's hand and went on.

The bairns were a great comfort to you at the time. Wee Walter, and wee George, and Meg's bairns, they used to come from Sheringwall and spend their holidays with you. It made you think you were just newly married again. It was only when you looked out at the cottages and saw that they were beginning to get dilapidated, and that the folk who lived in them were mostly strangers, young couples with young families, that you realised that forty years had passed. You realised it, too, when you looked in the mirror, or at Wattie, or when you went to the well for water.

It was when you looked at Wattie that you realised it most. He seemed to get old and done that quickly. One day he was working as well and as cheerfully as he'd always worked, the next he was retired and sitting in the house, an old man smoking beside the fire, spitting on your clean grate and getting in your road, so that you would rage at him and tell him to get away to the smiddy-seat out of your sight. But he never complained.

None of us complained, though God knows we had plenty to complain about. There were only Kate's pay and Wattie's pension coming into the house. You took ill-out with having to take most of Kate's money, for a milliner's wages aren't big. It wasn't fair, you thought, that she should have to keep us. Was it not enough that any men she might have married had been killed without her having to take her dead brothers' places and keep her old folks, too?

There's Walter's army pension, of course. But it doesn't count. You never touch it. You put it in the bank every week. For Kate when she's old. You couldn't bear to touch it for yourself. It would be like living on the dead. You would be as bad, then, as those who killed them.

Whiles you thought about taking in a lodger, but you were too old to give a lodger the attention he would want, and you were too proud. You had never had to keep a lodger all your life, so why should you keep one when you were almost finished? You would never have demeaned yourself to do that. You would rather have starved.

We were never the length of that, of course, though sometimes we were hard put to it. But things got better after you turned seventy and got the pension, too. You were glad because it meant that you didn't need to take so much from Kate.

In a way, those last eight or nine years haven't been so bad. You've just had enough money to do your turn; plain fare and no luxuries; thank goodness Wattie and you aren't big eaters. And you've had plenty of memories to live on, happy memories as well as sad ones. And you've had your little jaunts. You jaunted more in the few years after the war than you ever jaunted when the bairns were young. Of course, it wasn't so easy to go jaunting in those days, for the old cable-cars came only the length of Acresgreen. But since they extended the rails to Harrisfield and then, since they've done away with the old cable-cars and got electric trams, it has been easier to get about. The only thing is that all this has happened after you are too old to get the benefit. But that's always the way. Things come too late. Like this new house you're going to. Everybody says, *You'll be better off; there's all the conveniences, running water and a lavatory inside, everything you need.* But what good is that to us when we're too old to enjoy them? What good is that when we'll soon be dead?

SIX PLAIN

A COUPLE of days before the flitting a letter came from Aunt Meg. She lived in Glasgow now, where Uncle Bernard had a small garage that he'd bought with the money that his old boss, Lord Shering-wall, had left him. Aunt Meg wrote she would of liked to come and see the cottages before Granpa and Granma quit them, but trade was bad and they couldn't afford it just now, and seeing they were all coming, anyway, to the Golden Wedding, what was the odds?

Aunt Meg always spoke about bad trade in her letter as if it was a friend of the family, a sorta unwelcome poor relation who'd planked himself on them and wouldn't move. You could always depend upon there being something about bad trade in her letters and about there being something about the Royal Family. This time she wrote:

" Did you see the lovely photograph of little Princess Elizabeth in yesterday's *Daily Mirror*? It was so sweet. She's such a nice child. I wonder if it's true those rumours that she's going to have a little brother or sister, soon? I hope so. The little Duchess is so sweet. I got a lovely calender at Christmas of her and little Betty, and it looks lovely above the mantelpiece in the parlour. I would like to get new curtains for the parlour, but trade is so bad I don't think I'll manage it meantime. My old rose ones will have to do. I've managed to get myself a new coat though, in preparation for the Golden

Wedding. Bottle green with a red fox fur collar. I don't half look a snip. It was rather more than I wanted to pay, but I said to hang with poverty. I was determined to be à la mode for once in my life."

" The best o' it is," Granma said. " Your Aunt Meg aye thinks she's à la mode."

" She doesn't half fancy herself," Aunt Kate said. " She thinks she cuts a dash every time she goes out."

" She'll no' be able to dash very far," Granma said. " She's got awfu' sair feet, like masel'."

This was at dinner-time. Granpa was sitting kinda dejected-looking, eating his meat all chopped-up, on account of him not having any teeth to chew it with. He was looking out at the green and the harbour. I guessed he was thinking he'd have only two more days to look out at them, so I said, " I ain't seen Stumpy McGregor around lately. Wonder what's happened to him ? "

" I met him just now," Aunt Kate said. " He's been in the house for the past week with the cold."

" Oh, my," Granpa said. " That's terrible."

" He says he'll be in to see you either this afternoon or to-morrow," Aunt Kate said. " He didn't want to come any sooner because he's been spitting up stuff."

" Dear, oh dear ! " Granma said, laughing.

" Forty cupfuls," Aunt Kate said, imitating Stumpy. " God knows where it all came frae ! "

" Ye surely stood and spoke to him for a while ? " Granma said.

" It was him who stood and spoke to me," Aunt Kate said. " I couldn't get away from him. It's a wonder I didn't catch the cold myself. He stood so long that I was able to count how many waistcoats he had on. Five waistcoats ! "

" Ye're haverin', Kate," Granma said.

" No, help my Jimmie Johnston! He had on five waistcoats. I counted them."

Granpa was beginning to cheer up. He liked a laugh. So Aunt Kate leaned forward and cried, " A traveller told me a joke to-day."

" Oh, they travellers! " Granpa said, and he leaned forward expectantly.

" You wire in and take your dinner," Granma said, " and leave your travellers and their jokes alone."

But Aunt Kate had to tell the old man the joke. I'd heard it before. It was the one about the guy who couldn't find his bedroom in a large hotel, and he came to a locked door, and he thought his wife had locked him out, and he cried through the key-hole, " Is that you, honey ? "

I thought Granpa was gonna have apoplexy, or whatever they calls it, when Aunt Kate told him the answer the guy got. Even Granma laughed a lot.

When he'd recovered a bit Granpa said, " That reminds me of the time when auld Sam Dippy shut himsel' in the water-closet."

" Ye've told Spike that story afore," Granma said.

But that didn't worry him none, and he started in to tell me it again. And, although I'd heard it at least a dozen times, I enjoyed it again. Besides, it kinda helped to take the old man's mind offen the flitting.

After Aunt Kate had gone back to work Granpa lay down on the sofa and Granma covered him with a plaid. I said I'd wash the dishes, and I told her to sit down and have a rest. She sat and read the *People's Friend*, and every now and then she'd tell me what was happening in the story she was reading. She was helluva interested in it. It was like most of the other stories in the *People's*

Friend, all about a dame, poor, but honest, who married a rich guy and all about what a swell time she had. "Ye ken it's a lot o' havers," Granma said. "But ye cannie help enjoyin' it. Ye wish it would happen to you, though ye ken fine that onythin' that's likely to happen to you'll be different from what a novelist would make it, for truth's aye stranger than fiction."

I couldn't help thinking, as I looked round the kitchen, what a change it was from the first time I'd seen it. Everything that could be packed was packed. The pictures was offen the walls and you could see the marks where they'd been. I'd never realised how faded the wall-paper was till I saw them marks.

The dishes was to be packed in a tin bath, so I got started to wrapping them up in old newspapers and putting them in. While I was doing this Granma got talking about Uncle Tom when he was a kid. It started when she told me about the time he'd knocked over the tub of clothes, and then she told me a lotta other tales about him. "I cannie think why he never came back," she said. "It wasnie as if he had done anythin' wrong, anythin' he should be ashamed of. He couldnie help havin' the wanderlust, of course. But he might ha'e let us know where he went to. It's awfu' to think that we dinnie ken where he is. Canada. Or Australia. Or God-knows-where. Maybe, he's dead, like his brothers. I couldnie imagine him no' bein' in the war. He went to the Boer War, so he would go to that one, too—the fool!" She was sitting, staring into the fire and pleating her apron the way she always done. "If he'd been in a book," she said, "he'd ha'e turned up the day or the morn with tons o' money and bought this house, and let yer Grandfather and me bide here the rest o' oor lives in peace." She laughed. "But

things never turn oot the way they happen in books.
So I don't suppose I'll ever get the chance to fall on the
neck o' the prodigal son." She rose and filled the
kettle. "It's funny," she said after a while. "I
wouldnie ken him though he was to come in that door
the now."

"Oh, I reckon you would," I said.

"How do ye ken?" she said. "Ha'e you had a son
that's been awa' for twenty-five years?"

That shut me up and made me think some. I guess
the old dame was right. People change a lot in twenty-
five years. I reckon Granma would be hard put to it
even to recognise Mom if she wasn't expecting her and
although she'd seen photographs of her, for Mom must
be pretty different now from what she was when Granma
last saw her. There's a big change from a stout, middle-
aged dame, with short skirts and shingled hair, and a
young woman with hair piled high atop her head and
skirts sweeping the pavements. So I reckon there
would be the same trouble to know Uncle Tom.
He'd be a middle-aged man now, stout, and probably
bald.

We was just gonna have tea when Stumpy McGregor
came in. He seemed to make it a habit to come in at
tea-time. Granma pressed him to have tea, but he
wouldn't have it. She was real annoyed about it, and
she said afterwards, why did he come at tea-time if
he wouldn't take tea, annoying people when he sat and
watched them eating.

Stumpy was full of himself and the cold he'd had.
"Dear, oh dear," he said. "It wass terrible. The
stuff was coming up in cupfuls. I wass never done
hoasting and hoasting, and there the stuff would come
out of my mouth. Forty cupfuls, Wattie, forty! I

never put up so much stuff in all my life. God knows where it all came frae ! "

" I havenie been so well maself, Stumpy," Granpa said.

But Stumpy didn't take the cue. " I had an awfu' pain in my chest," he said. " So I rubbed my breast with paraffin oil and then I put a copper pan on top of it, and that relieved me. But dear, oh dear, it wass terrible while it lasted. It's not all up yet either. I'm still hoasting and getting up some stuff."

" I havenie been so well maself," Granpa said again.

But Granma had had enough talk about illness for one tea-time. " I was fair scunnered," she told me after. So she said, " Havers, there's nothin' wrong wi' ye," to Granpa, and she said to Stumpy, " He aye likes to mak' himsel' oot worse than he is."

" How are ye yourself, Mistress Gillespie ? " Stumpy said.

" I'm as well as I'll ever be," Granma said.

" Ye'll be gettin' ready to go ? " Stumpy said, looking around.

" Ay," Granpa said.

" The day after to-morrow," Granma said. " When are ye goin' yourself, Stumpy ? "

" No' for another fortnight yet," Stumpy said. " It's time enough."

" Ye'll ha'e got yer key ? " Granma said.

" Ay," he said. " Number Twelve, Calderburn Crescent."

" The same street as us," Granma said. " We're number ten."

" That's fine that we're in the same street," Stumpy said.

" Nell Dippy's in number nine, across the road,"

Granma said. "And the McRaes and the Pattersons are in number seven."

"They must be puttin' all the folk from the cottages in the one street," Stumpy said.

"To make us feel at home!" Granma said.

"Ah, it'll never be like home," Granpa said, shaking his head. "Our hearts'll aye be down here. They'd be as well to take us all oot and shoot us."

"Havers!" Granma said.

"No, Mirren, no," he said. "I'm ower auld to be transplanted. I'll just wither and die up there."

"Nonsense," she said.

Stumpy had just gone, when we heard a motor coming along the row. It was a kinda unusual thing to hear cars there unless in the forenoons, when one or two bakers' and butchers' vans came, so me and Granma looked out. It was a big black limousine like I'd like to have if I ever make good, it was a swell piece of machinery. There was a chauffeur and another man, a big, stout guy, middle-aged, wearing a heavy tweed coat and with his hat sticking on the back of his head "I wonder who he can be?" Granma said.

"I dunno," I said. "But we'll soon find out."

The guy was making for Granma's door. I looked at her to see if she'd answer it, but she was standing there still, with her hand touching the cameo-brooch at her throat and there was a funny sorta look on her face. And suddenly, as I looked at her, I guessed this was my Uncle Tom come home like Granma had always hoped he would, rich and successful. Jees, I could of jumped for joy and I rushed to the door and opened it.

"Is this where Mrs. Gillespie stays?" the big stout guy said.

"Sure," I cried. "Come in."

I put out my hand, but he never noticed it. He brushed past me quick.

Granma was standing in the middle of the floor and there was tears in her eyes all ready to fall and roll down her cheeks. She sorta held out her arms.

" Tom," she said.

But the guy didn't rush forward and clasp her to his manly bosom, like what I'd expected. He took off his hat and stood there sorta undecided.

" Mrs. Gillespie ? " he said.

" Y-Yes," Granma said. " Don't you . . ."

I guess she was gonna say, " Don't you recognise me ? " but the guy said, " I'm a reporter, Mrs. Gillespie. I'm from the *Weekly Noise,* and I'd like if you could tell me a few things about these old cottages. I understand that they've been condemned and that you've all got to shift. So as you are the oldest inhabitants my editor would like a story and, maybe, a picture."

" Oh," Granma said, recovering herself pretty quick. " I thought you were somebody else. How stupid of me."

" I'm sorry," he said.

" So am I," she said.

Well, he got his story. Both Granma and Granpa entertained him for the next half-hour with stories of the cottages when they was in their glory. But I didn't listen much at first. I was helluva disappointed that the guy wasn't my Uncle Tom. I couldn't figure how Granma and me had leaped to the same conclusion that he was. But after thinking it over I guess it was on account of us speaking about Uncle Tom earlier in the afternoon, and Granma saying she wouldn't of known him. He was in our minds and Granma saw a resemblance that wasn't there, and him being in my mind, I

was ready to stop any middle-aged stranger and say,
" Howja, Uncle Tom ? " That's how I figure it, anyways. Maybe, one of them psychologists, like Walter
Anderson's always talking about, would figure it
different.

Anyways, it helped to take Granpa's mind off the
flitting. He was in his element telling the reporter
about all the things that had happened long ago. He
told him about Wiggy Wilson's wig getting knocked
off by the clothes' rope and about the time Nell Dippy got
chased by foreign sailors down among the fish-boxes.
And he even told him about Sam Dippy and the lavatory.
Granma was fair on edge, wondering what he'd say
next, but she did her fair share of telling stories. They
sure kept that reporter writing busy. I guess they'd
of kept him there all night, but he said he reckoned he'd
got plenty of local colour, and he lit out after he'd got
a photo of them when they was a bit younger, Granpa
standing awful stiff in his swallow-tail coat, with his
hand on Granma's shoulder, and her with a book in
her hand.

" It'll be in next week's *Weekly Noise*," the reporter
said.

" We'll read it in our new house," Granma said. " We
could have thought about a lot more if we'd just been
prepared."

After the guy had gone Granpa kept minding lots
more things he reckoned he should of told him. " If
he'd just let us ken he was comin'," he said.

" Hoots," Granma said. " Ye'd think he was writin'
a book aboot the cottages frae the way ye're speakin'."

" Well, I dinnie see why he shouldnie write a book,"
Granpa said. " There's plenty o' material for a book."

" A whole encyclopædia ! " Granma said. " It would

take anybody fifty years to write doon everything that's happened in the cottages durin' the time we've stayed in them."

"I've often thought aboot it," Granpa said. "If I'd just had the eddication. . . ."

It was a pretty good day the day they flitted. Granma was up at the back of six as usual. There wasn't no sense in her getting up so early, but she said she'd risen at six most mornings so she didn't want this last morning to be any different. I got up about eight, and I was having breakfast when Aunt Kate got up. She was going to her work in the forenoon, but she'd asked the afternoon off. She made an awful fuss of Granpa before she went out. "Eh, he's a nice auld man," she said, hugging him as he sat up in his bed, eating his breakfast. "Is he going to give me a wee kissy-wissy then? The last kissy-wissy in the cottages." Like he was a kid of two. I could of crowned her. It was a kicky-wicky *she* needed. But Granpa laughed and let her about smother him with a kiss. Then she went off at the toot, running along the row as fast as she could on account of her awful tight skirt.

I took down my bed while Granma was getting Granpa ready and dressed in his best suit that he hadn't worn for years. It smelled awful strong of moth-balls. He was none too keen to put it on, he said his old suit would do fine because he would have on his overcoat and nobody would see him. But Granma said he gotta have it on. "I'm no' havin' ye goin' to oor new hoose dressed like a tramp," she said. "What would folk think if they saw ye? Besides, ye'll ha'e to wear this suit oot. What guid is it goin' to be to anybody after ye're dead?"

" Oh, one o' the laddies'll, maybe, wear it," he said.

" I'd like to see them ! " Granma said. " I'd like to see their faces if ye offered it to them. It's auld-fashioned. Nobody has vents like that in their jackets nowadays."

" It would, maybe, do for their work," Granpa said. " It's a guid piece o' stuff. Guid tough cloth."

" Like maself ! " Granma said, laughing, and she imitated the fish-wife who used to come to the cottages years ago. She went round the rows with her creel on her back crying, " Fine fresh herring like maself, like maself ! "

" And she was anythin' but bonnie," Granma said. " She had cock-eyes, and her face was like that grate —only not so clean ! "

We got Granpa sitting all ready on the sofa, with his overcoat folded beside him and his bowler hat on top of it. Then Granma helped me to fold the bed-clothes. " Dinnie bother to take doon Kate's auld bed, Spike," she said. " We'll just leave it here, seeing that she's got a braw new bed and bedroom suite comin' this forenoon."

" It's a pity to leave it," Granpa said. " It's a guid auld bed."

" Where could ye put it ? " Granma said. " An' what guid would it be to us ? We're better to leave it here."

" We could sell it for scrap-iron," Granpa said.

" Scrap-iron ! " Granma said. " Hoo much do ye think we'd get for it ? Sixpence ! It's no' worth the bother."

Granma began to get herself ready, and by half-past ten she was all dressed, wearing a black luvisca coat she'd had for more than ten years, and that she hadn't worn much on account of her thinking it was too showy for the times she was out and dressed. And she had on a gold chain and gold earrings that Great-Granma Murdoch had left her. She sure looked a swell old dame. " Ye'd think we were goin' to a weddin'," she said. " Is it yours, Spike ? " she said, laughing.

I was surprised she should be in such a jolly sorta mood. She made a helluva lotta jokes. I reckon it was all eyewash, though, to cheer up Granpa. He was sitting on the sofa awful quiet, not even smoking his pipe. " What's wrong wi' yer pipe ? " Granma said.

" Oh, I dinnie think I'll bother wi' it, Mirren," he said slowly. " I would ha'e to spit an' I dinnie want to mess up your clean fireside."

" Hoots, spit awa'," Granma said. " That fireside's got the last clean it's ever goin' to get from me."

And she lighted a paper-spill for him and held it to his pipe. All the same he was awful careful not to spit on the grate ; he leaned forward every time he hawked and nearly over-balanced off the sofa trying to spit into the fire.

Aunt Bella came at eleven o'clock in a taxi. Granma and Granpa were going to her house for their dinner and tea, and they wouldn't go to their new house till night after all the furniture was shifted. Granma looked all around to see that everything was as it should be. " Ye'll mind and put everythin' on the lorry, Spike," she said.

" Sure," I said.

" Dinnie leave ony mess," she said. " I wouldnie like to leave a dirty house."

" Trust me," I said.

She went into both rooms and looked around. They were pretty bleak-looking with all the furniture standing ready to be carted out. There was a sorta moisture afore her eyes and I noticed as she pulled down her veil that she put her fingers over them to wipe it away. " Are ye ready, father ? " she said.

" Ay," Granpa said.

We had to help him up. Aunt Bella stood at one side of him while I helped him into his coat. It was tough going ; he seemed to have no power to help himself. Aunt Bella placed his bowler on his head, but he took it off kinda annoyed and put it on again himself. " Where's the mirror ? " he said.

" It's packed," Granma said. " What are ye needin' a mirror for ? "

" Here's mine," Aunt Bella said, taking a small one out of her handbag. " It's not very big, but, maybe, it'll do."

Granpa looked at himself and he gave his hat a tilt to the side. " Tcha ! " he said. " Richard's himself again ! " But he didn't laugh like I'd heard him laugh when he said that.

Aunt Bella took one arm and I took the other and we began to help him out to the taxi. He made us stop at the kitchen door and he looked around. " It's no' much o' a place," he said. He shook his head slowly, then we went on.

" Mind the step," Aunt Bella said warningly.

" I'm minding it, damn ye," he said, real angry. " Do ye think I've no' got eyes in ma head ? I'm gey far gone, but I'm no' blind yet."

We got him into the taxi and I thought he looked awful small sitting low down in the corner. Aunt Bella made to put a rug over his knees, but he shoved it away. " I'm not a bairn, Bella," he said. " If I want a rug I'll ask for it."

Granma came out slowly. She stood for a minute

or two on the pavement before she got into the taxi.
" Here's the key, Spike," she said. " Ye'll see and look
after everything."

" Trust me, Granma," I said.

I stood and watched the taxi crawl along the row.
Both Granma and Granpa were looking out the back
window, but they never waved to me, or to Nell Dippy,
though she waved to them like she was in a fire on the
top storey waving to the firemen. " It's awful," she
said. " At their time of life."

" Yeah," I said, and I backed into the doorway for
I'd plenty to do without getting into a conversation
with Nell. As I went in I saw that Stumpy had come
out and he was shouting, " I'll see you next week," as
the taxi passed his house.

I went up to the new house and let in the men when
they brought Aunt Kate's new bedroom suite. It wasn't
long before a crowd of dirty, snottery-nosed kids had
gathered round to watch. I guess Aunt Kate would of
taken a fit if she'd seen the way some of them put out
their dirty hands to touch the furniture when the men
put it down on the pavement. I reckon it was a good
job it was pretty well covered with brown paper. But
that didn't stop one kid from tearing the paper offen
one piece to see what like it was. I was all set to fetch
him a clip on the ear, but one of the men on the lorry
saved me the trouble. " See here, you little bastard,"
he said. " If you don't get out of here I'll kick your
arse." It didn't shift the kids, but they stood back a
bit after that.

I was back in the old cottage and had the kettle boiling
when Aunt Kate arrived. She'd brought some cold
meat with her. " Did the bedroom suite arrive all
right ? " she said.

" Sure," I said.

" Do you like it ? " she said. But before I could say whether I did or didn't she went into ecstasies about it. " Oh, it's gorgeous," she said. " Simply gorgeous. I never saw such lovely furniture, it's fit for anybody, it's fit even for the Duchess of York. Oh, help my Jimmie Johnston, I won't know myself when I'm lying in the bed. It's lovely. And it was that cheap, too. Only eighteen pounds. Imagine, eighteen pounds for all that lovely furniture ! "

I spread a newspaper on the table. All the dishes were packed except a couple of cups and a couple of plates.

" Is the tea ready ? " Aunt Kate said. " I'm simply starving. Honest, I could eat a scabbed cat, I'm that hungry. I brought boiled ham with me. Do you like boiled ham, Spike ? It's lovely boiled ham. The man in the shop told me it was just freshly boiled. ' It's just like yourself,' he said. Really, I didn't know where to look. I didn't know whether he was kiddin' or not. ' That'll do you,' I said, ' you're kind of fresh yourself.' Oh, he laughed and laughed at that. Really, he did. Help my Jimmie Johnston, I never saw a man laugh so hearty. He got that red in the face I thought he was goin' to burst. Really, I never saw such a man to laugh."

Aunt Kate could go on like this for hours, just like she'd been wound up, so I sat back and prepared to endure it while I ate. " Did my father and mother get away all right ? " she said. " I'm that glad they had Bella's to go to and didn't need to be here when the furniture was goin' out. I hope they didn't break down or anything, did they ? It must have been terrible for them, really it must. Fifty years is a long time. I feel it myself. Of course, I'm quite pleased to go, too, you know. Really, I am. But it's when I think about them. . . ."

And so on till I was in a state between going to sleep and going mad. Aunt Kate just has that effect on you. As I listened I speculated about the guy she'd once been in love with. I wondered what had happened to him, and I wondered what he'd of thought of Aunt Kate if he'd married her. If he had, I reckon I'd of been kinda sorry for him.

I sure was glad when the lorry came. It was a friend of Uncle Jim's who was driving it, and Uncle Jim and George was there, too. George always welcomed a chance to get a half-day off the wireless college.

We wasn't long in toting out the furniture. We would of been quicker, but Aunt Kate kept getting in the way, fussing around and hoping we wouldn't bump it. Uncle Jim began to lose his rag and he said, " For God's sake, Kate, go and sit down on yer backside. Ye're more trouble than help. What'll it matter if they get a bit bump ? They're that well scratched already that another scratch or two'll never be noticed."

Aunt Kate was real mad. " Speaking like that to me before the strange man," she said.

" What difference does the strange man being here make ? " Uncle Jim said. " Ye'll get spoken to worse than that afore ye leave the face o' the earth."

At last everything was on the lorry except the frame of the old iron bed in Aunt Kate's room. I'd never realised what a small house it was until I saw it empty. It wouldn't of made one decent-sized room. Pete only knows how Granma and Granpa had reared seven kids in it. It's a wonder they ever grew up at all ; the cramped space would of been enough for them to shrivel up and die. No wonder they were all rarin' to get out and fend for themselves.

We'd let the fire die out, so Aunt Kate raked the ashes out and put them in the bucket with a lot of other old rubbish. She was gonna leave the key with Nell Dippy, so's Nell could put out the bucket when the ash-cart came around the next day. " I think that's every-thing," Aunt Kate said, looking around. She opened her bag and gave her mouth a few licks with her lip-stick, and she was putting on her hat when she stopped and said, " Oh, I'd better put some whiting on the windows."

" What ? " George said.

" I'm goin' to put some whiting on the windows so that folk won't be able to see in," she said.

" What difference will it make ? " George said. " There's nothing for them to see."

" I'll have to put it on," she said.

" Don't be daft," he said. " You're finished with the house. You won't see whether folk look in or not."

" But I promised my mother I'd put it on," she said. " She wouldn't be able to sleep if she thought people could see in."

" Come on, Kate," Uncle Jim cried. " We cannie keep the lorry standin' here all day."

But Aunt Kate rummaged in a box on the lorry and she brought out a tin of whiting and a rag and started to rub the windows. George looked at me and shook his head. " She can save herself the trouble," he said. " All the panes'll be broken in a day or two."

But Aunt Kate never let on she heard him. Uncle Jim lighted his pipe and muttered, " She's a thrawn bitch. She's like her mother there."

Both me and George got rags and gave some of the panes the once over so as to help Aunt Kate along. George fooled around more than he helped. He kept waving the rag like a flag and singing, *I wanta be happee, but I won't be happee till I make you happee tooooo!*

"That's enough from you, cocky!" Aunt Kate said.

At last she was ready, and after a final look around she locked the door. "Ah, the puir auld hoose!" she said. "Many's the time I've locked this door."

"And many's the time you've sworn at it when you were coming in late at night and it squeaked!" George said. "Come on, hurry up!"

So after we'd given the key to Nell Dippy we got on the lorry beside the furniture, and with a few hoots and some backfiring, we started off along the row, leaving the cottages behind, and up the hill towards Calderburn.

SIX PURL

REALLY, I can hardly believe I'm sleeping in another
house, I've slept that often in the West Room.
Help my Jimmie Johnston, it seems funny not to lie
and count the baskets of roses on the wallpaper, or to
listen to the war blind flapping between the window
and the sewing machine. Oh, that war blind ! Many
a row my mother and I had about that blind. I made it
during the war out of heavy red flannel, it was fine for
hiding the light. After the war was over I wanted to
put it away, but Mother wouldn't hear tell of it. " Ye
dinnie need to fash yoursel' makin' it doon into a dressing-
gown," she said. " Where ha'e you time in the mornings to wear a dressing-gown ? Just let it bide where it
is. It's fine for keepin' inquisitive folk frae lookin' in."
I was daft not to put my foot down ; I wasn't a bairn,
though my mother seemed to think I was. But I
didn't bother ; I let her alone. The blind didn't
hurt me, though often I'd rather not have had it ; I'd
rather have seen the stars and the lights of the harbour.
The blind stifled me and it didn't let any air into the room.
Thank goodness, I don't need to put it up in this house.
This is my own room, furnished with my own money,
and I'm going to do what I like with it. I think I'll
buy silk curtains for the window. Those were beauties
I saw in the Store and they weren't dear, either. Twenty-
five shillings the pair. Lovely lemon curtains. They
were gorgeous. And I think I'll buy an eiderdown

quilt to match them. It'll keep me fine and warm. This is an awful big bed, really I feel fair lost in it. I thought the old iron-bed was big, but this beats it. I wish I had somebody in it with me. But I'd think it funny if I had ; it's such a long time since I slept with anybody. Not since I was a kid of seventeen, or so. Of course, I've had Magda and Kathie sleeping with me, but that's been only occasionally, when they were here on holiday ; it's not the same as sleeping regularly with somebody. A fortnight in the year. They used to stay longer when they were kids at the school. I used to love when they came. I was in my element dressing them and taking them out. I touched and arranged their clothes as I used to touch and arrange my dolls when I was a kid myself. It was just as if they were my own bairns, and I used to pretend to myself that they were. My bairns and Harold McAllister's. . . .

Harold and I were in the same class at school. He was a quiet boy, an only child. The McAllisters lived in number seventeen, two doors along from us, and when we were wee, Harold and I used to come home from the school together. He used to wait at the girls' gate for me ; he was more like my brother than my own brothers ; Arn was so much older, and Walter, although he was only two years older than me, was always away fighting or something, and had no time for me. But Harold always waited for me and he took my hand and we walked home sedately across the square and down the green-steps. Some of the other boys used to call, ' Lassie-boy ! ' after him—the word, sissy, wasn't in our vocabulary then—but Harold never heeded them. His ears used to get red, but he looked straight ahead of him, his face pale and his dark eyes looking at the road in front. I used to keep a firm grip of his hand, afraid the other boys would do something—trip us both up, or pull our school-bags off our backs—but Harold would say, " Never heed them, Katie." And we would march on till we came to the steps.

Then we clattered down them, free, safe from the rough boys. We knew that we were safe and the boys knew that, too. But that didn't stop them leaning over the dyke and crying, " Lassie-boy ! " or " Katie Gillespie's got on her red knickers. Yah ! Yah ! Here comes the bull ! "

How I hated those red knickers. I seemed to wear them for years and years. They were too big for me when I got them. They'd been bought for Bella, but she'd never worn them because they were too small for her. They were too big for me when I got them, so I had to wear them longer than I would have had to wear them if they'd been bought for me. I thought they were never going to wear done.

Harold left the school at the same time as I did, and he went to work in the sawmill. All the boys in the cottages invariably began to work in the sawmill. Before long some of them left it to go to other jobs, but others stayed on. Harold was one of the ones who stayed on.

I was apprenticed to Miss Maggs, the milliner, at Acresgreen. I'd always had a notion to make hats ; when I was wee I'd far rather make hats for my doll than make anything else. My father often said it was like the women in the pictures in some French papers— all hat and nothing else—but my mother would tell him to be quiet and not go putting ideas in my head.

After we both started to work I didn't see much of Harold. His work at the sawmill kept him busy and his folk made him go to evening-classes. Not many of the lads in the cottages went to evening-classes, and this set Harold apart from them. He had never made friends with the other boys at school, and his being an only child, helped to make him lonelier than he might have been. Besides, he was a Catholic. The McAllisters were the only Catholics in the cottages, and this was why none of the other boys would make friends with Harold at school. Although they knew nothing of religious differences they understood that there was something outlandish about him because he was excused Bible lessons. And because they sensed that he was outlandish they determined to make him suffer, as people always try to make outlandish people suffer—make them pay for being different, as they made Arn pay.

The evening-classes made Harold lonelier than ever. There were no evening-classes in Harrisfield School at that time and he had to go to a school up town. Often he walked both ways, so his nights were filled ; he hadn't time to stand about at the head of the pier or at the smiddy-seat with the other lads.

For years after we left school I hardly ever saw him. I had my music lessons on Tuesdays and I practiced at least two other nights a week. If I ever went anywhere it was with my Mother or Bella or Meg. Mother was terrified to let me go anywhere alone.

The only place where I didn't have some other member of the family with me was the Sunday School after I became a teacher in the Primary. Both Meg and Bella had given up being teachers by this time, and both Arn and Walter had refused to be teachers ; they said they'd had enough of the Sunday School when they were young, and they thought they did very well because they were in the choir twice on Sundays and went to the practice through the week. So I was the only

Gillespie in the Sunday School. It wasn't that I was
fond of the Sunday School, but I was glad to get away
from the family ; it was a change. It gave me a chance
to be alone. That was impossible at home with us all
tripping over each other.

The only times I saw Harold were when I saw him
passing the window, or if we met in the row, or in the
square, and then we were usually in too big a hurry to
speak. But one Sunday, as I was coming out of the
Sunday School, I met him. He was coming home from
the Catholic Chapel in Leith. We walked home together, and we talked all the time. He told me about
his work and I told him about mine.

The next Sunday he was waiting for me when I
came out of the Sunday School. " I was passing," he
said, " and I knew it was about time for you to come
out."

After that he waited for me every Sunday, or I waited
for him if he hadn't arrived. And we got into the habit
of going for a walk instead of going straight home. We
would walk along the Low Road or down the pier, and
we would watch the sea-gulls swooping over the harbour
or perching on the piles of pit-props that lay beside
the railway lines. Sometimes we talked and sometimes
we didn't. It was all a matter of question and answer.
We never spoke of anything but our work and his
classes, and sometimes I told him about the shows Bella
took me to see.

Harold was always interested in them ; he never had
time to go to the theatre or music-halls, even if his
parents would have allowed him. But he'd have liked
to have gone. And he listened to everything that I
told him.

One Sunday he was leaning on a capstan at the end

of the pier and I was telling him about *The Merry Widow*,
which I'd just seen. It had been raining and the planks
of the pier were all wet, soggy and black, with the white
sea-gulls' droppings scattered over them like polka
dots. It was February, and there was a cold, cold wind
blowing up the Firth. I sat on a fish-box and leaned
against the wall of a goods shed, crouching against it to
escape the wind. My hands were deep in my muff and
I didn't dare take them out to push back the tendrils of
hair that were whipping against my cheeks. Although
it was cold, I thought it was lovely to be there with
Harold ; better than being at home helping my mother
to make the dinner, with an apron about smothering
me in case I dirtied my Sunday dress. There was
nobody on the pier but ourselves. I leaned my head
against the corrugated iron of the shed and I looked at
Harold.

He was nearly eighteen. He was the same height as
me, and he was slim and wiry ; his navy-blue suit was a
ready-made one and it hung on him, making him look
as if he were dressed in his father's clothes. But I
didn't care about the suit ; I didn't think it odd. It was
his face I was looking at. It was a nice face, with soft
down sprouting on the chin and the cheeks. He had
long eyelashes—" Far too good for a man," I thought
—and his nose was straight and thin, a bit reddened at
the tip by the east wind. One of his feet was on top
of the capstan and he leaned his elbow on his knee, his
chin in his hand as he looked out at the sea and the spray
dashing against the breakwater. Away, beyond the
breakwater, we could see the Island of Inchkeith, and
behind it, the open sea. And there was a heliotrope haze
hovering above the horizon.

" I wish I saw you oftener, Katie," he said suddenly.

" Why ? " I said.

He took his foot off the capstan and stood erect, his hands behind his back. " I don't know," he said. " I'd just like to see you oftener."

" So do I," I said.

He came and sat beside me on the fish-box. There wasn't much room on it ; it was narrow and very rough round the edges. My corsets were nipping my hips. But I didn't want to move ; I leaned against the shed and closed my eyes. Harold began to stroke the fur of my muff. " Poor old cat ! " he said softly.

" It's not a cat," I said. " It's real seal-skin."

" It's wet," he said. " It's all spray."

" Is it ? " I said.

" Feel," he said.

I drew out my hand and stroked the fur. It was damp and cold. Harold put his hand on top of mine for a moment. " Your hands are warm enough, anyway," he said.

He stood up quickly. I wondered why he was blushing. And I wondered if he'd hear the thumps my heart was giving ; they were terribly loud. I couldn't think why they should be so loud. I'd never noticed my heart beating like that before, unless after I'd been running. And I had been sitting quite still for a while.

" It's cold," he said. " I'll race you to the top of the pier."

And away we went, jumping over railway lines and sleepers, jouking around wagons and sheds, and jumping over holes, where the wood of the pier was beginning to rot. Harold was well ahead of me. I had an awful job with my long skirts and with carrying my muff. I was quite out of breath when we got to the top of the pier. My heart was thumping at a great rate now, but I no longer noticed how loud the beats were.

" When'll I see you again ? " Harold said, as we went up the brae to the cottages.

" Next Sunday, I suppose," I said. And then, without thinking, I said, " Unless you'd like to come to your tea this afternoon and I'll play the ' Merry Widow ' music for you—if my mother'll let me, that is ! Grace gave it to me."

" I'd love to come," he said.

My mother said nothing when I said I'd invited Harold to come to his tea. All she said was, " It's a good job there's plenty in the house. Walter'll not be home for his tea. That's one good thing."

I'd been expecting her to say something, so I was as pleased as Punch. But later on, when I was coming in after emptying the dirty dish-water down the siver, I heard her say to Bella, " She's too early begun wi' lads. She doesnie need to fash hersel'. Seventeen. Just a bairn."

I pretended I hadn't heard her, but it spoiled my afternoon. Before he came, I was terrified that Mother wouldn't be nice to Harold, and I imagined all the different kinds of frigid receptions she could give him. But I shouldn't have worried. She spoke to him in the same way as she'd have spoken to any of the other young men in the cottages coming to their tea.

Jim Anderson was there, too ; he was courting Bella at the time. He spoke away to Harold, trying to draw him out and to make him feel at home. Jim was well enough at home himself ; he came about the house for years and years, courting Bella before they finally got married. It was funny that Meg and Bernard were the same ; they didn't seem in a hurry. Not like a lot of the young fry nowadays. Help my Jimmie Johnston, they just rush into marriage as if they were rushing away to a dance. Things were different then. . . . But were they? Really, I think Harold and me would have been as daft as some of the young ones nowadays if we'd just got the chance.

My father was awful nice to Harold, and he asked him what he was studying at his evening classes, and asked him if he had joined a trade union yet, because if he hadn't it was high time he did. Bella chaffed him until his ears were like red roses on either side of his face. But Arnold didn't say much, and that was strange for him, for he always carried on at a great length at the table, joking and imitating folk: always on the point of upsetting the milk jug, or the tea-pot, till he had my mother fair up to ninety. But now he sat and looked at Harold. Only once do I remember him saying anything and that was, " You're fairly growing, Harold. You've become a man all of a sudden. And a handsome man, too. Eh, Kate ? "

I blushed and looked down at my plate. And Harold blushed, too. My father, and Jim, and Bella, laughed. But my mother sat quiet, saying nothing. I knew that she didn't want me to have anything to do with Harold because the McAllisters were Catholics. She was wondering, as she sat there, how she was going to put a spoke in his wheel. It wasn't only because she thought I was too young to get married. That had nothing to do with it. She knew that neither Harold nor I were thinking about getting married ; we were both too young to think of such a thing just then. But she knew that although we weren't thinking about it just then, it wouldn't be long before we did. Nothing would stop us from falling in love, and once that happened nothing would stop us from wanting to get married. And no daughter of hers, she was determined, was going to marry a Papist.

After tea I asked if I could play the piano.

" If you play hymns," my mother said.

" Oh," I said, making a face.

" Hymns or nothing," my mother said.

" But I wanted to let Harold hear *The Merry Widow* music," I said.

" He can hear it again," she said.

" Oh, mother," I said, trying to coax her. " Please. Just for once."

" Ay, what harm will it do ? " Bella said.

" There's going to be no music but sacred music in this house," my mother said.

" Listen now, that's being auld-fashioned," Bella said. " Nobody bothers about that nowadays."

" I bother," my mother said.

" Come down off your perch for once, Mrs. Gillespie," Jim said, laughing. " It'll do none of us any harm."

She sniffed, just like Grandmother Murdoch, and I expected her to throw back her head like the Captain's Lady and give us all a sermon. But Jim had won the day. She couldn't refuse him anything. It was the devil-may-care way he looked at you and his cheery grin, and because he was Tom's friend. My mother always remembers that. To her he's Tom's friend long before he is Bella's husband, and Walter's and George's father.

" Well, you can play *The Merry Widow*," she said. " But nothing after that but hymns."

While I was getting out the music I heard my father tell Harold that Grace was going away on tour with the provincial company, who were playing *The Merry Widow* in Scotland. He was fair proud of her. Grace was always his favourite.

I began to play the famous *valse*, and pretty soon they were all singing. Although my back was to them I could hear even my mother joining in occasionally. Bella was sitting on the sofa, between my father and Jim. I could see from the tail of my eye that Jim's hand was lying along the back of the sofa and that his fingers were beating time on the buttons down the back of Bella's blouse.

I played *The Merry Widow valse* two or three times because they all wanted it, then I played the other pieces. I remember *Vilia* the best. . . .

> *Capture your joys as they fly,*
> *Soon will they fade and die.*

Soon will they fade and die. . . . Ay, they fade quickly enough. As soon as I'd finished *The Merry Widow* pieces, Bella said, " Play *Bumpetty-Bumpetty-Bump, Here Comes the Galloping Major !* "

But my mother put her foot down. " Hymns now or nothing," she said. That was my mother all over. She never seemed to lose control of herself. Once she'd made up her mind to go a certain length she'd go to it, but no power on earth would make her go any further.

She had made up her mind that she wasn't going to let me have anything to do with Harold, and she did her best to carry it out. She did all she could to keep me from seeing him. It was impossible to see him through the week, so on Sunday nights I started to go for walks after the kirk with Betty Taylor. That was what I told my mother. I had to tell her something so that I could get out with Harold.

Really, I wonder what Magda and Kathie Ashe would
do if their mother tried to keep them tied to her apron-
strings the way my mother tried to keep me ? They'd
have something to say about it, I bet. Help my Jimmie
Johnston, I can't imagine, looking back at it, how I
came to be so soft.

But I can't imagine either, how I had the nerve to do
what I did. I don't know how I kept from showing
that I'd been away for a walk up the West Road and down
the Gipsy Brae with Harold, when I said I'd been at
Acresgreen with Betty Taylor. I was simply terrified
that my mother would find out. Really, I was. Simply
terrified. I thought about it from one week's end to
another, imagining that my mother had asked Betty
Taylor where we'd been on Sunday, and that Betty had
said she hadn't seen me. But as soon as I was out with
Harold I forgot all that.

It wasn't that we spoke much when we were out.
We just walked along, arm-in-arm, and if we saw anybody coming that we weren't sure about we let each
other's arms go. The West Road in those days was a
fairly dark road, with an occasional farm cottage showing
a feeble light, and the moon and stars shining through
the branches of the trees. And the Gipsy Brae was
darker still. I'd have been terrified to go down it
alone. I still would be terrified. Long ago the gipsies
had often camped at the foot of the brae between the
quarry and the sea. There are no gipsies now, but
their reputation still remains. As Harold and I walked
down the brae I kept as close to him as I could
get, clutching his arm. The trees sighed above us
and the dead leaves rustled beneath our feet. From
the hedges on either side came whispers, and sometimes a glowing cigarette-tip showed that couples

were sitting on the bank, in the shelter of the hedge.

But Harold and I never sat : we always kept walking. Only once did we sit down   I'll never forget that time. And it's not only because of what happened that I remember, but because of what happened after.

We'd been meeting like this every Sunday night for months, all through the spring and summer, and now the winter was on us again, and we'd kissed only once or twice—short, sharp kisses that meant nothing, stirred nothing, like touching your lips with a wet cloth. But that night it was so mild that when we got to near the foot of the Gipsy Brae Harold suggested that we sit down for a minute and rest.

We sat in a hollow of the hedge.   The twigs caught in my hair and when I leaned back my hat got pushed to one side ; I could feel my hat-pin dragging at the roots of my hair.   The moon was shining through the trees.   The little branches between it and us made it look as if it were all cracked.

" Look ! " I whispered.   " The moon's cracked."

" It's like the globe of the world in the school," Harold said.   " Those lines the twigs make are like the boundaries of countries."

" But when we begin to move and come out into the open," I said, " there'll be no boundaries."

We sat silent for a long time.   Then I began to shiver. My arms trembled in time with the moonlit patterns on the road.

" Cold ? " Harold said.

I nodded.   I was preparing to get up and get on our way when Harold drew me close to him.   He was trembling far worse than I was.   " Katie," he whispered. " Katie."

I lay still against him. He kissed me. I lay and watched the cracked moon. The silly, cracked moon, it had watched over lovers like us for hundreds, for thousands, for millions of years, the silly moon, the lady moon, Luna, had it ever been kissed like this? Harold kissed me again. It wasn't like the kisses we'd given each other up till then; it was a slow kiss, lingering. For a moment or two I felt that I was going to choke for want of breath. Then Harold began to push me slowly back. I could feel the twigs of the hedge scratching my neck. His arms were strong and crushing me, and my breasts were squashed against his chest. I tried to keep my balance, but I couldn't.

"Watch," I said.

But he didn't stop. "I love you, Kate," he whispered, "I love you." And his hands began to move about me. He was cupping my breasts with his hands. I was on fire. I remembered all the things my mother had told me, and I wondered if this was what she meant. I was terrified I was going to be sick. I wished Harold would stop it. I was sure I was going to be sick. I wished his hands would stop stroking me like that. And I wished he wouldn't stop stroking me. I wished he'd go on for ever; kissing and stroking me, his long fingers fiddling with the buttons of my dress, tickling me.

"Don't," I whispered. "Don't."

But he didn't stop. He was lying on top of me. I was terrified I was going to be smothered. I wanted to lie there and never move, but something stronger than that ecstasy made me give Harold a push.

"Don't," I said again.

And I pushed him off and sat up. I was afraid. I'd never realised love would be like this. I'd always thought love would be gentle and soft, with kisses, something sad and rather melancholy. I'd never thought it would be like this, fierce and exhilarating. I'd never thought of a man's body being there, so vital and so insistent, beneath his clothes.

I brushed the dust and dead leaves off my skirt, and I straightened my hat and my blouse. My hands were trembling so much I could hardly fasten the one button Harold had succeeded in unfastening. Harold stood beside me, silent, trembling a little. I didn't look at him. I looked up at the moon. The boundaries were still there. We began to walk on.

"Katie," Harold said. "What's wrong? What's all the hurry?"

"It's time we were getting home," I said.

We walked for a while without touching each other. Then he took my arm gently. "Are you angry, Katie?" he said.

"No, I'm not angry," I said. "Only — I was afraid."

"So was I," he said.

And we kissed again there in the middle of the road, tight, tight against each other as if we would never let each other go. Harold's arms pressed so tightly around me that they hurt. And he murmured words and snatches of sentences between every kiss.

But that was the last time we kissed. When I went home I saw that there was something wrong. My mother was sitting beside the fire with a face like a summons. My father was polishing his working-boots ready for the next morning. Arn and Walter weren't home yet, and I was glad.

"Well, miss?" Mother said. "This is a fine time to come in at on a Sunday night."

"It's only twenty-past nine," I said.

" Only twenty-past nine ! " she said. " An' is that not late ? "

I said nothing.

" Answer me, ye impiddent hussy," she said. " I asked ye a question."

" Now, Mirren," my father said.

My mother never let on she heard him. If anything his soft warning only aggravated her anger.

" I asked ye a question, ye limmer," she said.

I tried to unbutton my jacket, but my fingers were trembling. Oh, it was a terrible, different kind of trembling from the way they'd been trembling half an hour before. I could feel myself shrinking, thinking my mother was going to strike me. And I wished the moisture would keep away from my eyes.

" It's not late," I said.

" It's not late, isn't it ? " she cried. " So ye've the cheek to tell me it's not late ! A limmer o' eighteen tellin' me it's not late ! "

" Neither it is," I said.

I was sure she was going to hit me and I cowered back. But my father said weakly, " Now, Mirren, don't be so hard on the lassie," and she turned upon him.

" You stay out o' this, Wattie Gillespie," she cried. " I'm perfectly able to manage my own house."

Then she said to me, " Where have you been ? "

I knew it was useless, but I said, " I was for a walk to Forthport with Betty Taylor."

" Ye're a leear," she said. " I saw Betty Taylor, wi' ma own eyes at the well, not half an hour ago."

So that was the end of my walks with Harold. After that my mother saw that somebody went with me everywhere I went. I never got a chance to see Harold

alone. Of course, I saw him. You couldn't live two
doors from each other without seeing each other now
and then. But my mother effectively put a stop to
anything more between us. I think she must have
spoken to Harold, for he never made any move to see
me again. I wrote to him and tried to tell him what
was wrong, but I didn't get any answer. I often wonder
if my mother opened any letters and kept them from me.
I suppose she did it because she thought it was for my
own good. She didn't want me to marry a Catholic.
She knew he wouldn't turn, and she was determined
that I wouldn't turn. And she knew how miserable
some of those mixed marriages turned out, with the
priests always coming, interfering, and making sure that
any children were brought up in the Roman Catholic
faith. She did it for the best. But I've never forgiven
my mother. We never spoke about it after that, but
although it all happened years ago it's still there between
us, unsaid. . . .

The McAllisters flitted to Leith not long after that,
and I never saw Harold after he left the cottages. I
saw the report of his death in the paper years after. He
was killed in the war. . . .

SEVEN PLAIN

THE first morning in the new house I had to think a minute or two where I was when I wakened. It was still dark. I lay and listened. There was a noise like thunder at the side of the bed, *bumpetty-bump*, *bumpetty-bump*. I lay still, wondering what it was. Then I recollected that the stair went up the other side of this wall. It was somebody from upstairs going out to work who had wakened me. I turned over and tried to go to sleep again. But I guess I wasn't in the mood. I was so used on the boat to jumping up all awake as soon as I was called that I couldn't turn over and go to sleep like I'd of liked to of done. I was sleeping in the back bedroom. It was a lot bigger than the East Room in the old cottage and I had the window open, like I'd always wanted, but had never been able to manage on account of it being so stiff in the old cottage. I stretched out, feeling good and fine. And I reached for a cigarette outa my jacket that was hanging on the bed-post. I lay and smoked, thinking it was a fine house, real airy and with space to grow.

After a while I got up and got dressed. I took a squint into the living-room. Granma was up and had the fire lighted. The kettle was boiling. "I had a look at that gas-stove in the scullery," she said. "But I didnie ken what knob to turn and I was feared I'd gas us all." Granpa was lying at the back of the bed in the living-room. He didn't open his eyes, and I reckoned he was sleeping. It was only half-past seven.

I went into the bathroom and had a real good wash. Jees, it sure was fine to splash around and to use as much water as you wanted, knowing it didn't need to be carried from the well. Besides, it wasn't the same as washing at the wash-hand-stand in the old kitchen; there was plenty of freedom in the bathroom to wash as much of yourself as you liked, not like in the old kitchen with everybody there. I wonder how my uncles and aunts did with no bathroom. It must of been hellish annoying sometimes.

Me and Granma were having breakfast when Aunt Kate came in. She was plenty het-up. "Who's been splashing the bathroom floor?" she cried. "Help my Jimmie Johnston, what a mess! And the walls are all splashed, too!"

"Ye dinnie need to shout, Kate," Granma said. "We're not all deaf."

"I'm not shouting," Aunt Kate said, awful icy.

"Ye surely dinnie hear yersel'," Granma said. "Whiles ye'd think it was me that was deaf and not you. Ye've surely risen off yer wrong side this mornin'."

"I didn't sleep well," Aunt Kate said snappily.

"Yer new bed," Granma said, and she chuckled. "Ye would have grandeur!"

"That has nothing to do with the water on the bathroom floor," Aunt Kate said.

"Aw, forget it," I said. "I'll clean it up after you've finished. There wasn't no sense in me cleanin' it up and then you goin' in and splashin' it again."

"I don't intend to go in and splash it," she said. "I'm going to wash in the scullery."

And she did, too. She never used the bathroom. She always gave her face the once-over with a bit of flannel in the scullery and there she was with her toilet

finished. And she was always riding me for making
a mess in the bathroom. But hell, a guy couldn't
always watch what he was doing. Anyways, I didn't
see why Aunt Kate should make such a god of
the bathroom. What was it for if it wasn't for
washing in ?

But she was like that about most everything. You'd
of thought the new house was a show-place. She was
terrified it got dirty, and she was always running around,
making one helluva fuss, supposed to be cleaning by
her way of it, though really it was Granma who did all
the hard graft. Aunt Kate would of made a first
class gaffer, no matter where she went. I guess the girls
in the shop she was in must of felt like dropping a brick
on her often. Her bedroom was all knick-knacks and
gew-gaws, photos of Gary Cooper, and photos of Greta
Garbo, and photos of all us kids when we was young.
We sure looked a lotta hams. There was Bernard
Ashe, with his tongue sticking out, and George Anderson,
with a sailor suit and a white muffler around his neck on
account of him having a boil, and me with a big cap and
knicker-bockers when I was five, just like an old man
cut down, Aunt Kate said. Jees, I sure was glad Mom
never had any of us kids taken with nothing on when
we was babies, for Aunt Kate would of had them stuck
up in prominent positions as sure as fate. She had
bought lemon-silk curtains and a lemon eiderdown for
the bed, and she was terrified they'd get dirty. She
didn't sleep with the eiderdown on top of her, she folded
it up every night and put it on a chair in case it would
get crushed. And she rolled up the rugs every night,
too, and put them under the bed. It was Magda Ashe
that told me this when she came to the Golden Wedding
and was sleeping with Aunt Kate. Magda said she got

a fright the first morning when she jumped outa bed
and touched the cold linoleum.

All the same, I blame Granma for this habit of Aunt
Kate's.   Granma rolled up the rug in front of the living
room fire every night, trying to save it as much as
possible.   She'd done this for years, and George told
me Aunt Bella did the same.   So no wonder Aunt
Kate did it with the rugs in her bedroom; she reckoned
she was being thrifty.

It took us a few days to settle down, but at the end
of the first week we had everything ship-shape.   Granma
settled down pretty quick and it wasn't long before she
was lighting the gas-cooker with complete success.
She reckoned it was swell to get hot water straight from
the tap and not to have to go outside to the lavatory.
She was real pleased with the house.   But Granpa
wasn't so pleased.   The hell he was.   He was always
grumbling to himself.   Granma was always looking
out of the windows at the flittings that were going into
the other houses in the street and telling him to come
and look.   She sure enjoyed watching those flittings.
" I thought our furniture was bad," she said.   " But
when I see some o' they folk's stuff I think our auld
sticks are fit for a palace.   Look at that auld bed.   It's
no' half as guid as the auld yin we left ahint in the
cottages.   Come here and see it, Wattie."   But Granpa
never moved from the sofa.   In the cottage the sofa
had been at the left-hand side of the fire, but in this
house it was at the right-hand side and when Granpa
wanted his pipe offen the mantelpiece he had to put up
his right hand instead of his left.   This sure didn't please
him, and he was always grumbling about not being
able to find anything in this damned house.   Granma
did everything she could to humour him, but it made

no difference. Granma sure had a hard time between
him and his grumbling, and Aunt Kate and her cleaning
madness. And then, both of them with their deafness,
she must of been awful tired roaring at them sometimes.

Granpa sorta cheered up after Stumpy McGregor
flitted into the next stair. He sat at the window and
watched Stumpy's furniture being taken off the cart,
and when the usual crowd of kids gathered around he
got real mad at them. I reckon he wished he was able
to go out and give some of them the Order of the Boot.
And I reckon Stumpy wished that, too. The kids in
the cottages had been used to Stumpy's pin-leg, but them
kids here wasn't used to it, and they kept calling names
after him, and shouting to each other to come and see
the guy with the wooden leg. " Hey, mister ! " one of
them cried, real impudent. " Is your head made of
wood, too ? "

" Young scalliwags ! " Granpa said. " I just wish
I could gi'e them whatoh."

Another flitting that interested the old man no end
was the flitting belonging to the people across the passage
from us. Jees, I near faded away when I saw who it
belonged to. I thought at first I was dreaming, but
when I cried to Aunt Kate she soon let me know I
wasn't.

" Help my Jimmie Johnston ! " she yelled. " It's
Sarah ! "

And it sure was. Sarah the drunk dame, with the
bottles, I'd seen in the tram the first night I came to
Edinburgh. In the flesh.

" But I thought she had a house at Calderburn already,"
Aunt Kate said.

" I reckon she had," I said.

" That was six months ago," I said. " Maybe, she

had a row with that dame and got six months
for it ! "

" Maybe," Aunt Kate said. " We'll soon find out,
anyway."

And we did. And that was exactly what had happened.
Sarah—her other name was Clancy—had had no end
of a row with the dame next door to her, and she'd been
lifted and she'd got thirty days for breach of the peace.
And when she'd got out the jug she'd applied for a
transfer to another house.

" And she had to land here ! " Aunt Kate said. " Help
my kilt, as if we hadn't enough to worry us ! I guess
we'll have some trouble with her."

" I guess so," I said.

Aunt Kate took on real bad about it, but Granma and
Granpa didn't worry themselves none. " Ye dinnie
need to speak to her or ha'e onythin' to do wi' her,"
Granma said.

" It's all very well saying that, Mother," Aunt Kate
said. " But whether you want to take notice of her or
not, she's the kind of woman who'll take notice of you.
Really, I can't get over it. I don't know what the
Corporation are thinking about letting a woman like
that come to stay beside decent folk."

" The woman has got to bide some place," Granma
said.

Granpa said nothing. He sat and looked outa the
window. He sat there sometimes now when it wasn't
too cold. He could see the end of the breakwater and
the middle pier between the houses they was building.
But he was always lamenting and saying it wouldn't be
long before his view was completely blocked.

Stumpy came in every day or two and told Granpa
all that he saw when he was walking around. He sure

got around some, game-leg or no game-leg, and I reckon he knew every labourer and joiner working on the houses. " They tell me that we're goin' to be all shut in," he told Granpa mournfully. " They're goin' to build right down to the West Road and shut out our view o' the sea."

" Ay, man, do ye tell me," Granpa said. " They might ha'e left us that."

Both of them shook their heads and stared at the floor. Most times they sat silent, for they'd known each other so long that they didn't need to make polite conversation. Sometimes, if they were both in a good mood, they'd talk about the cottages and about folks they'd known. Other times they'd talk about their ailments. They always began like that, asking for each other, and sometimes they went on to talk of other things and sometimes they didn't. Usually their talk would go like this :

" How are ye to-day, Wattie, man ? "

Granpa would shake his head slowly. " I haven't had passage to-day," he would say awful polite.

" Oh, dear, oh dear," Stumpy would say. " Maybe, you'll get it yet."

" I hope so," Granpa would say.

" Ye cannie expect to go every day," Granma would say tartly. " It's not as if ye were a big navvy and takin' a lot o' exercise. Ye dinnie even eat enough to keep a sparrow alive far less make it go to the w.c."

After that Stumpy would tell them how many cupfuls of stuff he'd brought up that morning. " I cannie get sleepin' for it," he would say. " It's awfu'. Man, things never were like this afore."

" If only they'd left us alone in the auld cottages," Granpa would say. For both he and Stumpy reckoned

that all their ailments had got worse since they came to
Calderburn.

Sometimes Granma listened to them and sometimes
she didn't. She'd plenty to do without heeding them,
what with cleaning up the house and making the dinner.
Aunt Kate expected it to be standing ready on the table
as soon as she came in. And it had to be piping hot.
Jees, I don't know how she managed to swallow it so
hot. No wonder her nose sometimes went like a red
lamp. It couldn't of been good for her digestion, all
that hurrying and swallowing stuff so hot.

She did the same at night when she came in. She'd
gulp down whatever Granma had got ready for her tea,
and then she'd tie an old cloth round her head and she'd
put on an overall. And there she was all set to work.
From the way she started in to beat the rugs and clean
the windows you'd of thought the house was the dirtiest
in Calderburn, and you'd of thought that Granma had
never touched it. The funny thing was that Granma
did far more cleaning than Aunt Kate, only she didn't
beat the big drum about it. To hear Aunt Kate, though,
you'd of thought that Granma was a cripple. " My
mother's not able to do much, you know," she'd tell
folks. " I have to do most of the work myself.
Really, it's a job sometimes, having to do housework
when you come home tired after working all day.
But, help my Jimmie Johnston, somebody's got to
work."

One thing I'll give Aunt Kate credit for. She washed
the common passage every week, a thing that Granma
simply wasn't able to do. And it was over the washing
of this passage that Aunt Kate had her first passage of
arms with Sarah Clancy.

The passage was supposed to be done every week,

and the two tenants on the bottom flat were supposed to take week about. But Mrs. Clancy never took her turn. At first Aunt Kate washed the passage every week, her own turn and Mrs. Clancy's, but pretty soon she began to complain about it. "It's not good enough," she said. "Sarah'll have to take her turn. It's her kids that dirty the passage, anyway." So one day, when she met Sarah in the passage, she plucked up courage and spoke about it. But when Friday came and Sarah hadn't taken her turn Aunt Kate wrote to the Sanitary Department about it. Two or three days after a dame with horn-rimmed glasses and a prim voice came down and looked around, and said that both tenants must take week about. "It says so in the missive," she said to Granma.

"I know that," Granma said. "But does she know?" and she nodded at Clancy's door. "You'd better speak to her about it."

"I will," the dame said. "And I'll send a ticket down from the office. When you've washed the passage you'll hand the ticket to Mrs. Clancy, and when she's washed it she'll hand the ticket to you, so you'll both know when it's your turn."

The ticket came all right. It had—*It is your turn to sweep and wash the common passage and stairs this week. By Order.*—printed on it. Aunt Kate washed the passage on the Friday night, then she went to Clancy's door and knocked. There was no answer for a helluva long time. Then Sarah appeared.

"Good evening, Mrs. Clancy," Aunt Kate said in the posh tone she spoke in to her customers, and she handed the card to Sarah.

Sarah looked at it. "What's this?" she said.

"It's the card about the passage," Aunt Kate said,

sweet as honey. " Please hand it back after you've done the passage next week. I did it to-night."

Sarah didn't answer. She slammed the door in Aunt Kate's face.

She washed the passage next week all right, but she sure made a swell job of it. There was so much water when she'd finished that you could of swum in it. " Help my Jimmie Johnston ! " Aunt Kate cried. " It's a good job I've got my Wellingtons on."

We waited for Mrs. Clancy to hand back the ticket, but she never did. So after Aunt Kate had washed the passage the following week, she went to Sarah's door and knocked. She had to knock three times before the dame appeared.

" Well ? " Sarah said.

" I've done the passage, Mrs. Clancy," Aunt Kate said. " So you won't need to hand me the ticket, but I'd be obliged if you would hand it in or hang it on the handle of the door after this, after you've done the passage."

" It's torn," the dame Clancy said, just like that, the words snapped out like a pistol shot.

Aunt Kate was kinda taken aback. " Oh ? " she said.

" Ay," Sarah said. " Yin o' the bairns tore it."

And she banged the door in Aunt Kate's face.

Well, Aunt Kate didn't want to write to the Sanitary about it, so she waited to see if Sarah would take her turn the next week. She didn't. Aunt Kate waited till the Monday and then she washed it herself. Aunt Bella was awful mad about it. " You fool, you should write to the Sanitary about it," she said. But Aunt Kate said no, she'd give the dame another chance. And she got Walter Anderson to print a ticket like the one she'd got from the Sanitary and she hung it on Sarah's door.

All the same Sarah didn't do the passage the next week, nor did she hand back the ticket. Aunt Kate was furious. "She's not going to be allowed to let her kids tear that lovely ticket," she cried, and she went to Clancy's door, prepared for battle. As usual she had to wait an age, and she was boiling over when Sarah opened the door.

"Mrs. Clancy," Aunt Kate said, real icy and keep-your-distance, "I want that ticket, and I want you to know that if you don't take your turn of washing the passage after this I'll call in the police."

Sarah looked at her. "Do ye ken that I'm gonna have a bairn?" she said.

"By the look of you I'd say that you were going to have two or three," Aunt Kate said. "But that doesn't alter the fact that the passage has got to be done. You can't expect me to do it every week. For one thing your children dirty the passage more than anybody else in this stair."

"Ye're a damned leear," Sarah roared.

"Don't roar at me," Aunt Kate said, cold as a lump of ice. "I won't stand it. I'll go to the police."

"Ye can go to hell if ye like," Sarah cried.

"There's a fine, you know," Aunt Kate said.

"A fine night!" Sarah said, and she roared and laughed at her own joke, and her belly shook so much that heaven help what was in it.

"Give me back that ticket," Aunt Kate said. "I'll have none of your impudence."

But Sarah laughed and slammed the door in her face. Aunt Kate was all het-up when she came into the lobby, where me and Granma had been listening to everything.

" I'll write to the Sanitary at once," she cried. " I'm not going to stand it. I've never been used to dealing with such folk. Really. Do you ken that I'm gonna have a bairn ? she says ! A bairn ! I hope she has triplets. It would serve her right, and it would give her some work to do. She's a lazy bitch."

And Aunt Kate sat down and wrote to the Sanitary Department again. This was a week before the Golden Wedding, and it was just one of a lotta things that Granma and Granpa had to put up with in their new house. Another thing was the kids. Especially the Clancy kids. Aunt Kate declared that their mother put them up to it. They never missed an opportunity to cry after Aunt Kate when they saw her in the street and they were always chalking things about her on the walls of the passage. But the trouble was that we could never catch any of them at it. And it was no use going to Sarah and accusing them. She was the kinda dame, who'd of gone at once to the police and accused you of libelling her kids.

For ages before it happened, Aunt Kate was all set to make a splash at the Golden Wedding. She wanted to hire Harrisfield Church Hall. But Granma put her foot down good and hard. " We're for no sprees, Kate," she said. " We're ower auld to be bothered wi' them."

" But we'll have to have a party," Aunt Kate said. " And a dance."

" We'd look fine dancin', wouldn't we ? " Granma said. " Where would yer father be able to dance wi' his rheumatics, and me wi' ma feet that sore I can hardly walk ? "

" But nobody's expecting you to dance," Aunt Kate said. " You can sit and watch."

" There was no dancin' at oor weddin'," Granma said.
" And there was no dancin' at oor Silver Weddin', so
there'll be no dancin' at this one, either."

And nothing Aunt Kate said would make Granma
budge. " We're hirin' no hall," she said. " And
we're no' invitin' anybody. We'll ha'e plenty here wi'
the Ashes, and the Andersons, and oorsels."

Aunt Kate was real mad at this. " We'll have to
invite somebody," she said. " Stumpy McGregor'll
have to come in. And we'll have to ask Nell Dippy,
I suppose. Not that I want her, but we can hardly get
out of it, we've been neighbours for so long."

" Ay, we'll ha'e to ask her for her mother's sake,"
Granma said. " Puir Maggie Dippy was a guid
neebor."

" Will we ha'e to ask Truth ? " Aunt Kate said.

" Oh, I dinnie think we need to ask him," Granma
said.

" Of course, we'll ask Matt," Aunt Kate said.

" Of course," Granma said.

So it was settled. There was to be no spree and
Granma said she didn't want any presents. There was
just to be a party in the house. But that didn't prevent
Aunt Kate from lashing out and buying herself a new
frock. " Ye've surely plenty o' money ? " Granma
said. " I'm sure ye're no' needin' any new clothes."

" It's my own money," Aunt Kate said huffily.
" Surely I can do what I like with it ? "

" Of course," Granma said. " But ye dinnie need to
greet aboot it when it's a' done. Mind, siller's yer best
freend."

" Ach to hang," Aunt Kate said. " I'm going to
enjoy myself before I'm too old."

" Ye've been ower long in thinkin' aboot it," Granma

said. " Ye should ha'e kicked ower the traces long ago."

Aunt Kate said nothing to this, and Granma got started in to pokering the fire. She made a helluva clatter about it, I thought. There was no call for all that noise.

A couple of days before the anniversary a parcel came from the Store, with a lot of shoes on approval for Aunt Kate to look at. Her frock was blue and she was gonna buy blue shoes to match. There sure were some dandy pieces of footwear in that parcel. Aunt Kate was all over them like a kid with a box of candy. And like a kid she didn't know what pair to choose. She selected a pair at last and tried them on. And she walked back and forward a few steps on a newspaper spread over the linoleum in case the shoes would get soiled. " What do you think of those, Spike ? " she said.

" They're swell," I said.

She looked down at them and she screwed up her face. " What do you think of them, Mother ? "

" They're very nice," Granma said.

Aunt Kate took another walk back and forth. " They're kind of tight," she said.

" Ye'd better no' take anythin' tight," Granma said.

Aunt Kate looked down at them. They were swell numbers, blue suede with gold buckles. " Do you like them, Dad ? " she said.

" Ay, they're bonnie shoes," Granpa said, and he leaned forward to get a better view of them.

Aunt Kate turned and looked at me. She shook her head from side to side, her lips tight together and stretched out like in a smile, only it made her face look like nothing on earth. " Eh, he's a dear auld cratur'," she said. And she swooped down on Granpa and kissed him, near choking him with tobacco smoke. "He's the nicest, sweetest old man I know."

" Havers ! " Granma said.

Aunt Kate tried on another pair. "What do you think of those, Spike ? " she said.

" They're all right," I said. I was beginning to get a bit fed up. She'd had them off and on so often. " I like them, too," she said. " Only—" and she looked at the first pair she'd had on, " I like those ones." And she tried them on again. Granpa and Granma sat quiet and watched the operation, as Granpa called it. But I wished she'd hurry up and make up her mind. " Oh," she said suddenly, " I can't have those—the dye's coming off them, and that'll never do. Really, they'd never do at all. My feet get so sore with standing in the shop. I'm frantic with them sometimes."

I was beginning to get frantic with her, but I did my best to control myself. She must of noticed at last that I was beginning to lose patience, for she laughed and said, " I'm a devil when it comes to picking shoes. I never know what pair to take. You'll be saying I'm terrible, Spike."

" You're telling me ! " I said.

She went back to the first pair again. " Really, I like those," she said. " Not because Spike says he likes them. I really do like them."

" Well, why not take them ? " I said.

" They're kind of tight," she said.

" Well, they'll get looser once you begin to wear them," I said.

" I don't know," she said. " I'm feared to take them, really I am."

And in the end she didn't take them. She didn't take any of them. She packed them all back to the shop.

She said she'd just wear her old back court shoes. "The girl in the Boot Department won't be very pleased," she said. "I made her turn out nearly the whole stock of blue shoes before I picked out those ones. But, ach to hang, that's what she's there for."

But I reckon it would of been a different story if Aunt Kate had been the girl in the Boot Department. I know she went off the deep end completely when people made her take hats outa the windows and then didn't buy them. I've often noticed, though, that it's those kinda folks who don't like to be put to any bother themselves who always make the most bother for other people.

The Golden Wedding was at the end of April. By that time Granpa had gotten kinda reconciled to the new house. "It's no bad," he'd say grudgingly. "Plenty o' conveniences, ye ken. But I'd ha'e been perfectly happy to ha'e bided in the auld cottages." And, although he sat now at the window and looked out at everything going on, you could see that his mind was still down there at the foot of the hill beside the harbour. The Golden Wedding sorta took his mind offen the cottages. At least it took his mind offen them to the extent that he was tickled pink to think he was gonna celebrate his fiftieth wedding anniversary and that he was gonna see Aunt Meg, and his grandchildren from Glasgow. But the Golden Wedding made him think of the cottages, too, for he was bound to speculate about all that had happened to him in the last fifty years.

By good luck the anniversary landed on a Friday, so Aunt Meg and my cousins were coming for the week-end. Uncle Bernard wasn't coming with them on account of trade being so bad. "I'm just as well pleased," Granma said. "He's an awful blether, yer Uncle Bernard, and he aye upsets yer grandfather wi' his talk about all the fine gentry he's served with. Yer Aunt Meg will be plenty to put up with."

Aunt Meg and the youngest girl, Kathie, was gonna stay with Aunt Bella. Kathie was fifteen and she was still at school, a gawky sorta girl with pigtails. "It's a wonder you don't get those cut off and your hair bobbed, like everybody else," Aunt Kate said to her. But Kathie said her mother wouldn't let her.

"Help my Jimmie Johnston!" Aunt Kate said. "I thought that her who aye wanted to be in the fashion herself would of liked her daughters to be in the fashion."

Aunt Meg, evidently, had no say in the way Magda, the eldest girl, dressed. She was a real fashion-plate as far as she could manage. But I reckon she didn't get as far as she would of liked, for she worked in a draper's shop and couldn't have a very big salary. She was a year younger nor me, a pretty swell dame with dark hair and dark eyes. She was a honey. In fact though she was my cousin I could of fallen for her pretty hard, and I was all set to play around with her. But she gave me the frozen mitt. She wasn't having nothing to do with sailors whose boats was tied-up. The trouble with Magda was she'd read too many novels about shop-girls marrying rich guys. And she'd seen too many films and read too many film magazines about what the stars did when they was at film premieres. Like ninety-nine out of a hundred dames she reckoned she was gonna be a famous film star and she was just waiting for a producer to discover her. She was all set to begin. She knew exactly how to behave when admirers asked her for her autograph. And she had a charming smile that she practiced for an hour every day in front of the mirror and any other spare time she had. But she hadn't time to practise that smile where cousins was concerned. Not even cousins like me. I reckon I was kinda sore at her attitude. It was the first time I'd made a play for a dame and she'd given me the air.

Tony, the youngest kid, was a great guy for the mirror, too. He was only fourteen and I reckon it was kinda unnatural for a kid of that age to be always looking at himself and striking attitudes. He was still at school, but he was gonna leave at the end of the summer-term, and he wanted to be a ballet-dancer. The hell he did! No wonder Aunt Meg got real annoyed at him. "We're for no ballet-dancers here," she said. "Away and not be silly! Where could you be a ballet-dancer? You've got to start when you're a bairn and it takes years of training. A butcher, or a grocer, or a mechanic'll be more in you line."

"It won't," Tony said. "I can dance. I know I can dance. I'd never get out of the bit if I became any of those things you say. I've no intention of dirtying my hands in this world."

"Maybe, you'll have to dirty them plenty in the next world, shovelling coals!" George Anderson said.

"You can go into private service," Aunt Meg said. "You can be a footman, or a valet, or a butler, and you won't need to dirty your hands then."

"Private service!" Tony said.

Bernard, the eldest guy, was seventeen. He helped his father in the garage. Me and him got along real good. He talked sensible, like George Anderson and me, about football, and motor-bikes, and dames. But Tony and Harry was more like Walter Anderson, they talked highbrow and I was mighty uncomfortable with them, though I got a good laugh at them when they fooled around.

Harry was sixteen. He worked alongside his father and Bernard in the garage, but he wanted to be a novelist. He was full of plans for books he'd write sometime. Two of them he told me was to be called, *Black Bastard*, and *Son of a Bitch*. I asked if he'd written any of them yet, because if he had I'd like to read them. But he said he hadn't written any of them. " But when I do," he said, " oh boy ! there'll be fireworks. The critics'll have something to say. I bet somebody'll say, ' Another young cock has come to crow on the dunghill of modern Scottish literature.' "

" I bet they will," I said. " If they're anything like the titles ! "

There was an awful stir in Granma's that Friday afternoon. The Ashes was all over Granma and Granpa because they hadn't seen them for about a year. And they was all dying to know how they was liking their new house. " Fine," Granma said. " I'd wonder what was up wi' me now if we found ourselves back in the cottages. I dinnie ken what I'd do without the hot water or the gas-cooker."

" Ah, but it was fine in the cottages," Granpa said. " They would ha'e done oor turn fine."

" Havers ! " Granma said.

" We were ower auld to be transplanted," Granpa said, shaking his head. " There's only one thing for it now."

" Nonsense, father," Aunt Meg said. " You'll have a long life in front of you up here. I'm sure it's very nice. You get a fine view of the harbour from those windows. There's plenty to see here that'll keep you lively."

" We were kept lively enough in the cottages," he said.

" Ay, we were kept lively sometimes ! " Granma said, laughing.

"It's different altogether up here," Granpa said.

"There's one thing," Granma said. "We'll ha'e no trouble wi' the lavatory key here. Do ye mind the time one o' the bairns went awa' back to Sheringwall wi' it in his pocket?"

Granpa chuckled at the recollection, and everybody else laughed. "That was Harry," Tony said.

"It was not," Harry said. "It was you."

"It'll not matter who it was," Granma said. "It all happened years ago. But we had an awful job till the key was sent back. We had to get a loan o' the Dippys' w.c. I mind it was an awfu' job aye havin' to go and ask Nell for the key. Yer grandfather had just taken a dose o' salts before we found out about it, too!"

It sure was a packed house when we was all there at night. There wasn't enough seats to go around and we had to get a loan of some chairs from Stumpy McGregor. Even then us younger ones sat around anywhere or on each others knees. I was itching to get Magda on my knee, but she was too darned high and mighty to sit on anybody's knee. She was too snooty even to help her mother, and Aunt Bella, and Aunt Kate, to hand round the trays with drinks, to drink the old folks' healths.

Stumpy proposed the toast. You sure would of thought it was coming from the sole of his one foot, and he wheezed the whole time. "Dear, oh dear," he said. "This iss a happy night for me . . ." And so on and so forth. I reckoned he was never gonna get done and give us a chance to drink what was in our glasses. Not that it made much difference. It was only some kind of light wine. Only the old ones got whisky, because Aunt Bella said, "It's poison for boys ! " But me and Bernard sampled the whisky later, on the sly.

After the toast we all sat around. Nobody seemed to know what to say. Granpa was looking into the fire and Stumpy was wheezing away and wiping his mouth with the back of his hand. Aunt Kate was eyeing the creation Nell Dippy had appeared in, and always giving another self-satisfied look at her own blue frock. I guess she was wondering what rag-bag Nell had dug her frock outa. It sure was some model: red velvet with the velvet all rubbed away in patches. And Nell had a bit of dirty yellow lace round her neck, put there I reckon to save her washing the dirt outa the wrinkles. Matt Renton had on a frock-coat that was going green. He had brought his dog with him, and it was snuffing around at everybody's ankles. I calculate Aunt Kate hadn't been any too pleased when she saw it. " Oh, it's you and your dirty dog, is it ? " she said to Matt when she opened the door to him.

We looked more like we was at a funeral than at a wedding, so Uncle Jim said, " What about a tune, Kate ? It'll liven things up."

She didn't need any coaxing, and all us young ones gathered around the piano, and we bawled and shouted while she thumped on it. *The more we are together the merrier we will be.* That was the song we kicked off with, and by the time it was finished we was all feeling a bit livelier.

The music-stand beside the piano was made out an old orange box and it was covered with cretonne, and it was chock-full of music. Every bit of music Aunt Kate had ever possessed was in that stand, from the " Piano-forte Exercises " she'd had when she was a kid, with Katherine Gillespie written on them in big, school-kid writing, to the latest pieces of jazz. I reckon there wasn't many tunes that had been popular in the last thirty years that wasn't in that stand.

She played all the tunes that was the rage then. *Weary River*, and *There's A Rainbow Round My Shoulder*, and *Lover Come Back to Me*. I reckon she'd of played all night if she'd played what everybody wanted her to play. Kathie wanted *Moonlight On The Colorado*, and Tony wanted *The Pagan Love Song*, and Harry wanted Beethoven's *Minuet in G*. But Granma said that was enough for the present; it was time we had supper.

The table was all set. There was a one-tier wedding cake in the middle and there was so many other things on the table that we couldn't of sat down at it even though we could all of got round it. Aunt Bella and Aunt Meg and Aunt Kate began to hand things around. Granma wanted to help, but they made her sit down between Granpa and Stumpy, on the sofa. She sure looked a swell old dame as she sat there, with her black silk blouse and her gold chain and Great-Granma Murdoch's gold earrings. You wouldn't of guessed she was seventy-nine and that she'd come through all she'd come through.

We was all so busy eating for a while that we hadn't time to watch what anybody else was doing. All the time Aunt Bella, and Nell Dippy, and Aunt Kate talked. You'd of thought they was trying to drown each other out. I can't figure how they managed to talk and eat at the same time, but they all managed to shift plenty. Bernard put away a lot, too; he had a swell time. So had Matt Renton. I can't figure where he put it all.

You could tell when they was all beginning to feel they'd ate enough, for more and more they began to join the chorus of Aunt Bella, and Aunt Kate, and

Nell; and pretty soon you could hear only Aunt Kate above the din of voices. I reckon it would of taken an explosion to drown her out. The only ones who didn't talk were Granma, and Granpa, and Stumpy, and Stumpy wasn't talking because he was wheezing so bad.

I couldn't help looking at Granma and Granpa, and thinking that although this was happening on account of them they might as well not be there for all the notice anybody was taking of them. And I wondered what they thought about it as they looked around the three generations; what they thought of Uncle Jim and Nell Dippy talking about chances for the Derby, of Walter and Harry talking about Virginia Woolf and Freud, of George and Bernard talking about the match between the Rangers and the Hearts, that we was gonna see the next day, and of Aunt Bella and Aunt Meg talking about the films they'd seen lately. What was they thinking about?

SEVEN PURL

Oh, the auld hoose, the auld hoose,
What though the rooms were wee?
Kind hearts were dwelling there
And bairnies fu' o' glee.

THE old man wished that Kate wouldn't sing that
song; it brought the moisture to his eyes, and no
matter how hard he tried he couldn't prevent the tears
from falling down his cheeks. He looked into the fire
and spat, hoping that nobody had noticed the tears.
Not that it would matter, he supposed. They would
say, " He's an auld man. What more can ye expect ? "

It wasn't the first time he had wept, anyway. But the
last time had been so long ago and the occasion so unlike
this one. The tears then had been a different kind of
tears from the tears now; they had been tears of rage
and frustration. He still pressed his lips together in
anger when he remembered them, though it was forty
years or more since it had happened.

It was in 1889, after the London dockers' strike. He
had been fired by the account of that, stimulated by the
courage of Ben Tillett, and Tom Mann, and John
Burns. He had burned to do something like that for
the men in the sawmill, something to alleviate their
condition. A strike seemed the only solution. Why
shouldn't it succeed when the dockers' strike had suc-

ceeded, and the Bryant and May match girls' strike?
It couldn't fail.

He was full of enthusiasm and he. went around the
mill agitating, calling upon the men to follow him and
strike for an increase of wages.   But they were apathetic.
They agreed that their lot was a hard one, that they had
bad hours, and that they were poorly paid.   But they
didn't appear to want to do anything about it.   They
hoped that somebody else would do it for them.   Their
minds could visualise a future state of affairs wherein
they were given a square deal, good hours, good pay,
leisure, but none of them had the courage or the will-
power to attempt to bridge the gap.   Some of them said
what was the use?   The condition of their fathers had
been similar to their own, and if it had been good enough
for their fathers it was good enough for them.   Others
said they believed their condition could be bettered,
but they didn't see why they should bother themselves
about it just to help other people.   This was when Wattie
pointed out to them the advantages they would give to
their children.   They said their children could fend
for themselves, as they had had to fend for themselves.

Wattie talked to them quietly and he talked to them
wildly, trying by curses to rouse them from their apathy.
He called them fools and he called them slaves.   He
sneered at them for being afraid of Sir Malcolm.   He said
they didn't want to better their condition; that they
were like pigs content to wallow in their own dirt.
He said that all they wanted to do was to sit back and
open their mouths and let other men, bolder than themselves, drop the plums into them.

In the end his scorn and his eloquence won and they
had a strike.   But it was a poor kind of strike.   Within
three days more than half of them had gone back

sheepishly to work. They were not trade union men, because Sir Malcolm wouldn't have trade unionists. They had no " strike pay " and in a week they were all back at work except Wattie.

The following week he went back, too. There was nothing else for it. There was nothing in the house and there were the bairns to feed, and Mirren was expecting again. It was a simple story. Starvation or the boss's terms. He knew, as he went in crestfallen to interview the foreman, that millions of men before him had had to choose the same terms, and that millions of men after him would have to do the same thing as long as their fellow workers wouldn't stick together and fight for their rights. But he never felt more like a whipped dog than when he lowered his eyes before the gleam of triumph in the foreman's eye and muttered " I doot I'll ha'e to gi'e in, Curly."

And that night, instead of going straight home, he went up the Gipsy Brae and there, safely in the darkness, he wept as he hadn't wept since he was a child.

And now, sitting here, with his children and his children's children around him, he wondered if it had been worth it. Maybe, I'd have been better to have kept my pride, he thought. We couldn't have been any worse off on the parish than we were when I worked for something I despised. It's a terrible thing when a man has to choose between his manhood and his bairns' hungry bellies. . . .

> *You and me sweat and slave,*
> *Body all achin' and wracked with pain. . . .*
> *But Ol' Man River, he jest keeps rollin' along.*

" Play *Ro-Ro-Rollin' Along* now," Tony said.

" No, play *The Merry Widow valse*," Kathie said.

Kate reached out and placed *Ro-Ro-Rollin' Along*, on the piano. "I'll play this," she said, then she took *The Merry Widow valse* and put it away under a pile of music, out of sight. "We're for no old music to-night," she said. "Except Scotch stuff to please your grandfather."

Tony sat on the edge of the table and he swung his legs and made patterns in the air with his feet, and every now and then he took another squint at himself in the mirror.

> *No need to hurry, no need to worry*
> *That things are gonna go wrong.*
> *Like the birds that sing I dream of spring*
> *As I'm ro-ro-rollin' along.*

But I've got to hurry, I've got to worry. I'll be leaving school in another two months. It's time I began to train. I should have been training already. It's hopeless, you fool. You'll have to be a butcher, or a baker, or a candlestick-maker. But I won't. I'm going to be a great ballet-dancer. Tony Ashe, the famous ballet-dancer. No, it'll need to be more Russian. Ashmanikoff. Hell, no, that would give folk the chance to say something funny about ash pans. Ashe . . . Ashe . . . Ashevski. Ashevski, the famous dancer, who has danced with Pavlova . . . I wonder if I'll ever dance with Pavlova ?

> *Birds in the trees seem to twitter Louise.*
> *Each little rose tells me it knows*
> *I love you . . . Louise.*

Maurice Chevalier in *Innocents of Paris*, with Magda
Ashe. Well, that's impossible now. But there's no
saying what might happen in a year or two. Maurice
Chevalier in . . . What? Oh, it won't matter. Something about love. With Magda Ashe . . . No, this
would be better. Maurice Chevalier and Magda Ashe
in whatever it will be. Or—oh, boy, I wonder if this
will ever happen? Magda Ashe in, Something About
Love with Maurice Chevalier . . . You know, that's not
a bad title.

"I saw *Silver Wings*, that new musical comedy, last
week," Magda said. "It was lovely."

"Really," Kate said. "It's not been here yet.
Edinburgh is sometimes awful late in getting things.
The last good musical show I saw was *New Moon*."

"Oh, it was lovely," Magda said.

"It was gorgeous," Kate said.

"Harry and I went to see *Journey's End*, a fortnight
ago," Tony said. "Oh, it was gorgeous. All about
men getting blown to bits and getting gassed. Really,
it was gorgeous."

"It was lovely," Harry said.

"Help my Jimmie Johnston, it was divine," Tony
said.

Both of them shrieked with laughter when Magda
and their Aunt Kate glared at them.

> *Look down, look down that lonesome road*
> *Before you travel on.*
> *Look up, look up. . . .*

That's what I'm doing, isn't it? Looking up.
Though not heavenwards! Black Bastard, by Henry

W. Ashe, is a masterpiece. Another young cock has come to crow on the dunghill of modern Scottish literature . . . Look down, look down that lonesome road . . . But it won't be lonesome any more then. . . .

"They're nice houses," Meg said. "I'm sure my mother and father are very comfortable here. They've got every convenience. They'll be taking a new lease of life."

"If they'd only got it ten years ago it would ha'e been better," Bella said. "They're ower auld now to readjust themselves. I think my father would be far happier in the cottages."

"So would I," Nell Dippy said. "It's terrible the class o' people that are here. Right bad lots most o' them. The man across the passage frae me has been in the jail. Oh, he's a terrible bad lot. He speaks at they Communist meetings at the Mound. He'd like this country to be like Russia, full o' Bolsheviks and God-knows-what, killing Sir Malcolm Harris and the Lord Provost—even the King and Queen."

"Isn't that terrible?" Meg said. "What's the world coming to?"

"There was an awful row in our stair last night," Nell said. "And this Bolshie was at the bottom o' it. He was givin' his daughter a row because she didn't come home till half-past eleven. I heard him roaring that it wasn't the thing for a lassie of fifteen to come in at that time. Oh, it was an awful row. The man up the stair got the polis to them, and two bobbies came after twelve o'clock. Wakenin' up the whole stair with their noise at that time o' night! Why can folk no' ha'e their rows in the middle o' the day?"

The moon is new, but love is old.
This aching heart of mine is calling
Lover, come back to me. . . .

Really, those two girls get on my nerves giggling like
that. I know they're laughing at me. Little jades.
After all I did for them when they were young. Taking
them out and dressing them. Really, the younger
generation! I'm sure I wouldn't have dared to laugh
like that at anybody older than myself when I was their
age. Really, when I think of the money I spent on those
two when they were kids. And on Walter, and George,
and Bernard, and Harry, and Tony. And now they all
laugh at me and crack jokes about old maids. Really,
I don't know what I'd like to do to them. They don't
need to laugh. Maybe, they'll be old maids themselves
yet. You never know. They won't know till the time
comes. I didn't think when I was their age that I was
going to be an old maid, either. I used to laugh at
Aunt Isabella, and Aunt Sybil, and Aunt Katherine,
and call them mouldy old maids of school teachers.
When I was like Magda I was dreaming of getting married
to Harold, planning what I'd wear at my wedding, and
how I'd dress my children, and what I'd give Harold
for his breakfast. I love you, Katie, he said, I'll always
love you. He had on a black tie with thin blue stripes
and a celluloid collar. The collar was chafing his neck
and I stroked the reddened bit with the tips of my fingers.
That's lovely, he said. But you'd better stop, somebody's coming. Somebody's coming. I've had to
keep an eye open for other folk all my days. First it
was my mother. And then, after I'd lost Harold for
good, it was an eye for my nephews and nieces. Dressing
and sorting them as if they were my own bairns, pre-

tending to myself that they were. I'll never forget the
time I took Magda and Kathie to Portobello to see the
pierrots on the promenade. They had fawn coats with
black velvet collars and their hair in long curls. Kathie's
hair had pink bows at each side and Magda's had blue
ones. They each had a wee handbag, and I'll never
forget how they marched into the biggest ice-cream shop
on the Prom. for halfpenny cornets. Really, I could have
died of shame. It was funny, of course, the way they
came out, shutting their bags as if they'd been buying
the whole shop. But I could have hit them as they walked
along the Prom. sucking their cornets and dripping
ice-cream on their coats. Help my Jimmie Johnston,
I was in a fair panic, wondering what Meg would say
when I got them home.

And then when Kathie cried, " Oh, my bag ! I've
lost my bag ! "—really, I got up to ninety. Everybody
on the Prom. was looking at us as if it was me who'd
pinched her bag or something. I didn't know where
to look. What a commotion. I could have planted
her. " Where did you leave it ? " I cried.

" I don't know," she cried. " I don't know." And
she yelled holy murder. Oh, I fair wished the sea would
dash over the rails and carry her away. " Be quiet
now," I said. " Be quiet, there's a good girl. Aunt
Kate'll look for your bag, and if she can't find it she'll
buy you a new one."

" You don't need to bother," Magda said, cool as you
please, and sort of chuckling. " She's got it hanging
over her arm."

Really, those bairns. . . . When I think of all I've done
for them. And now they sit and look at each other, and
grin and jerk their heads from me to Matt. Really, it's
sad. That's the only word for it. Sad. . . .

Blue hills of Pasadena are calling me home,
Blue hills of Pasadena are calling me over the foam,
So my grip I'm gonna pack,
And find that little shack.

I've gotta get outa here or I'll go loopy, and hell knows there are plenty of loopy folks around here without me. Jees, if you ask me they're all loopy. What a buncha crocks for the bughouse. Aunt Kate and Walter, and Harry, and Tony. Jees, you wouldn't need to tell those three they was crazy, they'd jump down your throat like an avalanche. They all think they're geniuses. Jees, I sure am glad I'm not a genius. But I gotta get outa here. Quick. It's me for the first boat, no matter what like it is.

Why does my heart miss a beat
At some footsteps on the street?
It's the precious little thing called love.

" Aw, the Hibs are not worth watchin'," Bernard said.

" Aw, be yourself," George said. " They're the best team in the league."

" Howja make that out ? " Bernard said.

" I'm tellin' you," George said.

" They're lousy," Bernard said.

" Aw, come off it," George said. " Have you ever seen the way McRorie keeps the goal ? "

" Aw, him ! " Bernard said.

" Ay, him," George said. " You've not got a goalie in Glasgow to beat him."

" Aw, come off it," Bernard said.

" I'm tellin' you," George said.

" Aw, be yourself," Bernard said.

I'm not much to look at,
Nothin' to see,
Just glad I'm livin'
And lucky to be.
I got a someone crazy for me.
She's funny that way.

I wonder at our Kate doing herself up like that. I'm sure everybody's bound to know her hair's dyed. Everybody knows she had brown hair when she was young. Like me. Her, and me, and Tom, were the only dark ones, all the rest were fair. Painting herself like that, too. Of course, I don't blame her for trying to make the best of herself. But she makes such a poor attempt at it, she'd be better not to do it at all. I'd just like to hear what Bernard would say to me if I were to go home all dolled-up like that.

Don't wear a frown on old Broadway,
You've gotta smile on Broadway.
A million hearts beat quicker there,
A million lights they flicker there.
There ain't no sorrows on the great white way,
That's the Broadway Melody !

You've gotta smile on old Broadway. You've gotta smile on more than Broadway. You've got to smile right here in Calderburn, and you've got to keep on smiling the same as you've kept on smiling for the last fifty years. There's nothing else for it now but to keep on smiling till the end of the chapter. It would be silly to greet now. Your life has been hard enough without making the end of it any harder by thinking about all the sad bits and dwelling upon them. You'd find it hard, anyway, to separate the sad bits from the

happy bits. They're all jumbled up. They happened
like that, and when you try to remember them they
get more jumbled than ever. They come crowding on
top of each other, each memory, not bothering whether
it happened before or after the memory you've just had.
All the important ones are standing up like the peaks of
mountains, standing out of the valleys of everyday
things that are shrouded with mist, and your memory
leaps from peak to peak, backwards and forwards, and
if you trailed a thread behind you it would weave into
a pattern like a spider's web. And that pattern is
difficult to follow. It would be difficult for you to go
away back to the beginning and to march steadily on,
step by step, in the way your life would be told in a book.
No, you remember something that happened last week,
and then you remember something that happened when
you were a bairn; then something when you were a
young woman, and then something when you were a
bairn again. It's all jumbled up. Back and forward,
back and forward. It would take a gey clever person to
unravel it all. It's like a poem that you saw in a book
that Walter Anderson had. You've never been one for
poetry, although you read a lot. You've never even
read Annie Swan's poems, and you've read everything
else she's written. (A clever woman that. You mind
when you said to Bella, " She's a clever woman, Annie
Swan, she writes poetry," and Bella said, " Hoots,
mother, she'll ha'e nothin' else to do ! ") But this book
of Walter's was lying on the table and you looked at it,
and you've never forgotten one of the poems. You
can't remember the words, but you can remember the
sense. It was about Time, knitting and multiplying
the stitches. As if your life was a bit of knitting—a
jumper or a sock—and every incident in it was a stitch.

You thought it was very true. And you thought that there were a good many holes in your garment of life. Wee holes and big holes. Wounds. But some of them you've patched up yourself, and some of them have drawn together, knitted together again by Time. For Time heals everything and knits the stitches together so closely that sometimes you can see only the faintest trace of the wound. . . .

But Time hasn't made so very much change in you, except in a few of your beliefs, and in your health and looks. You're the same Mirren who stood at your attic-window in the Mitchell-Greys and looked at the red sky. You're the same Mirren who stood in front of the fire with Walter's medals in your hand. You're the same Mirren who stood before the window and peeled potatoes, and looked out at the green and the harbour, and watched the cottages slowly change. And, although all those Mirrens looked different to other people none of them felt any different to you. When you peeled potatoes you just felt the same as you felt when you threw out your arms to challenge the red sky ; when you looked down at the medals you felt the same as you did when you looked down at wee Walter lying so bonnie and fair in the bed between Arn and Tom. It was only Time that had changed ; not you. Time . . . something that cannot be measured by days or by months or by years, for yesterday may not be so clear as a day twenty years ago, and something said five minutes ago can be forgotten, while words spoken when you were young are still ringing in your ears. . . . Time.

> *Should auld acquaintance be forgot*
> *And never brought to mind*
> *We'll tak' a cup o' kindness yet*
> *For the days o' auld lang syne.*

EIGHT PLAIN

L ESS than a week after the Golden Wedding the *Red Biddy* got a cargo and we sailed for the Mediterranean. We was at a lotta different ports and when we came back to Britain we docked at Hull. Cinnamon and some of the crew went home for the week-end from there, but I didn't bother. I met a cute broad in a café, and me and her stepped around while the *Red Biddy* was in port. She was some baby, the butter-fly's wisdom tooth and everything. I had a swell time.

We sailed again for Alexandria and then we came back to Bristol. Every voyage we had we never seemed to touch Harrisfield or any place near it. But I didn't worry none.

It was nearly seven months after we first left that we touched Harrisfield again and we was paid off and the boat was tied-up. When we got ashore most of us went to the Tap and Cinnamon got more nor he could hold. It was kinda strange for him not to be able to keep his feet, but I reckon he must of been run down or something. Anyways, I was scared he *would* get run down on his way home, so I took him there.

His wife was real mad when we went in. She sat by the fire and didn't speak at first. Her reception wasn't calculated to make me feel at home and I was gonna leave as soon as I'd dumped Cinnamon, but he said, " Stop and get a cup o' tea."

" Oh, no," I said.

" Oh, but yo ! " he said.   " Ye might make a cup o' tea, Bunty."

" Ye can make it yersel'," Bunty said.

I said not to bother, I guessed I'd better be on my way.   But Cinnamon told me to sit down or he'd knock me down, and he began to trot around and tried to make the tea himself.   " It's a b—r when a man comes home from a voyage and has to muck in and make a cup o' tea for himsel'," he said.

" And it's a b—r when a man comes hame that drunk that he doesnie ken whether he's comin' up the stair on two feet or four," Bunty said.

" I reckon I'd better go," I said.   " My grandmother'll think I'm never comin' home."

" Sit still," Cinnamon said.   " We'll ha'e a cup o' tea and then I'll go along with you and pay my respects to Mr. and Mrs. Gillespie."

" Are you Wattie Gillespie's grandson ? " Bunty said.

When I said I was she got real friendly and started in to make the tea herself.   " Sit doon and no make a fool o' yersel', man," she said to Cinnamon.

" I thought that would be impossible," he said.

" Well, ye dinnie need to make yersel' look a bigger fool than ye are already," Bunty said.   " Comin' hame like that at this time o' day !   I expected ye three hours ago.   Folk that think ye're such a fine man dinnie ken what I've got to put up with."

" And you dinnie ken what I've had to put up with this last trip," Cinnamon said.   " First of all I had the 'flu——"

" But it flew awa' quick enough when ye got into the Tap ! " Bunty said.

" Then I had lumbago for a week," Cinnamon said. " Oh, I was bad.   Then to crown all I had constipation.

I had it for three weeks, and I tried everything. Salts, and cascara, and a great big dose of Black Draught. But there was nothin' doin'. So this mornin' I swallowed a bottle o' castor oil, and then I couldn't leave the boat. Oh, I was bad."

" Ay, ye're bad all right," Bunty said, laughing. " Here, drink up that tea and, maybe, ye'll ha'e constipation again."

After he got kinda sobered-up Cinnamon went along with me to Calderburn Crescent. Granma let us in. " Come into the room for a minute," she said. " Your grandfather's indisposed."

" Oh, I'm sorry to hear that, Mrs. Gillespie," Cinnamon said, awful concerned.

But Granma said it was nothing to worry about. " He's on the throne just now," she said, and she left us for two or three minutes in Aunt Kate's room. Cinnamon looked around, real amazed. " So this is Kate's room ? " he said. " It reminds me o' a bloody bazaar ! "

Granpa was in bed smoking his pipe when we went into the living-room. Jees, I sure was surprised at the change seven months had made in him. He looked awful small lying there in bed ; there was nothing of him under the clothes at all. His face was terrible shrunken ; you could see nothing but nose and beard. Before I went away he used to sit up quite perky and talk when folks came in, but he didn't sit up now. He shook hands with me and Cinnamon, but he made no move to carry on a conversation. He lay and he looked at his hands and he was always rubbing them together like he was cold. But I reckon he couldn't of been cold with all those blankets and the big fire there was. I reckon Cinnamon saw a big difference in him from the last time he seen him. He did everything he could to

get Granpa to liven up, but he sure had his work cut out.
Only when he mentioned the municipal elections that
was coming off the next week did Granpa show any
interest.

" Ye'll ha'e to go and vote, Mr. Gillespie," Cinnamon
said.

Granpa raised his hand. " It's out o' the question,
Danny," he said. " Ay, it's out o' the question."

" Will ye manage to go, Mrs. Gillespie ? " Cinnamon
said.

" I doot it," Granma said. " My feet are ower sore."

" I'd like fine to go," Granpa said. " It'll be the
first time I've missed votin'. They came last year wi'
a car and took me. But I doot I'll no' manage this year
car or no car."

" Kate'll go and vote," Granma said.

" Oh, ay, Kate'll ha'e to go," Granpa said. " Every
vote counts. I just wish I was able to go maself."

" Plenty o' folk are able, but they'll no' go," Granma
said.

" Ay, it's a big mistake," Granpa said. " They're
aye the kind o' folk who complain, too. They're aye
greetin', but they'll no' move a foot to help themselves."

" Who's standin' for this ward ? " Cinnamon said.

" There are three candidates," Granpa said. " A
Labour, a Communist, and a Conservative."

" At that rate the bloody Tory'll get in," Cinnamon
said.

" Ay," Granpa said angrily. " They cannie expect
anythin' else, splittin' the vote like that. When will
the workin' classes learn sense ? Squabbling among
themselves. Some are Labour, and some are I.L.P.,
and some are Communists, and they're all at each others'
throats. Why can they no' forget their differences for

a while and unite against the folk that are keeping them down ? "

" What else can you expect ? " Cinnamon said. " It's the way they've been taught at school. Taught a lot o' rubbish about kings and queens, and great battles. Taught to look up to their social betters. They'd far rather kiss Lord This or That's arse than shake hands wi' plain Willie Smith. Look at oor freend Stumpy."

" Ay," Granpa said. " Look at him. He's no' learned sense yet. I'm surprised at him, a man o' his years and experience votin' Conservative."

" I'm surprised at nothin'," Cinnamon said. " The more I look about me at the senseless things folk do, the more I despair o' mankind. Sometimes I think the best plan would be to go awa' to a desert island away from them all. But I think to myself, if I did, what would I get to laugh at ? "

There was a big change in Granpa, but there was a big change in Granma, too. She was beginning to fail. She didn't go about the house the way she used to. She had an awful job with Granpa. Most days he lay in bed, but sometimes he thought he'd like to get up, and then she had an awful job dressing him the same as if he was a kid. It sure took it outa her. Then there was Armistice Day coming around again. It always shook her up and made her remember things she wanted to forget. Two three days before it happened, she was liable to snap your head off at the slightest provocation.

You couldn't blame her, of course. Because for near a week before the 11th everybody was talking about it. Kids were selling poppies and you couldn't walk a yard without them trying to get you to buy one. The papers were full of what was gonna take place. They sure screamed it at you, so you couldn't forget that the

King was gonna be at the Cenotaph, and the Prince of Wales was gonna be at some other ceremony. The British Legion was doing this and the ex-service men were doing that. And General X wrote an article in this paper, and General Y wrote an article in that one. All about the glorious dead and a nation mourning, and telling folks what they should think about during the Two Minutes' Silence.

" A lot o' havers," Granma said. " As if folk who lost anybody needed a twa minutes' silence to remember them in. It's a farce. It only suits they generals who were well ahint the lines. It gi'es them a chance to air their uniforms and their medals.

I reckon Granma was right. I reckon it was all a racket put on by those folk who stood to gain something by it. It helped to awe a lotta simple folks who couldn't think for themselves. I reckon it was one of the things that made Cinnamon want to go to a desert island, but I reckon, too, that it was one of the things he got a big laugh outa.

I know I got a big laugh outa it myself. Especially the time the kid came to the door selling poppies. I guess it wasn't nothing to laugh about, but I couldn't help chuckling to myself when Granma cried, " No," and slammed the door in his face. I sure would of liked to see that kid's face.

But Granma's face looked kinda funny, too, when she came in from the lobby. " Maybe, I should ha'e taken one from him," she said. " It's not his fault, puir bairn."

But she sure said plenty to Aunt Kate when she came home at dinner time with a big poppy that had cost her a shilling.

Aunt Kate was, if anything, more deaf than ever.

She was still having trouble with the dame Clancy about washing the passage. And she was still trying the quack's cure for her deafness. She sure had a busy time of it. She told me so herself.

"Help my Jimmie Johnston!" she said. "There's an awful lot of work about a new house. You've no idea, Spike. It takes me all my time to get it done. My mother's not much help, you know. Of course she potters about. She cooks the meals and looks after your grandfather. But she's not much help otherwise. I have to do some of the work before I leave in the morning and then I do more when I come home at night. Really, I get fair fed-up sometimes. I like work, but help my kilt—sometimes there's so much to do that I don't know whether I'm standing on my head or my hands. I've an awful rush in the mornings. I put out the bucket first. Really, the dust-cart comes that early. It's here before eight o'clock. But I manage it. I just dive out of bed and put on my coat over my nightgown and dash out with the bucket. Sometimes my mother puts it out herself, of course. Then I get cleaned and have my breakfast. Then I take my lemons and my menthol. And then I put my plugs up my nose and do the dusting. Really, it says in the directions that I should keep the plugs in for twenty minutes. But how can I? I've got to rush away then to my work. I've to run for my car nearly every morning. I'm sure all the folk about here will know me; they'll think I'm always running."

"I'm sure they will," I said politely, and I watched her dust a vase that Granma had dusted just ten minutes before.

Another thing that distressed Aunt Kate was vermin. She was up to ninety because they discovered mice in the scullery. She bought a penny trap and set it, and it hadn't been set an hour before there was a big fat mouse in it. Aunt Kate got all hot and bothered, terrified to take it outa the trap. But it didn't take me long to get rid of it.

I set the trap again, and the next morning there was another mouse in it, about as big and as fat as the first one. "Help my Jimmie Johnston!" Aunt Kate said. "This is getting serious."

When she came home at dinner time she had another trap and she was lamenting because it had cost twopence. "Really," she said, "I nearly walked out of the shop without taking it when the wife said it was twopence. It's not worth it."

The next morning there was a small mouse in the old trap, and then in the afternoon it caught another one. They were both small mice. Aunt Kate looked at them and shook her head sadly and she screwed up her face with sympathy. "Poor little orphans," she said. "They would have to come out when their mother and father were caught."

We set the traps again, but there were no more mice. Aunt Kate sure went an awful length about paying twopence for the second trap, though. Jees, you'd of thought she'd been robbed. "I've a good mind to take it back to the shop," she said. "Twopence for that! Really, it's not worth it. It hasn't caught anything."

Not even the mice made Granpa snap outa the coma he always seemed to be in. He didn't even show much interest when Granma said, "We weren't bothered much wi' mice in the cottages." He just shook his head sadly. Most of the time he lay in his bed and slept. He was deafer than ever, and Granma sure had some job between him and Aunt Kate. Sometimes she didn't bother to shout to them at all; I guess she gave it up as a bad job.

Two three days after I landed I walked down to the cottages. I sure was surprised at the change. Most of the shutters and doors was offen the houses, and every window was broken. I kinda laughed to myself when I recollected how busy Aunt Kate had been whitening all the panes. Even the wood in some of the windows was out. Every bit of wood that could be taken away was away. All the old coal-bunkers that used to stand outside every door had been broken up, and the marks on the pavement where they'd stood was beginning to get overgrown with weeds like everything else. The grass of the green was about up to my knees, and though Granma said they hadn't been bothered with vermin in the old days there sure was plenty now. Human vermin, too. Gangs of kids from Sing-Sing was always down there, breaking up doors and shutters, chipping and sawing, breaking up every bit of wood they saw into firewood, and then they went around selling it for a penny or twopence a pailful. Granma was always answering the door to kids who wanted to sell sticks. She bought one or two pailfuls a week. Sometimes I wondered if she ever figured where that wood came from.

Sure enough, none of it came from her old cottage —yet. But it wouldn't be long, I reckoned, before it got smashed up, too. By the look of the door I could see that the kids had been making a determined pass at it, for it was all chips and dents. It wouldn't be long before it got knocked down. It was the only door standing in the cottages. I reckoned it was kinda tough, like the folks the house had belonged to.

The inside of the house wasn't in such good condition,

though. The paper was hanging off the walls and the plaster was broken and showed the wood behind. The fireplace was out. All the old grates had been sold to some scrap-iron firm, and I reckon they'd all go to help to make armaments. There was word, anyways, of a boom coming in munitions. All the bricks was lying around, and the big hole where the grate had been gaped like an open wound in the wall. I guess it would of broken Granma's heart if she'd seen it. About the only thing that still remained the same as it was when we locked the door was Aunt Kate's old iron bed. But it sure had been shifted about some. I reckon some of the kids had been trying to get it out, but couldn't. And I reckon it won't be there long after the door gets broken down. It's a wonder the guys who took the grates didn't take it with them. It would of helped to make swell bullets or guns. Kinda funny when you think about it, ain't it ? I guess Granma would of got a great kick outa it if she'd thought about it. And so would Walter, or George, or any of the Ashe guys, when you reckon how often they must of slept in that bed when they was kids. It's kinda funny to think any of them might get killed by a bullet made outa Aunt Kate's old iron bed.

I looked around for another boat, but it was tough going. All the boats was tied up. Everybody was going around moaning about bad trade, and every second man you met was unemployed or on short time. Aunt Meg moaned about bad trade in every letter, except in the bits where she went all lyrical about the birth of Princess Margaret Rose. Aunt Kate was just about as bad. They weren't selling enough hats to suit her. " Ye'd think it was your shop from the way ye go on," Granma said. " What are ye worryin' about ? Ye cannie drag folk in by the scruff o' the neck and make them buy hats if they dinnie want them."

When I wasn't looking for a boat or at the pictures with George I worked in Granma's garden. They weren't used with a garden, and Aunt Kate made an awful to-do about it, wondering how she was gonna manage to keep it tidy. " As if I hadn't enough work in the house already ! " she said. But Uncle Jim and George had dug it up and then they'd sown grass seed on it. Uncle Jim said that would be real easy to keep once the grass had grown—if it got peace to grow for the kids ! They sure didn't aim to let it grow, but Granma and Aunt Kate did their best to keep them from climbing over the railing and trampling over the grass. And it wasn't looking too bad. I pottered about in it and I got the fresh air if I got nothing else. I got some good laughs, too. Especially at Nell Dippy and Truth.

Nell spent most of her time, like the other dames around there, in hanging outa her window and calling to everybody that passed. I reckon she knew everybody in Sing-Sing. All the message-boys, and coalmen, and van drivers knew her, and they waved to her and shouted. She hung outa the window so much she caught the cold and she had it bad just then and had to get the doctor. We didn't see her for two three days, so I asked Truth how she was when I was working in the garden and saw him coming shambling up the street. I didn't ask him because I cared two hoots how Nell was, but I knew it would give Granma and Granpa something to talk about.

Truth sure was some picture. I reckon he would be about fifty, and I reckon he hadn't shaved for weeks. You didn't need anybody to tell you he was simple. But I guess he wasn't simple enough to work. He didn't like work. He said as much when he hung over the rails and watched me working in the garden. He complained about the tough time him and Nell had had trying to get their garden dug when they first came to Calderburn. "It was awful," he said. "All the ground about here was hard, but ours was the baddest bit."

I was near choking when I went inside. I can't figure how I didn't laugh in his face. The baddest! My grammar ain't so good sometimes, and I don't know yet when to put *were* and when to put *was*, but I sure wouldn't of said *the baddest*. The hell I would.

I gave Granma a good laugh about it. "What did he say about Nell?" she said.

"He said she was gettin' on," I said. "He said the doctor said he would see her in two or three days if he didn't see her name in the paper before then."

"He's an awful comic, Dr. Brown," Granma said, laughing. "He'd be just takin' a rise out o' Nell. He would ken fine there wasnie much wrong wi' her. I doot it'll be a long time before her name's in among the deaths in the *News*."

"Did ye hear that, father?" she shouted to Granpa. And she repeated the joke to the old man. But he didn't appear to see the humour in it he once would of seen. He just shook his head and looked at his hands and mumbled, "Ay, man do ye tell me." And then a while after he said, "It's a long time comin'." I reckon he was thinking that the time when his name would be in the death-column was long in coming, and it kinda gave me the willies to hear him. It was kinda pathetic to see him. I reckon I wouldn't like to live so long if I was gonna be so helpless when I was his age. I'd rather die in my prime. It was awful to see

anybody who'd once been as intelligent as Granpa turning
so childish.

I stuck it for three weeks and then I began to wonder
how I was gonna stick it any longer. It was no life for
any young guy like I am staying with those two old
folks and Aunt Kate, and if it hadn't been for Aunt
Bella, and Uncle Jim, and the boys, I don't know what
I'd of done. I was at Henderson Gardens most of the
time. I even got kinda pally with Walter. I reckoned
I'd rather listen to him talking about Cubism, and
Picasso, and lesbianism, than sit and watch Granpa
lying in bed and Granma hobbling about slowly, waiting
on him hand and foot. It was kinda pathetic I guess.
There they was with nothing to live for, eating and
sleeping, wakening up in the morning with the same
ahead of them as had happened to them yesterday.
It was all so goddamned useless that I reckon I should of
been in a state between rage and pity at the emptiness
and frustration of their lives. But I went off to Henderson Gardens at every opportunity. Living in Calderburn Crescent was just too much like living in a funeral
parlour.

When Granpa did speak it was always about the
cottages, lamenting and wishing he was back. Though
God only knows how they'd of managed if that had been
the case. Granma had plenty to do with him in this
house, attending to all his wants, where everything was
handy, water and lavatory, and things. But I don't
figure how she'd of managed in the old house.

It kinda cut both ways I reckon. Because it was
because they'd had to flit that Granpa was failing so
sudden. Or was he? Wouldn't he of failed just as
quick living in the cottages? He was an old man.
Eighty-three. He was no chicken, I guess it was time

he handed in his checks. I reckon he thought that, too. That's why he didn't make no move to snap outa the semi-coma he was in most of the time. I reckon he thought the quicker he went the better for all concerned. Kinda like those stories you hear about some animals —I just forget which ones it is—sacrificing themselves for their young.

Granma wasn't like dying, though. She was a real tough old dame. All the same, I guess that if Granpa was to kick the bucket she wouldn't be long in kicking it after him. After he'd gone she wouldn't have nothing to live for no more. That's the way I figure it, anyways. Maybe, I'm mistaken. I guess nothing Granma would do would surprise me. I wouldn't be surprised to find her tacking around like a merry widow when I go back to Calderburn.

But when that will be Pete only knows. I reckon I'll never be back now.

It was George who said to me why not try Leith Docks. He went with me one day and we trailed around looking at all the boats that was tied up. It looked pretty hopeless. " I guess you'll have to try your hand at somethin' else, Spike," George said. " Those boats look as if they were stuck in the water."

" I guess so," I said.

" Join the army," George said. " You're fine and big, and you're dumb enough. You're just the kinda guy they want."

" Join it yourself," I said.

" No, I'm goin' to wait till they come and beg me with tears in their eyes," George said.

" Maybe, you won't have too long to wait," I said.

We was laughing and fooling, and talking about my

future career as the only American general in the British army when somebody said, " Hey, buddy ? "

This was a sailor looking outa the port-hole of a boat. We'd never noticed him, we'd been so busy fooling. I guess we both got a kinda start, it was that funny to see anybody on any of the boats except an occasional old watchman guy.

" States, buddy ? " the sailor said.

" Yeah," I said.

" Lookin' for a ship ? " he said.

" Yeah," I said.

" You found it," he said.

And I had, too. She was *The Charleston Coon*, all ready to sail. She'd lost one of her crew, the poor guy had died, and they was having trouble to get somebody to take his place. None of the unemployed sailors in Leith figured they wanted to go to the States with a boat that wasn't coming back. But that didn't worry me none. I counted the letters in *The Coon*'s name. Seventeen. That figured out to eight.

" My luck's in," I said to the sailor. " Lead me to the old man."

We sailed that night. It was so sudden and I had such a rush packing my kit I didn't have time for any tearful farewells. And that sure suited me. The only thing I was kinda sorry about was because I hadn't time to go and say good-bye to Cinnamon.

" Ye'll be back sometime, laddie," Granma said.

" Sure, I'll be back," I said.

But I know that even though I do go back I'll never see her or Granpa again. I thought about that as I leaned on the rail as we got out into the Firth. The lights of Leith and Edinburgh lay behind us. Away to the right were the lights of Harrisfield Harbour.

Behind the harbour was a band of blackness where the cottages lay.   And behind that on the hill were the lights of Calderburn.   You could see them quite plain ; row upon row of lights, like the lights of a barracks or a prison.   But pretty soon I knew they would all go out, too, and everything would be dark the same as it was dark at the cottages.

EIGHT PURL

WALTER ANDERSON leaned on the wall of
the West Road and looked down at the cottages.
The green steps had been walled-up. Behind him the
tenements of Calderburn lined the road. From bright
windows without blinds came the raucous blares of
wireless loudspeakers, and from lighted doorways came
shrill yells and harsh, humourless laughter. Children
still played in the gutters ; though it was late nobody
seemed interested enough in them to drive them home.
The smell of a fish-and-chips van was wafted down the
road towards him, and the greasy tang made him wrinkle
his nose with disgust.

Below the road the cottages lay in darkness and quiet-
ness. They were as if they belonged to another world ;
another world and another time. The pale moon-rays
coming from behind a bank of cloud lighted their
desolation, showing the great gaps in the roofs, the
broken tiles and rafters, the black holes that once had
been doors and windows. And the moonlight casting
a sickly pallor over the rank grass that covered pavements
and rows made it look like slime.

The sea was like polished coal and the lights of the
harbour were like a necklace of yellow diamonds on its
black bosom. Its sheen under the reflected light from
the black bowl of the sky drew away the attention from
the cottages, softening their ruins, shrouding them
decently.

Once again Walter compared the scene with Gold-smith's *Deserted Village*. It was hard to believe that people had lived there once : that these hovels had housed children who had laughed and played where vermin were crawling now : that young men and women had loved, and old people had died beneath the rafters where birds were roosting. What strange sights had they seen ? What stories could these old bricks, from which the plaster was rain-washed, have told ? They had seen the births and deaths of at least three genera-tions. They had seen young men depart full of hope and vitality for the far colonies. They had sheltered other men who had plodded on dully, day after day, doing the same thing year in and year out. They had heard the skirl of the pipes and the deeper braying of brass bands. *Good-bye, Dolly, I must leave you*, and *Keep The Home Fires Burning*, had echoed along the now silent rows, calling insistently to the youths, calling for them to leave their peaceful roofs and go far away . . . To what ? They had seen some of those same young men, young no longer, return maimed and disillusioned. They had seen mothers who had wept and fathers who had cursed because of others who had not returned.

What had they not seen ? What variety of human hope and endeavour was foreign to them ?

Vanity of vanities, saith the preacher ; all is vanity. For now the cottages lay dead and silent. They were the past. And those they had sheltered belonged to the past, too. They were dead, and most of them were forgotten. Soon there would be nothing left to show that they had ever existed. *For man cometh up like a flower and is cut down*. . . .

He was the third Walter who had stood here. *One generation passeth away and another generation cometh, but*

the earth abideth for ever.   And he wondered if they, too,
had stood here and dreamed of what they were going
to do with their lives.   Had they ever meditated, as he
was meditating, about the vanity of human wishes ?

His grandfather must have done so often.   In his last
years he must often have thought about his early
ambitions and of what they had come to.   He had
planned great things, hoped for great things, but what
eventually had come of them all ?   He had raised a
family, he had worked and he had died.   And what
remained, except some of those seven children, to show
that he had ever lived at all ?   And those children
—what had they dreamed of ?   Some of them had
dreamed of fame and fortune ; they had aspired to great
things.   But what had come to their ambitious hopes ?
His Uncle Tom had disappeared like a handful of ashes
blown by the wind.   And his Aunt Grace and his
Uncle Arnold—surely those two of all those lives in
the cottages had deserved a better fate than to die as
mediocrities ?   And the others—all those lives that
had lived in the cottages ; lived and loved, married,
and died, and gave birth.   Where were all those lives
now ?

And what of the younger lives who had come from
those others ?   Spike and his brother and sisters, the
Ashe children and George, and himself ?   Would any
of them live to fulfil any of their grandfather's hopes ?
Spike ?   No, Spike had only the wanderlust.   George
had it, too ; they were seed of old Captain Murdoch.
Only Magda, and Harry, and Tony, and he, had the
divine spark—or had they ?   Did they merely think
they had it ?   Would they, too, wither away into oblivion
as their Aunt Grace and their Uncle Arnold had withered ?
And even if they had the divine spark, would it catch

fire ? Would a tiny flame, perhaps, spring up and throw some light on those who had given them birth ? Or were they, too, doomed to obscurity, to darkness, to eventual desolation and dust ?

They were seed of his grandfather's seed. They were in flower, strong and full of hope. Would the flower bear fruit ?

NEIL GUNN 1891 – 1973
THE SCOTTISH COLLECTION

THE LOST CHART
A cold war thriller set in the Scottish city of Glasgow shortly after the
Second World War, '*the Lost Chart*' moves on two distinct planes –
the physical and the metaphysical.

THE LOST GLEN
The famous novel on the decline of Highland ways and values
in the 1920s.

THE OTHER LANDSCAPE
'*The Other Landscape*' returns to the familiar setting of the Highlands
but with a new element of dark humour.

THE SILVER BOUGH
Archaeologist Simon Grant comes to the Highlands to investigate an
ancient cairn. A stranger in a strange part of the country, he finds that
there are barriers to understanding between him and the people
of the community.

SECOND SIGHT
The setting is a Highland shooting lodge, whose occupants are depicted
in stark contrast to the local people. A violent death is foreseen.
But whose? How? When? The drama is played out against a
background of strange mists and elemental landscapes.

OFF IN A BOAT
'*Off in a Boat*' logs the adventures of a man, who at a critical point of his
life, throws caution to the wind, and with his wife as Crew, navigates his
way round the West Coast of Scotland.
Whilst Gunn masters the art of sailing and anchorage, the Crew
explores the possibilities of the camera.

Other titles in the SCOTTISH COLLECTION

THE BRAVE WHITE FLAG *James Allan Ford*

THE LAST SUMMER *Iain Crichton Smith*

THE SCOTTISH COLLECTION OF VERSE
VOL 1 to 1800 *Ed Eileen Dunlop & Antony Kamm*

THE FIRST HUNDRED THOUSAND *Ian Hay*

DUST ON THE PAW *Robin Jenkins*

THE MERRY MUSE *Eric Linklater*

MAGNUS *George Mackay Brown*

THE BULL CALVES *Naomi Mitchison*

EARLY IN ORCADIA *Naomi Mitchison*

THE CHINA RUN *Neil Paterson*

WHERE THE SEA BREAKS *John Prebble*

A GREEN TREE IN GEDDE *Alan Sharp*

TIME WILL KNIT *Fred Urquhart*

WALK DON'T WALK *Gordon Williams*

SCOTTISH BIOGRAPHIES

BURRELL: PORTRAIT OF A COLLECTOR *Richard Marks*

AS IT WAS (Autobiography) *Naomi Mitchison*